'*The Upstairs Room* is the real thing. Frightening and clever and full of atmosphere'
Susan Hill, author of *The Woman in Black*

'A very impressive debut . . . a strikingly unusual, unsettling narrative that makes you want to read on to the end'
Michael Frayn, author of *Spies*

'An incredible read. Clever, chilling, I couldn't put it down'
Joanna Cannon, author of
The Trouble with Goats and Sheep

'A gripping and impressive story of mounting terror. Spell-binding'
John Carey

'Kate Murray-Browne is a wonderful writer and *The Upstairs Room* is a brilliantly evoked, sure-footed debut about loneliness, compromise, illness, housing, ambition, jealousy, failure and love – not to mention a terrifying room'
Robert Williams, author of *Into the Trees*

'I loved *The Upstairs Room*. It's so suspenseful and creepy and confidently paced, and psychologically and socially acute, and really gets under the skin of the gentrifying city'
Lottie Moggach, author of *Kiss Me First*

THE UPSTAIRS ROOM

KATE MURRAY-BROWNE lives in London.
She studied English at Cambridge University and
worked in publishing for ten years before becoming
a freelance editor. She is also a visual artist and has
exhibited work in a number of different galleries.
The Upstairs Room is her first novel.

THE UPSTAIRS ROOM

KATE MURRAY-BROWNE

PICADOR

First published 2017 by Picador

First published in the UK in paperback 2018 by Picador
an imprint of Pan Macmillan
20 New Wharf Road, London N1 9RR
Associated companies throughout the world
www.panmacmillan.com

ISBN 978-1-5098-3759-5

1 3 5 7 9 8 6 4 2

A CIP catalogue record for this book is available from the British Library.

Printed and bound by CPI Group (UK) Ltd, Croydon, CR0 4YY

For Chris, with love and thanks

LONDON, 2013

It was there from the beginning, the day they first saw the house. Eleanor noticed the smell first. It wasn't unpleasant, just strong: the smell of age, of yellowing, of brown-grey, of damp. It was persistent – not the kind of smell you could get rid of or, she thought, get used to.

It was early July, a heatwave. Everything was bleached and parched; the whole city drooped. Eleanor's face was pulp, her neck and kneecaps slick and slippery, as she stood in the hallway, trying to imagine it as hers.

In the photographs, the house had looked grand: a Victorian terrace, steps up to the front door, huge bay windows. Close to, it was shabby. Chunks of plaster had come away from the front windowsill, and moss was starting to grow underneath, as though it was decaying from the inside. Paint was peeling off the window frames. The front door was an unsettling shade of yellow.

The estate agent, Michael, showed them into the living room at the front of the house. The vast window, which had seemed so luxurious from the outside, now felt exposing, vertiginous: just a membrane between them and the street. There was a fireplace surrounded by dark green tiles with an electric heater jammed in its centre, and elaborate cornicing edged the ceiling. 'Really nice period features here,' Michael said and Eleanor could sense Richard's excitement.

The walls were pea green and the carpet a dense red. The colours were dull yet insistent; murky and bright. She could see the paint puckering near the skirting boards, in stiff peaks like blown flowers. By the window, it had formed a clean slit, as if someone had dragged a knife down the wall. 'Of course, the decor's getting a bit tired,' Michael said. 'It could do with some TLC.'

The sofas were ancient and large, covered in faded pastel blankets made of thin, used felt. Double doors led through to a kitchen looking out on a bare lawn. Baby-blue cupboards with red plastic handles in the shape of crosses, which made Eleanor think of hospitals. A side table draped in lace. *We'd need to strip it bare*, she thought.

They proceeded through the house. The basement, empty now, had been converted for a lodger – a bedroom, living room and a shower room under the stairs. It looked hasty and cheap, as though the shower might come away from the wall. 'Can you imagine converting this into a kitchen/dining room?' Michael asked. Richard could. 'I don't know if you guys like entertaining but imagine knocking all this through, dinner parties looking out onto the garden . . .'

They moved back upstairs. A greying bathtub. Heavy curtains. Everything – beds, armchairs, banisters – weighed down with blankets and quilts. Eleanor imagined touching them; they would be clammy. Four bedrooms. 'So, the vendors are a family, a couple with a little girl, no onward chain. They want to move really quickly on this one, which I'm guessing is going to be good for you guys too. You've got kids, right? Two girls, lovely – a bedroom each for you and your little ladies and then you've got a spare room, or a study . . .'

They were on the top floor. Eleanor began to feel slightly peculiar here – it was almost airless, as if they were too far from the central nervous system of the house. There was only one room he hadn't shown them. Michael stopped with his hand on the door and said, 'OK, so you're gonna need to use your imagination with this one.' He stumbled; there seemed to be a little resistance from somewhere and then the door gave and swung open too fast.

Inside, the walls were covered in writing – a child's writing. The name 'EMILY' appeared again and again in capitals, sometimes very small, sometimes huge, covering almost all of the white. There were frantic scribbles – large clouds of line – and faces: dwindling to pointy chins with tiny dash-like mouths and enormous eyes.

Despite the blaze of black ink on the walls, the rest of the room was curiously still. The bedspread – a cheerless shade of pink – was smooth as glass. A collection of toys, which struck Eleanor as vaguely old-fashioned, was arranged in a neat pile on the pillows. There was no other furniture, only a leather suitcase in the corner of the room.

Richard laughed uneasily; Michael was embarrassed. 'Yeah, so this isn't quite . . .' he attempted. 'You know what some kids are like.'

'This isn't normal though,' Eleanor said. 'Why didn't someone stop her?'

'Well, the vendors are a bit . . .' He stretched his mouth out into a triangle. 'But all you need is a coat of paint and that room's as good as new.'

*

They were silent in the car. Eleanor was anticipating the argument they were going to have. She felt helpless, defeated before they'd even begun. The four bedrooms, the outside space. The area, the schools. Transport links. *It didn't feel right*. What does that even mean? There's a housing crisis. Prices are rising every month, every week: they're rising right now. *I just didn't feel comfortable there*. We're running out of time. *The smell. The upstairs room!* You have to look at the potential. We could make a fortune on that place. *Acquisitive, greedy*. Irrational.

She felt empty. They were on the move now, however much she wished they weren't. The house they'd moved to after they got engaged, where they'd brought their children home from hospital, was no longer theirs. The moment they'd given notice, it had lurched into the unfamiliar. Its flaws and eccentricities became unbearable when there was no point fixing or tolerating them. She had never felt less welcome than in the house they had seen that afternoon, but she was unwelcome in her own home now. And she knew their resources were slowly depleting – time, energy, child-care, love.

It was only when they were getting ready for bed that it surfaced, vivid and sharp: an image of the kitchen sink, surrounded by perfectly clear, sterile metal. She tried to picture the bathroom and was certain it was the same: she could see unbroken plains of enamel, unpunctuated by signs of life.

'Think about it, Richard, there was nothing: no washing-up liquid, no toothbrushes, no soap. It was empty.'

Richard threw his shirt on the chair in their bedroom. 'They were probably just tidying up before the viewing. Shoved it all in a cupboard.'

'I don't think they live there any more.'

'He said they did, didn't he? Michael, I mean.' Richard got into bed. 'If anything, it was *too* lived-in.'

As she brushed her teeth, Eleanor thought of those blank surface and the deep, dark paint colours. The feeling of

4

compression on the top floor; the writing on the wall. There was something not quite right, awry. She just didn't know how to articulate it. By the time she came back in the bedroom, Richard had already turned out the light.

ONE

1

Zoe made her way through the damp streets, trying to ignore the dislocating feeling making her want to turn back. It was becoming familiar, this sense of constantly working against resistance, and easier to tolerate. She forced herself forward, reminding herself there was nowhere else she ought to be.

It was September now, summer was over, the weather and light were on the turn. Things were starting to happen – she'd been offered a job, one that had a tinge of optimism about it. And on Monday, Martin, one of the lawyers at the property development firm where she was temping, had said he thought he'd found her a place to live.

Martin was the only person at work who talked to Zoe. He was always slightly performative, as if being the kind of man who was nice to the receptionist was important to him, but it was better than not being talked to at all. She was explaining how hard it was to find somewhere to live in London, especially if you were on your own and didn't make much money. He'd sympathized glibly and said things like 'housing crisis' and 'millennial' and 'Generation Rent', enjoying his foreign vocabulary. And then he told her about one of the other lawyers who worked there, Richard, who'd just bought a house and needed to rent out the basement, to save money for a big renovation project. It felt like one of the most positive things to have happened to her in months.

When Martin had said 'London Fields', that too seemed auspicious, but now she was here it felt uncanny to be returning. Zoe deliberately took a route past the flat she used to share with Laura and tried to peer through the windows. The blinds, with the same tangle of slats at the bottom, stopped her looking into the bedrooms, but the kitchen cupboards were the same, and the drying rack that hung over the sink was still there. She could see mugs hanging from the hooks that she and Laura had screwed into the bottom of the cupboards. It was reassuring, as well as surprising, to see that it hadn't changed. The pub opposite had a new name and the paint was darker and slicker. She saw flowers on the tables and a blackboard listing things with chorizo in them. The corner shop had become a wine bar.

She knew the street Richard lived on – Litchfield Road. She and Laura used to joke that they would live there one day, as if their lives would grow and expand at the same pace as London, and for a while, they used its name as a synonym for luxury or desire. Walking down it again, she realized it was more idiosyncratic than she remembered, broken up by mansion blocks and council estates, untrimmed hedges and thick coats of ivy. Its grandiosities now seemed faded and absurd: plaster lions guarding the steps, pillars topped with gigantic pinecones, wrought-iron balconies with peeling paint, cornicing. The large bay windows started to glow in the weakening light.

She found the house and climbed the steps to the front door. She'd expected it to be smarter – she associated Richard with the bland polish of the office. The door was an unfashionably bright colour. The bell had a sing-song tone that went on too long. She saw a shape enlarge in the mottled glass.

A woman answered – Mrs Harding. Eleanor. Zoe wasn't sure what she'd thought a lawyer's wife ought to look like – beautiful or ostentatious perhaps – but this woman wasn't either of those things. At first sight, she was unremarkable: her face was pale and slightly flat, and she had dark-blonde, fine, shoulder-length hair. Her clothes were casual: a blouse, dark jeans and loafers. You could easily not notice her, Zoe thought, and it was only after she followed Eleanor into the house that she saw how thoughtfully chosen everything was: the print on her blouse was subtle and unusual; her jeans were smart and well cut. She wasn't imposing or unfriendly, but Zoe could tell she wasn't the kind of person who made things easy.

She led Zoe into the front room. Something was not quite right. Eleanor was gathered and tasteful, and this room, with its garish walls and sagging sofas, was the opposite. She was at odds with her own home.

Eleanor wasn't cold exactly, but she was distant as she poured Zoe a glass of wine. 'And what are you up to at the moment?' she asked distractedly, the openness of the question making Zoe freeze, not knowing how to start. Zoe tried to explain about her new job and why she needed somewhere cheap to live, while Eleanor just looked mildly puzzled, as if she didn't properly understand. Zoe supposed that was reasonable; she didn't make that much sense to herself at the moment. When she asked about the house, Eleanor answered fully and said nothing unusual – they'd only just moved, had two girls, Rosie and Isobel, one and three, major renovations were planned – but her tone was guarded and she shut down the small talk a little too quickly: 'OK, shall I show you the basement now?'

Behind her on the stairs, the hall light on the crown of her head, Zoe noticed that Eleanor's hair was highlighted, delicate little stripes of colour reaching almost to the root. She recognized it from when she used to get her own hair done at a salon, before she left her job and had to do it at the sink. She wondered if, underneath, Eleanor's hair was mouse-coloured, like hers.

At the bottom of the stairs, there was a small landing and two doors, one leading to a bedroom at the back of the house. There was the base of a bed; two tartan boxes on wheels; an ornate, unsteady-looking dark wood wardrobe; and bars on the window, which looked out onto the garden. The lawn was raised, almost out of sight, and the window faced the tiered concrete banks leading up to it. There were one or two pots, filled with bare soil.

Eleanor took her round the room, apologizing brusquely. 'The view's not much, I'm afraid; the garden's fairly low down our list of priorities at the moment. The furniture's just what we've got spare, but we could come to some arrangement, if you had things of your own you wanted to bring. It's just a shower room through here, but you could use our bathroom from time to time, if you wanted. With that sort of thing, we're going to have to work it out as we go. Richard and I have never had a lodger before so we don't have house rules or anything like that. And of course, we want this to suit you too.'

Next door, there was a living room, with mismatched armchairs and a sofa, looking out on a narrow, walled-in yard. Zoe felt a surge of excitement when she saw a door leading out to it – her own front door! – until Eleanor pointed out that there were no steps up to the street: 'We'll have to share the entrance upstairs, I'm afraid.' The room was half the length of the house and to Zoe it seemed like a ballroom.

Eleanor turned to her and asked directly, 'Do you have a boyfriend?'

It sounded like a request for information, rather than an attempt to be friendly. She said she didn't, the words feeling raw and new in her mouth.

'Because we'd have to have some kind of rule about overnight guests. Unless, I mean, if there was someone long-term . . . perhaps we could discuss it.'

Zoe hadn't thought about overnight guests. Eleanor seemed to be trying to politely ask if she had sex with a lot of people. She didn't, at the moment, but she didn't want to rule it out. She said it wouldn't be a problem, and then worried that sounded even more peculiar – that Eleanor might think she was some kind of recluse.

Zoe pretended to assess the room, praising the fireplace and the large windows, asking pragmatic questions about bills and council tax, while she tried to work out whether she could live there. She felt dejected and elated at the same time. It was unequivocally grim: a dark, worn-out basement below someone else's home. The furniture was a collection of things that had descended to the ranks of the unused and un-wanted: awkward inheritances, second- or third-bests. There was a strange smell, as though everything had reached an age when it would never get clean: just too much sweat and skin. But it would be hers. She had never had more than a room to herself before.

The basement could have felt claustrophobic, but to Zoe, it seemed secluded and comforting: her own private cave. She could imagine herself at a desk, looking up at the street, peaceful, writing . . . But besides all that, she was determined to make this life she'd chosen work. And then there was the fact that, right now, she had no other options. She'd been house-sitting and sleeping on sofas, plugging the gaps in other people's lives, while they went on trips, changed flatmates or partners. She was pleasantly surprised by all the transition around her and the opportunities it threw up, but she couldn't rely on it. Really, there was nothing to consider.

'It's perfect. Perfect for me, I mean. I'd love to live here, if, you know, you and Richard are happy with that.'

An expression of pure relief crossed Eleanor's face and then disappeared. She motioned for Zoe to follow her upstairs and began talking about moving dates and bank details. Something on the landing caught Zoe's eye. She didn't know why; it was small, almost imperceptible. Without thinking about it, she crouched down. It was writing. Pencil on white plaster, just above the skirting board. The hand was shaky but insistent, escalating from a cramped 'E' to a flamboyant 'Y'. It was discreet, but defiant as well. It said, 'Emily'.

Eleanor spoke quickly and surprisingly sharply: 'That isn't anything to do with us. A family lived here before we did – that must have been the little girl. We'll wash it off before you arrive.'

There was a pause. Eleanor said, 'It isn't anything to worry about, you know.'

It was only later, when she'd left, that Zoe realized Eleanor hadn't shown her the rest of the house.

2

Richard couldn't remember when he first became aware of Zoe. He remembered putting money in the envelope for Amanda's leaving present and feeling vaguely sorry: Amanda was patient and kind, and when clients came into the building, they often said, 'The lady on your front desk's lovely.' And he noticed when her place was taken by a younger woman, who didn't look quite right. When she agreed, in an amiable but slightly blank way, to order a bike or look after a package, he didn't absolutely believe she would. He was mildly surprised to see her there, week after week, but truthfully, he didn't think too much about it. Sometimes he felt guilty for not making more of an effort with the people that surrounded him; he wondered if he ought to be more like Martin, who called the men in the postroom 'Chief' and said, 'Morning, you,' to the woman in the coffee shop, but he never managed it. So when Martin came in one morning, pointed a finger at him and said, 'Sorted out someone for your basement: Zoe,' he had no idea who he was talking about.

It was embarrassing to have to be introduced to Zoe, given that he walked past her every day. When he looked at her properly for the first time, he saw immediately why she didn't fit: there was something hopeless and inauthentic about her attempts to look smart. There was a hole underneath her bottom lip, her pale blue nail varnish was chipped, and the white shirt she wore was thin and slightly too big. She also looked absurdly young. Martin had told him she was twenty-seven and it made him feel exhausted. Most days, he still believed he was in his late twenties, but looking at Zoe's unlined skin, it became very clear he wasn't and hadn't been for some time. He was disarmed by how loquacious she was: she seemed genuinely interested in living in his house, which was extraordinary, but she was also bright and interesting, telling him that she'd resigned from a job in marketing without another one to go to, so she could 'focus on more creative stuff'. She was temping on reception but she was about to leave because she'd just been offered a job in an art shop.

It immediately felt necessary to make it clear that he was not an ordinary lawyer, and in an almost involuntary non-sequitur, he blurted out: 'I'm part-time here, you see, because I'm also working on a Master's in Renaissance Studies. I'm going to do a PhD next year, if I get funding. I'm going to become an academic.' Suddenly, in front of Zoe, this plan, which in his head seemed so audacious and had sustained him for the last two years, was punctured and collapsed. *I'm going to become an academic* – even his career change sounded dull. But still, he came away from their encounter buoyed, and a little charged. He wondered if Zoe might bring something to the household, do more for them than simply solve a financial problem.

*

The day after it was decided, Richard made his way home with a rare bubble of elation rising inside him. He had been ambushed by spontaneous bouts of happiness since they'd moved: from the day they'd first seen the house, it had felt like a charm or fate. He knew not everyone could see it – they were the only people to offer in the end – but that only made it more special. It had a light only visible to him.

After years of feeling restless and in the wrong place, things were starting to take shape. He was now a family man – a status that still felt new and unreal, but that he liked: it gave him ballast and purpose. He'd found the courage to make changes – not the wild, dramatic life changes he'd once longed for, just a series of adjustments, year by year: part-time hours, starting his MA.

And now they had the house to hold everything together. If he ever felt anxious and questions started crowding in – what would he do if he didn't get funding, what if he couldn't find a job, what if it was just another dead-end after all – he would remember the house. He hoped they would never have to sell it, but they would know it was there if they needed it: a London property they'd renovated during a housing boom. A shrewd investment; one success he could be sure of. All he had to do was make it work.

He was building a maquette in his imagination. He spent hours moulding and stretching it, extending rooms, constructing walls, creating doors, skylights, staircases. He filled it with kitchen islands, roll-top baths and king-sized beds. He wallpapered, upholstered, sanded floorboards and painted skirting boards. He spent days thinking about 'Cat's Paw' versus 'Lamp Room Grey', whether Fired Earth tiles were a good investment, and if they should paint small rooms in strong colours. He could spend days tiling an imaginary kitchen.

It was true they hadn't planned to buy somewhere that needed so much work or borrow so much money, and he knew that Eleanor was still unsure, almost squeamish, about it. And she'd been worried about finding someone for the basement. Although he hadn't said anything, it had made him anxious too, this unusable, expensive space beneath his house, decay and hopelessness emanating upwards. He couldn't imagine anyone wanting to live there. But now he had found Zoe, and she was fascinating and creative and intelligent. Perhaps she would even help with babysitting.

He put his key in the yellow door, thinking about paint colours – dark grey, perhaps, or navy – and door furniture. It was a Wednesday evening and he felt the lightness he always felt, knowing he was finished with the office for the week. He now faced two whole days working on his Master's in his new study: the epicentre of the life he was building. He saw Eleanor sitting on the floor of the living room, playing with Rosie and Isobel, and felt a rush of excitement and love. He was certain they were all at the start of something. He just needed her to see it too.

3

Zoe moved in the same week, on Saturday. Her mother drove her and although she knew she ought to be grateful, it was frustrating to start a new life this way: getting a lift from your mum, aged twenty-seven. But she didn't have a car or enough money to hire a van and anyway, she couldn't drive, so she sat in the passenger seat, watching the rain make little broken lines on the window, becoming gradually more rigid.

'It's nice round here, isn't it? Pretty houses,' her mother said. 'We used to think Hackney was the back of beyond.' Zoe thought about replying but didn't have the energy and then it was too late: the remark sank into the silence. She was preoccupied with how she was going to defend herself when her mother saw the basement – not even a basement flat, effectively someone's spare room. The shock, the disappointment, entreaties to come back home. She was working herself up into a self-righteous rage thinking about the conversation they were going to have: her mother would tell her she was crazy, paying rent to live in this place when she could have her old room in Kentish Town. Zoe would tell her that she didn't understand – this was just the way it had to be, if you wanted to live by yourself in London. Her mother would be appalled by the dingy carpet, the miserable

19

furniture; Zoe would be scornful of her bourgeois obsession with soft furnishings.

Richard let them in and Zoe felt horribly juvenile as he and her mother talked cheerfully about his children, stamp duty and the congestion charge. Richard must have been closer in age to her than her mum, but all his stabilizing forces – his family, his mortgage, his wealth – put him in a different league. He offered to help unload the car but her mum said there wasn't much, and they made their first procession down to the basement carrying boxes. Zoe gingerly turned the door handle to her new living room, thinking how ludicrous it was that she'd agreed to live here when she couldn't properly remember what it looked like. She hoped that the reality might be an improvement on the half-formed impression that had stayed with her all week, but it wasn't: it was worse. She wanted to cry, as she took in the grime and the gloom, and braced herself for her mother's reaction. But all she heard was, 'Oh, this is lovely!'

Her mother put down the box and walked round the room, patting the mantelpiece and peering out of the window.

'All this space to yourself – this is going to be wonderful. And Richard seems nice. Look at this fireplace!'

She stood in the middle of the room and put her hands on her hips.

'I think this is going to be great, Zo.'

Zoe tried to detect a false note, but she seemed completely sincere. Had she been expecting something worse? Was this really all she thought Zoe was capable of?

'Why don't we get you some furniture? I mean, this is all very nice, but you might want a few bits of your own.'

'I don't think I need anything, Mum.'

'It might make it feel more, you know, yours. I would –

help you.' She paused. Zoe's mother very rarely offered to help with money and it didn't come naturally to either of them. It had been the three of them for so long, Zoe, her mother and her brother Peter, that they'd felt almost equal – even though her mother was in charge, the triangle was small and its points were close. Now she said, 'I helped Peter when he moved. Not much, but . . . I'd like to do the same for you.'

'But Peter was buying somewhere, getting married. This isn't the same thing.'

'No, but this is your place now. You're getting settled too, in your way.'

'But it's not— This isn't the end!'

She laughed. 'Well, I don't think it's "the end" for Peter either.'

'Maybe you can do it later on, when I'm a bit more sorted?'

Zoe wanted to tell her that something else was going to happen, that she wasn't going to spend the rest of her life in a stranger's basement on her own, that it would get better than this. But she couldn't quite see the way. She just wanted her mother to leave. And, after some token unpacking and small talk that gradually wound down into silence, she did. Zoe sat on the ageing duvet on her bed, the boxes on wheels so light they tried to skate apart and away from her. She pressed her fingers onto her eyelids and tried to regulate her breathing. She didn't want Richard or Eleanor to hear her cry.

*

On Sunday, Eleanor came down and asked Zoe if she'd like to meet their children, Rosie and Isobel. Zoe made a show of leaping up enthusiastically, even though children made

21

her nervous. She had an automatic, craven desire to be liked by them, as though they could expose some unsavouriness in her. Eleanor had mentioned the possibility of her helping with babysitting and she wanted to ingratiate herself, but she'd only babysat once, for one of her university tutors when she'd graduated. It had been stressful and relentless: the two-year-old had done a shit in the garden and the dog started eating it.

Rosie and Isobel looked older than she thought a three- and one-year-old ought to look, although, really, how would she know. Eleanor told her that Rosie was small for her age, but she looked uncannily grown-up, like a miniature adult. She had an elfin, slightly sad face, and she clutched Eleanor, who dredged the answers to Zoe's questions out of her, saying, 'You're three, aren't you, Rosie? Oh dear. She's not normally like this.' When Zoe started admiring Isobel's smock, for something to say, Rosie came out from behind Eleanor's leg and pushed Zoe and told her to go away. Zoe was mortified, which only increased when she saw that Eleanor was too. 'She's still a bit unsettled from the move,' Eleanor said apologetically.

Isobel was just over one, what Zoe would have thought of as a baby, but she was large, slightly hulking, already walking and babbling. She looked exactly like Richard. Zoe knew that this was normal and apparently cute, but it was disconcerting to see a man's face on a child.

In the last year or two, Zoe had noticed people starting to ask if she wanted children. When she said she didn't know, they would say, 'You're probably too young, aren't you?' which might have been reassuring, but only reminded her that one day she wouldn't be, particularly as nurses at family planning clinics had started talking about 'leaving things too late' or 'wasting your fertile years'. They never even asked if she had a boyfriend, as though that was the least important aspect of the whole business. Looking at Isobel made her shiver: surely you had to be careful who you chose to do this with, if it meant staring at that person's face for the next eighteen years.

*

On Monday, Eleanor was at home when Zoe got in from work. She'd told her that she worked four days a week at a publishing company and had Mondays with the children. She was sitting cross-legged on the sofa, her computer resting on a cushion on her lap, talking on her mobile phone. Rosie was lying on the floor on her back, gripping an iPad, fixated on something colourful and frenetic on the screen.

Eleanor looked startled, as though she'd forgotten Zoe lived there, but carried on with her conversation. Zoe thought about going downstairs, but went into the kitchen instead – she was seduced by what Eleanor was saying, in a low severe voice. 'It's 0145 – are you writing this down? – 01458 723 66 . . . I think it's better if you speak to him direct actually, rather than us having a three-way conversation . . . Well, they're not comparable projects, are they, that's the point.' Zoe made a cup of tea and lingered over it, turning the bag in the water, thinking how satisfying it must be to be paid to make decisions and have people act on them. 'Well, that's just going to have to move, I'm afraid. My department's stretched enough as it is.'

'You're home early,' Eleanor said when she'd finished. It sounded accusatory, but Zoe didn't think she meant it to.

'Well, the shop shuts at four, and it's actually not too far on my bike so . . .'

'Of course, sorry, you said.' She shut her laptop. 'This isn't how we spend the whole day. It's just now's Isobel's nap, so it's a good time for me to catch up with things at the office, keep on top of things so tomorrow isn't too hellish. We're only going to watch one more, aren't we, Rosie?'

Zoe didn't know what to say, so she just smiled and got the milk out of the fridge.

Eleanor darted off the sofa to pick a chocolate wrapper off the floor. 'We don't normally have chocolate for tea either. But today was a bit tough, so . . . it's a treat.'

'Sure,' Zoe said. She waited for Eleanor to ask her something about her day, but she didn't say anything and the tea was resolutely made. 'See you later then,' she said and retreated downstairs.

*

The shop didn't open until ten, so Zoe found she could avoid the family in the mornings, although she would often be woken up before they left the house, by some high-pitched debate about shoes or porridge. She would go into the deserted kitchen, looking with curiosity at the remains of their breakfast time: puddles of milk on the high chair. An electric toothbrush on the table. A lipstick in the fruit bowl.

On Thursday, she was surprised to find Richard at the kitchen table, but remembered that he worked part-time too: he was an 'in-house lawyer' at the property developer but devoted Thursdays and Fridays to his Master's. She saw that he was looking at door handles on his laptop before he quickly shut it down and jumped up to start making coffee. She got a cereal box out of her cupboard self-consciously, trying not to get in his way.

She had to brace herself for the tenor of the conversation: he questioned her intently about the art shop, how she'd ended up temping on reception and why she'd left her original job in marketing, although she didn't get a chance to speak for very long before he reinterpreted what she'd said. 'Completely right. Completely right, Zoe. If something's not the path for you, you have to leave. If you feel like you're turning into the kind of person you don't want to be. And you know, it only gets harder as you get older, have more responsibilities.' He gave her pointless advice, like not to get a mortgage – 'it traps you, Zoe' – which seemed as useless as telling her not to buy a pony. He started talking to her about writing, and she was slightly puzzled that a dissertation could provoke the kind of agonizing creative process that Richard described, and also that he spoke in such collegiate and reverential tones, as if Zoe were an expert. She liked to think of herself as broadly creative – she worked in an art shop after all, she was friends with a lot of artists and she often thought about trying to write something – but she felt he'd got her wrong somehow. She didn't want to disappoint him, though, so she was generally supportive and encouraging and he seemed happy enough to talk while she listened.

*

On Friday night, they had friends over, a couple, and Zoe sat in her room, marooned and hungry: she was too embarrassed even to walk past the kitchen to leave the house. She tried to read a book or write, but all she could think about was food and she found herself idly taking in snatches of conversation from upstairs: 'You're talking five, six hundred pounds if it's a genuine Danish design'; 'Bibury's properly beautiful – it has a trout farm.' The couple left early and when Eleanor and Richard had gone to bed, she crept out to the corner shop to buy crisps and ate them in bed, feeling absurd.

At the weekend, there were swimming lessons and birthday parties and trips to the park. The logistics were discussed endlessly, so it was easy enough to know when she had the house to herself and how long for. When she was sure it was empty, Zoe emerged from the basement to explore upstairs.

Eleanor still hadn't shown her the rest of the house and she was too shy to ask, even though it made her feel mildly uncomfortable living in a house she hadn't fully seen. She used the bathroom on the half-landing and stood at the turn of the stairs, prickling with curiosity, afraid of getting caught. She didn't even know what she wanted to see: it would just be bedrooms and bathrooms, after all. The study Richard had talked about.

She went back downstairs and contented herself with inspecting the ground floor. It felt strange, the living room, because they still hadn't done it up. The walls were the same dense colours. She was sure they hadn't chosen the ancient sofas that seemed too big and formless, dominating the room, sinking into the floor. The ephemeral things clearly belonged to them, and they were solid, expensive and tasteful. And there were so many of them: butter dishes, rolling pins, knife-sharpeners. A pastry brush. Their bin was shiny and gargantuan, but it didn't shut properly; the lid had to be weighed down with a dented can of Waitrose oxtail soup. She opened the fridge: Fairtrade coffee kept shut with a hot-pink plastic clip, brightly coloured pouches of baby food, apple juice cartons, supermarket gnocchi. A tube of medical cream. Half a lemon with a circle of ochre round the rim.

They looked younger in their wedding photo, but not too much – Zoe guessed they had got married not long before Rosie was born. Eleanor wore a very plain white gown with cap sleeves and her hair was neat and smooth, no loops or curls. Richard wore a top hat and tails: his outfit was fussy and didn't sit well on him. It looked as if they'd come from two different weddings. They stood on a lawn, Richard behind Eleanor, with his arms around her. The pose was a little stiff – they were smiling but it was hard to tell if they were happy.

She set the photo down and saw that Richard had left his laptop open on the kitchen table. Up until then, she'd only looked at things they had on display, which she'd told herself wasn't wrong. There would be no justification for looking at his computer. She gingerly touched the trackpad anyway. The screen came to life, and suddenly she was reading an email from Eleanor to Richard: 'Carol can't do Friday night, shall I try Mum? Let me know if you want me to pick anything up from the supermarket.' No preamble or kisses. Why weren't they nicer to each other? Zoe had sent emails to her ex-boyfriend that were warmer than that. She heard the key turn in the door and sprang back, her face hot. The hall filled with noise and she slipped out of the kitchen, waving tentatively, keeping her face turned away, retreating to the basement only half noticed.

4

Eleanor knew they needed Zoe. She knew they were lucky to have her. She was – relatively – discreet and tidy, had different working hours, went out a lot. She could barely have intruded less, but Eleanor wanted to ignore her completely, and she couldn't. The first week she was there, Eleanor found herself irritated by any trace of her at all: foreign salad leaves in the sink, her bicycle in the hall. It was vaguely repulsive, finding bits of a stranger in your house. A hair that was too long, glinting and brash. A Brazil nut caught in the dishwasher, smooth and damp like a tooth.

It made her feel self-conscious too. She hadn't chosen the strange paint colours or the ancient furniture, but it was still her house – it ought to represent her in some way. She felt embarrassed seeing its eccentricities through Zoe's eyes. She'd stopped noticing their broken bin lid, but now it looked slovenly or slightly demented. Most of the time she didn't have the capacity to worry about what Zoe thought of them, but when they crossed paths, she felt exposed, as if Zoe was observing her. She reminded herself that Zoe was unlikely to be interested.

Eleanor knew Richard was more curious about Zoe and she was grateful for it – she was happy to outsource the task of being friendly to him. Occasionally, she wondered if she ought to feel anxious about his interest – it felt almost arrogant or complacent not to and she was constantly reminded to be wary, by magazines, her friends, her mother: 'Darling, what are you thinking? Asking a young woman to come and live with you. It's madness.'

'I don't think I need to worry about Richard, Mum.'

'No, perhaps you don't.' Her mother had sighed.

But jealousy was something she didn't really feel any more – perhaps another thing that had been obliterated in childbirth, to make room for the terror and love – and when she'd met Zoe, the night she came to look round the house, she knew straight away Richard didn't fancy her. She was pretty and slim; she wasn't thin exactly, but she was rangy, long torso, small breasts. She wore things Eleanor would never have contemplated at any age – loose jeans that hung below her hip bones, rolled just above the ankle. A complicated arrangement of vests, a long cardigan. Her hair was dyed red and there was masses of it, pulled back in an elastic band. Her skin was the kind that was so pale you could see its workings: veins, blood vessels, shadows. She had a stud in her lower lip and her eyeliner was wonky. She was so far out of their range of experience, it would have been like Richard saying he fancied a flamingo.

Richard had insisted that they invite Zoe to have supper with them and they arranged it for her second week in the house. Eleanor didn't have the energy for it, but she knew Richard was right: they ought to do it. In the end, Isobel wouldn't settle and Eleanor spent most of the evening upstairs. After she'd got her back to sleep, Eleanor sat on the edge of their bed and found herself folding back, feet still on the floor, too tired to either get up or get on the bed properly. She could hear Richard talking – 'Writing is like giving birth, Zoe. Editing is infanticide' – and she closed her eyes and thought she might just pause here a bit longer. She would be surprised if Zoe were enjoying herself, but at least she couldn't accuse them of not trying.

*

There were other things to worry about. The house was hungry for resources. Richard's savings account had collapsed in just a couple of months. Even her own savings, which had always seemed quaint and decorative compared to Richard's, had to be drawn in. Richard promised her they could be replenished – he calculated obsessively, compiling budgets and timetables and year plans. He checked property websites compulsively: 'It's gone up in value by thirty thousand – we've made thirty thousand already.' But it couldn't be translated into anything real. They still had to live there.

She knew Richard had plans for the house. It was a vision Eleanor couldn't quite access, no matter how many times he asked her what she thought. He drew floor plans and wrote lists and columns of figures at the bottom of the gas bill or on the backs of envelopes. They watched *Grand Designs* every night. Wallpaper samples arrived in the post.

She couldn't make herself care. She tried to remember if she ever had – she must have done once. She used to pride herself on her taste and had enjoyed choosing clothes – this wasn't so different surely: it was still colour, forms, lines. But since Rosie and Isobel, she'd lost her appetite for it and now relied on old clothes, her previous self's good choices.

She'd enjoyed buying things for their old house and had fought with Richard over the furniture he'd inherited from his family home. His parents instinctively disapproved of anything that hadn't been validated by history, so everything they owned was dark and solid, heavily upholstered, floral. The pieces Richard saved were hard to accommodate: chairs that were too delicate to sit on, enormous china lamps, endless side tables. She'd wanted things that were clean, minimalist and modern, things Richard's mother called 'awfully plain'.

Now the only thing she cared about was ridding the place of the people who'd lived there before. She had never had any contact with them – the sale had been completed through the estate agents and the solicitors – yet she felt unbearably intimate with them. They surrounded her, intractable, from the depressions in the seat of the sofa to the dirty red carpets: little constellations of grease spots in peculiar arrangements that Eleanor couldn't connect or read. Richard had negotiated with the lawyers that the owners would leave the house part-furnished. He said it was a good thing – they couldn't fill a four-bedroom house with what they already owned and he didn't want to have to buy cheap placeholders or rush decisions about colour or style ('a sofa is a *huge* commitment, Eleanor'). They got rid of the beds, but he convinced her to keep everything else.

The first day in the house, when Eleanor started to unpack, she'd seen that they'd left behind smaller belongings too. Blankets and quilts remained draped over the armchairs. She found a mousetrap, the dirty rubber tubes of a shower extension. A shower cap in the bath, stained pale brown at the edges. A dress for a doll behind the sofa, grubby pink velour with a white lace collar.

When she went back to the upstairs room, the room with the writing, she noticed that someone had left a row of small objects on top of the suitcase in the corner. It was an idiosyncratic collection: a tiny amber tortoise 'the size of a thumbnail. A tea cup from a doll's house. A corner of wallpaper from the hall. A hairnet. A scrap of pale grey fur. She touched it gingerly: it had the sinister softness of real pelt.

The spaces between each one were perfectly even: they looked deliberately placed. A neat line of pebbles, also carefully spaced, in size order, sat in front of the suitcase.

Richard told her to just throw away everything she'd found.

'Can we really though?' She looked at the quilt. It was an elderly patchwork, with the floral pattern fading to white in patches and grubby brown lines following the fissures of the seams. 'This is handmade. And this' – she held up the doll's dress, gingerly – 'what if they come back for it?'

'They can't. It's not their house any more.'

'It doesn't feel like it.' She touched the shower cap experimentally with her fingernail. 'I don't understand why they would leave all this stuff behind.'

'They just didn't want it any more. Stop overanalysing.'

Eleanor knew she was pressing on a bruise – it already felt dangerous to expose too much of her ambivalence towards the house. Richard turned back to his laptop screen, and she turned back to the boxes.

*

A month later, Eleanor was walking back from the corner shop and an open doorway caught her eye. It was a house a few doors down from them, one where the basement had been properly converted into a flat. A woman, Eleanor guessed in her seventies, black fabric stretched tight across her body, stood in the doorway of the basement. Her eyes were locked on a large black cat sitting on the steps leading up to the street.

The woman was gripping a white plastic handle screwed into the side of the doorway and breathing heavily. Eleanor moved tentatively towards the top of the steps.

'Would you like me to pick the cat up for you?'

The woman nodded. Eleanor took the steps slowly, cautiously, not wanting to scare it.

'Grab her!' the woman said. 'Quick, before she goes out in the road!'

Eleanor wrapped her arms around the cat and lifted it up. It hung there limply, as though its legs had suddenly stopped working. Struggling with its weight, she carried it down the steps and deposited it in the hallway. As she set it down, she had a sudden vision of the woman shutting the door behind her, trapping her inside. She turned round, relieved to see the light from the streetlamps.

'Bless you, dear,' the woman said.

Eleanor stepped back outside and held out her hand. 'I'm Eleanor,' she said. 'We've just moved into number 52.'

The woman was still gripping the handle. '52? Finally got rid of it then, did they?'

'Oh, did you know them? The previous owners?'

The woman made a face. 'Not really.'

'Why, what was wrong with them?'

She glanced quickly back into the house. Eleanor could hear the sound of the television; the woman clearly wanted to return to it. 'Just not my cup of tea, dear. Not sure they were anyone's cup of tea, if you know what I mean.'

'Oh, were they—?'

'Bless you, dear,' she said again. 'Good night.' The door closed and Eleanor stood still for a minute, before making her way back up to the street.

5

Zoe met Adam at the art shop, although later they would disagree about it – he would say they didn't meet until she came to his studio. But she remembered that Friday, a late September day when the weather was unusually warm. She could still see him taking off his jumper and the defined muscles at the top of his arms; she remembered the jolt in her stomach followed by immediate embarrassment.

She'd been offered the job at the shop the week before she moved to Litchfield Road and it had felt right somehow – enjoyable, steady, faintly bohemian, but not something that would tie her down or set her on a particular path. Laura had a friend who worked there and suggested he recommend Zoe when he left. She knew she wasn't the obvious person for the job – it had been years since her art foundation course and she hadn't painted anything since then – but she imagined herself saying, 'I work in an independent art shop in a warehouse in Hackney Wick' and thought it told the truth about her, or part of it at least. It was only later she discovered that when she said it, people would ask her if she was an artist and she would say no and the conversation would falter.

She had always liked the shop too – in the days when she and Laura did most things together and had no particular plans, Zoe would go in with her and hang around while she chose her paints. Laura told her that the shop kept going because they were specialists in a kind of resin that was difficult to get anywhere else, and that the owner, Duncan Evering, was a respected, if not famous, sculptor. There was a workshop at the back where Duncan made work to order for artists: moulds, casts and plinths.

Zoe would look around while she waited for Laura – she liked reading the names of paint colours. Certain colours – Burnt Ochre, Rose Gold Lake – gave her a kick in the stomach. But her favourite shelves were the ones that made the shop feel like a laboratory or a coven: bottles, tubs and jars filled with liquids and granules and pastes. Rabbit-skin size, Liquin Original, thixotropic alkyd primer.

She was grateful to Duncan for hiring her, particularly when she wasn't an artist; she told him she was a writer, which was not entirely true, but it was more plausible and made her feel less fraudulent. He seemed delighted by the idea – he told her she could write in the shop when it was quiet – and she felt guilty. At first, she'd been keen to learn about their stock and she'd fantasized about buying some of the materials and making something herself; she wasn't sure what. Duncan had even mentioned teaching her how to make casts, so she could help him in the workshop.

On her first day, alone in the front of the shop, she felt as though she could breathe more easily. She scrawled in a notebook and felt her mind stretch and loosen. It was euphoric, marvellous and then, quickly, it wasn't. The days were long and sprawling, a waste ground of time, barely punctuated. She had craved space, now she had too much. She stopped writing and roamed around the shop, restless and bored. Some days, she wanted to stick a scalpel in her arm, just to prove she existed.

Zoe had only been working there a month when Adam came in and was still a little unsure of what she was saying as she explained the difference between resin samples to a Spanish artist. The door opened; she looked up and he smiled at her, openly, generously, gorgeously. He waited by their sculpting tools section and Zoe tried to concentrate on what she was saying and also keep looking at him.

He had dark hair that was somewhere between long and short, and a beard. He wore the uniform of all the young men that came in to the shop: a navy cable-knit jumper, narrow, faded grey jeans and workmen's boots. He was small, maybe only five foot eight, slight and a little hunched; he didn't seem to want to take up space, or assert himself. He waited patiently for her to finish. Zoe became even more conscious of what she was saying, pitching her voice at him, trying to sound competent and informed.

Finally, the other customer left and Zoe was able to turn her full attention on him. She smiled intently, willed him to need help or advice, to ask her something, anything, but he knew what he wanted and brought it over to the counter. She was alert and nervy as she served him; ordinary tasks – putting the figures in the till, finding a plastic bag – became charged and meaningful. He had a spot on his cheek. She wanted to squeeze it. She handed him his change and carrier bag, and he left, oblivious.

*

She didn't think too much about it: this sort of thing had been happening a lot. It was now ten months since she'd left Rob, but the separation had destroyed her and she'd been reassembled awkwardly; she kept finding bits of herself in unexpected places. Just before the break-up, she had got so unhappy that the idea of sex didn't disgust her exactly, but was a bit off-putting, like something rich and queasy when you're not hungry: liver, undercooked eggs, black pudding. She'd forgotten why she ever liked it in the first place. And then as soon as they'd broken up, she'd been hit by a ferocious and peculiar sexual energy. All her senses were stirred up, vivid and overwhelming, and she could suddenly feel everything. Bizarrely creative sexual fantasies about unlikely people still came to her, fully formed, almost like dreams. That morning, she'd stopped at the lights on her bike and noticed that the cyclist in front had one leg of his jeans rolled up. She wanted to lick his ankle. Unfamiliar kinds of passion flared up all the time – she was almost getting used to it.

*

That evening, she went back to Litchfield Road and listened to Eleanor and Richard argue about Tupperware. It was so bland, she became perversely curious and then found herself taking sides: Eleanor was right, if you put it through the dishwasher at work, it *would* eventually get lost. The kind with flaps on the lids *was* expensive. The argument eventually wound down, unresolved, and she waited until everything was completely silent before going upstairs to make herself supper.

She went to bed early and woke up a few hours later, with an immense pressure on her chest. She felt disorientated and confused, unlike herself – the only thing she was certain of was that something was very, very wrong. She didn't know where she was; then she saw the wardrobe at the end of her bed rearing up and remembered. She tried to reach her phone to call an ambulance, but couldn't move. Her body remained stuck in the foetal position. She tried to shout for help. The pressure on her chest was getting worse; she was running out of time. She strained as hard as she could, but it was as if her body was coated in steel. Eventually, something yielded and she heard herself shout.

Almost immediately, the pain in her chest disappeared and as certain as she had been that she was dying, she suddenly knew that she wasn't. She was still terrified, she just didn't know what of. Her body wanted to sleep, but she forced herself up – the thought of slipping back into that frozen state was unbearable.

She paced around the room to keep herself awake. As her eyes adjusted to the dark, the forms of the furniture and indistinct piles of things on the floor seemed malleable, animistic: the carpet felt cold and unfamiliar underneath her feet. She opened the curtains, letting the concrete banks and the flower pots take shape in front of her, and wanted to wrench the bars off the window. She went to the doorway and stood at the threshold, looking up at the stairs, feeling the pressure of the unseen, unknowable rooms above her.

6

Eleanor wasn't sure exactly when she started to feel ill, or rather, when it distinguished itself from general feelings of unease. It was gradual, like the heat and light draining out of a room, and part of her thought it had been there all the time, from the day they moved in. Moving was inevitably exhausting and Rosie and Isobel's sleep had been disrupted, so she expected to feel bedraggled and used up in the first few weeks. She didn't think about it. But even as things started to settle down, the feeling that something wasn't quite right intensified. It became articulated, insistent, unignorable.

She noticed the nausea first, the day she cleared out the upstairs room. She'd put the job off, concentrating instead on the rest of the house. She'd bleached and scoured its folds and creases – the insides of cupboards, underneath tables, door hinges, skirting boards, grouting. She baulked at the idea of getting quite so intimate with the house, but felt better when it was done, even though she knew it was never going to be quite enough. She'd thrown the blankets, the shower extension and the mousetrap into a black bag, quickly, as though they were scalding. A few things seemed too personal to throw away, like the quilts and the doll's dress – in the end, she put them in a pile next to the suitcase in the upstairs room, now the only room they weren't using.

She had no idea what to do about it. She stopped referring to the house as four-bedroom, and when she showed people round, she said the room was a storage cupboard. There was a sliding lock on the outside of the door and she considered keeping it shut, trying to forget it was there.

But she could feel it above her, pressing down on the house. They had been living there for six weeks and she knew if she put it off any longer, she would never do it; she got Richard to take the girls out on Saturday and went up by herself. As she opened the door, she felt a little resistance, as though something was pushing back from the other side. Then all at once it gave and she was inside.

It was now empty, apart from the suitcase in the corner. The writing and drawings on the walls still made her shiver, but looking again, she realized the work was more intricate and careful than she'd thought. Among the frantic scribbles and untethered relentless lettering spelling 'Emily', there was obsessive cross-hatching, elegant spirals, a face with hundreds of tiny lines emerging from the mouth. Mostly the faces were unmoored but sometimes they were placed in a careful row, like a chorus, diminishing in size, five or six sets of eyes staring intently. Among the faces were drawings of birds: some elaborate with thick, bold feathers and some so simple they were almost foetus-like symbols, repeated all over the walls. The more she looked, the more Eleanor was drawn in. It was fascinating, weirdly beautiful.

She shut the door behind her and noticed that the wood on the inside had been damaged, as though it had been attacked – there were scratch marks in the paint and the wood was splitting. Eleanor thought again about the lock on the outside. She tried to think of a benign explanation for it being there, but couldn't.

She turned to the suitcase and the strange procession of objects on top. Its soft brown leather was concave; there was something inside it. It seemed wrong to throw it away without knowing what it was. Perhaps it was something precious, and if she were keeping the quilts . . . But she was afraid to open it, and still afraid of moving the objects.

It was then that she noticed she was feeling sick: mild waves of nausea, discreet but pronounced. There was a light dull ache in her head. She wanted, badly, to leave the room.

But she had promised herself she would deal with it, and time was short. She got a screwdriver and removed the lock. She tried to wash the walls, but it was no good; the ink was indelible. On Monday, she bought some cheap white paint and applied it during Isobel's nap, as the mild ache in her head turned into a defined pain and nausea lurched in little choppy waves. She wondered if it was the paint fumes. Still the writing and drawing showed through. She tried again the next evening after work, and again the night after, but three coats later, the writing was still clear. They would have to wallpaper it, but Richard refused – it was madness to make a huge aesthetic decision like wallpaper when they hadn't even decided how they were going to use the room. Eleanor gave up and went back downstairs, shutting the door behind her.

*

The following weekend, she found herself alone in the living room – Richard had taken Rosie to the supermarket and Isobel was sleeping. She had things to do – hundreds of things – but she sat still for a moment, luxuriating in the pause. It was a bright day and the sun was coming in

41

through the bay window. Eleanor stretched in the light like a cat, marvelling at the way it fell on the walls, bleaching the paint until the green was almost pleasant. She began, cautiously, to enjoy the house, as though the sun was something it had created and was offering up to her. Then she noticed a mark at the bottom of the wall. She moved closer, breath quickening, as though she knew what she was about to find. There it was: the name 'Emily' in the corner of the living room. The writing was smaller, in pencil not ink, and it was discreet, lurking by the top of the skirting board, the letters shaky and small. Eleanor ran to the kitchen for a cloth and scrubbed until it was simply a mark, no longer legible. Then she sat back down, her heart alive in her chest.

The writing on the ground floor was obviously done in secrecy, but as Eleanor discovered, it was no less compulsive. Behind the door of the living room. Above a door frame. In an alcove. The scrawls were like vermin: Eleanor became alert, vigilant, every smudge leaping out at her. When she saw the familiar faded pencil, it made her jump, even though she had been looking for it.

Soon, they were swarming at her and she couldn't understand how she hadn't seen them before. She imagined them blooming on the wall; an imperceptible trace deepening until it was impossible to ignore. Some instinct propelled her to look behind the sofa and she found an infestation: scrawls, a face, 'EMILY' in capitals. As she ran to the kitchen for hot water and detergent, Eleanor wondered how Emily had managed to move the sofa by herself. An image of a giant child with unnatural strength came into her head. Maybe Emily was a disturbed adult. Maybe she had drawn on the walls and her parents had moved the sofa there to hide it. But they fitted the space covered by the sofa exactly. Eleanor wondered if she was the first person to see them.

She found herself retching behind the sofa. She tasted vomit and swallowed.

She pushed back the sofa and knelt next to it, shaking. A headache engulfed her, a pulsing, living thing. She felt the strongest propulsion to leave the house, to get up and grab her coat. She told herself not to be melodramatic, and waited for it to subside.

7

The shop had been open an hour and a half, and there had been no customers. Zoe was just facing another blank morning, when Duncan asked her to make a delivery. This, at least, was new. A van came for deliveries in the mornings, but this piece hadn't been ready in time and it was urgent – could she take it to Dalston in a taxi? Zoe was embarrassed by how excited she was by the prospect: fresh air, a taxi ride, an encounter. Duncan took her out to the workshop to show it to her – it was a plinth, so smooth and white and perfect that she was afraid to touch it. He wrote down the name of the customer for her – Adam Cunningham – and she wondered if he would be the man that had come into the shop a few weeks ago, who she still thought about sometimes when she heard the door go and somebody different came in.

It was bright but cold; the air was sharp on her face, exhilarating, as she handled the plinth into the back seat of the cab. The taxi dropped her on a narrow street off Kingsland Road, opposite a warehouse building with a set of bright yellow double doors. She pressed the button on the intercom, a man answered, and she looked up at the windows while she waited for him to come down. She could see pot plants, cut-out paper shapes stuck on the glass and strange plaster lumps on the windowsill.

The door opened and it was him. She felt suddenly self-conscious, as if by wanting this exact thing she had actually made it happen; as if her desire was so obvious, it had somehow brought him here. She was relieved when it became clear he didn't remember her from the shop. He smiled and something shifted inside her.

She offered to help him carry the plinth upstairs. They eased it up the narrow concrete stairwell together, intricately synchronizing their movements as the weight passed between them. It felt like they were dancing. Two floors up, he unlocked another door, they went up one more flight of stairs together, and then they emerged into the best place Zoe had ever seen.

It was a space so vast it couldn't properly be called a room: an entire floor of a low, wide warehouse building. In its centre, there were two giant rumpled sofas, kitchen units and a dining table, but they only dented the expanse. The rest was taken up by studios, divided by low MDF partitions. Zoe could see easels and lightboxes, fabric, desks, radios, sewing machines, printing presses, bicycles, canvas and books. It smelt of white spirit.

'This is your studio?'

'It's a live/work space. My bedroom's that way, and my studio's just over here.'

He led her towards the back of the room and they set the plinth down in the middle of a small square area, filled with strange forms. There were some she could identify – a hunk of tarmac, a bent piece of drainpipe – and some she half recognized. There was a perfect white plaster circle with the centre pulled up and folded over the rim; it looked like a drooping witch's hat or a used condom. A collection of rusting metal sheets stood in a washing-up bowl. There were drawings pinned on the walls, tools, pens, maquettes, notebooks, scraps of paper, diagrams. A plaid shirt and a huge navy jumper that looked like it might be handknitted hung on a hook next to goggles and gloves. A pair of trainers splashed with something thick and white sat under the desk. Zoe felt unexpectedly calm. She had the strongest sensation of being home she'd had in months.

'God, this place is *amazing*.'

He looked pleased. 'I'll show you round if you like.'

*

He took her round the other artists' spaces, telling her who they were and what they did: they had names like Ursula and Cora and Oscar and they made sculptures out of felt or did 'performance stuff' or were working on PhDs about conceptual art. She saw giant abstract paintings, boulders of paint encrusted on palettes, half-full tubs of primer. He showed her his bedroom, which had barely more than a bed and a clothes rail in it. His lack of possessions might once have made her suspect a lack of personality; now, she took it as a sign of authenticity.

Adam pointed out the remains of the building's life as a factory: a board which still had the marks of people clocking in and out. He opened what she thought were windows but turned out not to be: they were doors opening straight out onto the sky with no barrier or balcony – 'this was how they'd get heavy goods in.'

They stood looking out at the drop and she felt the sun on her face. He asked her how long she'd been working at the art shop.

'Oh, couple of months? Something like that.'

'I thought I hadn't seen you before. Are you an artist too?'

'No.' She tried to say it resolutely, but it still sounded strange.

'Oh – so how come you work there?'

She thought about evading the question, like she normally did, but she decided to be honest instead. It was worth trying, and this place felt so far away from real life, a fantasy world where people wanted to do things and just did them.

'Well, I used to work for a charity, in communications. You know: PR, marketing campaigns, that kind of thing. It was fine, I mean, I liked it, but it was never really what I wanted to do. It wasn't going anywhere, the job was never going to change and I used to want to be a writer, but I . . . lost sight of that some time ago. I don't know what happened really: I just had this moment of clarity and realized that if I didn't leave, I'd be there forever. And I didn't want that. So I left.'

'You just quit? That's really brave.'

She preened involuntarily, even though it wasn't true. Resigning hadn't felt brave; it had felt ridiculous. She would have given anything not to do it, and had spent years trying to avoid it, finding ways to anaesthetize herself against the boredom and sense of wasted time. And if she hadn't broken up with Rob, it might never have happened, but her life had been so bent out of shape, it felt as if one more change wouldn't matter. She didn't tell him that she woke up in the middle of the night, fearing that this wasn't 'space to figure out what she wanted to do', it was the substance of her life and would stretch on and on with nothing to mark or coordinate it.

'So how come you ended up working at Evering's?'

'Well, at first I couldn't stand the idea of a permanent job so I temped for a bit, but for these really corporate places and I always felt a bit . . . well, like I didn't really fit in. And then someone told me about the Evering's job and I really loved the shop so I just went for it. I thought it would be more straightforward, and useful, I guess: selling actual things to people that wanted them instead of, I don't know, tweeting and email-newsletters and arranging meetings and worrying about whether my boss liked me. I used to think working for a charity would feel meaningful, but I still found myself wondering whether anything ever made a difference or if it did, whether I was the best person to be doing it . . . I was still getting sucked in by it, even without particularly caring about it, and I thought if I didn't have all that *noise* going on, I could find something I really did want to do. Although I haven't yet.' She looked down. 'Maybe that sounds really stupid.'

'God no, I think about this sort of stuff all the time. I'd love to do something more meaningful.'

She looked at him sceptically. She couldn't imagine living there and feeling like that. 'Really?'

'Yes, definitely. I love making work, but I don't particularly like having to explain it to curators or do funding applications or write another fucking artist's statement. Some people really thrive on that side of things, and maybe I did too for a while, I don't know. Now it's just tiring, having to remind people you exist all the time. And my friends from home own houses and have kids and dogs. Sometimes I wish I had an ordinary job, then I could just make whatever art I wanted and not have to go round talking about it all the time.'

'What sort of ordinary job would you do?'

'I really want to do something *physical*.' He made a vague wrenching mime with his hands. 'I see those men who cut down parts of trees – you know what I mean, what are they called?'

'Tree surgeons?'

'Yeah, them. I see them and I'm, like, aching. That would be such an amazing job.'

She looked down at the trees lining the street, the orange leaves luminous in the sunlight. 'Why don't you do that then?'

'I don't know – it looks pretty terrifying, hanging off a tree with a fucking massive chainsaw. I think you can get quite seriously injured.'

She laughed. 'That's a bit pathetic.'

He looked at her and smiled. 'Maybe I'm not as brave as you.'

'Ha, I don't know, I'm not really brave. It's not exactly dangerous sitting in Evering's. And it can get really boring.' She could smell the grilled meat from the kebab shop opposite. She felt hungry and remembered that she would have to go back to work; she felt a depression in her stomach.

'Do you not like it then?'

'Bits of it. I like the space. And Duncan. And sometimes interesting people come in the shop.' She stared straight ahead when she said it but she couldn't stop herself smiling. She was almost certain he was too.

'You must get more time to concentrate on writing though.'

'I suppose, yeah . . . but I still don't know if writing was really the thing I wanted to do either.' She laughed, to disguise the fact that this was the most honest thing she'd said in a long time. 'I just wanted something more, I guess. Something of my own.'

'It sounds like you're an artist, Zoe. We all want that. That's why we do it. We want something of our own.'

She turned to him, inordinately, cravenly flattered. *It sounds like you're an artist*: it was as though he'd said *it sounds like you're really good in bed*. It was so seductive to have someone explain you to yourself. A feeling rose in her, pure and bright, and she thought she might kiss him and stay there forever. And then she thought about how kind Duncan was to her and how she couldn't really untether herself from one of the only things keeping her in place – and then the feeling got alloyed and confused and she looked away. 'I guess I'd better get back to the shop.'

'OK.' He shut and bolted the doors and they walked back towards the stairs. They stood opposite each other and she was certain that this time she wasn't deluded or hyper-sensitive: there was something between them.

'Hey, it was nice to meet you.'

'You too. Thanks so much for showing me round. I really love it here.'

'No problem. Come back any time.'

He paused. He tried to sound off-the-cuff, but she could tell he had prepared it.

'We're having a party next Friday? Just a house party. You should come? I mean, if you're not already doing something.'

She said that that would be nice and they exchanged numbers, while she tried to hide how pleased she was. When she got out into the street, she found she was running. Her excitement had reached a pitch that was almost distressing. How was it possible to get so high on a building, on walls and ceilings and space? The sun turned everything pale gold – the tarmac, the tower blocks, the terraces – and the basement and the shop seemed sepia in comparison. She looked up at the sky: in one direction, it was white touched with the very palest blue, and in the other, there were inky grey clouds edged in light. She felt more hopeful and more unstable than she had for weeks.

8

Soon, the nausea was there all the time. It was there when Eleanor woke up and when she went to sleep. Mostly, it was dull and consistent – a low-level queasiness leaving her just enough energy to wash and dress and get Rosie and Isobel out of the house, to prepare meals and put the washing on, reply to emails, take meetings, keep on top of the publishing schedule, send thank-you cards and read picture books, but she was performing it all through a slight haze. She was never quite present; everything was tinged. Every movement, every gesture or smile, came just a little bit less easily and with a delay only perceptible to her. Some of her resources always had to be directed to dealing with the hard, bright thing in her stomach that refused to settle, and the delicate nubs of pressure on her head and face. At the top of her nose, above her ears, the back of her skull, like small fingers prodding insistently.

And then sometimes, if she had been at home for a few hours, it was intense: so intense that the pain in her head made her want to cry and she was actually sick, suddenly, violently. Something would rise up inside her and she would have to run upstairs to the bathroom, with Rosie behind her demanding to know what she was doing. She would throw up with the door open. Sometimes she couldn't even manage that and would be sick in the nearest place: in the sink, a canvas bag or, once, into her hands. There would be a moment of light-headed relief, on her knees, clutching the table leg, Rosie asking, 'Why did you *do* that, Mummy?', Isobel screaming. But it was just a moment's silence before it started again, slowly accumulating until she couldn't properly listen or feel or think.

At first, she told Richard when she felt ill, and he was sympathetic and tried to help: he arranged for her to rest on weekends, persuaded her to take days off work, made her cups of hot water. But nothing helped and soon, it was happening so often that they both ran dry – she was bored even saying the words: 'Just a headache, and feeling sick again.' It became clear that resting every time she felt sick was not an option: she couldn't stop participating in life altogether. She just had to live with it.

*

Richard encouraged her to find out what it was. She took four pregnancy tests. She went to see her GP and smiled politely when a friendly, detached young doctor told her that moving house was as stressful as divorce or losing a loved one. Eleanor listened attentively while she talked about rest, staying away from alcohol, drinking lots of water, scheduling in me-time, getting Dad or Grandma to help a bit more.

She did neck stretches. She stopped eating sugar. She tried yoga. She went to alternative practitioners: paid people to touch her head or her feet in a certain way, and put needles in her wrists. They at least took her seriously and there was something seductive about being listened to, but the treatments didn't help. After each session, she wondered how long she could continue with this: sitting on low wicker chairs, turning the limp, softened pages of cheap magazines, worrying about the time off work, taking off her tights, lying down, enduring something overly intimate, then putting her card in the machine and feeling her overdraft expand.

Her doctor had told her to come back if it didn't get better in two weeks; she tried again. She was told she had a virus and just needed to rest. The third time, the doctor seemed actively bored, as Eleanor explained the same procession of symptoms. She reminded herself that they probably had patients with cancer in their waiting rooms, but she was firm, as she'd promised Richard she would be, and insisted that they give her tests. They tested her for various conditions, none of which quite described what was happening to her. The results came back negative. She wasn't surprised. She'd always known, somehow, that they would.

*

Every time she tried something, a small part of her remained fatalistic, because there was something she was keeping to herself. An unwelcome idea was forming in her head. When she felt sick, she had a strong desire to leave the house. Even just outside the front door, gulping at the air, she felt as though something was slowly returning to her body, an elixir injected into her bloodstream. At first she thought it was the fresh air or a change of scene. But eventually the distinction became clear: when she was on the street or at the office, the park or the shops, she felt herself getting better, stronger. The illness was at its worst, its least endurable, when she'd been in the house all day. She found herself making excuses to leave, going to coffee shops, inventing things they needed from the supermarket, walking the children round the park in the rain, while Rosie cried and begged to go home. She felt ill in the house and better when she was away from it. She didn't see how she could explain this to anyone – certainly not to Richard.

It had to be her imagination. The next time she felt ill, she decided to ignore it. It was a Saturday and Richard had taken Isobel to Rosie's swimming lesson. Leaving the house would be so easy – she could just go, unencumbered by buggies or nappies or arguments about coats. But she resolved to resist it. It would be ludicrous to waste these precious free hours walking round the block, when there were so many other things she needed to do.

She emptied the dishwasher, feeling the familiar discomfort turning to nascent queasiness. She tried to distract herself. She tidied the children's toys away, while it bloomed to a full, perfect nausea. The tiny stains on the carpet made her retch. *Mind over matter*. The grip on her head became cruel and insistent. She wanted more than anything to go outside. She put up the drying racks and took the washing out of the machine. The nausea rose. The green of the walls seemed to intensify, until it was almost overpowering.

She thought of the miscarriage she'd had before having Isobel, how she'd not had any time off work, taken Rosie to her playdates, bled into her black trousers while talking to a mechanic about the broken washing machine. Wasn't that worse than a headache and hadn't she coped? Wasn't labour worse? Wasn't that just what women did, withstood physical pain in silence – had IUDs fitted, period pains, morning sickness, abortions and didn't talk about it? And now, this illness which didn't even have a name was flooring her.

She began to panic; this couldn't be true, it wasn't sustainable. She had to be able to stay in her house. She stared at the clothes hanging on the drying rack, barely able to remember getting them out of the machine, astonished to have completed the task without collapsing. She found herself standing in the bay window, watching the cars going past. Then suddenly she was grabbing her coat, clutching her handbag, fumbling with keys. She opened the front door and staggered down the steps, drinking the cold air. She doubled over outside the gate. *Two minutes. Then I'll go back in.* But before she knew what she was doing, she was running down the street.

9

Zoe sat on Laura's sofa, corralling loose bits of tobacco with her fingernail. They were looking at old photographs and being careful with each other. Laura had spread the pictures out on the coffee table like a safety net, to remind them of a time when the way they felt about each other had been simpler. She'd taken the photos for an art project when they were at university: they were of Zoe in a black dress holding a melon. Zoe remembered how seriously they'd taken it, and felt embarrassed and wistful.

Laura lived in an eighties ex-council house in Hackney Wick, which she shared with four other artists. The linoleum in the kitchen was covered with swirls of dirt, like a garage floor; there was always washing up in the sink and the living room smelt of smoke and takeaway. The house was cluttered with slightly sinister artworks – there was a plaster model of a small boy riding a horse in the hallway, which Zoe found particularly unnerving, and there were paintings of people puking and shitting in the upstairs bathroom. But there was something domestic and collaborative about the house too: people sat around and smoked and watched TV together and had conversations about drugs or art. The downstairs loo was broken and there was talk of turning it into a camera obscura, though no one had got round to it yet.

Since they'd moved out of their flat in London Fields, Laura had experimented: she'd shared an attic room in a hostel in Shoreditch with five other people, and listened to her roommates having sex on the mattress next to her. She'd lived in a warehouse space in Hackney Wick with no internal walls or kitchen and a communal shower block, putting up curtains between the beds and cooking on a camping stove, the Olympic Stadium looming. 'I get now why people live in houses,' she said. It made Zoe envious and grateful at the same time: the way she felt when she saw Laura's paintings.

Laura had just got a part-time job in arts administration, which was dull, but gave her a regular income and time to be in the studio. As a set-up, it was more mundane and less outrageous than either of them had imagined their lives would be when they were in Brighton, taking photographs, posting poems they'd written to each other, swimming drunk in the sea, and drinking lapsang souchong from a thermos on the beach. But for the first time ever, that kind of quiet purpose and security looked deeply appealing and, though she wanted to be happy for Laura, it made Zoe feel like she'd done things the wrong way round.

She'd been gingerly telling Laura about Adam and had passed over her phone so she could read his texts: he'd sent her the details for the party and a picture of the plinth with a sculpture made out of nails on it, in a gallery. She had told him how much she loved his work and wanted to impress on him how much seeing his studio meant to her, but she couldn't find the words. She kept wanting to say 'fantasizing' and 'stimulating' – as though there was a chemical in your brain that produced sex words when you fancied someone. He said he wanted to read her writing. She wished she hadn't told him about it.

'It sounds like he likes you.' Laura handed back her phone.

'Do you think?'

'Oh, come on, he's clearly flirting with you – "oh, look at my plinth, can I read your poems."'

'I just don't really trust my judgement at the moment.' Zoe put her phone back in her bag. 'Do you think I should go to the party?'

'Of course – you have to.'

'I won't know anyone. I'll look desperate.'

'You won't, don't be silly.'

Zoe hesitated. 'Why don't you come with me?'

Laura had her tongue out and a Rizla in front of her mouth; she stopped and put it down. 'Zoe, you know I would. But I'm seeing Nick on Friday.'

'Bring him?'

Laura just looked at her. Then she picked up the Rizla again and said, lightly, 'How's it going in your new place? What are the grown-ups like?'

'They're OK. I like her, Eleanor, but she's quite intimidating. She buys clothes from Jigsaw. And she wears a watch.'

'God. What about him? Is he good-looking?'

'Um . . . maybe, I don't know. He's just one of those people – I mean, you just wouldn't ever think of him like that.'

'But it's working out OK there?'

Zoe hesitated. She couldn't truthfully say she liked it. After she'd moved in, she'd scrubbed and hoovered and bleached, but the rooms never seemed to get entirely clean: the brown-grey lines on the enamel and the black spores between the tiles refused to shift. The carpet and the walls felt coated. Even the dust wasn't normal – it was browner and denser than ordinary dust. It made the light grey fluffy kind seem clean.

And she'd found more writing on the wall, the name 'Emily' again, this time above the skirting board near the electric fire. A day later, she'd found another scrawl, slightly larger, in the bedroom, beside the wardrobe. Then one night when she was reading in bed with a cup of tea, she saw the same writing on the wall, next to her pillow. It made her jump and then she was wide awake. She couldn't understand why she hadn't noticed it before. She left the marks there for a few days; it seemed a bit obsessive to care about writing on the wall if you could barely get it together to hoover. But she couldn't completely forget about it, particularly at night, just before she fell asleep; knowing Emily's name was burning into the wall beside her bed. Eventually, she gave in and got some warm water and a cloth. Kneeling beside her bed, she wondered if it had got bigger. The letters definitely seemed to be sprawling outwards.

But saying this aloud to Laura would mean she'd have to confront it. She had nowhere else to go; she had to make the best of it. So she just said, 'Yeah, it's good; I like it,' unconvincing and evasive.

They looked at each other for a moment; Zoe thought Laura knew she was lying, but didn't know whether she was going to say anything about it. She wasn't sure she would like it either way, so she said: 'Sorry I was being stupid before. I am going to go to the party on Friday.'

Laura picked up her cigarette. 'I know you are,' she said.

10

Richard tried to tell himself that it didn't matter. It was a minor work frustration and it was Wednesday evening anyway; he should just forget about it, turn his attention to his Master's. But he still seethed the whole way home, furious about what had happened earlier that day: the disagreement about the adequacy of the indemnity insurance, how Martin had undermined him, the way it had ended up looking like he was being unreasonable, when actually Martin was being cavalier. He was mainly furious with himself for caring at all. He had thought that publicly disassociating himself from work would make him happier and calmer, give him a sense of perspective, but it hadn't. It made him feel worse, in fact: now he was caught between things, neither one nor the other.

He told himself what he always told himself: that he was on a different path, that he had different values, that there were more important things than money and status, like creativity, passion and family. When he spoke to Zoe about it on Thursday and Friday mornings, he believed it, became almost zealous in his commitment to this way of life. But he couldn't always hold those ideas in his head and the fact that they so often deserted him made him doubt himself.

Truthfully, when he was around Martin, he couldn't access them at all. All he wanted was to feel successful again.

He found Eleanor at the kitchen table, drawn and white-faced. Rosie and Isobel were watching television.

'Eleanor, I thought we said we weren't going to allow—'

'Richard, just don't, OK?'

He took his coat off and dropped it on the sofa. He went into the kitchen, trying to put off the next question – it made him feel anxious and exhausted already, but he asked anyway. 'How are you feeling?'

Eleanor grimaced. 'Sick again.'

'Actually sick?'

'Three times.'

'Well, that's less than yesterday – maybe you're getting better.'

'I don't think so. I think it's getting worse. I wasn't sick at all after lunch yesterday.'

'Well, you look better.' It wasn't true; he didn't know why he'd said it. He filled the kettle and switched it on.

'I really don't feel it.' She slumped forward on the table.

'You'll feel brighter tomorrow.'

He was annoying himself with his glib, unassailable positivity but he couldn't manage any other response. Eleanor's illness frightened and frustrated him at the same time – its mysteriousness, its namelessness, the way it refused to follow a pattern or logic. He just wanted it to go away and at first, he had applied himself to the problem, suggested resting and time off, sourced advice from colleagues, sent her articles about possible causes of headaches. He'd tried to suppress his irritation at the defeated air with which she tried things – she never seemed to believe anything would work.

The only other thing he could think of was a private

doctor but he didn't know how they'd pay for it – they needed the money for the house. All that was left was sympathy, but that felt useless and flaccid, saying 'sorry' and 'poor you' over and over again when it didn't change anything. He just had to save enough to get started on the building work – as soon as they could make the house feel truly theirs, things would be better. Eleanor would be happier and less run-down.

'By the way,' she said, 'I found some more Emily writing today. But in the kitchen this time.'

'Really?' His tone sharpened involuntarily. 'OK, well, we'll wash it off.'

'I've washed it off.'

'So that's fine, then.' He was still sounding shorter than he meant to. He took a deep breath and tried to soften his voice. 'Do you want a cup of tea?'

'No, thanks. You don't think it's weird?'

'She was just a child being naughty, writing her name on the walls. It doesn't mean anything.'

'It doesn't give you the creeps?'

'No! Come on, Eleanor, please. Can't you just put up with it for a bit? It's really not long till we can get started.' He thought about his spreadsheet and didn't know if that was true. They hadn't saved anything since they moved in; the plan was already set back by two months. 'I know it's not right at the moment, but it's going to be great.'

She looked around the room. 'Sometimes I don't know if it's ever going to feel like ours.'

'Eleanor! I'm trying, OK? We'll get rid of all this crap, I promise you, it'll be unrecognizable by the time we've finished. But you have to try too – you can't be so negative about it all the time.'

Eleanor pressed her fingers into her temples; she looked

like she was in pain. His frustration turned to guilt, which seemed to stop him saying anything. The moment passed. The television programme theme music started.

'OK, come on, you two, bath-time!' Eleanor scooped up Isobel and took Rosie screaming away from the television. He got out his notepad and started drawing floor plans, soothed by the simple act of committing marks to paper, creating something.

*

Later on, when the children were in bed, he showed her his notepad. 'I had an idea about the extension – maybe we could make a little room for you, here, above the kitchen, like a study?'

She came and stood behind him, and looked over his shoulder. 'What would I do in a study?'

'I don't know. Your work? Editing?'

'I don't do any editing these days. It's not really part of my job any more.'

'You could read there or . . . OK, maybe it could be a dressing room – we could put a . . . thing for your shoes in there or a wardrobe or something.'

She laughed. 'Richard, I barely have time to get dressed in the morning!' She peered at the notepad. 'It's miles from our bedroom anyway. I thought that was going to be a utility room.'

'Yes, but I figured out a way we can get a bit more room under the street – like 48 have done, look next time you go past – so we can have the washing machine there and then we can have a room for you.'

'I think we probably need a utility room more.'

'Well, we can think about it.' He closed the notebook and started tapping at the computer. 'Can you just have a look at this? I'm thinking of adding it to the mood board for the sitting room. Also, did you know you can get skylights that shut automatically when it rains?'

'We don't have skylights.'

'We will do! When we convert the attic. Come on, Eleanor, we've been through this so many times.'

She kissed the top of his head. 'Sorry, I just can't keep up with it – it feels like the plans change all the time. I still feel sick – I'm going to go and lie down, OK?'

Richard lingered in the kitchen longer than he was supposed to. Eleanor had warned him about keeping it free for Zoe after they'd eaten: 'We need to give her her own space, Richard, or she'll move out.' He heard Zoe on the stairs and knew he should leave, but he felt listless and stuck. She hovered uncertainly in the doorway. 'Sorry, I'll get out of your way,' he said, without moving.

'No, no need! I'm just on my way out, actually.'

'You look nice,' he said, without really thinking about it, and then regretted it when she blushed.

'Oh, right, thanks . . .' she said.

Richard was suddenly aware of everything – his glasses, the remains of the children's tea on the table, his strange little drawings on the notepad. She filled a glass of water from the tap and gulped it. He said, 'Oh, well, have a nice time!' and when the door went, he felt slightly altered. It was as though the light had gone out of the house, but he could feel it still, burning the back of his neck.

11

On Friday, the shop was unusually quiet and Zoe spent the day in a state of restless anxiety, which intensified with each unused hour. She was dreading the party – certain that it would be humiliating in an unspecified way – but she couldn't face another evening in the basement, or telling Laura that she'd been too scared to go. Besides, if she didn't go, nothing would happen. Maybe nothing would happen if she did, but then: something might.

By the time the shop shut, she was so wound up and understimulated, she didn't know what to do with herself: she thought she might arrive at the party and grab Adam's crotch or punch him in the face. Back at Litchfield Road, she tried to wash off her nerves in the shower. She hadn't shaved since the end of the summer and was only half aware of the hair on her legs. Looking at them properly, the hairs were startlingly thick, black and delineated; under her arms, it was dense and springy. She got rid of it all, soaped her arm-pits and the backs of her knees three times, cleaned between her toes, cut her pubic hair with nail scissors till it was just a shadow. When the shower drained, the foam was grey with clumps of hair, like dirty snow. She still felt jangly; she wondered if she should make herself come before she went out.

She tidied her bedroom, even though she knew no one was going to see it – however well the evening went, it was unlikely that Adam would leave his own party to come back to London Fields to have sex with her. She tried to find something to wear that was glamorous, unconventional and understated, and when that seemed impossible, she decided that understated was the most important quality and put on a black T-shirt dress and Doc Martens.

As she'd got older, she'd got less interested in what she looked like, gradually shedding hair straighteners, natural highlights, fake tan, padded bras, thongs, tops that were low at the front and high enough to show her flat stomach and the jewel in her belly-button, now also long gone. It was mainly a relief to lose all these things: she'd got a kick out of going out and knowing that she looked good, but it never felt entirely real – like she was dressing up as a good-looking woman and getting away with it. Eventually, pleasingly, it started to matter less. She supposed it was partly to do with being with Rob for so long. Now, she wondered if she ought to have been more vigilant. Maybe her appearance looked strange or inappropriate outside the context of a six-year relationship, like a family nickname or a private joke.

She walked to the party, winding through the streets behind Kingsland Road, her heartbeat getting louder, repeatedly asking herself what she was doing. Eventually she came to the yellow doors opposite the kebab shop. She forced herself to press the buzzer and a distorted voice that could have been Adam's, or anyone's, answered and the door opened. Zoe made her way up the stairwell and saw a small, morose-looking man standing in the door frame. He looked older than her, with dark, close-cropped hair and large glasses. He didn't smile. She introduced herself again and told him she was a friend of Adam's. He nodded and let her in.

She realized immediately that she had made a mistake. There were a few gestures to a party – low lights, music, a strand of fairy lights half-heartedly draped over one of the studio partitions – but it was not a party, yet. The room was empty apart from six or seven people sitting on the sofas, none of whom was Adam.

She took them in, with an increasing sense of dread. Their collective look was severe and deliberately unfashionable, as if they were trying to trick you into dismissing them before they revealed their inherent social value. They were a mass of shirts buttoned up to the top, cardigans, large glasses; everything was bottle green, navy or check. The girls wore items of intimidating ugliness, like tartan slacks or a black velvet jumpsuit. Zoe felt naive in her black dress and eyeliner. They smiled nervously, as though her presence was slightly embarrassing, which she supposed it was. The man who'd let her in muttered, 'Sorry, what did you say your name was?' and she repeated it loudly, addressing the group on the sofa, smiling fiercely. They introduced themselves guardedly, as if they were prepared to retract this small gesture at any moment. She was wondering what would happen if she just turned around and walked out, and then Adam appeared from the back of the room. He saw her and smiled, and it was intoxicating. She knew then that she would stay.

*

She thought it would impress Adam if she got on with his friends, so she attached herself to the group on the sofa and applied herself to the task. She talked to Oscar, who made drawings: he'd tried to paint, but just found himself stabbing the canvas. ('I mean, sure, there is some creativity in destruction, but . . .') She talked to Ursula about the experience of making your own felt and what she thought neon colours signified and to Anna about her performance piece involving junk food. She didn't particularly want to talk about herself, so she questioned them vigorously and they seemed happy to talk. After an hour of smiling, sympathizing and praising, she realized she was exhausted. It had finally become a party: it was crowded, the music was loud, and she was drunk. Adam was on the other side of the room; she got up and walked towards him, unsteady and determined.

He caught her eye and smiled at her, as if she were the best thing he'd ever seen and for a moment, she believed that she was. He introduced her to the person he was talking to but she and Adam quickly discarded him, drawing closer, talking intently, ferociously, about nothing much. She said things she'd said thousands of times before, about London, her job, university, but when she spoke to him, all the words became vivid and new. He kept finding ways to touch her; when he did, it felt like his fingers left marks on her skin. The party swelled and coursed around them, and she realized people were dancing.

After a while, she started to feel frustrated. There was a strange eddying between them: he would touch her hand or the small of her back, and abruptly remove his hand. They would move closer again, and he would pull away. She didn't want to talk all night. But she had no idea how she was going to get him to fuck her at a party in a warehouse where all the rooms had MDF walls.

'Hey, you never sent me any of your writing,' he said.

'I don't know, I'm not sure if I can . . .'

'Come on, I sent you that picture of my sculpture.'

'That's different.'

'How?'

Because you're a real artist.

'Come on, just tell me a couple of lines of something. You must be able to remember something.'

Something was forming in her mind; it was stupid, she was drunk. 'Just a sentence,' he said. 'Anything.'

'I'll write it down for you, OK?'

She found a receipt in her bag and he found a pen. She carefully wrote down part of a poem she'd written six years ago.

He took it and read it in front of her. It was excruciating and sublime.

'I really like it, Zoe. Can I keep it?'

'Hey Adam, where's Kathryn?' A bearded man in a plaid shirt appeared out of nowhere. Adam introduced him to Zoe, but all she could think was: *Kathryn*. The way he'd asked. Adam looking mortified, pulling his hand away. It was all so obvious.

'She's in Edinburgh.'

'Oh, right. Is she just visiting uni friends?'

'She's moved back. She's doing a Master's.'

'Seriously? Anna never told me that.'

'No, well, she has.'

'And are you OK with that? The whole long-distance thing?'

He grimaced and did an exaggerated shrug. 'I don't love it. But you know.'

Zoe stopped listening. She felt foolish, flattened. She'd got it wrong; of course she had. She wanted to snatch the poem out of his hand. She interrupted and told Adam she had to go. He followed her through the crowd and down the dark grey stairwell, not speaking. When they got to the front door, they just looked at each other.

He took her hands, tenderly, apologetically. His skin still felt like nectar and she wouldn't see him again; maybe she should just enjoy this feeling while she could. And then there was that moment, that exquisite moment: their mouths almost touching, an inch apart, as if they were attracting and repelling each other at the same time, rapidly evaluating the consequences of going forward or back – and then plunging and kissing. Zoe felt both transported and utterly grounded; his mouth tasted curious and exotic, like nothing on earth, and also like beer.

She pulled away. 'You've got a girlfriend.'

'I know. I'm sorry.'

He pushed her up against the concrete wall. It was cold and uncomfortable, and Zoe thought this was the most exciting thing that had ever happened to her. She was kissing him ferociously, not sure what she wanted from him: just more; more something, more everything. But he was saying goodbye.

'Zoe,' he said hopelessly, and something happened to her when he said her name. 'I really like you.'

'Me too,' she said. And then it was over, the heavy door closed behind her and the air was biting and damp. She walked to the bus stop in the rain, drunk, desperate, sad, happy.

12

It was slowly getting worse. Eleanor could almost manage it, as long as she planned enough time away from the house. She was out for ten hours on Tuesday to Friday, a shot in the arm that left her just sturdy enough to get through the evening and the night. Weekends were more difficult, but she was strategic, making sure the stretches inside were not too long, or at least punctuated by a walk to the park or a trip to the shop. If she was desperate, she stood in the door-way to the garden, even though she and Richard had both decided it was too dangerous to have it open in case the children attempted the steep, rickety staircase down to the lawn, which he promised to have replaced by spring. More often she found herself drawn to the front of the house, away.

Just when she thought she had it under control, some-thing would go wrong. It would rain, Isobel wouldn't stop crying, Rosie would be furious about her coat. She'd be trapped, and then it would erupt suddenly: thick black liquid crashing at the sides of her head as she threw up in the wastepaper basket.

They had a weekend in Oxfordshire planned to celebrate Richard's birthday and Eleanor used that as sustenance, fantasizing about an entire night within a different set of walls. She imagined them driving there, the distance between herself and the house slowly expanding. She felt she could breathe more easily. They would go to Richard's parents for a few days over Christmas and their best friends were getting married in the new year – any pleasure she took in the idea was now overtaken by the excitement at the prospect of another night away.

*

Mondays, her day with the children, were truly difficult. Rosie and Isobel confined her to the same small trail of coffee shops and parks surrounding the house, always calling her back with their demands or quirks. She had felt this before of course, but never particularly minded it; sometimes even enjoyed the less dynamic way of life. Now, she felt tethered.

The Monday before they went away, she argued with Rosie on the bus. Rosie wanted her to pretend to drive the bus, but it was crowded and Eleanor felt self-conscious, so she said not now; Rosie demanded and Eleanor refused. She tried to distract her but Rosie was tenacious and it went on and on. Why hadn't she just pretended to drive the bus? But they were struggling for something else now: Rosie had been wilful and aggressive all morning – ice cream now; do real drinking, not pretend drinking; not that cup; draw a curly-wurly, that's not a curly-wurly – and Eleanor was finally, pointlessly, resisting. Rosie was becoming anguished, on the verge of screaming, and Eleanor felt a familiar compressed nub of shame and panic that drummed at her sides.

She didn't know why she was finding it so difficult. Feeling ill must be something to do with it – a headache and being sick made everything harder. She couldn't remember when Rosie's tantrums had started, but they seemed to have increased dramatically, in volume and intensity, since the move. Eleanor found it impossible to explain how shocking and draining she found it. When she tried to talk to Richard about it, the words turned light and insubstantial as soon as they left her mouth, just as they did when she mentioned it to friends or other mothers. She could only bring herself to talk about it in a jokey way, and everyone responded accordingly, jolly and dismissive. It was a phase. Rosie would grow out of it.

She was so embarrassed, she wanted to get off the bus immediately, but didn't think Rosie would manage the walk. She made herself wait until they were two stops from home, but Rosie refused to get off and it was a few minutes before Eleanor managed to get her out of the doors with the buggy. She told herself that all children had tantrums; that it was normal. Struggling to keep hold of Rosie's hand, terrified she was going to go wild and run out into the road, it didn't feel normal at all.

Rosie had been a sweet, easy baby and a sweet little girl. At two, she had had a perfectly triangular chin and large eyes and matted hair and Eleanor knew she was enchanting, to strangers as well as those who loved her. She was naturally extroverted, which Eleanor admired, but found puzzling – it was so unlike her or Richard. Rosie would wander around tables in cafes and steal people's straws and hand lumps of sugar to them. When Eleanor swooped in apologetically, she saw people crane towards Rosie, real delight on their faces.

She was now nearly three and a half. Her hair was darker and her face had become paler and more serious. In some ways, Eleanor loved the way she looked even more: she looked less like a child in an advert and more like Rosie. But she was different in other ways too. The move had made her inconsolable: she cried when Eleanor put her toys in boxes and at the sight of her bedroom without any furniture in it. When she saw the movers load Isobel's cot into a van, she screamed and wet herself. Eleanor waited for her to settle down in Litchfield Road, but sometimes she was afraid something had permanently altered. In the new house, Rosie was belligerent, hostile, fierce.

Eleanor dragged Rosie down the street, while she howled and screamed; Isobel had woken up and was crying too. Eleanor thought of all the things she could have done differently, how she could have avoided this. It was her own reaction she found the most disturbing. Why hadn't she just done what she was asked? Not because it was a strategy or she believed it was the best thing for Rosie, but because she couldn't bear to. She had instinctively wanted to assert herself. There was something mutinous and egotistical rising up in her and she didn't particularly like it.

Eleanor had never thought she was stubborn or self-important; that was not how she saw herself. Everyone talked about motherhood as a great change, and she had changed – of course she had – but privately, she feared that she hadn't changed enough. She desperately wanted to be calmer, more self-effacing, more accommodating – all the things that mothers were supposed to be. She didn't feel like a mother; she felt like a person with a child, and it frightened her. She began to wonder if this had always been true. Perhaps she had just been lucky that Rosie and Isobel were easy and she could bury her incompetence, a grave, miserable secret. Now things had got difficult and she was being exposed.

*

Rosie was calmer when she got home, but Eleanor's nerves were still frayed and she felt a sharp surge of irritation when she opened the door and saw Zoe had left her bicycle too close to it: there wasn't enough space to get the buggy in. She left Isobel on the step and wheeled the bicycle forward. Gripping the handles, she felt a disturbed kind of envy. She remembered cycling to work, flying through London, as close to weightlessness as she'd ever come. Zoe's bicycle felt light and graceful in her hands, like an animal.

'I can't cycle now I'm a mum,' someone at work had said to her when she was pregnant with Rosie. 'Maybe dads can, but I just feel I owe it to my kids to stay alive.' This had never occurred to Eleanor, and she tucked it away, while she observed how other mothers behaved. Her colleague was right, it turned out, and she was grateful that someone had alerted her to it: mothers don't cycle. She hadn't minded, hardly registering the moment when she decided it was silly to have her bike taking up space if she never used it and that she should get rid of it. She propped Zoe's bike by the radiator and tried to shake off her feelings as she went back outside to get the buggy.

Later that afternoon, it started to rain. Eleanor had been counting on another trip out towards the end of the day, but when she heard the gentle tapping at the window, she felt real dread. Within a few minutes, the windows were rattling and draughts were coming through the cracks. They were marooned.

She was in the children's bedroom. Zoe had got home half an hour ago and Rosie was still volatile; she didn't want to risk Zoe overhearing another tantrum. The nausea was getting worse; she wondered if she was going to be sick. It would only be an hour and a half until Richard got back – as soon as he was home, she would fake a need for something from the shops and walk up to London Fields. She thought, longingly, about the weekend away.

She was trying to play shops with Rosie, while Isobel pottered around the room. Isobel seemed curiously attracted to picking up anything that might cause her harm and Eleanor was constantly having to get up and stop her. Every time she turned her attention away from the game, Rosie became furious. 'Play *properly*, Mummy!'

'One second, Rosie, be patient,' she was saying, just as Rosie sank her teeth into her arm. She was stunned: by the speed, the pain, the viciousness. When she managed to say something, her voice was loud and sharp and didn't sound like her own.

'Rosie, no! That's very bad – no biting!'

Rosie looked at her. Eleanor's arm was throbbing. She managed to speak more quietly but her voice was still strange.

'No biting, Rosie. We don't bite people. Say sorry.'

'No!'

Eleanor felt shaky and her eyes were swimming and she wondered again whether there was any point in arguing about it. Isobel started to cry and she tried to bounce and soothe her, unable to really give it her full attention. Rosie unexpectedly gave in.

'Sorry, Mummy.'

'That's OK, Rosie. Can I have a hug?'

She put Isobel down and held Rosie's small body in her arms, while Isobel sat on the floor and cried. Then she tried to continue hugging Rosie, while freeing one arm to dangle a garish green toy in front of Isobel's face: it had a bell and bits of plastic attached and it clicked and jingled in a way that temporarily seemed to help. Rosie pressed her fingers curiously on Eleanor's arm, on the mark her bite had left: an angry ring of red parentheses.

'Mummy's owie,' she said. Eleanor smiled gratefully.

'Yes, that's right! Mummy's owie.'

'Poor Mummy.'

'Yes, poor Mummy, but it's all right now.'

'Kiss it better?'

'Yes, OK, kiss it better.'

Rosie bent down and kissed it. Eleanor felt one of those strange unexpected surges of joy at the feeling of Rosie's clammy lips on her skin. Then Rosie bit her again even harder, and recoiled, with an expression on her face as though she knew she'd done the wrong thing and it delighted her. Eleanor didn't recognize her daughter at all. She heard herself scream – thin and high-pitched – and then she burst into tears.

*

She was still agitated when Richard came back. Rosie ran downstairs and flung herself at him, shouting 'Daddy!' Eleanor followed her as fast as she could, carrying Isobel.

Richard held Rosie in the air. 'Hey, Rosie-posie! Have you had a good day?'

Eleanor stared at him, thinking that her distress must be imprinted on her face, that he would notice and ask how she was. But he was tickling Rosie, while she shrieked.

'Richard, Rosie bit me,' she said.

'What?'

She remembered Zoe and motioned for him to go into the kitchen. She hoped Zoe hadn't heard any of the noise from upstairs.

'Rosie bit me,' she said quietly.

'Oh, Rosie, you're a cheeky monkey, aren't you? You bit Mummy?'

'She can't go round biting people!'

'No, you're right. Mummy's right. No biting, OK, Rosie?

We don't bite people.' He put her down and got a glass out of the cupboard. He looked at Eleanor properly for the first time.

'Eleanor, what's wrong? I know it's not good, but she's only little. I'm sure it's just normal toddler behaviour. I don't think you should make too much of a big deal about it, otherwise she'll start doing it for attention.' He nodded at Rosie. 'It's six thirty. Shouldn't we start doing their tea?'

'I think I need to get something from the shop first. Can you watch them for a sec? Sorry, I know you've only just got in.'

'Eleanor, it's pouring, you'll get soaked!' he called after her as she grappled frantically with her mac in the hall cupboard. 'We must be able to do something with what we've got in the fridge.'

'Sorry, sorry!' she said, slamming the door behind her. She started running down the street, knowing she was going to be sick, not wanting any of the neighbours to see. She reached the dark, empty expanse of London Fields and vomited by the railings. Someone stopped and asked if they could help her and she said she was fine, horrified by the mess she'd made on the pavement, feeling too disgraceful to accept help.

'Are you sure?'

'Food poisoning,' she said, so they didn't think she was drunk, and they walked on.

Her hood had fallen back and wet hair plastered her face. The rain felt like medicine. She tipped her face upwards, as if to get as close to the sky as possible.

Later, after she'd put Rosie and Isobel to bed, she consulted the internet. Biting was perfectly normal, a phase, but she'd handled it badly, of course. She had made a fuss and that wasn't what you were supposed to do. She should have resisted the urge to cry out or get angry. Used positive words and a positive tone of voice. Distraction. Star charts. Hand puppets to demonstrate kind behaviour. The website acknowledged that it could be very painful, being hit, kicked, punched or bitten, but she should try to conceal the agony. She sat at her computer and cried.

*

The next day, the stones started. Eleanor was taking Rosie and Isobel to nursery, navigating the buggy out of the narrow doorway. Rosie was clutching her juice carton and howling, 'I don't want it!'

'Well, give it to me then, Rosie, you don't have to have it.' Eleanor held out her hand.

Rosie cried louder and held on to the carton even tighter. 'I don't *want* it!'

Eleanor sighed, as she made her way down the steps. 'What is it you don't want, Rosie?'

There, at the bottom, were six pebbles, lined up in size order, deliberately placed.

'I want you to go away! I *hate you*!' Even though Eleanor was becoming used to this, it still cut her, somewhere. She didn't have time to think about why the stones were there or what they might mean. She kicked them to the side before manoeuvring the buggy out into the street.

Two days later, they were there again. Rosie was calmer, and Eleanor noticed how strange it was, how carefully they had been lined up. She didn't have a free hand, so she pushed them away with her foot. The next time they appeared, she let go of Rosie's hand and bent down. 'Stay there, Rosie! Just one second!' Half afraid to touch them, she made herself pick them up and put them out on the street.

The next day, when she saw them, she put them in her pocket, carried them to nursery with her and after she had dropped the children off, put them in a bin three streets away.

Richard told her it was probably kids messing around. She couldn't quite believe him, but it was another thing she had to learn to live with, along with the headache and the biting and the feeling of not quite being there. She let them accumulate, these discomforts, because she didn't know what else to do.

13

When Eleanor told her they were going away for the week-end for Richard's birthday, Zoe had been thrilled. She had never been alone in the house for that long and it felt like a rare luxury: she could cook a proper meal, have a bath, watch television, and spread herself on the sofas without feeling furtive. But when she unlocked the door to an empty house on Friday afternoon, she realized she didn't particularly want to do any of those things. The stillness of the house unnerved her – she missed the usual background of shrieks and splashes and raised voices. Her bike stood alone in the hall, no longer having to share space with the buggy. A white plastic horse with blue wheels stood in the middle of the living room.

She had been living there for two and a half months and she still didn't find the house any easier. She couldn't sleep properly. She had never been a good sleeper – Rob had said that she talked during the night, indistinguishable babbling or nonsense, like when she'd told him there were eggs under the bed. Occasionally, she'd seen figures in the room and woken up shouting. But it was different in Litchfield Road. She had woken up paralysed again, twice, which left her with a kind of restless claustrophobia: she thought she could feel the earth pressing in around her. The figures she saw had taken on a particularly vivid shape: she had started dreaming that there was a girl in her room, a child, around seven or eight, with tangled black hair and an intent expression. She paced at the foot of Zoe's bed or stood in the corner by the wardrobe. In her dream world, Zoe recognized her: it was the girl who had written on the walls, Emily. In daylight hours, she told herself she'd just been spooked by the writing and that was why her subconscious had conjured up this image. But the dream had an unusual character: it would settle on her in the moments before falling asleep, as her thoughts gradually became pliable and soft, and it was real and sharp, like a vision. She would wake up astonished to find the room empty. It made the prospect of a night alone in the house even less appealing.

She thought about ringing Laura, but stopped herself: she'd been calling a lot lately, with neurotic, inane questions about men she'd met, including Adam, even though it had been two weeks since the party and she'd heard nothing from him. ('Should I text him?' she asked. 'I'm not even going to dignify that with an answer,' Laura said.) Zoe didn't know if she was pestering her, and the thought was so intolerable, she couldn't risk it. In Brighton and in their London Fields flat, their friendship had been a kind of partnership, with an understanding that they were always available to each other: Zoe was never truly alone or at a loose end unless she wanted to be. She'd squandered that, she supposed, by moving in with Rob, but even so, she didn't know anyone who had that sort of friendship now. And she couldn't bear the thought of Laura pitying her.

She decided to try and make the most of the night in, even though her spirits were slowly dropping. She never cooked properly at Litchfield Road because she was afraid of getting in the way; she compiled salads and heated up soup. To mark her weekend alone, she made pasta, which she overcooked. It was gluey and slippery, but she ate it anyway, too much of it, and felt worse.

Zoe had never had a bath in the upstairs bathroom, although Eleanor had told her more than once that she could. She decided this would be a good moment to try it out. The bath looked reasonably clean, but as it filled up, she noticed a gauzy film across the top, little foreign hairs coated in bubbles. She got in anyway. At the foot of the bath, there was a blue plastic lobster, which had escaped the net bag bulging with other bath toys, and a used blister plaster – the white, expensive kind that emulated skin. Its milky, spongy centre was coloured with ochre from the blister and it had two wrinkled fingers sticking out on either side. Zoe touched it experimentally, without knowing why.

She lay in the water, idly reading the labels on the bottles clustered in front of her. It started to feel uncomfortably intimate, learning about all the problems Eleanor had to solve: fine, limp hair; dull, tired skin; roughened hands. She thought about her own cheery, brightly coloured set of bottles downstairs, which were too cheap to address specific flaws, and was grateful for them.

When she got out, she looked at herself in the mirrored cabinet above the sink, nearly tripping over the small pink plastic stool covered in stickers. Something moved at her feet and made her jump. It was a used cotton bud, wet, bent and yellowed at one end. She opened the cabinet. There was an open box of tampons and the packet was a colour she'd never even seen before – super super extra plus or something. They were vast and squat, like bullets. She didn't know why they were so enormous, but assumed it was something to do with childbirth. *I'm never having children*, Zoe thought.

She dried off and put her clothes back on and rinsed the bath, trying to remove any trace of her being there. Then, although it was disgusting, she picked the plaster up between her fingernails and put it in the bin, feeling instinctively that it was Eleanor's and that she would be embarrassed when she came back and found she'd left it out. She felt sad thinking about Eleanor's limp hair and blistered feet, even while feeling jealous that she could afford superior plasters.

Stepping out on the half-landing, Zoe remembered, again, that she'd never been past this point in the house before. She hesitated. There was no possibility of being caught; this could be her only chance. She turned and went up another flight of stairs. The doors on the next floor were all shut. She paused again, and then opened one of them.

Eleanor and Richard's room revealed almost nothing, only containing a large bed with a tasteful duvet cover, a wardrobe and chest of drawers. There were some heavy, faded red velvet curtains, which Zoe was sure belonged to the previous owners. A delicate, tall-backed chair with Richard's crumpled trousers on it. She opened one of the wardrobe doors. A dirty clothes basket, the arms of Richard's shirts sticking up, like someone calling for help. Eleanor's clothes, filed in rows: linen, silk, buttons. Everything was navy, camel, grey or rose – even the colours looked expensive. She pulled something out, a silk shirt with a Peter Pan collar and 1930s print, and held it up against her.

She went next door to the children's room. It was the opposite: overfull, with vast crates of books and piles of coloured plastic. The empty cot and small bed unnerved her. There was a doll in the middle of the cot – Zoe picked it up. Its body was made of greying fabric filled with beans, but its limbs and head were plastic. It hung limp in her hands:

staring eyes, pouting mouth. She dropped it back in the cot and went up to the top floor.

Again, the doors were shut. She chose the back room first this time, and found herself in Richard's study. It was small, just room for a double-stacked bookcase, a desk and a landscape of cardboard boxes. The desk had clearly been chosen with some care: it was an antique, dark wood, with a green leather surface. Zoe thought of her small folding table downstairs and felt childish and amateur. Next to his computer was a leatherbound notebook with the initials 'RWFH' on the front. There was a stack of library books with words like 'Renaissance' and 'Critical' in the title. She put down the notebook and shut the door behind her.

Zoe felt profoundly uneasy. It was something about being on this floor of the house; she had gone too far, the altitude was too high. But there was only one room left. She turned the handle and had to push harder than she thought to open it. She gasped when she stepped inside, taking in the blank staring faces, the frenetic childish scribbles, still visible through the paint. She noticed a suitcase in the corner, with a pile of quilts next to it and a curious row of objects on top: an amber tortoise. A piece of fur. A hairnet.

For a moment, Zoe was unable to move. Then she heard a loud crashing noise – something in the house had fallen or collapsed. Dizzy with shock, she backed out of the room. She wanted badly to escape downstairs, but forced herself to look in every single room she'd been in. She had to find the source of the noise.

There was nothing: the rooms were still. Her bicycle was upright in the hall. The front and back doors were closed. She opened the curtains of the bay window, but there was nothing in the street. She went to the window at the back of the kitchen and cupped her hands around her face to look out into the garden.

Back in the basement, she sat in her armchair, knees up against her chest, listening to her heart beat. Maybe it was normal for children to write their name on the wall – she wouldn't know. But it wasn't normal writing. It was unhinged. And why had Eleanor and Richard left it like that, like some kind of shrine?

Zoe wondered if she had imagined the crashing noise; she was sure she hadn't. She couldn't help feeling that it was something to do with her. What if she had disturbed something? What if she had invited something in? Then she had an awful thought: she wasn't sure if she'd shut the door behind her. She told herself she must have done; there was no way she could bear to go back up there. She just hated the idea of it staying open, contaminating the rest of the house.

*

She woke on Saturday morning, alone and exhausted. She had dreamt about the girl again, this time in the upstairs room – the details were hazy, but the mood stayed imprinted on her: some combination of fear and distress. She'd bought eggs for breakfast the day before, but she didn't feel like being upstairs for any longer than she had to. She didn't have the energy to go to the shops, so she made milkless tea, and a bowl of dry cereal, retreating downstairs to eat it, trying not to think about the upstairs room.

It was her brother's housewarming party that afternoon; he and his wife, Alice, had just bought a flat in Walthamstow. She hadn't particularly wanted to go and had half thought about making an excuse – now, she wanted to get away from the house.

She still felt some trepidation, as she sat on the train, clutching a pot plant. Housewarmings were becoming more frequent now; it wasn't just her brother, some of her friends had managed to buy places too. In the last year, Zoe had absorbed a lot about buying property, without really wanting to. 'I feel like I'm becoming so boring about it,' Peter said. *You are*, Zoe thought. There was always so much to say, and none of it interesting: chains collapsed, people were inefficient or unscrupulous, things got gazumped and gazundered.

Everyone was pushed out from the centre of London, and in return gained staircases and spare rooms and space. It was something she couldn't quite comprehend – the amounts of money involved were fantastical and yet somehow people found ways to do it. Often it was obvious how – some combination of wealthy parents, wealthy partners and well-paid jobs – but sometimes it felt like everyone knew about a secret store of money that she couldn't access. She'd stand in richly furnished rooms, bemused at where it all came from – cashmere rugs, faux retro radios, statement cushions.

It was the first time she'd been to Peter and Alice's new flat, the top two floors of a large Victorian house. The stained glass in the front door and the pretty tiles in the porch made Zoe envious before she'd even been let in. Alice was waiting for her at the top of the stairs. She looked delighted to see her; Zoe remembered how much she liked her and felt guilty for feeling jealous of her front door. She was led up another flight of stairs to an enormous room: huge bay windows, a kitchen island, dining table and sofas. She'd arrived more or less on time (this was another new development: parties that started at 4 p.m.) and there were only a few scattered guests, talking quietly and conservatively. The statement cushions were taut.

Alice handed her some wine in a plastic cup and Zoe went over to say hi to Peter. She had always got on well with him, despite, or maybe because of, the fact she felt he was very different from her. Mostly, she was pleased that he chose things that were stable and secure because it meant she could be chaotic and creative by comparison. Buying property was a Peterish thing to do: like getting married or knowing about contents insurance or washing up, while she did Zoeish things like leaving her job and splitting up with Rob, and being so unhappy at Peter and Alice's wedding that she got drunk and cried, and was sick on her brides-maid's dress. But now, in this large light room, she wondered, as she had a lot recently, whether it would be better to be less like Zoe.

He was recounting the story of the house purchase to a friend Zoe hadn't met before, a thin frenetic man in glasses and a suit. Zoe had heard the story before and didn't par-ticularly want to hear it again: its protagonist was a land transfer document. But at least she only had to half-listen and could produce outrage and sympathy at the right cues, while trying to work out who else she knew who might have been invited, how likely they were to come and when they might arrive. She tuned back in to hear Peter's friend say:

'The market's incredible at the moment. My mortgage is a thousand a month and I'm charging seventeen hundred in rent.' He didn't say *You do the math* or *Kerrching!* but the implication was clear.

'You've got to deal with tenants, though,' Peter said.

'Oh right, yeah, they're a nightmare. They don't look after anything. I was there last week, yeah, and the bath-room was *covered* in mould. They hadn't been opening the windows! They just don't care.'

'Well, it's not their house,' Zoe said, and then regretted it. She didn't particularly want to have an argument.

'You'd think they'd care about where they're living, though.'

Zoe felt too tired to dispute it. 'Yes, you would,' she said.

'How about you, where do you live?'

'I live in East London . . . near London Fields?'

'Whoa. I didn't think anyone could afford to buy round there any more.'

'I rent.'

'Renting's even worse though, right? That whole area's nuts at the moment.'

He was looking at her, waiting for her to justify herself, and she wished she could make something up – *I'm a lawyer for a commercial property developer* – but Peter was there, and he wouldn't believe her anyway.

'I rent a room from a family – well, two rooms actually, but we share some of the living space.'

'You're, like, what, an au pair?'

'No, more like a lodger, I guess.'

'Oh right.' He looked at her with both curiosity and disdain. 'I didn't think you got lodgers these days.'

'Is it still going all right there, Zo?' Peter asked.

I can't sleep in the house and I think it might be haunted. 'It's fine,' she said. 'I mean, I love the area and it's close to work.'

'What do you do?' Peter's friend asked.

'I work in an art shop.'

'Oh, right – are you an artist?'

Zoe began to find it difficult to speak. She got away as soon as she could, saying she had to get another drink, but after she'd refilled her cup, she didn't know who else to talk to. She spotted Alice's sister, Annie, who she'd met a few times before. It wasn't a particularly appealing prospect, but she went over anyway.

Alice was exceptionally normal, in a way that Zoe often found comforting and endearing, and only occasionally frustrating. Annie was superficially normal, but with a slight, indefinable air of lunacy. She was only twenty-eight, but she already had two children, which Zoe thought was entirely unnatural. She had her back to Zoe and she was juggling a baby; her husband stood nearby trying to control their toddler. Zoe realized too late that she had a phone pressed between her ear and her shoulder. She wanted to walk away, but Annie had turned round, held up her palm in front of Zoe's face and mouthed 'Wait' with unnerving urgency.

'Yes, well, I didn't appreciate finding out about your kidney from someone else, Daddy. Daddy – Daddy, what I'm *saying* is—'

Zoe felt foolish but Annie's eyes were pinned on her and she didn't feel she could walk away again.

'Look, I've got to go now, I'm at the housewarming . . . Alice and Peter's . . . Yes, you *did* know, Daddy. OK, speak later . . . yes, yes, love you, bye. Zoe! Hi! So sorry about that.' She hugged her, which was awkward with the baby between them. 'Here's Benjie!' Annie held him up, a little too close to Zoe's face. There was something goblinesque about him, ears sweeping out, upturned nose, wide mouth.

'Hi, Benjie!' Zoe said.

'This is Zoe, Benjie. Zoe is Aunty Alice's sister. Well, sort of sister. Sister-in-law. Say hello to Zoe, Benjie. Say he-lo. He-lo. He-lo.'

Zoe smiled and waited.

'He-lo. He-lo. Say he-lo. He-lo.'

Annie held him closer to Zoe's face.

'You can give him a kiss.'

'Oh – can I?' She leaned in and placed her lips on his clammy cheek, feeling idiotic. She pulled back slightly too quickly and tried to shift the focus away from her. 'Is it going well, then? With the two of them?'

'Oh, well, you know, it's hard work! Hardest thing I've ever done. But it's amazing, seriously. How are you anyway? I don't think I've seen you since the wedding.'

Zoe blushed, remembering how drunk she'd been, how Alice's other bridesmaid had had to help her with her dress, and how kind Alice was about it, which made it worse. She thought she saw Annie trying to hold back a smile and she knew she was remembering it too.

'No, I know. I'm good, thanks.'

'Are you still working for that charity?'

'I gave that up. I'm working in an art shop now.'

Benjie wriggled in Annie's arms; she struggled to contain him.

'Oh, right. I didn't know you were arty.'

'Well, I'm not really . . .'

'And what about your boyfriend? Is it . . . Rob?'

'Yeah, that's right. We split up, actually.'

'Oh, shit, yeah, of course, Alice did tell me. Sorry about that,' Annie said, pulling the baby's hands away from her hair. 'How long were you together?'

'Nearly six years.' She was more practised at talking about it now, but her voice still wavered. It took her by surprise; she didn't expect to still be upset by it.

Annie looked down at the baby's feet. 'Oh no! Odd socks! Is that Daddy? It's Daddy, isn't it. Silly Daddy! Are you seeing someone else?'

'No – not at the moment.'

'Oh no,' she said, dispassionately. 'Well, I'm sure you'll find someone. Do you want kids?'

'I'm not sure . . .'

Annie held Benjie up to Zoe's face again. 'But they're so CUTE.'

'Definitely, I know. But I'm not with anyone at the moment so . . .'

'You should start thinking about it, though. I mean, I'm sure it was the best thing to split up, if what's-his-name wasn't the right person. But you have to get a move on – the good ones get snapped up eventually.'

Zoe drained her plastic cup of warm wine and told Annie she had to get another drink. She realized if she kept aborting conversations like this, she was going to get really drunk.

She poured herself some wine deliberately slowly, and waited by the kitchen island, unmoored. Somehow having another conversation was unthinkable. There was a spare room next door, a kind of study, where she had put her coat and bag. She got out her phone. No one had called her. There was no one she felt she could call.

If she were a stronger, better person, she would go back in, apologise to Peter, make convincing excuses. Instead, she put on her coat and left as quietly as possible. She'd only been there half an hour.

*

On her way back, she thought about Peter and Alice, and Annie, and the man making £700 a month from tenants who didn't open the bathroom window. She knew it was unfair to feel resentful: Peter and Alice had got their deposit for the flat because Alice inherited money when her step-mother died. It wasn't as though Zoe and Peter came from different worlds, after all. She might still meet a man with a wealthy dead step-parent.

Zoe wasn't sure if she would ever have a chance of owning a house, whatever she did, but she also knew she wasn't trying very hard. If this was what she really wanted, she should be pursuing someone available, not daydreaming about someone who had a girlfriend and lived in a warehouse. She should be trying to be a success, not leaving her job because she felt like it. She had done all this by instinct, rather than choice, and what if she did want it after all? It looked nice, but where did the resources come from? Where did you find the capacity to deal with bathmats and light fittings, cushions and fridges? An entire person, with preferences, desires and responsibilities, ex-girlfriends and uncles, kidneys and feet? All she had was herself, and two rented rooms, and she was full to bursting.

At Walthamstow station, she felt her phone buzz. It was Adam, telling her that he had been thinking about her and reading her poem and asking if they could meet. She was euphoric and then helpless with rage at how easily he could floor her. She thought *oh God yes, yes please*, but she scrolled through her phone book and pressed Laura's name. She would consider all the options, even if she already knew exactly what she was going to do.

14

The weekend away had been gorgeous – just not in the way it was supposed to be. Eleanor didn't care about the hotel or the birthday meal or that Richard's parents had taken Rosie and Isobel for the night. All she could think about was wellness: the seductive feeling of being nourished, strengthened from the inside. She felt more alive than she had in weeks. Richard told her it was the proper night's sleep and she pretended to agree. She wanted to believe that he was right, that it would last beyond the weekend, but when she got home and it began again, she wasn't surprised. Within days, it was worse than before.

The Monday after they got back, Rosie threw pieces of Lego in her face and pinched Isobel. Eleanor tried to stay calm, not make a fuss, pretend it didn't hurt, but the familiar panic throbbed inside her and she found herself close to tears. Rosie leapt on her back and sank her teeth into her shoulder. It was surprisingly difficult to get her off; she wondered if it would bruise. *This is normal, a phase*, she told herself, trying to suppress the feeling that it was something else.

Her private fear was that Rosie found the house as difficult as she did. At first, Eleanor had been relieved that Rosie loved her new nursery, but now, it felt ominous. Rosie would scream and cry when Eleanor came to pick her up or have a tantrum on Saturday mornings when Eleanor explained that there was no nursery today. Eleanor remembered the way Rosie used to run into her arms when they'd been apart, clutching her tight, as if they hadn't seen each other for years. It had been wonderful and oppressive and cloying. She ached for it now.

By the end of the day, Eleanor was frayed and her shoulder was still sore. After the children had gone to bed, she decided to try and talk to Richard. 'We need to talk about Rosie's biting,' she said and then laughed, an unnatural, high-pitched sound, at having to say such an unappealing thing.

'OK, let's talk then.' He sat down at the table and something about the way he did it, the show of being magnanimous, made her furious. She stood opposite him, picking at the skin around her nails.

'I just . . . I don't know what to do any more. What if she does it at nursery?'

'Have you asked them about it?'

'They said she's been fine. She's not biting other children. Just me.'

'Well, that's OK, then.'

'It really hurts, Richard!' She pulled at the neck of her top to show him the mark on her shoulder. The red had faded now – it was just a few grey indentations, the skin barely punctured. Even she could see it didn't look serious.

Richard paused. 'Why don't you ask work if you can go back full-time? They could go to nursery five days. To be honest, the extra cash would be pretty helpful right now.'

'I can't do that!' she said, scalded. 'I'd lose my one day with them.'

'But if you're not enjoying it.'

'I *am* enjoying it!' They stared at each other, and she wondered if either of them were going to acknowledge how untrue that was. 'And anyway, it's not about whether I enjoy it, it's about . . . being there, I don't know.' She looked away.

Richard said gently, 'Rosie does seem to be doing really well at nursery. Maybe she'd be happier . . .'

Eleanor couldn't imagine how she would face people, having to go back to work because she couldn't even manage one day a week on her own with her children. Because they couldn't even manage one day with her. It was unthinkable. Besides, she was lucky to work part-time; she knew that. She was always careful to be grateful, because things were always worse for someone else and she didn't want to upset or offend anyone by complaining. She was grateful to be able to go back to work, grateful to work part-time, grateful that she could leave at five every day. Grateful that her children were healthy; grateful that she could have children at all. Even when she remembered sitting in the hospital waiting room during labour thinking, *This is the worst experience of my life*, even when she felt sick catching sight of something the same blue as the midwives' uniforms, she was still grateful that she had not had to have an emergency caesarean and that no one had died. She was grateful that her mother lived nearby, and that Richard helped. She knew that gratitude and counting your blessings were important for staying positive. It just made it impossible to ask for anything more.

The conversation had run aground. She went to the fridge, got out a head of broccoli, and wondered when they'd lost the knack of being honest with each other. When they'd got married, she'd decided to take Richard's name, partly because if they had children, she wanted them to share a family name. 'We can be Team Harding,' Richard said. She had never felt less like they were a team. They were on opposing sides, constantly bargaining with each other, pitching for their share of the resources of their marriage: time, money, sense of identity. She was afraid of what she might lose if she tried to describe how confused and conflicted she was.

Richard got out his laptop; he said he was working on his essay, but when she looked over, she saw the little squares of paint chart colours on his screen. She chopped the broccoli and tried to think of something cheerful or interesting to say. She had so little energy left.

She knew about the importance of taking care of your marriage after you had children, and about quality time and date nights, and she also felt that it was her responsibility to provide these things. She would try and organize more nights out for the two of them, just as soon as she started to feel better. But truthfully, that wasn't what she missed most. She missed moments when they'd suddenly be intrigued by each other, spooning out conversation like honey from a jar, happy and loquacious. Her head on his stomach, listening to the gentle mechanical noises. The things she used to tell him that now seemed too trivial: 'I thought about cabbage but I got cauliflower instead', 'My feet got cold when I was waiting for the bus.' They piled up, unused, as she listened to Richard click and scroll.

*

Eleanor had met Richard eighteen years ago, at Cambridge. It was the first week of term and she had been invited to a meeting to formalize their timetable. She was more disorientated than she'd ever been, cowed by the beauty, age and scale of everything, and horrified to discover she was the last to arrive. She sat down, her face hot, sneaking furtive glances at the other students. There were ten of them, but it might as well have been a hundred: she was only able to pick out a few faces. One or two she'd been introduced to: a girl with peroxide-blonde hair and a nose stud; a tall thin boy, cross-legged, hunched over, tapping his foot rapidly against the chair leg. She noticed his glasses were dirty.

The tutor initiated a 'friendly little discussion' about English Literature to 'get to know each other' – it was not a formal tutorial, but it was clear that they were being tested or testing each other in some way. There was a small awkward silence and Eleanor's discomfort became almost hysterical, before one of the students she'd met before, a boy called Dominic, started talking, in a loud easy voice. Eleanor forced herself to speak, hating how her tongue had thickened and how weak and tentative she sounded. Then the boy with glasses spoke. He wasn't rude to her exactly, but he was on the cusp of it, managing to be both challenging and dismissive at the same time. She loathed and admired him; he later admitted he could barely remember her being there. Dominic responded, calling him by name – Richard. They clearly knew each other and dominated the rest of the session with a style of passive-aggressive argument that would become very familiar to her. She didn't speak again. Eventually, they were given the times for their term's tutorials – their tutor called them supervisions – and put into pairs: she was with Richard, of course.

Eleanor had never given this decision much weight; she assumed they would have come together some other way. It was only later, as their marriage lengthened and deepened and their lives hardened, that she began to think about it again. If it hadn't been for that initial pairing, perhaps nothing would ever have grown between them. Perhaps one of them would have met someone else before it had been able to. She didn't like to think that nearly two decades of her life were due to a whim, a quirk of logistics. But sometimes, when she met someone's eye, felt something in her stomach and thought she saw the ghost of another life rear up, she wondered if it really did all hang on that fine a thread, after all.

At first, the supervisions were her worst hour of the week. In front of the tutor, Richard would behave as if she wasn't there, directing his conversation at Dr Franklin only. Eleanor could barely keep up with his trains of thought and floundered when she had to speak. She dreaded the end even more: they were twenty-five minutes away from college and had no choice but to walk back together. The walks were uncomfortable, interspersed with heavy silences. Richard would ask her opinion about their course, their tutors, the reading; she would start to stumble, inarticulate; he would interrupt and then tell her what he thought. She tried to initiate small talk, but he seemed immune to pleasantries. As soon as they reached the edge of town, she would invent an errand and escape.

It was halfway through term that things started to change. Eleanor had found Cambridge utterly overwhelming. She'd gone to a girls' school and had got used to things being restricted – men, calories, ambitions. University seemed limitless by comparison. People were trying to display, rather than disguise, their intelligence. They talked brashly about politics and philosophy and had opinions about things that Eleanor didn't know it was possible to have opinions on: Rwandan politicians or whether Shakespeare was overrated. It was nothing like the sixth-form common room and conversations about blow jobs and toast. It was far too much but at the same time, intoxicating.

She hadn't known it was possible to transform so quickly. She made her first real friend: Amy, the girl with peroxide hair who Eleanor had originally thought was far too dynamic and self-confident to be interested in her. She discovered that although Amy knew a lot, about whisky and punk and Israeli foreign policy, she didn't know how to cook. Eleanor tentatively started to teach her things: how to sweat onions, spinach reduces, bouillon is better than stock cubes. She took Amy to get her supermarket loyalty card and explained when it was worth spending more money and when the cheaper brands were OK. In this way, they became close: Eleanor softening mushrooms in a Woolworths pan, drinking wine from a mug and listening to Amy deride the other members of the English group, particularly Dominic and his right-wing chauvinistic view of the world.

Eleanor's relief at being happy and somewhere approaching comfortable was so intense that she became chatty – gregarious even. She was playing a part and although she wasn't sure it suited her, it was convincing everyone, sometimes even herself. 'I can't imagine you being shy,' someone said to her, and she was amazed at how easy it was to fool people. She still felt out of her depth, but she was getting used to that feeling, managing it; even, sometimes, enjoying it. She had unfurled.

Most weeks, she ended up running into Richard on the way to supervisions, but she stopped finding the prospect of walking together horrifying. She wasn't intimidated by him any more; she began to suspect that he was being deliberately opaque in order to sound more intelligent than he was. It wasn't that she was too stupid to understand him; it was that he didn't want to be understood. Even Dr Franklin seemed to have trouble following him sometimes. Eleanor interrupted if one of his monologues started alienating her and became more articulate if he asked her opinion. He became more considerate, more willing to engage. It felt like he was beginning to respect her.

Once they were in a seminar or tutorial, everything shifted. The softness and consideration were gone and Eleanor became subdued. She was still in awe of his confidence, while hating it at the same time, and still nervous around Dr Franklin, who made his preferences clear. He listened intently to Richard, and then seemed to mentally put his feet up when she opened her mouth. And when she bumped into Richard in the college bar, looking horribly uncomfortable, she would try out her chatty girl routine on him, to no effect. It was impossible to think they'd ever had a satisfying conversation.

But the walks to and from Dr Franklin's were a hinterland – neither fully social or academic, it was a small space in which they were more truly themselves. Cautiously, they started to arrange to meet so they could walk together and Eleanor found herself looking forward to it. She began to garner personal details about Richard and lined them up in her mind like treasure, not sure yet of their particular value. She learnt he grew up in Oxfordshire, he went to boarding school and his house had a boot room. His parents were doctors and his sister was planning to go to medical school; he felt like a black sheep. He wanted to be a playwright and was trying to work up the courage to have one of his plays put on at Cambridge.

At one point, Richard started complaining about the standard of contributions in their seminar group – Dominic came under attack, and he didn't think much of Angela. 'Well, I do my best,' Eleanor said jokily, and he said quickly: 'No, you're good. I mean – not brilliant. But good.'

She felt like he'd kissed her.

15

Zoe had thought about Adam constantly since the party. Remembering how he touched her back, the kiss in the hallway, the way he said, 'I really like it, Zoe. Can I keep it?' could absorb her so completely that she became useless, only able to stare straight ahead, submerged. She'd replayed everything he'd said to her as they stood in the open doorway in his studio – it was one of the most compelling conversations she'd had for months. *We talked as if we'd known each other all our lives.* Actually, the opposite was true. It was so much easier to speak like that, fluent and unvarnished, when you didn't know someone at all.

She wondered if Adam had split up with his girlfriend, but even if he had, she couldn't imagine where it would end up. Breaking up with Rob had been agony, but she'd also been deeply relieved. It was intensely relaxing not having to constantly adjust your behaviour to fit to someone else's. After that disastrous New Year's Eve, she stayed in their flat by herself for two months and went feral: undressing in the kitchen, leaving her vibrator by the bathroom sink. She didn't shower and shovelled cereal into her mouth on the sofa. If she took a mouthful that was too big, she regurgitated some back into the bowl. She gave in to every pathetic little desire she had, simply because she could and every time she caught herself doing something weird, selfish or disgusting, she felt a deep sweetness inside her.

She didn't have the resources to start all over again – to argue about bathroom cabinet space or go to someone's cousin's wedding. When her friends complained about their partners' habits, she felt secretly joyful that this was something she didn't have to contend with. Sometimes when Laura talked about Nick – 'when I'm with him, I just don't see the point in doing anything else' – she felt a kind of longing, but then she thought: *wait till you know him better*.

She asked herself why she was going to meet Adam. What did she want from him? Sex, of course – masturbation got boring after a while. But that wasn't really what was drawing her in – it was something in between sex and love: contact, connection or at least the illusion of it. It was the way his hands felt on the small of her back. She wanted him to climb into bed with her and hold her, put his hands on her face, his mouth on her cunt, and then leave her alone. But was that really worth all this, this distraction, sublime anxiety?

*

They arranged to meet on a Friday night, at a pub just behind the warehouse. By then, she was slightly tired of the whole thing: how restless and helpless it made her, how consuming it was trying to work out what he wanted from her, with so little information. When she saw him, sitting at one of the tables in the corner, she was immediately disappointed. She'd forgotten how small he was, and how real. The image she'd had of him suddenly felt puffed up and fake, like a Disney prince. Then he saw her and smiled, and she wanted him again.

She sat down and started flipping her lip stud back and

forth with her tongue, like she was wobbling a tooth. She hadn't done it for years; she thought she'd trained herself out of it. They made disconnected, fractious small talk and she wondered again why she was doing this. All the looseness was gone; it was as if they'd never had a satisfying conversation.

There was an excruciating pause and then he said, 'I'm so sorry, Zoe, about the other night. I should have told you I had a girlfriend. I was so embarrassed when Tom came over . . . I really didn't want you to find out like that.'

So this was how it was going to be. She was going to be pitied and rejected and she hadn't even properly asked for anything. She wished there was some way of doing this that wasn't quite so humiliating to her.

'It doesn't matter,' she said. She wished she hadn't come.

'No, it does,' he said. 'I wanted to explain things to you. I do have a girlfriend – Kathryn – and I definitely should have made that clear from the start, but— It's kind of complicated with Kat and me. I don't know if we're going to stay together.'

'I'll hang on then, shall I?' Her sarcasm was flat and reflexive, and she regretted it: she didn't want to sound bitter.

'No! I didn't mean it like that. OK, look, the thing is, we met at school. And I know that makes it sound serious – I mean, it is serious, in one way . . . But it's not like we've been together that whole time – we've broken up a few times because – well, lots of reasons. And things really aren't going well right now. She's an artist too and I used to think that was a good thing, like, we both understood each other. But she kind of follows her work in a way that's – ruthless is too strong a word, but . . . single-minded, definitely. I mean, we all have to be dedicated, I get that, but if she gets offered a residency out of the country or if she needs to be in the studio twenty-four hours a day before a show, she just goes and does it. It's like I always come second. So, we've ended up spending a lot of time apart and recently it's started to feel like she doesn't want the same things as me, fundamentally. I don't want to be thirty and stuck in this half-hearted on-again off-again thing; if we're going to stay together, I want to do it properly. I want to get married one day, I want kids. I was telling her this – that I want us to decide if we're going to give it a proper go or not – and then she tells me she's going to Edinburgh for a year! And that was just— I'd had enough. I mean, we said we'd try, but I'm kind of running on empty now. Do you see what I mean? We are still together, technically, and I definitely should have told you that. But it's complicated.'

He looked at her imploringly. She was too cross to speak. She'd come all this way, spent all this time worrying about it, just to hear him complain about his relationship. She didn't want to talk about his girlfriend; she wanted sex. Eventually, she said what she thought she was supposed to, trying to sound reasonable and detached.

'It sounds really difficult. But I don't think we should see each other if you're still together.'

'You're right, I know. I shouldn't have invited you to the party and . . . all the stuff in the stairwell. I tried to stop myself texting you, I really did. It's just you're so beautiful and I was so impressed by all that stuff you said about your job. I feel like I'm surrounded by people who are just trying so hard to *be* something the whole time and you seem . . . I don't know, like you follow your own light. You seem happy to be yourself.'

For a moment, she was surprised by how wrong he'd got her. Why on earth would he think she was happy to be herself? Then, in an instant, she was struck by his flattery and all she could think about was that he thought she was beautiful. She was disarmed and hated that that was all it took.

'If it was another time . . .' He looked down at the table. 'I wish we'd met at another time, that's all.'

Then, with none of the electric slowness of the kiss in the stairwell, their mouths were mashed onto one another's, in a frenzied, wet embrace, and she was there, exactly where she'd wanted to be, in the moment she'd fantasized about for weeks. He bought drinks that they didn't really want and they talked glibly about how they shouldn't be doing this and what a mistake it was, and then he was asking her to go home with him and she was unlocking her bike outside. She could see, hear and feel everything – the lock hitting the railings, the flash of the front light, desperate excitement and the cold air on her face.

*

The bed was somewhere between a double and a single and there wasn't really room for both of them. Zoe lay awake, her torso crushed against Adam's, watching the tangerine light come through the thin curtains, thinking about the night before. It had been fun – not transcendental, but fun. He was the first new person she'd slept with in a long time – she didn't like to think about the last time too much. There'd been moments when she'd felt detached from it, and she was surprised and disappointed at how demure and polite she became. 'Sorry about my beard,' he said when he went down on her and she'd said it felt nice, even though it didn't. But then there had been moments she'd loved, not just the thrill and novelty of thinking *I am having sex with a man* but times when he'd turned her on and she'd lost herself in it.

When Adam woke up, she was embarrassed: by what they'd done, the things she'd said when she was high on lust and possibility, the sheer foolishness of going along with something with such a stunted future. She supposed this awkwardness was just the price you paid for sex, like a hangover, which she also had. She suddenly felt homesick and thought hungrily of the long, whole, perfect day ahead, and all the things she could do with it: drink tea, ring Laura, make herself a bacon sandwich. Maybe even do some writing. It had been fun last night, pretending to be the very best version of herself, but she couldn't sustain it much longer. She didn't want to be here any more.

Then she realized she was wet between her legs. Not a slick, gluey wetness, but something less viscous, drenching and uncontrollable. She tracked back wildly: it probably had been about a month. What an idiot. She pulled away and put her hand between her legs. It felt how she expected, but she didn't know what to do next – she didn't want to pull her hand up covered in blood.

'Are you all right?'

She was mortified and wished she wasn't. The word 'period' made her think of Year 8, sanitary towel bins and her mum. There must be some elegant or hip euphemism but all the ones she could think of were silly or disgusting. She thought of Rachel in *The Rachel Papers* misquoting the Lady of Shalott: 'The curse is upon me.' She wondered if she could work in a literary allusion. He probably hadn't read it.

'I think my period's started – I'm really sorry.' The politeness again.

Embarrassment was usually infectious, but Adam seemed immune to it. Rob used to ask her if she was OK, in an anxious, hushed tone that suggested he thought her body was a bottomless pit of horror. Adam just asked if she had tampons and then offered to go out and get her some. He sounded so unruffled, she agreed. She didn't even have any cash to give him. When he left, she thought about trying to get across to the bathroom, but she would have had to walk through the kitchen and she could hear his housemates having breakfast. She stayed in bed, luxuriating in being alone.

*

After that, she didn't go home. They went out to the kitchen, where there was a small group at the table: Oscar and Ursula from the party, and a small woman in a dressing gown with a stripy towel on her head, who turned out to be Oscar's girlfriend, Katy. Zoe felt her presence cause a hum of discomfort. She didn't mind. It was almost enjoyable.

They chatted inconsequentially for a bit and then everyone began to move: Ursula was teaching a felt-making workshop in Bethnal Green, Katy went to dry her hair and Oscar went back to his desk. Adam put some toast on for her. The winter sun was coming in through the windows. He came up behind her and tried to kiss the back of her neck, but she turned her head at the wrong moment and he kissed her underneath her jawbone instead. She could feel his mouth there long after he'd moved away. She tried to stop herself smiling.

Zoe realized she was happy. Maybe this was the answer: sex and affection, with no commitment or compromises. She could still have something of her own. She would never have to go to the supermarket with him. He would never take anything away from her.

After breakfast, she went into his bedroom to collect her bag and they agreed not to have sex again, at least not while he was still with Kathryn. She didn't believe it. It wasn't over yet, the two of them. He had to get the train to Edinburgh, to sort out the messy, exhausting business of his decade-long relationship; Zoe didn't envy either of them. She shut the door behind her and was plunged into the beauty of the day to herself. Bacon. Tea. Sunlight.

16

It started in the dead hour. Three o'clock, after lunch, when every cell in Richard's body felt heavy, pulling him down. His frame sagged. It happened every afternoon, but it was intolerable the days he worked at home and every cure had failed – drinking water, turning off the heating, salads for lunch. He'd consulted the internet, Googling 'afternoon drowsiness', and got some faintly unrealistic advice – stick your head out the window, share a joke with a colleague. The morning contained some sort of charge and he could attack his dissertation for a few hours. On Thursday afternoons he had a seminar, which wasn't ideal but it forced him to be active. But on Fridays, alone in his study, he would start to slow and the sentences would become stunted. He became conscious of the untamed, unexplored space surrounding him – the attic above him and the room next door – and he found himself standing at the window, looking over the quilt of gardens and the backs of houses, the maze of drainpipes and aerials, the uncoordinated protrusions of kitchen extensions.

Occasionally, he wondered if it was the room that made him feel like this. It was cramped, a little overfull, and although he'd tried to protect the space, he was hemmed in by cardboard boxes and temporary bookshelves. It had become a repository for those liminal possessions no one knew what to do with: postcards, orders of service, a staple-gun, a pair of flippers. He was never relaxed or at peace, the way he always imagined he would be.

Eleanor thought there was something strange about this floor of the house. He'd told her over and over again that there was absolutely nothing wrong with it, that the writing on the walls next door was just a slightly weird child messing around. He didn't say that it unnerved him as well.

Richard didn't usually have much time for the concepts of 'space' and 'moods' or 'energy', but he found himself reaching for those words instinctively. It felt almost more difficult to breathe here, as though the air was slightly contaminated, and something was always compelling him downstairs, away. Once or twice, Eleanor had joked about the upstairs room being haunted. He didn't believe in ghosts – that was central to his identity, like not believing in fate or karma or homeopathy. And yet, if he was honest, he'd been slightly too quick and defensive when he rejected the idea.

Last Thursday, when he'd gone into his study, the door to the upstairs room had been wide open. He shut it again, certain that Eleanor hadn't been up here and that she wouldn't have left it open. Keeping the doors shut upstairs was one of the things that was important to her, like matching crockery, or candles or guest towels. He didn't want to ask her in case he unsettled her even more. At his desk, he'd had a strange feeling that nothing was in the right place; he thought his notebook had been moved and his pen. It was just a feeling, there was no evidence for it and the rational part of him longed to dismiss it; yet his discomfort remained, unarticulated.

He couldn't write, so he started to scroll back and assess what he'd produced. That was always the worst part. The afternoon was ahead of him, theoretically two or three hours' work was there for the taking, but he knew that worryingly soon the streets would be filled with chatter and screams from the primary school across the road and he would have to confront the fact that the day was beginning to conclude. Zoe would come home. Another ninety minutes or so, and Eleanor would be back with the children and then: resignation. Whatever he was left with was the sum of his achievement. This was what the day – and with it time, money, his family – had been sacrificed for.

As he was casting around for something to distract him from the inevitable despondency, the lights went out. It was a grim day, overcast and raining, and the room was filled with a bluish-grey gloom. He got up and tried the switch at the wall, and then the desk lamp. Nothing. He went out and clicked the switch on the landing. Success. A blown fuse. Drawn to the sterile comfort of the electric light in the hall, he headed downstairs.

The fusebox was in the basement, on the landing between Zoe's bedroom and living room. Richard hadn't been down there since Zoe had moved in. He opened the box, flicked the switch and paused to see if it would trip again. It didn't, but instead of going upstairs to check the lights, he stayed where he was, occupying this place that was both his and not his.

The door to Zoe's bedroom was wide open. She clearly hadn't been expecting anyone to come down here and something about that assumption irritated him: it was their house, after all. The staircase and the landing couldn't be considered fully hers, just as the kitchen and the living room weren't fully theirs. There was something provocative about the open door. He stepped inside.

To say it was a mess was an understatement. The duvet

was rucked off the bed, exposing wrinkled, stained sheets and a pyjama top, one arm flung out. The bottoms lay at the side of her bed, where she'd stepped out of them, a wrinkled figure of eight. When he got closer to the bed, he noticed her underwear was inside her pyjamas; it looked like she'd pulled them off in the same movement. There was a reddish-brown butterfly imprint on the gusset. Her things were scattered all over the room, like a garbled description of a woman: an inside-out skirt, a single boot, a wire coat hanger, splayed tights, a small black bra with a lace trim.

Richard was mesmerized. All this intimacy, just lying all over the floor. He could almost see her getting out of bed in the morning, tracing her path from the trail of belongings. He knew, and had come to terms with the idea, that Eleanor was the only woman he would ever have sex with. He hadn't thought that she was the only woman he would know like this, about all the other kinds of closeness he was giving up.

He went back out into the hall and stood at the foot of the stairs for a long time. Then he opened the door to Zoe's living room and went in. It should have been less of a transgression than the bedroom, but somehow opening the door seemed to be going too far, as though his fingers might burn dents in the handle.

The living room was tidier, but he counted six mugs: four were hers and two belonged to him and Eleanor, which really annoyed him. One of the mugs was a third full of the weird red tea she drank and it had solidified into a sort of milky jelly. Another had a hard black-brown disc stuck to the bottom, light green spores of mould on it. Richard badly wanted to reclaim them. There were two bottles of wine on the mantelpiece and a tumbler next to them, with a sticky red residue at the base. There was a white plastic fold-out table in the corner, piled with notebooks and paper. Was she writing something extraordinary down here, while he was struggling to eke out a single paragraph upstairs?

He felt sick and full up, cross and guilty, and he went back upstairs to his desk. He was out of the slump now, but he still couldn't concentrate. Something had altered. His mind was working horribly fast, with no real progression.

*

Mostly, Richard tried not to think about his younger self. He was just grateful that he was no longer the same person, with that unappealing inheritance of hubris and self-doubt he'd shouldered at Cambridge. He tended to think more about the future than the past, about what was missing rather than what was lost. But sometimes, in the wrong light or the wrong space, he wondered if they were the same thing after all.

The first time he kissed Eleanor, he thought it was a mistake. It was one in the morning and they'd come back from a dinner to celebrate Amy's birthday. He'd been slightly annoyed with Eleanor all evening: she was sparkier, looser, more silly than he'd ever seen her before. It was April, halfway through the third term, and he now felt he knew her well enough to see that her garrulousness was an act. It felt like a betrayal of the private, sincere friendship they'd been building steadily over the two twenty-five-minute walks a week. And, although he was getting better with practice, this kind of party still made him ill at ease. Eleanor seamlessly fitted in.

It was a mistake because he wanted to fall in love, and he knew that Eleanor wasn't the sort of girl he could fall in love with. Since he'd arrived at Cambridge, he'd had fierce spontaneous crushes: on Cara, who had blonde hair and wore red lipstick; Juliet, who wore turbans and modelled for life classes; the red-haired girl who sat in front of him at Dr Cooper's 9 a.m. lectures. For a while, he revelled in these wild, obsessive feelings, picturing himself as a romantic hero, plagued by unrequited love, but they quickly became dissatisfying. He could never turn them into anything tangible or solid. He became shy and clumsy around these girls and all too aware of the gap between who he wanted to be and who he really was. He wanted to be witty and razor-sharp but the words left his mouth sounding unfathomable or insulting. When he had a conversation with any of them, it was as if there was a pane of glass between them.

He had barely noticed Eleanor. She wasn't very pretty, she wore ordinary clothes and she was quiet. It was only in the second term, when they had been walking to supervisions together for some time, that he noticed he was starting to enjoy talking to her. She was cleverer than he'd given her credit for. She was funny and sympathetic. The newest and strangest sensation was how comfortable he felt around her and how much he liked himself when he was with her. He only occasionally said things which made him wince when he remembered them, like the time he'd complimented her by mistake and hurriedly tried to take it back in case she somehow exploited the weakness.

It wasn't just that he liked being with her, there was a charge to their conversations too. He didn't fancy her because she wasn't the kind of girl people fancied: she wasn't exotic or lively or remarkable. He supposed they were friends; it was just a wholly inadequate word for what was going on between them. It didn't feel like any friendship he'd ever had. The amount he looked forward to the walks wasn't normal. And when he saw her in seminars or lecture halls and they caught each other's eye, he felt that there was something connecting them, a level of vibration that only they could sense. They belonged to each other in some way. It was disturbing.

When he woke up in her bed the morning after Amy's party, sweaty from sleeping in his clothes, they kissed again, and this time it was more tender and intuitive. The next time he saw her, they got drunk and ended up in bed together, in their clothes, again. The third time it happened, he woke up before her and watched her sleeping and wondered why he was trying so hard to resist how he felt about her. The realization was instant and overwhelming: it didn't matter that she was not the kind of girl he had imagined ending up with. She was not some unattainable bloodless figure; she was here and he was in her bed and he was happy. Within a week, he was fully, properly in love.

*

Love was an ambush. It was like everyone described and at the same time utterly unique. Every song was about him, and yet he still couldn't fully articulate what it was that was so perfect about Eleanor. They stayed up all night talking, skipped lectures and had sex in the afternoons. Ordinary things, like drinking a coffee outside the English faculty library, became emblazoned and delineated with her. Everything he'd ever cared about became unimportant; nothing would ever matter as much as being in bed with Eleanor, her sitting astride him wearing his T-shirt. He had sex for the first time. He felt mildly jealous of her ex-boyfriend, and even that was intoxicating. He had a love rival. He was starting to live.

The sharpness and brightness of his feelings intensified

until they were almost unbearable and then gradually, inevitably, they began to dim and dull. His focus widened and the rest of the world reopened to him. The structure of his life re-formed. He started going back to lectures and tried to make amends for all the work he'd missed. In some ways, it was a relief; he could work and eat and sleep again. He wasn't going to fail his exams. Things weren't the same as before – his life had still changed monumentally, it was just recognizable again. And Eleanor was still funny, sympathetic and clever, and he started to admire things about her that he hadn't noticed before, like the way that she was practical and robust. No one had ever suggested that you could find these qualities attractive in a girl. She was less volatile than him and, although she said she loved him, she hadn't lost herself in the way he had: it meant she was always slightly enigmatic in a way that was very appealing. They still had sex and it was still good, though it was becoming a more reliable, comfortable kind of pleasure, like a cup of tea or a pasta bake.

Towards the end of his second year, he and Eleanor celebrated their first anniversary. Now, he disposed of years casually, but then it had been a landmark of gravity and significance, positioning them as 'long-term', an achievement Richard hadn't dared hope for. He took her out for dinner in the smartest restaurant he knew, which in retrospect didn't seem that smart. Eleanor had worn the black dress that she wore for formals, and for Amy's birthday dinner. They talked about what they were going to do when they graduated, though at that point it felt adult and abstract, like a conversation about political systems or philosophy. He said that he wanted to study more, possibly abroad; Eleanor thought she'd go to London and try to get a job,

'something to do with reading and writing, I don't know.'
'I'd miss you,' he said, and they smiled, widely, infinitely,
at the thought that they might mould their lives around each
other. It had felt exciting, then.

17

Eleanor wasn't surprised when things started to move. Feeling ill made everything gauzy, and they were tiny things, easy to explain away. She'd find a door wide open when she thought she'd shut it. The cutlery in the wrong compartments; her house keys in the fridge. She thought that she'd left a plaster on the side of the bath when they went away for the weekend – she hated doing things like that, even though she knew that no one would see it: it made her feel out of control and slovenly, and it worried at her more than was rational as they drove away for the weekend. When she got back, it wasn't there. She knew her handbag was on the sofa – she could see herself dropping it there when she came in – but when she turned round, there was an empty space. She gaped at it, worried she'd left the front door open and someone had come and grabbed it while her back was turned. But the front door was shut. She ran upstairs and saw her bag on her bed and could only stare at it, uncomprehending. She could have put it there – of course she could – but her memory was blank.

She told herself it was the illness making her slow and confused. Sometimes she'd even catch herself in a daze: pouring fresh milk down the sink, about to scrape food remains into an open drawer. But that wasn't what it felt like. It felt like the house was active. She didn't expect things to stay as they were when she left them – a house with five people in it did not stay still. She expected crumbs on the bread board, depressions on the sofa. But this was something else.

Everything was out of place. A spoon in the oven. A pair of nail scissors in the bread bin. Feeling her way through the cloudy water of the washing-up bowl, Eleanor's fingers touched something familiar and wrong. She fished out her glasses, dripping, covered in soap and grease. Three days later, she looked down at the cup of tea she'd made, and saw something solid and glistening floating towards the top. She dredged it out with a fork, half knowing: it was the salmon skin from their plates, thick, silver, gorgeous, hideous.

*

Every so often, she'd find the pebbles there on the front step; she couldn't discern a pattern to it, but just when she thought it might have stopped, they were there again, a perfect line in size order. Once or twice, she stood at the window, to see if she could catch someone putting them out, but she didn't have time to watch for very long and on the days she was looking out for them, they never appeared. She carried on, as the year started winding to an end, patiently moving her things back to the right place, getting rid of the pebbles, managing her time in the house, trying to detach when Rosie sank her teeth into her arm again.

One Sunday, she was making a cake, when she opened one of the bottom kitchen cabinets where they kept the mixing bowls and found a saucepan. She held it in her hands, certain, so certain, that she had taken it out of the dishwasher that morning and put it back in its correct place, the cupboard above the sink. Still, she asked, 'Richard, did you put this here?'

He looked up from his computer. She could see rows of tiny bathroom taps on his screen. 'What?'

'This saucepan. Did you put it in the bottom cupboard?'

'I haven't touched it.'

'I don't understand how it got there then. I would never have put this there. It isn't the place.'

'Zoe must have done it.'

'Mummy!' Rosie pulled at the hem of her jumper. 'Not that! The bowl!'

'Just one second, sweetheart. Zoe doesn't use our pans, Richard. She has her own cupboard. And she doesn't cook – she makes salads and things.'

'Maybe she cooked last night.'

Rosie started pummelling Eleanor's thighs. 'Mummy, come on!'

'Mummy's just talking, darling, let Mummy finish talking. Zoe was out last night, we heard her come in, remember?'

'Maybe she cooked when she got back. Or this morning when we were out.'

'I just don't think it's very likely!' Rosie was hitting her leg harder and it was starting to hurt. Eleanor knew she had to act soon to avoid another tantrum. She could feel the corners of her eyes getting hot and full.

Richard got up and stood next to her. He touched her shoulder gently; she jerked away. 'Eleanor, I don't understand. What's the matter? Come on, Rosie, calm down – we will in a minute, sweetheart. You just put it in the wrong place, Eleanor. It's a mistake. It's OK.'

'I just don't think I did!' She was trying so hard not to cry.

'*Mummy!*'

'OK, fine!' she said, and got the bowl out of the cupboard and banged it on the worktop, and then felt guilty. Richard was looking at her and she knew he was on the verge of speaking, but he changed his mind and went back to his computer. She got the sugar and flour out of the cupboard, carefully, not trusting herself to get even this right, and tried to stop her hands shaking.

What else could she do? They had bought the house just over three months ago. It was supposed to be their 'forever home'. 'You'll have to carry us out in a box,' Richard told the conveyancer cheerfully. They had no savings left; they couldn't even afford a removal van. It was where they lived now: they'd wallpapered themselves in and shut the gate. But it was rejecting her, like an unwelcome transplant. And she had no idea why.

*

She went to bed early that night and just as she was starting to drop off to sleep, there was a shriek from the children's room. It was a sound like nothing she'd ever heard before. She leapt up and rushed in. Rosie was sitting upright in bed, shaking and crying uncontrollably. Eleanor reached out to her and Rosie recoiled. She didn't seem to recognize her. She had an unfathomable expression of pure terror; she looked straight past Eleanor, staring at something which seemed to horrify her. Eleanor looked round instinctively but the wall behind her was blank. Every time she reached out, Rosie got even more wild and tried to push her arm away.

'What the hell's going on?'

Eleanor was only half aware of Richard behind her. 'I don't know! She won't let me anywhere near her!'

Isobel had woken up and was crying now too. Eleanor picked her up and rocked her, pleading with Rosie – 'it's OK, you're OK, you're all right, calm down' – but she was having no effect on either of them. Rosie was behaving as if she wasn't in the room, her eyes fixed on the thing she could see by the door. It was hideous to watch. Eleanor handed Isobel to Richard and tried again to reach out to Rosie – 'Please, Rosie, you're safe, I promise you!' – but she pushed her away again, hard this time. Her agitation seemed to increase. Eleanor didn't know how much more she could bear, but she had no idea how to stop it.

Rosie's screams started to taper out, turning into small moans. She was breathing heavily and making little whimpering sounds. Then she lay back down and slept.

'Jesus, what was that? Was she having a nightmare?' Richard asked, handing back Isobel.

'I don't know,' Eleanor said, rocking Isobel in her arms. Isobel's crying began to fade and the ability to comfort her effectively felt blissful. She put Isobel back down in her cot with relief, knowing it would be hours before she would sleep herself.

Instead, she sat in bed with her laptop, headache drumming in her skull, consulting the internet. Eleanor discovered that night terrors, like biting, were common. She had again done the wrong thing: trying to intervene had probably frightened Rosie more. She should have stayed calm and waited till it was over. She didn't understand how on earth that would be possible. It was normal, a phase, she'd grow out of it. *But what if she doesn't?* she thought. She put her laptop on the bedside table and curled up on her side. The worst thought came later, after she'd been lying awake for some hours, her head throbbing. *What if Rosie really could see something after all?*

18

Richard was woken up at five by Eleanor getting out of bed. At first, he was irritable; he'd slept badly after Rosie's nightmare. He heard Eleanor retching in the bathroom and felt a familiar kind of despair. She appeared in the bedroom, white and puffy, damp and weak, and lay down next to him. He pretended to be asleep. Then he heard her crying.

He turned over and took her hand. Immediately, he knew that this was different. She said she had a headache again, but this time it was so intense, it hurt to move her head or speak. He tried to stroke her head – she pushed his hand away and cried. He went to get her tablets and water – she sat up shakily and swallowed them, then jerked up and ran to the bathroom. He heard her vomit. She came back and lay down again, tears on her face.

Later, he couldn't think exactly how he knew it was serious. Serious enough that he rang his office to tell them that he couldn't come in. He took Isobel and Rosie to nursery, agitated by the thought of Eleanor at home alone. Rosie caught his mood and wet herself in the street.

At home, Eleanor was vomiting compulsively. Eventually, there was nothing left and her body could only perform a kind of simulation, arching as if possessed and then collapsing on her side. He panicked about dehydration and made her drink water, but she threw it up again immediately: thin contaminated liquid shooting out of her like she'd burst an artery. All the useless resources he marshalled – cups of hot water, more paracetamol, anti-nausea tablets – ended up expunged from her body. He worried she would have to go on a drip. She started bringing up bile, then blood.

Richard sat at the end of the bed, enmeshed in indecision. He wanted to take her to hospital, then thought he was overreacting and then wanted to go again. He didn't know what he would do about the children. He typed things into search engines and questioned her intently about her vision or rashes. The day passed quickly and slowly: a drawn-out, endless round of vomiting, sleeping and crying. He kept thinking that things would get better and then he realized that another hour was slipping out of his grasp and nothing had changed. He had to collect Isobel and Rosie and he still didn't know what to do – he was afraid of leaving Eleanor to go and get them, afraid of not being able to look after them properly at the same time as looking after Eleanor, afraid of their distress at seeing her like this. He asked Eleanor what she wanted but she could barely speak. He tried to think of people he could ask for help: his parents were too far away, his sister would be at work. Eventually, he did the one thing he had been trying to avoid: he rang Eleanor's mother.

*

Richard remembered lying on his back on the grass by the river in Cambridge, Eleanor's head on his stomach. They'd said they were going to work and Eleanor was reading and writing in pencil in the margins. She was focused and self-contained; he was envious. He'd brought a book too, but he could only read if he held it at an uncomfortable angle to block out the sun, and he couldn't concentrate anyway: all he could think about was the colour of the sky and Eleanor's hair. His pen lolled on his chest, next to her face. He was trying to fight the urge to distract her, when Eleanor shut her book and said, 'By the way, I ought to warn you: my mum's a bit unusual.'

They were heading to London that weekend; he was going to meet her mother for the first time.

'Unusual how?'

'She's just not like a mum. She does weird stuff.'

'What kind of stuff?'

'She pisses in the garden.'

'What? Why?'

'She's sort of a hippy. She says it's more natural, but I think it's just that she's lazy – when she's in the kitchen, she can't be bothered to go upstairs to use the bathroom. And she's an attention seeker.'

'So you don't get on with her?'

'We get on OK. She's just always disappointed in me – she wants me to be more gregarious or daring than I actually am. She's got a much more colourful life than I have. I think she'd rather it was the other way round.'

When he met Carolyn, he understood: she was flamboyant, garrulous and beautiful – proper, deep beauty that never diminished, even as the tiny vertical lines set in around her mouth, her hair got coarser and wilder, and the veins on her hands stood prouder. She was kind, but flirted with him insistently and he hadn't known what to do – he knew that he was expected to flirt back, but he just wasn't that sort of person. He couldn't flirt with his girlfriend's mother. He became stiffer and more awkward in response and she tried harder. Eleanor affected a kind of detached superiority that he'd never seen before, which irritated Carolyn and made Eleanor seem immature. The whole evening was mortifying.

Over time, Carolyn began to see him as a product of Eleanor's dreadful banality and enthusiastically disapproved of his job and his wealthy parents. He thought she was irritating and hard work, and not half as charismatic as she thought she was. Eventually, all conversations returned to her. She refused to hear about the wedding – 'if you try to talk to me about marquees and button-holes, darling, I will literally go insane. I do not want to hear those words in this house.' When Eleanor told her she was pregnant with Rosie, she shrieked, 'Oh God! I *can't* be a grandmother! Not yet.' She was tiresomely neurotic about food, trying to find excuses to skip meals, always following a new regime. 'I'm only eating citrus fruits this week,' she said as Eleanor put a shepherd's pie on the table. Richard often found himself losing patience, but Eleanor was more accepting and tolerated Carolyn with grace and stoicism. It made Richard love her even more.

They got on better after Rosie and Isobel were born. She refused to be called 'Grandma' or to babysit – 'I won't be left alone with them, Richard. I don't have a maternal bone in my body; you ask Ellie' – and she enjoyed saying things like 'Children are such absolute *shits*, aren't they.' But she softened when she saw them, and would get totally absorbed in their company. She clearly loved them – there was just an unspoken agreement that they would never draw attention to it.

*

Richard was floundering when he spoke to her, but Carolyn was calm and practical. For the first time, he appreciated her forcefulness: she insisted that he drive Eleanor to her house and then go to nursery to 'pick up the monsters'. He poured Eleanor into the back seat of the car, putting seatbelts and blankets around her horizontal body. When they arrived, Carolyn drew Eleanor to her with an affection she normally reserved for Isobel and Rosie. The next morning she called her doctor out – Richard could only imagine the mixture of flirtation and stubbornness that had got him out on an emergency home visit, to see a patient who wasn't even registered, and he couldn't help but be grateful for it. The doctor told them it was probably a virus and that she would get better. Richard was relieved that Eleanor wasn't going to die but angry that there was no concrete word to describe what they'd been going through. He wanted a diagnosis and a cure – something potent that would ensure it never happened again. At least some acknowledgement that his fear was justified. But Eleanor was slowly recovering – the pain in her head was still intense, but she was vomiting less and it was clear she wasn't in any danger. The crisis had passed.

19

'She's walking! Oh, thank God for that – can I stop playing Florence Nightingale now?' Carolyn got up and kissed Eleanor on the cheek, which was uncomfortable for both of them. 'Honestly, I wasn't cut out for this. How are you feeling, darling?'

'Much better, Mum. Still tired.'

'Well, don't be going home to those dreadful children of yours just yet. Let me make you a cup of tea.'

Eleanor sat down wearily at the fold-up kitchen table. She was wearing her mum's old dressing gown, and the ratty towelling on her skin conjured up a memory so indistinct it was simply a feeling: her small face and body pressed into the fabric. They had never really had a family home – she barely remembered their house in Parsons Green, where she'd lived with her mum and dad until the divorce, and then it was flat after flat, circling the same patches of Hackney and Stoke Newington. And now they were in Carolyn's 'bachelor pad' – the small flat she'd bought three years ago. But the furniture never changed; it shuttled around northeast London with them, and the chairs and the curtains and the fish slice contained her childhood. She looked at the kitchen scissors on the magnetic strip and she could feel her tiny hands clutching the great loop of orange plastic, the long silver swoop of the blade ahead.

When she'd first arrived at her mum's flat, she'd been slipping in and out of sleep. She would wake up not knowing where she was, not knowing where Rosie and Isobel were, and she'd panic, before remembering. As she started to get better, the panic subsided and she felt more rational: to be apart from her children was less like a tragedy, more like something not quite right, askew. And as she got stronger, the moments she had to remind herself that she was on her own – that she could sit still, linger over breakfast, not rush in the shower – were accompanied by an acute pleasure. It was such a luxury to step outside your own life. Ordinarily, she didn't think much about what things were like before she'd had children; it felt so far away, she sometimes thought she genuinely couldn't remember it. Sitting at the table, watching her mum switch on the kettle, take down the Alton Towers mug, open the rusting tea tin, she started to reconnect with the person she used to be.

Carolyn had always told her she wished she'd never had children. Eleanor refused to take offence, partly because she knew Carolyn was trying to shock and she didn't want to satisfy her. Carolyn said it destroyed your identity and your creativity, and she spoke fondly and evangelically about the imagined lives she might have had if she hadn't met Eleanor's father. She saw inadequate mothering as a mark of character.

Eleanor grew up thinking that Carolyn was vaguely demented and that she, Eleanor, would do a better job of being a woman. Part of that would be embracing motherhood. But now she had children, she found it was harder than she thought to do it well and there was no way to prove she was making a better job of it: there was too much doubt. It pleased her when the role seemed to fit, but inside, she knew she didn't match up. When she had told Richard that Carolyn was 'not like a mum', she had known exactly what she meant by that; now she was less certain. She had been so sure of the ways Carolyn was deficient, but it was less easy to say what she ought to have done instead. She also couldn't comprehend how Carolyn had brought up a child on her own, and even though she didn't always think she had done it well, she was reluctantly in awe of it. She didn't want to admire her mum – it was easier just to get annoyed with her – but sometimes it was unavoidable.

*

'I've never seen you like that,' Carolyn said, putting the mug of tea on the table. 'As a child, you were so robust.'

Eleanor said nothing and took a sip of tea. Her jaw was still slightly strained from days of throwing up.

'Where on earth do you think you picked it up from?'

Eleanor looked down. For a moment, she wondered if she could tell her. If she could say, *It's all the time. I'm ill all the time. I hate it, I can't function, I can't enjoy life and no one will listen to me. But it's there every day and I'm scared it's something in the house . . .*

'Is it those kids, do you think? The things you pick up from small children – they're like vermin.'

Eleanor looked up again. 'Yes, something from the nursery. I think that's probably it.'

*

Recovery was sublime. She was tired but it was an exquisitely pleasurable tiredness because she could feed it. She lay on the sofa in her mum's dressing gown, took naps. She remembered what sensation was like: iced water at the back of her throat, salted butter on her tongue. She became euphoric from it all: glorious showers and cups of tea and clean sheets. Her mum made her hearty comforting meals, which she wouldn't eat herself, and Eleanor had never tasted anything so delicious.

The feeling was addictive; she became actively afraid of losing it. But she knew this wasn't right – the flat was too small, Carolyn was getting on her nerves and she longed to be back with Isobel and Rosie. She wondered if the illness had been nothing to do with the house at all – maybe it *was* just a virus, lying low, that had now expressed itself fully and was gone. She *had* been run-down. Perhaps she could now finally begin to appreciate the house. Richard was right: it was an opportunity, a blank canvas. They could make whatever they wanted from it.

She felt brand new when Richard came to pick her up. She held Rosie and Isobel close to her and joy invaded her body so violently, she cried. For a few days, she was rejuvenated, bursting with energy. The small jobs that used to defeat her were now enjoyable – she gathered up the empty bottles in the bathroom, sticky with shampoo, mouthwash, hair wax, and washed them out and recycled them. She turned the bed covers back every morning and opened the window, to air the bed. She bought mothballs for the cupboards and made sweet potato mash for the freezer.

Then she grew tired again, but not the healing tiredness of the past few days – a different, more familiar kind. At first, she refused to accept it – *it can't be, I can't, I can't do this* – but her cranium began to feel swollen, live, growing outwards. The nausea nagged at her insides. Her head became heavy and full and then there was the pain, thick and black, swelling and receding. Again, she would shut the

KATE MURRAY-BROWNE

front door behind her and sit on the steps outside her house
or go to the nearest park and sink onto a damp bench,
gasping. Eleanor was afraid. She was now certain: there was
something in the house.

TWO

1

In the new year, Eleanor became single-minded, devotional, in her mission. She was going to cure the house. Nothing mattered more than this. On Mondays, she put Rosie and Isobel in front of the TV for as long as she could; at work, she did as little as possible, while she compulsively trawled the internet. She learned about 'sick building syndrome' and 'indoor pollution', but none of it described her – people complained of asthma or breathing difficulties, but no one talked about vomiting or migraines. She read about illness caused by ley lines and water currents underneath the house, about dowsing, copper rods, feng shui and crystals. She bought house plants, covered mirrors, burned incense and changed the position of their bed.

She realized she'd always treated the house squeamishly, afraid of disturbing it or finding something she wouldn't like. She decided to confront it. She checked the pipes and the boiler, pulled out the cooker and the fridge. She took out drawers, cleared shelves, unscrewed cupboard doors. Nothing went unearthed, apart from the basement; she wondered if there was a way of asking Zoe if she could spring-clean it, without sounding peculiar or rude. She didn't know what she was looking for: mould, a leak. Something growing, something broken.

She bought a hygrometer to test the damp levels. She read that mites and spores could live in soft furnishings, so she gathered up the towels, stripped the beds, took down the curtains, pulled the covers off the sofas. She washed and dry-cleaned continually, shampooed the carpets, stuffed old clothes, cushions and duvet covers into bin bags. She bought new mattresses on credit cards. Zoe came home one Monday and found her working dementedly, washing the walls – the sofas nude, their mattress in the hallway, the cooker half out of the unit. Eleanor half registered how strange it must look. Zoe hung around the doorway, curious, and then said tentatively, 'Are you spring-cleaning?'

'That's right,' Eleanor said, clipped, wiping sweat off her face with her elbow, not stopping to take her rubber gloves off. She thought about saying something else, but she just wanted to get back to work. Zoe smiled nervously and went downstairs; Eleanor turned back to the wall.

*

It was during the excavation that she found the notepad. It was lodged behind one of the radiators in the living room, halfway down, at an angle – she thought it had slipped rather than been placed there. She levered it out with a wooden spoon and as she held it in her hands, she found she was shaking. It was an ordinary, spiral-bound, lined notebook. The pages were starting to stiffen and yellow. Someone had tied a pencil to a piece of string and attached it to the wire.

It was filled with handwritten notes: tasks and shopping lists. Eleanor felt uncomfortable as she read it: its banality only made it more intimate. It was mostly unremarkable: *Cabbage, ring Susan, check bank balance, David. Pay Sarah, sausages, tins toms, Margot.* But almost every list contained the name 'Emily'. Eleanor's stomach dropped sharply each time she saw the letters. *Emily food, Emily appt, Emily haircut. Emily shoes.* No other name appeared so frequently. She was dominating the house. Her stomach dropped as the words *prescription, hospital, treatment, pills* appeared again and again.

Eleanor read every page carefully, not sure what she was trying to find. There was the odd menu plan – *Mon: fish fingers, Tues: bolognese, Weds: stew*. About a third of the way through, she found a note to someone, as if the notepad had been left out for someone to see. It was functional and unaffectionate: *This is the package for returning, don't forget the recycling bags.* At the bottom, it said, *Emily not good.* She found five or six more, full of imperatives, equally unrevealing until the last line: *Emily very bad; bad night last night – Emily; Emily WORSE today.* In the last, the writing became slightly wayward: *WORSE* was underlined twice, two diagonal lines that nearly scored through the paper.

*

Eleanor put the notebook in a kitchen drawer and felt it there, luminous and quivering, for the rest of the day. She grew more and more agitated the closer it got to evening. She was thinking about it as she shampooed Rosie's hair, listening to her scream, saying, 'Not long now, darling, I know you don't like this bit,' detached and automatic. The words 'Emily WORSE' played in her head while the well-worn sentences of Isobel's picture books slid out of her mouth. As soon as she had got them both to sleep, she ran down the stairs, jerked the drawer open and put the notepad in front of Richard as he sat at the kitchen table. He flipped through it, ostentatiously disinterested. She sat opposite him, arms folded, heart beating loudly.

'So?'

'So, there was something wrong with Emily! This proves it.'

'We knew that. All that writing – clearly something wasn't right. And actually, this doesn't prove anything at all, if you think about it. "Emily very bad" – she was a child! She was probably just badly behaved. Going through a phase.'

Eleanor thought of Rosie and her 'phase'. Her stomach lurched briefly; she ignored it.

'But all this stuff about hospitals, treatments . . . What if it was something more than bad behaviour? What if she was ill?'

'It doesn't mean anything. Could have been athlete's foot for all we know.' He skimmed the notepad back across the table to her. 'Just chuck it. Stop thinking about it.'

Eleanor took the notepad back and folded the pages over carefully, one by one. 'But so much, Richard. Every single day. And the lock on her bedroom door – this wasn't a happy house.'

'She was clearly . . . too much in some way. They were just at the end of their tether and they locked her in her room. It's something people do.'

'What people? What people do that?'

'I know it's not something you or I would do. I'm not saying it's nice. I'm just saying it's more common than you think.'

'I feel like something was seriously wrong. What if she died?'

'Well, then that would have been very sad. But there's absolutely no evidence to suggest—'

'What if she died in the house?'

'What if she did? Eleanor, it's a Victorian house! People

will have suffered, and grieved, and died, and had babies, and fallen in love – all in this house. All in any house we could possibly live in. It doesn't mean anything.'

Eleanor said quietly, 'I feel like in this house it does.'

Richard was still for a minute. Then he got up and put his arms around her.

'Why can't you just forget about it? They're a different family. They might have been unhappy but we're not. Why can't you just enjoy the house?'

*

The notepad made Eleanor hungry for information. The next Monday, she went into Richard's study and got out the documents from the house sale. She reread the surveyor's report, but found nothing unusual. Physically, the house was healthy.

She thought back to the sale, raking it over for clues. Little peculiarities, submerged at the time, now began to surface. On the second viewing, she'd asked the estate agent directly if the family were still living there. He'd said they were and she'd been satisfied, but now his tone – cautious, evasive – preyed on her. They were moving away, he'd said, and weren't going to buy somewhere new until they'd settled. 'I feel like they're not telling us something,' she'd said to Richard, on the tube to the solicitor's. 'We don't even know why they're moving.' 'It could be anything,' he'd said. 'Maybe they're splitting up. Maybe one of them lost their job.'

Fleetingly she'd thought it was strange, to have no contact with them, but the sale had been smooth and quick. They had been compliant, acquiescing to anything Richard tried to negotiate. The estate agents had said they were in a hurry; the house had been on the market for months. They were the only people to make an offer. Richard was proud of this; she found it unnerving.

Now, she wished she'd asked more. The contracts for the sale gave the names of the previous owners – Claire and Steven Ashworth – but no forwarding address. She put their names, and Emily's, into Google and trawled through every result but could find nothing that fitted. They had left no trace. She knew rationally that this was not unusual, but it felt almost vampiric not to have made any impact on the internet, like having no reflection in a mirror. She rang the estate agents and asked for their details; they were polite and apologetic but said they couldn't give out that information because of confidentiality. She found the name of their solicitor in the correspondence about the sale: she rang and said she needed to get in touch with their clients urgently. At first they were reluctant to help, but she persisted and they agreed to forward a letter. She composed it hurriedly, simply asking them to get in touch with her, and sent it off, only half expecting anything to come of it.

The next evening, after the children had gone to bed, she told Richard that she needed something from the shop, to steal a little time away from the house. Walking back, clutching her plastic bag of unwanted goods, trying to absorb as much air as she possibly could, Eleanor passed the flat of the neighbour whose cat she'd rescued. The basement window emitted a blue glow from the television screen and she saw the shape of the woman through the net curtains, on her sofa. The curtains were ratty, with a gash in them. Eleanor stopped. She didn't have long. Impulsively, she ran down the steps and rang the doorbell.

Her hands twitched by her sides as she waited for the woman to come to the door. It took a long time, and her breathing rasped when she finally answered. Eleanor felt bad for disturbing her, for forcing her to get up when move-ment was clearly difficult, but it was overwhelmed by a fiercer desire: to *know*. She tried to sound calm, measured and polite, as she introduced herself again and explained which house she was from.

The woman gave no indication that she remembered meeting her. She did not introduce herself; she just stared impassively, getting her breath back. 'Oh. You all right?' she asked, grudgingly.

'I'm so sorry to disturb you, but I need to get in touch with the people who lived in our house previously – the Ashworths? Do you have their new address or a phone number . . . ?'

The woman shook her head slowly. 'No. No, I wouldn't have anything like that.'

'Would anyone on this street? Was there anyone they were friends with?'

'Not that I'd know. Goodnight, dear.' She started to shut the door.

'But— Sorry! I'm so sorry to keep you, did you know anything about them? I thought I remembered you saying that there was something . . . something odd about them?'

The woman paused.

'I didn't know them, dear. I mean, the girl wasn't right, you could see that much. But none of them were right, really.'

'In what way?'

'Oh, there was always something going on in that house. The mother was cold, you know, snappy, though I expect you would be running round after a little girl like that.'

'What was wrong with the girl? Was she ill?'

'She was . . . disturbed, I suppose you'd call it. Mind you, the whole house was disturbed. There was always noise coming from upstairs, always something going on. I don't get out of the house much these days, but if I was going past, you know, to the shops and that, there was always something. Some commotion.'

The cat sidled past her and out of the door. It ran, surprisingly fast, up the steps.

'Now you've gone and done it!'

'I'm sorry, I'm so sorry.' Eleanor dropped her carrier bag, raced after the cat and picked her up, putting her back in the doorway. The woman turned away from Eleanor and pulled the door to, so it was just ajar.

'Go on, get back inside, you! Shoo!'

'I'm sorry to keep asking, but what sort of—?'

'I don't think I can help you. I didn't know them, like I say.'

'But—'

'Bless you, dear. Goodnight.' She closed the door and Eleanor was left outside. She picked up her bag and dug her fingernails into her palm.

2

When Eleanor told Zoe they would be away for another weekend, this time for a wedding, Zoe rang Adam and invited him over. She regretted it as soon as he said yes. He'd only been to Litchfield Road once – they'd both been drunk and had frantic, unsatisfactory sex before falling asleep. She woke at half past five and was horrified at the thought of Eleanor and Richard finding out he was there. She oscillated endlessly about whether to try and sneak him out of the house before they got up, if he could scramble out of the front area or if she should just wait until they'd left for work. In the end, she let him sleep, watching him anxiously, listening to the noises above her, willing Eleanor and Richard to leave as quickly and quietly as possible.

He had never spent much time in the house and she was afraid of what he would think of her when he saw it properly. It was an arrangement that was haphazard and squalid, without being particularly bohemian or exciting.

They had been seeing each other for over three months, even though he still hadn't broken up with Kathryn. Their sporadic, drunken encounters quickly gained a rhythm; they'd stopped talking about how they shouldn't and accepted that they were. It was more or less working. She could still send herself dizzy with anticipation twenty-four hours before they saw each other. Certain things he said to her became precious and she would repeat them during the day like incantations. Sometimes, late at night and alone, she got jealous and angry that he was with Kathryn, and sometimes she tried to imagine having a proper relationship with him, but not for very long. She knew that something would have to change to accommodate that and she was afraid of upsetting the balance, even more of losing that obsessive feeling. It would go eventually, she knew that – she just wanted to keep hold of it for a little longer.

'Is it strange living here?' he asked, looking round her bedroom, and she became immediately defensive.

'Strange how?'

'You know, is it a weird situation? Being a lodger?'

'It's fine. I don't see them that much,' Zoe said, without telling him that she had to try very hard, all the time, to keep it that way.

'But you share the kitchen? And the front door?'

'I've got my own bathroom,' Zoe said.

He looked round the room again. 'It's great,' he said, unconvincingly.

She led him upstairs, so that she could cook supper for him. She hoped this would make it better somehow. Maybe the cosiness – the home-cooked food, Eleanor and Richard's nice things, watching their giant television – would be sufficiently different to feel exotic, like role play.

'Whoa,' he said, when he stepped into the living room and she remembered how strange and shabby the furnishings were. 'I thought you said they were rich?'

'I don't know if they're rich exactly. Anyway, they didn't choose it – it was like this before they moved in. They just haven't got round to doing it up yet.'

'No, I can see.' He pointed to the green walls. 'This colour is intense.'

He wandered into the living room and started inspecting things, and Zoe watched him from the kitchen, getting irritated. He picked up Eleanor and Richard's wedding photo and put it down again, making a noise that was somewhere between an expression of curiosity and a laugh. She began to feel protective and worried that Eleanor and Richard might somehow find out or sense this: she had invited a stranger into their house and allowed him to mock them. Adam pointed at one of their framed prints and said, 'Rothko would go fucking mental if he could see this.' Zoe smiled and said, 'Ha! yeah,' and started peeling potatoes.

She'd put a chicken in the oven before he came round, but she'd never cooked one before and got anxious about food poisoning. She overcooked it: the meat was bloated and lost its taste, and the potatoes were flabby and chalky at the centre. They sat opposite each other at the dining table, eating off Eleanor and Richard's expensive crockery, aping something that was not available to them, because they were the wrong generation and would never have that sort of relationship. 'This is really nice,' Adam said, and she thought they both knew that it wasn't.

After they'd eaten, they sat on the sofa, which had lost any kind of physical robustness and sank beneath their weight. She flicked through the TV channels; everything seemed garish and too loud. She could see the chicken carcass in the kitchen, and thought about all the good meat still on the bones. It would have to go in the bin. She supposed Eleanor would make soups and pies and packed lunches for the children. It felt impossible.

'You must find *this* weird though,' Adam said. 'Being in someone else's living room.'

'I told you, I don't come up here that much. Just when they're away.'

'Still . . .'

'Yeah, well, if I had a room in a hipster East London warehouse, I'd live there. But I don't. So I live here. There's a housing crisis, you know.'

'I know,' he said, and looked at her curiously.

It wasn't going well, and the point of them being together was that things went well – there was nothing else to hold them in place. And because she felt that it was her responsibility to keep them afloat, she did the thing she had been considering, but knew she shouldn't really do.

She reached out and touched his arm, as if impulsively. 'Hey, do you want to see something *really* weird?'

He looked startled, which was what she wanted.

'Come on.' She grabbed his hand and led him into the hallway, and up the stairs.

'Are we allowed up here?'

'Well, they never said I wasn't. But obviously I wouldn't do this if they were here.'

Scaling the house felt like an expedition; she began to feel nervous and excited. She opened the door to Richard and Eleanor's bedroom. They'd changed the position of the bed and there were a few incongruous touches: incense on the windowsill and a strange throw covering the mirror. She was surprised; she wouldn't have thought either of them would be into that sort of thing. But otherwise it was the same: blank and forensically tidy, apart from a couple of Richard's shirts on the chair. Adam seemed fascinated, and she was relieved to have got his attention back. He put his palm flat on the bedlinen, experimentally and reverentially. 'I can't believe people actually live like this,' he said.

He walked over to the chair and picked up one of Richard's shirts. 'Cufflinks,' he said, almost to himself.

She showed him the children's room and he got angry about their toys: 'Kids don't need this much stuff, *surely*. It's like there's this *conspiracy* to make sure only rich people procreate.' She picked up the hideous doll and threw it at him playfully. *Oh Zoe, what are you doing*, she thought.

'Kids are so fucking *creepy*,' he said and then she knew she'd made the right decision.

They went up the next flight of stairs, and Zoe felt again that peculiar hike in pressure on this floor of the house, or maybe it was just nerves. She showed him Richard's study and together they took in his books, his desk, his MacBook Pro. 'I bet he doesn't use half the features on that,' Adam said.

When they were outside the final room, she said, 'OK, are you ready for this?' She felt the same curious resistance from the door, as if something was pushing against it, but then they were inside and Adam was silently taking it in. She could tell he was astonished, and she felt pleased.

'What *is* this?'

'I don't know. It must have been from before they moved in; their kids aren't old enough to write.' She touched the walls; they felt cold. 'You can tell they've tried to paint over it.'

He moved towards the suitcase, with the strange array of objects lined up on top. Zoe noticed that the pile of quilts next to it had a doll's dress on top; it made her shiver. She instinctively felt they shouldn't touch anything, but he crouched down in front of the suitcase and picked up the piece of fur. 'Jesus.'

'Careful. Don't stir up the evil spirits,' she said, trying to make it sound like a joke.

He stood up. 'This is like an installation. Why did she do this?'

'I don't know. I guess she must have been disturbed in some way? But I don't know where these things came from.'

'Whoa.' He pointed to the door: it was split and beaten at the bottom, as though it had been scratched and kicked. 'That's fucking *dark*, man. Like, this girl really wanted to get out.'

Zoe hadn't noticed that before. The pleasing jitteriness was now giving way to fear. It was all right for him to enjoy it, but she had to live here. She wished she hadn't shown it to him.

'What's in the suitcase?'

'I don't know; I haven't opened it.'

He looked at her flirtatiously. 'Do you want to?'

She nodded and he moved his hand towards it.

'No—!' she said and he laughed.

'Are you scared?'

'Yes! Aren't you?'

'Of course. But I also want to know what's inside.'

'Go on then.'

He lifted the objects off it and placed them on the floor beside it. Zoe watched to make sure he didn't disrupt the order; she wasn't sure what she thought would happen if he did, but it felt important. He slowly unbuckled the straps and lifted the lid. She was relieved and slightly disappointed: it was just paper.

Hundreds of sheets of paper, thin and scrappy and torn at the edges. Not in neat piles, but stashed in clumsily. Some of the larger sheets were in scrolls and there was a stack of exercise books, but most were loose.

It was clearly the same person who had drawn on the walls. Zoe saw the same faces, though some had lines slashed across the cheek or a cross over the mouth. There were paintings done in thick, rough black brush strokes, showing hunched, foetal figures with giant eyes. A page with hundreds of black crosses on it. And birds, so many birds – always in the same position, prone on their side, never in flight. It made her shiver.

She opened one of the exercise books – it was full of biro line drawings that got simpler and stranger, until there was only a semicircular line with a loop at the top. One page had only three biro lines, made so forcefully they'd torn the paper, like cuts.

'Hey, some of these are good.' Adam started talking about 'outsider art' and 'the cobra movement', but Zoe stopped listening. The hunched figures were staring at her. Finally, she couldn't stand it any more.

'Adam, come on – let's just put it away and go downstairs. I'm really freaked out now.'

He looked her in the eye. 'Do you believe in ghosts?'

'No! Of course not. Why, do you?'

'I don't know, not ghosts exactly. But I sometimes think spaces, sort of, hold on to energy. It feels different up here, from the rest of the house. I mean, something bad happened, right? That's obvious. And this girl's energy, maybe it's still here. There must be something wrong with the room. Otherwise they would be using it.'

Her heart was hammering now. She wanted sex. Not in a way she'd ever wanted it before; this wasn't a normal craving. She'd heard people say they'd wanted sex to prove they were alive, but it had never made sense to her; now she understood. It had nothing to do with desire; just a need to reassure herself that her body was warm and full of

151

blood. She wanted to ward off death. It was so primal and consuming she thought she might fuck anyone who was in front of her right now.

She kissed him, and hoped that he would think it was charmingly spontaneous and unpredictable. He turned her round and pushed her face against a wall and put his hands down her skirt. Arousal mixed with adrenaline and there were noises she'd never heard before coming from her throat. She was on the floor and he was pulling at her clothes. The faces on the wall stared down at her, pale and indistinct behind the layer of paint, but definitely there, and she felt dizzy and light-headed. It wasn't pleasurable in any sense she knew – it was rough and stimulating and obliterative, exactly the way she wanted it to be.

They lay on their backs on the floor, half dressed. 'I wonder what the evil spirits will think about *that*,' he said and she laughed, even though she was still afraid. She was short of breath, though she could pretend that was just from the sex. They picked up their clothes and ran downstairs. In the safety of her bedroom, they became hysterical, deranged. They sat on the edge of the bed, she bent forward over her knees and he lay on his back shaking. She laughed so much it caused her pain; she rocked catatonically, unable to breathe. Eventually, they were still. 'We've got to get out,' he said. 'It's too weird here.' She got her things together hastily, but when she closed the front door behind her, she felt a kind of private dread: she would have to come back.

3

Eleanor hadn't felt well, exactly, at the wedding: she'd felt tired, shaky, in recovery, but inordinately grateful not to be in pain. The headache faded and her strength came back as soon as they drove away from the house. It was genuinely moving seeing Amy and Dominic get married, but that pleasure was diminished by the fiercer delight at not being in the house. She was privately euphoric. She felt restored when they came back and Rosie seemed more content after her night with Richard's parents. They had a relaxed Monday together, and Eleanor remembered how it used to be: enjoying Rosie and Isobel's company, the way they could casually make her heart burst. But as the evening came round, the accumulating weight of the house became too much and a thin, faint pain covered her head like a cap. The following Monday was hard again: Rosie worried at her little finger as though she was trying to bite it off, and had another night terror, this time for several torturous minutes. Eleanor resigned herself to staying awake long after Rosie had gone back to sleep, fizzing with anxiety.

The next day, when she came to pick Rosie and Isobel up from nursery, Rosie didn't want to leave. It was starting to happen regularly now. She was shrieking: 'I don't *want* to go home! I hate you! I hate home! I want to stay here!'

'Ah, it's cute she likes it here so much,' one of the nursery assistants said, embarrassed, and Eleanor could only just manage a smile as she dragged Rosie out into the street, pleading with her to stop crying.

Eleanor tried reasoning, cajoling and distracting, but by the time they got to Litchfield Road, Rosie was still anguished. She was trailing some way behind Eleanor and Isobel, making consistent rough, rasping wails, her mouth a thin line of horror. Eleanor received it like artillery, a deliberate, measured attack. She ignored it, partly because she vaguely believed it might be the right tactic – she wasn't making a fuss! – but also because she had no idea what else to try. She felt ashamed when they passed anyone and tried not to meet their eye. The panic was steadily rising; it was all she could do to keep it down. Rosie was now incomprehensible to her: even if she stopped crying, there was no way of telling whether she would start again or bite Eleanor or put Isobel's elephant in the bin. She was an utterly irrational force and Eleanor felt entirely alone.

As they got near the house, Eleanor caught sight of a woman she thought she recognized. She was with two children, a boy and a girl, a little older than Rosie. Eleanor was too slow to look away and their eyes met. She thought the woman looked concerned and at the same time a little critical, though that could have been her imagination. Then the woman stopped outside a house opposite theirs, and got her key out. Eleanor became interested. She maintained eye contact and smiled ruefully, an unspoken apology for Rosie.

'Are you all right there?' the woman asked. Her tone wasn't entirely sympathetic but Eleanor behaved as though it was.

'I don't know what else to do! She won't respond to anything when she's like this.'

'How old is she? Three? Four?'

'Three and a half.'

'Oh, that's a tricky age! My two were always pretty good, thank goodness, and we were very strict with behavioural charts – have you tried anything like that?'

'We've never managed – Rosie, come on, darling, it's all right – we've never managed to get anything like that in place.'

'Oh, you really ought to. I mean, as I say, my two never really went in for this sort of thing, but you need to have a system . . .'

Rosie seemed to be running dry, intrigued by the woman and the older children. The wailing slowed and turned to a quieter rasping until it stopped altogether.

'There we are, Rosie. OK, good girl,' Eleanor said, swamped in relief. Then she held out her hand.

'I'm Eleanor. We've just moved across the road, number 52.'

'Number 52, now which . . . ? Oh God, not the madhouse?'

'The what—?'

'Oh sorry-sorry-sorry-sorry! I shouldn't have said. That was just what Mark and I used to call it, because, well . . . Did you know the people you bought it from?'

'No, we never met them—'

'Mummy!' Rosie pulled at her trouser leg.

'I'm just talking, Rosie – let Mummy finish talking.'

'I'm Joanna, by the way,' the woman said. She looked at her watch. 'Do you have time for a quick cup of tea? Or do you need to get back?'

Eleanor did need to get back but her excitement was mounting. She could find out more about the house, and perhaps Joanna might become a friend. It would be so nice to have a friend close by. Maybe they could spend some Mondays at her house. Perhaps she would help her handle Rosie.

'Are you sure you don't mind?'

'No, absolutely not! It would be great to have company. And they can have a bit of a run around before their tea. Come on in.'

'OK, then, well, that would be really lovely,' Eleanor said, manoeuvring the buggy into the hall.

Joanna led them downstairs into the basement kitchen. She opened the door to the garden and let her children – Amelia and Jack, Eleanor learned – out with Rosie, where there was a slide and a trampoline.

'We can keep an eye on them from in here. What kind of tea would you like?'

Eleanor kept one eye on Isobel, who was tentatively exploring, while she surreptitiously took in Joanna's kitchen. Everything was ordinary, cheerful and smart – white wood, purple flower patterns, coasters, table mats, mug trees. It was not austere and refined, like the plans that Richard had for their house, nor minimal and clean, like the things she would have chosen years ago. It was the sort of house a family with two young children should have; it seemed to fit Joanna exactly. Eleanor might once have been privately condescending about it. Now, she would give anything to live there.

They talked in the way they were accustomed to, with frequent interruptions, and about the usual things – the schools, the area, their houses – until Eleanor felt brave enough to try and ask about number 52. She tried to keep her voice light and jokey.

'So did you say our house was called the madhouse?'

'Oh God, I'm so sorry about that! I should never have said a thing! It's just the mum who lived there before and her kid, they were a bit . . . sort of nutty, you know. So Mark and I had this joke . . . But that was a long time ago, I mean we can't have seen them for, what, a year? It's not since you've moved in, God, no.'

'How were they nutty?' Eleanor said, watching Isobel stagger towards Joanna's kitchen cupboards.

'Oh, well, it was the little girl, really. She was appalling! Screaming, crying, making all sorts of noise. Look, all kids can be a nightmare at times, can't they? But there was something . . . unnatural about her. Jack! Jack! Rosie's go, OK? Let Rosie have a go.'

'It doesn't matter,' Eleanor said, desperately hoping this train of conversation wouldn't be derailed.

'No, Jacky, she's our guest! We don't treat guests like that, do we? Sorry, what was I—?'

'The people that lived in our house?'

'Oh yeah! So this little girl, she was a couple of years older than Amelia, I think, though it was hard to tell, really. But the way she behaved! Weird noises, all the time. And I tried to be friendly with her, you know, the mum, because some women find it difficult, don't they? It was clear she wasn't coping – she just looked exhausted the whole time. Really haggard. And I never saw her! I don't know where the girl went to school – Amelia! *Amelia!* You're supposed to be the big girl, Amelia. Thank you! Thank! You! – but I'd never seen her at any of the play groups round here or anything like that. So if I saw her in the street, I tried to be friendly, but she made it difficult. She just wasn't . . . responsive. And then there was this incident with the little girl— Jacky!'

Eleanor raced across the room. 'Isobel! Not in your mouth, darling, OK? No, no, put that down, that's Joanna's. Sorry, what was the incident?'

'Oh, well, we got talking in the street – I was inviting them to our Christmas drinks – I mean, to be perfectly honest, I don't know what we'd have done if they'd come, but I thought we've got to *ask* her. And the little girl was, well, how she normally was, but more *animated* somehow. A bit kind of frantic. She was growling and flapping her arms about like this and then she bit Amelia.'

'Iso! Iso? Why don't you play with this instead? Look, this one. Sorry – she *bit* her?'

'Yes, she just went for her! Like: *pow*! It was . . . savage, really, that's the word. Brutal. She drew blood. And the mum didn't even apologise! I couldn't believe it. Amelia was howling and this woman was just standing there.'

'Maybe she didn't know what to say.'

'But she had this look on her face. Sort of hard. Cold. So after that, I just thought, OK, I won't bother then. I mean, this was, what, God, two or three years ago now? So Amelia was little, and as I say, this girl was older; well, she was bigger anyway. And I just thought, if she's dangerous, Amelia and Jack have to come first, right?'

Eleanor nodded, mute, rattling a toy in front of Isobel's face.

'Look. Some kids aren't easy. I know that. But you'd go past at ten in the evening. And there's a light on upstairs! And you could hear the crying from outside. Our two would have been in bed for hours by then. And sometimes you do think . . . Look, I'm not saying it was her fault. There could have been all sorts going on that I didn't know about. But children are like little sponges. They pick up on everything and there was something not right in that house. I'm sure of it. Jacky! Jacky! I'll come over. OK. Good boy.'

'What about her husband?'

'Oh, you never saw him! It was always the two of them

together. I saw him out and about once or twice – again, this was a few years ago now – and he looked *awful*, poor man. You know, unwell. Not that I'm really surprised; I'm sure it was no picnic living in that house. Jacky! Right, that's it!'

She got up and intervened, and it was hard for Eleanor to ask her anything more. The conversation moved on and Joanna gave Eleanor lengthy advice about dealing with tantrums: a long explanation of a complicated reward system involving jars and bits of pasta.

'I managed to stamp it out in Amelia and Jack very early on. But a lot of it's you, you know. I mean, look at Rosie now! You've relaxed, and so has she.'

Eleanor watched Rosie running with Amelia and Jack, shrieking. She did look sublimely happy. Eleanor and Joanna talked more about the area and then the conversation dipped, so Eleanor asked the question that now carried with it a different kind of tenderness. 'And what do you do? Do you work?'

'Well, I used to work in TV, but I'm a full-time mum now. I went back to work after Jack, but it became obvious after a while that it just wasn't possible, you know, with two of them . . . Mark's job is pretty full-on – he doesn't get home till eight most nights – and we couldn't both have done that kind of job. I'll probably look for something part-time when they're older but, to be honest, I want to be the one picking them up from school. Do you know what I mean? I know it's not right for everybody, but I want to be that kind of mum.'

'I can understand that,' Eleanor said.

'How about you, do you work?'

'I work in publishing. Four days a week. Iso . . . Iz, darling. Come on, we've got to go home soon.'

'Oh. Well, lucky you,' Joanna said, insincerely. 'Still, four days is a lot, isn't it? And even if you're just working nine till five, it's a long day in childcare. You're just picking them up now, aren't you?'

'I don't really know how else we'd do it . . .' Joanna was looking at her, and it was clear that it was important to her that Eleanor express some kind of regret or unhappiness. It would be so easy to do. *I envy you, I don't really enjoy my job, we wouldn't survive on my husband's salary.* It was partly true. Why didn't she just say it? It was the kind of amelioration she used to offer up without thinking, but now she was just very, very tired.

Joanna looked pensive. 'I did worry, you know, about how I'd cope not working, you know, losing my identity and all that. It's such a big shift. But I did cope. And now I can be the kind of mum I want to be.'

Eleanor half smiled. 'I don't think I know what kind of mum I want to be.'

Joanna looked at her blankly and didn't repay her expression of honesty; Eleanor felt foolish and bluntly angry. She sensed that Joanna might not be a friend after all. As she strapped Isobel into her buggy and prayed that Rosie would agree to come home without a fuss, she was thinking again about Emily.

4

Richard knew he shouldn't go back to Zoe's room, and he also knew that he was going to. He was starting to accept that his study days, which had seemed like enormous gifts, giant plains of time and space, didn't always make him feel particularly good. When he was alone in the house, he felt himself alter, in tiny cellular adjustments, and after a few hours, the mood was there, definite and intrinsic.

He was constantly aware of the basement. As the day went on, its presence became more and more insistent, and then, when the dead hour was particularly oppressive, he found himself standing in Zoe's bedroom again, staring at her tights.

It was still a mess. The duvet was contorted in a different position; her things had orbited round the room. There was a black bundle at the foot of the bed – light, slightly silky material. A cascade of pyjama bottoms; tights forming wrinkled cocoons. He went over to the wastepaper basket and looked inside: on top of crumpled tissues, an empty contact lens solution bottle and a cloud of red hair, sat a fat, slug-like condom.

Richard had only used a condom twice in his life, the first two times he'd had sex with Eleanor, before a detached, delicate conversation about former partners, in which they'd agreed that it was OK not to: Eleanor was on the pill, Richard was a virgin and Eleanor's last boyfriend had been too. In the six months before they'd met, the condom in his wallet was simply currency: the potential for pleasure and sophistication compressed in a tiny foil package, but never exchanged. It felt like tempting fate and foolish to have it there at all, and as it turned out, he never needed it. When he and Eleanor became a couple, he threw it away without a note of regret: he had a girlfriend, a badge of maturity that had always seemed some way off, something he'd have to build towards or earn. It was only much later that he started to feel that the condom in the wallet had represented other things too – spontaneity, daring, inconstancy – and perhaps he had never fully cashed it in.

It took Richard a moment to realize that Zoe must have disregarded Eleanor's rule about overnight guests. He felt briefly disgusted at the idea of a stranger coming into his house and then outraged at the thought of Zoe ignoring them, and then impotent as there was no way he could confront her about it.

He went into the living room. There was a small pile of nail clippings on the arm of one of the chairs, a scattering of little commas, white with patches of blue paint. Crumpled tissues with violent fleshy smears and streaks of black hovered on the seat of one of the armchairs, along with a mirror and two sticks of make-up. He itched to move them, with a surge of frustration – why didn't she *care* about upholstery? – followed by a kind of envy: how freeing it would be not to care. He moved, this time more determinedly, to the writing desk. There were some thin sheets of lined paper, with sprawling, almost incoherent handwriting on them. He picked one up:

I'm only going to say this once and if you disagree, I'll never say it again. I think you should split up with your girlfriend and go out with me. This is why:

1. I really like you

2. I think you really like me

3. I think we could have fun together

4. You don't really seem to like your girlfriend very much

The rest of the page was blank; he turned it over but it stopped there. He picked up the paper lying next to it.

I know all the reasons we shouldn't be together, but I can't stop thinking about you. I didn't want to say this at the time, but the sex with you was mindblowing, the best I've ever had. I feel like there's definitely something between us – and that we could be something special together.

And another:

What makes you think you can just use me like this? I know what you want: you want to stay with Kathryn and carry on fucking me. Well, that's not going to happen. I think it's fucking disgusting that you would go to Edinburgh and see her after we'd been together on Saturday. How can you be so unfeeling – not just of me but of her! OK, obviously I don't really care about her that much, but we didn't even use a condom the first time. What if I had a disease that you gave her? I mean, I don't, but I could have. That would be a really horrible thing to do.

Richard thought, *Jesus, she shouldn't say any of that.* He set the last sheet down carefully, praying it was the right spot, making a mental note to be more careful next time. He went back upstairs. The dissatisfied, introverted feeling had intensified, and it was not something he could convert to productivity. He sat at his desk, shifting restlessly, thinking about the last time he'd felt that strongly about anyone. He knew that what Zoe was going through wouldn't last and it didn't even seem to be giving her that much pleasure. But it was powerful and it pulled at him. The feeling was both new and recognizable; the blood relation of something he thought had gone away.

*

Richard had met Lucinda in his final year at Cambridge. He knew of her, of course; she was famous, in an insular circle that felt like everything to Richard at the time. She played the lead in every student play; he always saw her face on posters in town. She was the kind of person you noticed, absorbing their presence and identity without thinking about it.

When he heard that Lucinda was doing the same paper as him for their finals – Shakespeare and Performance – and they were going to be in Dr Williams's supervision group together, he was unsettled in a way he couldn't put his finger on. He and Eleanor had been together for eighteen months; there was no cause for other girls to make him nervy. It was worse when he discovered there would only be three of them in the group: the third student was Fiona Turner, who Richard had heard of for different reasons. She was always one of the top four or five students in the year ('she just works really hard', Richard would say dismissively). Although he was jealous of Fiona and slightly suspicious of her, he assumed she would be his natural ally. As it turned out, he was wrong about everything.

At their first supervision, he sat on a low sofa, opposite

Dr Williams, while Fiona sat in a high-backed chair, an awkward distance away. Her hair was pulled back in a scrunchie and she was wearing a purple fleece. They waited in silence, punctuated first by occasional small talk, instigated by Dr Williams, and then by her asking if either of them knew where Lucinda was, whether they were friends with her, would it be possible for one of them to ring her. He and Fiona shook their heads sullenly. Dr Williams had just said, 'Well, I think we're going to have to start,' before there was a knock at the door, Lucinda arrived and the whole strained, suppressed atmosphere blew apart.

She chose to sit on the sofa, next to Richard. 'Shall we start with the essay I put in your pigeon-holes?' Dr Williams said and Lucinda put her hand on Richard's arm and whispered, in the kind of whisper that made it clear she didn't mind being overheard, 'Can I share yours?'

Richard reacted as if her hand was scalding. She didn't wait for an answer and shuffled along the sofa, so her thigh was pressed against his. She bent her head over the photocopy to read. Her face was far too close. Her red hair was pulled back and he could see tiny hairs forming a fuzz around her hairline. She wore bright red lipstick and her face was covered with a fine white powder; underneath it, the trace of freckles.

Throughout the supervision, Lucinda was garrulous and expressive, gesturing wildly with her hands. What she said was often irrelevant and tangential, but Richard found it impossible not to be fascinated by her. She ignored Fiona, but seemed to listen when he spoke; once she even said, 'God, you're brilliant,' when he'd finished. When she said the word 'cunt', she leaned over and put her hands over his ears and laughed. It was stagey and inappropriate, and her fingers on his hair felt marvellous.

On the way out of the supervision, she questioned him intently about his reading and essays, as if there was a shared understanding that they were vastly superior to hers. Fiona walked pointedly ahead of them, emanating disgust. It had only been an hour and already they had formed a little unit against her.

Richard was flummoxed. In a just world, he should be in Fiona's camp, isolating Lucinda. Any independent observer would have put him at the Purple Fleece end of the scale. But perhaps Lucinda knew this, and he had underestimated her need for an ally.

When Richard saw Lucinda in the student theatre bar at the weekend, she was actively uninterested in him, to the point of being rude. He approached her expectantly, primed for more flattery and physical contact, and she almost recoiled. He was cut by her callousness, but then, a small part of him was unsurprised – of course, why would she acknowledge him in public? He felt foolish but in a familiar, resigned way. In the next supervision, she was warm again, touching his hand, praising his ideas. She was rude about someone they both knew ('I swear to God, she's so boring, when she speaks to me, it's like she's shitting in my ear'), and Richard, shocked and amused despite himself, felt himself yield. Later that week, she came up behind him in the library and kissed him on the cheek; he yelped, she laughed, he was embarrassed. In the student bar, she ignored him.

It continued like this for weeks and it made Richard irritable – she was trying to draw him in, but lazily; she couldn't even manage to do it consistently or well – but when she trained her beams on him, it was irresistible. He started to think about her all the time. At the end of every supervision, at the bottom of the stairwell, they would speak for a few minutes, before she had to go. He treasured that conversation, spending all week storing up things to say to her and forgetting them when he was there. Every morning, he thought about bumping into her in the street or the library or Sainsbury's. He imagined the conversations they would have in fine detail. He fantasized about there being a very good reason she was rude to him in public, something they would laugh about together later. If he said something Eleanor found funny, he tucked it away to impress Lucinda with. His whole week revolved around Thursday afternoons.

For a long time, he managed to hold Lucinda and Eleanor in his head at the same time: truly loving Eleanor, truly obsessed with Lucinda. But his image of Lucinda enlarged and brightened, leaving no room for Eleanor. He started to wonder if he hadn't made a mistake two years ago. That he'd been wrong to settle for someone who hadn't immediately made his heart leap. He didn't know if he believed in love at first sight, but all the love stories he'd ever heard began with a spark or eyes meeting across a crowded room or wild attraction. When he and Eleanor talked about how they first met, he told her he liked her from the first time he'd seen her in their tutor's room. It felt ungallant to say that he didn't remember her being there. She saw through it and teased him and they forgot about it. It felt ominous now.

The nights when he'd lost sleep over Eleanor felt like a lifetime ago. When those feelings had faded away, it seemed natural, inevitable, and he hadn't minded. He'd just assumed that he wouldn't feel that way about anyone again and it didn't seem to matter that much: he'd gained other things. Now, it seemed impossible to live without – that kind of energized obsession that turned every Thursday into a festival and obliterated whole hours of the afternoon.

When they reached the summer term, it became clear that his time with Lucinda was finite. It seemed unlikely they would stay in touch; if he didn't do something, he would never see her again. He didn't think about what or where it would lead. It just seemed so important not to let her go. At each supervision, he told himself it had to be this week – he would ask her to have coffee with him or if they could see each other over the summer; make some gesture that felt honest and true; do *something* – and then he let the moment go by, resolving he would do it next week.

After their final supervision, they stood opposite each other in the courtyard; she was oblivious and it felt impossible to speak. His heart was beating fast and he put his hands in his pockets to stop them shaking. 'Well, I guess this is it!' she said cheerfully. She hugged and kissed him: an inappropriately defined kiss, lips wet on his cheek, as wonderful as it was unsettling. He still didn't say anything. He told himself it didn't matter, as she turned away and waved: it was stupid of him to think anything would have happened anyway. At least he'd avoided making a fool of himself. But he was surprised by the strength of self-disgust that rose in him as he watched her walk away.

After that moment in the courtyard, caught between desire and cowardice, everything shifted. Eleanor started to make him restless. He was outgrowing her; the whole thing was tired. He told himself Lucinda had just been a crush, that it was normal to have crushes, and anyway she wasn't a very nice person, and yet he knew if he'd had the chance, if he'd been braver and luckier, he would have discarded Eleanor for Lucinda in a second. Even three years later, he'd bumped into Lucinda at a party, and he could feel himself getting pulled in again.

They were on the brink of entering the real world, where

everything would be larger and different and harder – he couldn't imagine him and Eleanor surviving it. They were probably going to split up and that frightened him, because it would be sad and gut-wrenching to actually separate. Then he realized they didn't have to break up straight away, that he could let it run while it was still convenient for both of them. Once he'd decided that, he felt better. They would sit it out and then go their separate ways.

5

Eleanor tried not to look at Rosie differently, but it was impossible, when she went wild and bit her, not to think about what Joanna said: *the madhouse, unnatural, something wrong, the incident.* She thought about the neighbours on either side of them; surely they would know more about the house and the Ashworths. She began to work up the courage to approach them.

They had not made much effort with them since moving in – she'd suggested putting a note through the door inviting them round for a drink, but Richard was protective of the house, not wanting too many people to see it before it was finished. The idea lost momentum. The woman at number 50 lived alone – she was grand and imposing and reminded Eleanor slightly of Richard's mother. Occasionally, she saw young men bounding in and out of number 54 and they smiled at her warmly, although they never stopped to say hello. She decided to start with them.

Eleanor made her way up the steps to their front door and rang the bell. There was silence, then the sound of loud, rapid footsteps on the stairs and a man flung open the door, saying, 'Yup?' He had the round, smooth face of a teenager, but was wearing chinos and a shirt with wide blue stripes – Eleanor guessed he must be in his early twenties, his first job, something well paid. His shirt was open at the navel – she could see a triangle of smooth brown flesh. He leant forward in the doorway, his hand still on the catch, bobbing with enthusiasm, and Eleanor found herself recoiling slightly, from his height, his good looks, his buoyant, entitled manner. As she introduced herself, he took his hand off the catch and stood up straighter, deferring to her in a way that made her feel elderly.

'Oh hello, Eleanor! I'm Jamie.' He was speaking to her the way she expected Rosie and Isobel's friends would, in twenty years' time. 'You're from next door? Yeah, I've seen you around – you've got little kids, right?'

'Yes, that's right.'

'We were talking about you guys, actually, the other day, cos we've seen a red-haired girl come out of your house, with a bike? Is she, like, your au pair or another daughter or . . . ?'

'She's our lodger.'

'Ah, right, OK! We didn't get how you all fitted together.'

'What about you – do you live here by yourself?'

'Ha, no! I mean, I wish, right. There's four of us – me, Luke, Hannah and Joe. It's Han's house – her dad bought it for her after uni and we all moved here together.'

'And do you like it here?'

'Yeah, it's *fucking* cool round here, man.' He caught himself and although he didn't actually apologize, he looked embarrassed. Eleanor was mortified that he thought he couldn't swear in front of her.

'Look, I'm sorry to disturb you, but we're trying to get in contact with the people who owned our house before us – the Ashworths – and I just thought they might have given you a forwarding address?'

'The family? No – we didn't really know them. They

moved out before you guys moved in, so we didn't really overlap that much.'

'When did they move out?'

'Like, six months before you got here, maybe? The house was empty for a little while anyway.'

'I don't suppose you know why they moved?'

'No idea. Well, actually, Luke had this theory about – hang on—' He turned back into the house and bellowed 'HAN!' so loudly that Eleanor started.

'What?' A girl appeared from the back room, holding a mug of tea. Eleanor guessed she had just come in from work; she was wearing an expensive-looking suit, clear tights and no shoes. Her dark blonde hair was loosely corralled in a low ponytail. Eleanor saw a row of high-heeled shoes in the hall; she noticed the labels and felt briefly insecure.

'Han, mate, do you know when Luke's back? It should be around now, right?'

'He's not in tonight, remember? He's seeing that Soul-mates girl.'

'Oh yeah, I forgot about that! Han, this is Eleanor, from next door. That red-haired girl's their lodger.'

'Oh, right. These guys are *all over* your lodger,' she said, disdainfully, as if this reflected badly on Eleanor. She turned to Jamie for a reaction, and he went red. 'Han . . .'

'What? You are.'

'Eleanor was asking about the family that lived here before them?'

'Oh, them! Christ, they were mental! Well, the girl was.'

'Ah, come on, Han, she was just a little kid.'

'I've got a *nephew*, Jamie, I know what kids are like. They're not like that.'

'What was wrong with her?' Eleanor asked.

'Oh, it was just . . . everything! The way she moved, she

made these weird noises all the time, like sort of shrieks and animal noises, but really loud . . . I'm not saying I'm, like, a shrink or anything, but there was something really wrong. You could just tell. And the mum looked like kind of a bitch, and you never saw the dad.'

'They *were* weird,' Jamie said. 'We used to talk about them a lot. Like, there was always a light on upstairs. Even if you were getting in, like, three, four in the morning, the light was always on.'

'Whereabouts upstairs?' Eleanor asked, even though she knew.

'The top floor. And I just thought it was weird, cos you'd think they'd all be asleep at that time, right, a young family?'

'Yes, you would,' Eleanor said, the words barely more than a murmur.

'I wish Luke was here, man – you should talk to him! He had the room next door to them at the top and he could hear crying and stuff, through the night, but not like normal crying. It used to freak him out. Something definitely wasn't right. But Han, didn't he think there'd been some kind of accident there? Didn't he say he saw an ambulance outside the house, just before they moved out? He thought the little girl had died.'

Jamie had relaxed again and was leaning forward, enthused by the story. Eleanor wanted to back away.

'Luke *says* he saw an ambulance,' Hannah said. 'He *says* the girl died.'

'Yeah, OK, Luke can talk a lot of shit sometimes. But I reckon *something* happened. He definitely thought there'd been an accident anyway. And I kind of thought, actually that makes sense, because why else would they want to leave so quickly? I mean, it's weird to move out of somewhere before you've even put it on the market, right?'

'It is weird,' Eleanor said, feeling her insides coil.

'So it was empty for ages and Luke was all like, oh my God, the house is definitely haunted, the girl's spirit is coming back, they're never going to sell it . . . He said he heard noises coming from that room, like, *after* they'd moved out.'

'Jamie,' Hannah said. He registered Eleanor's expression.

'Oh! Oh, that's just Luke, man – I mean, like I say, he's full of shit. You know, maybe the ambulance stuff was real, but that could have been anything. And you guys have been all right there, right?' He laughed nervously. 'No things flying round your head? No strange tappings on the wall at night . . . ?' He knocked the door frame.

'No – no, nothing like that.'

'Why do you need to get in contact with them anyway? Is something wrong?'

'No, it's just – house business, you know, problems with the sale – I won't bore you with it. Look, thank you very much for your help.'

'Sure, no problem, it was nice to meet you! You guys should all come round for, like, a drink or something some time?' He looked at Hannah for approval; she withheld it.

'That would be lovely,' Eleanor said, secure that it would never happen.

'OK, well, cheers then, Eleanor! Cheers, bye.' He shut the door and she made her way back down the steps, her mind swarming.

*

Eleanor let herself back into the house. Richard was at the kitchen table on his laptop; he stood up when she walked in.

'Where did you go? You said you were just going to walk round the block.'

She took off her coat in a daze and dropped it on the sofa. Her mind was overfull; she knew telling him about the neighbours would cause an argument, but the words spilt out of her mouth.

'Richard, you have to hear this: I spoke to the people next door – they think there was something wrong with the girl here.'

'You went round to the people next door?'

'Yes, to ask them if they knew—'

'Eleanor! What's wrong with you?'

'They think there was an accident here!'

He turned away and started emptying the dishwasher loudly, letting the plates clatter. She stood in front of him at the kitchen worktop. 'They think that Emily might have died! That that's why the family moved out.'

'Hang on, they *think* there was an accident. They don't know.'

'But they were gone a full six months before they sold it – don't you think that's interesting? We thought they weren't living here!'

'I don't think that's interesting at all, actually – there could be a hundred reasons why they would have done that.'

'Aren't you curious, about what went on here before us?'

He put a handful of forks down on the counter. 'No! I don't want to know! It's our house now. And this isn't curiosity, Eleanor, it's obsession! So what if there was an accident? What if we do find out that Emily's alive or dead or whatever? What will that tell us?'

'I just want to find out why I'm feeling like this.'

'You're feeling like this because you're ill! It has nothing to do with the house!'

She came round the other side of the worktop and put

the forks away in the drawer, arranging them so they faced in the same direction, nesting together. 'They talk about the house to each other. Next door. They think it's haunted.'

'Well, there's one problem with that theory, isn't there: ghosts don't exist. And ghosts don't make people ill. My God, I can't believe we're even having this conversation – you have a degree from Cambridge University!'

She knelt down and opened a cupboard, took out the saucepan he'd put away and put it in the cupboard above the sink, inside a nest of larger saucepans. 'Doesn't it worry you, that people would say that about our house?'

'No. I've seen those guys next door – they're idiots. If a house is empty for any length of time, people will make up stories about it. That's all there is.'

She stood up and turned to face him. 'I just want to go back and speak to Luke. If I can just hear what he says . . .'

'You're not going back there, OK? They'll think we're mad.'

'Why?'

'Because you're acting like you're mad! Have you seen yourself? You look mad.'

Tears formed in her eyes. He moved towards her; she backed away. 'Oh Eleanor . . . Eleanor, I'm sorry . . . You're unwell, that's all I meant . . .'

She ran upstairs and locked herself in the bathroom. She looked at herself in the mirror. He was right; she did look mad. Her hair was dirty and coarse strands were coming away from the crown. Her face was blotchy and the skin under her eyes was pouched and scored with lines. Her jumper was covered in mysterious white stains – she couldn't even remember where from. She had never felt pretty, but she'd always felt presentable, together. Even when Rosie and Isobel were babies and her clothes were always covered in milk and vomit, she was as vigilant as she could be, washing and changing and neatening compulsively. Six months ago, she would have changed her jumper before meeting someone new. She'd unravelled without even noticing. What must they have thought of her, those people, so young, so callous, so sure of themselves? How could she go back?

Richard was outside the door. 'Eleanor, I'm sorry. I'm really sorry – I didn't mean it.' His tone changed when she didn't answer – he was speaking quietly so as not to wake the children or perhaps disturb Zoe, but he was beginning to get frustrated. 'Eleanor? I'm sorry, OK? Eleanor? Come on!'

She couldn't answer. She sat on the edge of the bath and waited till he'd gone back downstairs.

6

In Adam's bed, listening to him make her coffee in the kitchen and having some kind of passive-aggressive argument with Oscar about the bins, Zoe thought she had never been happier. Her body was slightly stiff from the narrow, uncomfortable bed, but the ache was familiar now, and pleasant because she associated it with him, like the soreness at the top of her thighs.

There was part of her that missed how it used to be: when whether or not she stayed the night was a genuine question. There was something dulling about having to carry around her contact lens case and toothbrush when she knew she was going to see him. She wanted to be spontaneous and romantic – she just hated having coated teeth and prickling eyes at the shop. But there was a pleasure in preparation, too. Shutting the door of Litchfield Road behind her and knowing she wouldn't be back for twenty-four hours, she felt something unconnected to Adam: a light holidayish feeling, and a kind of relief.

He came back in and handed her a cup of coffee. It was the same mug she'd used last time she was there – it had a line drawing of Brighton Pavilion on it and she said it reminded her of university. She didn't know if he'd chosen it deliberately this time, but she thought he might have and that thought made her uncommonly happy. The morning stretched ahead: long and full, touching and fucking and talking about nothing. Maybe they would go somewhere and eat something delicious.

But he didn't get back under the covers with her; he sat at the end of the bed and said, 'So I wanted to talk to you about something,' and she felt it all fall away, very fast. The bed and the mug and his face turned unfamiliar again, and she remembered that, really, he was nothing to do with her: she was still essentially on her own.

'I spoke to Kathryn last night, and she said she wants to come down for my exhibition in a couple of weeks.'

'OK.'

'So it probably isn't the best idea if you come to the private view.'

'I didn't realize I was invited.'

'I thought you might have wanted to come.'

'How can I if you don't invite me?'

He sighed. 'OK, look, this is kind of an unusual situation. She doesn't normally support me like this. Things aren't great between us, and it's only a group show – I just never imagined she'd be there. And so I was thinking that maybe you would . . . But what could I say, I can't say no. I'm really sorry, Zoe.'

She hadn't particularly wanted to go to his exhibition – in fact, going would have caused her huge anxiety. She would have been too conscious of not fitting in with his world, and she certainly wouldn't have enjoyed it. Not feeling obliged to go had seemed distinctly precious. It was proof that their arrangement worked. But now he'd set her against Kathryn, and she was losing. She didn't know how to behave.

'Get into bed.' She pressed her palm on the duvet next to her. They lay side by side, under the covers, drinking coffee together in silence, hips touching. Eventually, he said, 'I feel bad.'

'Don't – it doesn't matter.'

'I sometimes feel as though this isn't a great situation for you.'

'It's fine, I told you: I don't want a proper relationship. I just split up with someone. I'm not ready for anything more than this.'

'You mean Rob?'

She nodded. She'd only mentioned Rob once or twice; she was surprised he'd held on to the name.

'You never talk about him.'

'What should I say?'

'I don't know – I just feel like you know everything about me and Kat, but I don't know anything about Rob. I don't even know why you broke up.'

She ought to know the answer to this by now. Sometimes she'd think she'd found a story and she'd try to catch hold of it and nurture it, but then another one would form, contradictory and equally true. Maybe it started two, three years from the end, lying in bed next to him while he had a sneezing fit and becoming suddenly, involuntarily depressed: *Is this what the rest of my life is going to be like? Sitting here listening to him sneeze?* A conversation with Laura, when she admitted that it was fine, that she could carry on, but she didn't know if she could do it forever? Sometimes she thought it had been there in their very first conversation, at a party in Brighton, when she'd been drunk, talking too much and nearly spilt her drink. 'Careful,' he'd said, and held out his hand. But she knew if she tried to explain any of this to Adam, she would end up saying too much, feeling as if she was exposing herself, and even then not be able to properly articulate what she meant to say.

'I don't know. We just wanted different things.'

'How long were you together?'

'Nearly six years.'

'So it must have been a big deal then.'

'It's not that long. You must've been with Kathryn for, what, ten years?'

'Eleven. But on and off.'

'Did you see other people in between?'

'Sometimes. She did more than me. I think we last broke up – two years ago? And I dated this girl for a few weeks then, another artist, but it wasn't ever really . . . anything, you know? There just wasn't that much there. That was the last person I was with. Before I met you.'

She knew it was dangerous, inviting these ghosts into their conversation. Perhaps she should move them on, but she was curious and anyway, there didn't seem much point in trying to protect each other's feelings. That was something that proper couples did; what they had was more honest, more authentic.

He hesitated. 'Was I the first person you – you know – since you and Rob split up?'

'Yes.'

'It must have been pretty weird. After six years with the same guy.'

She hadn't realized she was cross with him, but she must have been, because she said, too sharply, 'Well, no, it wasn't actually.'

'It must have felt a bit strange—'

'I mean, it wasn't six years with the same guy. There was someone else in between.'

'Oh, what, did you break up with Rob before?'

She looked down. 'No.'

'Oh, what, you mean . . . while you were together? Jesus, Zoe.'

'What?'

'I'm just a bit surprised. That you would do that.'

'Adam, if *you're* going to lecture me about fidelity, then that's just—'

'I'm not! I'm not. Did he ever find out?'

'Yes— But I wasn't— Look, let's just leave it, OK? I don't actually want to talk about it.'

'But what happened, did you—'

'Hey, this is sexy: why don't I talk more about my ex-boyfriend and then you can tell me all about your long-term girlfriend?'

'I'm just interested in you!'

She leant back on the bed frame. 'This is supposed to be fun. Isn't that why we're doing this?'

'Don't you ever think it could be more than fun?'

'Adam . . .'

'Don't you ever think about doing this properly? Being together?'

She often thought about it, and sometimes it felt good, but never entirely real or true. It existed in an imaginary future, when everything awkward and misshapen about them had been smoothed out. She just didn't know how to get there. It worked at the moment, and Kathryn was part of it – she held the balance. There was no need to disrupt anything.

'Adam . . . come on. You can't ask me that while you have a girlfriend. You have to sort out whatever's going on with Kathryn first.'

'I know, but what you think kind of affects what I do and . . .'

'Adam! Please. I just want to have a nice time.'

'OK, fine.' He rolled over on his side and bit her shoulder. She felt something approaching warmth again, but the thing she wanted was no longer available; he'd neutered it. She had the same thought she always had when things went wrong: it was supposed to be simple and blissful and if it was becoming complicated, maybe she should just end it. Somehow, that felt impossible. She tried to stop thinking about it and concentrate on him kissing her neck. It almost worked.

7

Richard was sitting at the kitchen table, while Eleanor was getting the children ready for bed, calculating and recalculating, scrawling the figures on the back of an envelope, hoping that if he tried again, adjusted this column or that, they might tell him something different. But the answer was always the same: there was not enough money. He was half aware of his foot tapping, quicker and quicker, against the chair.

He was beginning to see how crude and optimistic his plan for the house was. He hadn't taken into account the reality of their lives: broken radiators, Amy and Dominic's wedding, dentistry, outgrown shoes. Every month, he told himself that these things were anomalies and they would start saving properly next month, but then there would be something else and he didn't know if it would ever slow down or stop. They had been in the house over six months and they were no closer to making it their own.

He thought about charging Zoe more rent, but apart from the fact that it was clearly unfair and he would find the conversation intolerable, they couldn't afford to lose her. He didn't know if they could find anyone else for the basement. They could scale back the plans for the house, but they would only do this once and they had to get it right. It needed to be perfect, not just for him and Eleanor but for future unknowable buyers.

He heard Eleanor on the stairs and put the envelope under his laptop, despite knowing that his scrawls wouldn't mean anything to anyone else. She had forgiven him for what he had said about meeting the neighbours, yet something about the argument had stuck. They were more polite to each other, and less honest. If he tried to talk to her about any of this, she would only become more negative about the house.

'How was that?' he asked.

'Not too bad tonight, actually. They both went down pretty quickly.'

'It all sounded very quiet.'

'I think I've come up with a solution to Rosie's thing about shampoo. I made her hair stand up in spikes, when the shampoo was on, and I showed her in the mirror.' Eleanor smiled. 'It really made her laugh and she started pretending to be a monster. So then we did a shark's fin and antlers and Isobel was laughing too . . . They were being really sweet.' She went into the kitchen. 'I just wish they were like that all the time.'

She got a frying pan out of the cupboard. 'Oh God, I forgot garlic. I'll have to go out.' She sounded almost serene.

'Are you sure?'

'Yes, I won't be a minute.'

'Do we really need it?' He came up and stood behind her. 'What are you making?'

'It's fine. I don't mind going to the shop.'

'But it's late – just make it without, or use extra chilli or something.'

She was putting on her coat in the living room. 'I really don't mind going. It won't take long.'

He opened the fridge. 'Come on, Eleanor, let's just put something together out of here.'

'I don't mind!'

He started pulling things out of the fridge. 'We've got loads of food. We could have pasta – or an omelette! Why don't you just stay in the house?'

They looked at each other for a moment and then she hurried into the hall. 'I'm not going to be long!' she called and he heard the door slam. He went back into the living room and watched her standing, just in front of the bay window, face tilted towards the sky. She turned round and caught his eye. They looked at each other and she walked on.

Richard sat back at the kitchen table, got his envelope out from under the computer and stared at it. He had to make the house how he wanted and Eleanor had to like it, because they didn't even have enough money to move. He tore up the envelope and put it in the bin. Then he started looking at carpenters online, trying not to worry about the amount of time Eleanor was away from the house.

'You were gone a while,' he said, when he heard the door go.

'Oh, they didn't have it at the corner shop. I had to go to the Kingsland Road.'

'For garlic?'

'It wasn't a problem.' She went back into the kitchen and put an apron on.

She made supper and Richard made plans for the house. 'Do you want to watch something?' he asked, after they'd eaten.

Watching television together now seemed like an event. They used to do it every night in the old house. He remembered Eleanor's head pressing into his stomach and it felt like a different universe.

'I'm not feeling too good actually. I might go out and get some fresh air.'

'Eleanor, you've just been out!'

'We should leave the kitchen free for Zoe.' She got up and started clearing the plates.

'We'll just shut the double doors. Or we'll watch something on my laptop upstairs.'

'I've got a headache, Richard. I don't feel well. I need the fresh air. Please!'

'I really don't see how fresh air is going to help. Why don't you just rest? Go to bed early?'

'It does help. It helps to be out of the house.'

'That doesn't make any sense. Why won't you just rest?'

'I don't care if it makes any sense or not! It's true.'

He listened to the door go and went up to his study. He thought he might at least get some work done on his dissertation, but he was listless and subdued. Eleanor's absence nagged at him; he hated the thought of her alone, wandering the streets in the dark.

It would be easier when the house was complete; she would be happier, he would be more relaxed. They could properly settle and finally find something that would help her headaches. He shut down his dissertation and made plans for the colours of skirting boards instead.

When he heard Eleanor come in, he was absorbed in coat stands and heated towel rails. He came down at ten, to get a glass of water, and saw Eleanor sitting in the bay window. It was open a crack and her face was pressed up to the glass.

'Eleanor, what are you doing? You're going to freeze!'

'It's fine. I'm perfectly warm,' she said, without turning towards him, though he could see the reflection of her face in the glass. He wanted to say something, but he didn't know what. He turned round and went back upstairs.

8

Usually, Zoe tried not to think about it. It was three years ago now, that night, and she could almost forget about it, until something sharp and wretched stirred in her stomach and she'd know it was still there. Now, cycling home from seeing Adam, thinking about what he'd asked her, she could feel it becoming dislodged again.

She had been afraid. That was really the only reason. It was her last night in London Fields with Laura; she was moving in with Rob the next day. She sat on her bed surrounded by boxes, the cardboard pale and soft with age. Two scratchy check laundry bags from the pound shop were bulging with clothes. She was holding a collection of things she'd found under the bed – socks, books, underwear – covered in a pale grey fur so thick that it had developed a structure of its own. She pulled it off.

The bedroom was pretty much done. She had to do the living room and kitchen next, but Laura was there. She'd never said she didn't want Zoe to move out, but she'd become quiet and distant when Zoe started talking about it. She was hostile to Rob when he came round. It broke Zoe's heart but also irritated her, which stopped her running into the living room and telling Laura that she didn't want to go. It was too late now, anyway.

She was afraid of moving and moving because she was afraid. She'd loved their flat more than she thought possible. She could see its flaws – the dingy carpet, the soft plastic leather sofa, the scratched perspex-topped kitchen table, the intolerably ugly kitchen chairs. You could see into the flat below through the floorboards in the bathroom, and in the living room there was a hole in the ceiling that workmen had knocked in the week they moved, exposing the innards of the partition. Presumably whatever they'd found was bad news, too bad to deal with, because it was just abandoned, and the landlord never answered their calls.

But she was proud of the flat and every small thing they'd done to improve it – Laura had made curtains and put them up, Zoe had bought an off-cut from a haberdashery shop that they used as a tablecloth. They ignored the hole in the ceiling and put a throw over the leather sofa; it kept sliding off and they kept pulling it back into place. They'd moved in in summer when London Fields was dense with people every day, the air filled with barbecue smoke and chatter. They went to Shoreditch together to get fringes cut, and bought vintage dresses from Broadway Market that never quite fitted properly. They bought oven cleaner from the pound shop and cheese from the farmers' market. They drank pints in the Dove and sat at the side of the lido in bikinis.

But it was temporary; they knew this from the beginning. The corner shop started selling expensive chocolate and taxis began to appear, sleek and incongruous, on Kingsland Road. The new Overground station was coming and the building works felt personal and aggressive, as though Zoe and Laura were being dug out. It opened the following summer, flanked by luxury flats. Zoe loved the low, dark, gun-metal grey of Dalston Junction station; the flash of orange hurtling across the sky above Middleton Road; the feeling of glimpsing behind the scenes as the train cut through the rooftops. The line extended, orange ribbon running all over London, with more and more connections. But people they knew had started talking about Clapton, Homerton, even south of the river. Zoe told Laura that their friend Jo and her husband were thinking about buying in Dalston. 'Oh, for fuck's sake,' Laura said. Jo and her husband were management consultants. Zoe and Laura were constantly worried that the landlord would decide to do their flat up and sell it, or rent it at market rate. Flyers and letters from estate agents came through the door, and they hurried them into the bin. They stopped calling about the hole in the ceiling.

Flatsharing was becoming a kind of game, a scramble for remaining space, and if you played badly or were unlucky, you were out, adrift. It had endless rounds, usually initiated when someone absented themselves to live with their boyfriend. She longed to stop playing, and sometimes she looked at studio flats, but she didn't know anyone who lived alone at twenty-five and she couldn't afford them anyway. The only practical solution was Rob: he kept saying they should move in together. He'd qualified as an architect and they could afford a one-bedroom flat if they moved a little further out, deeper into Hackney, away from London Fields. But that meant leaving Laura.

'You can't put your life on hold because of your friend,' Rob said. 'That's ridiculous. Laura's an adult, she'll work something out.'

'But what? What will she do?'

'I hate to say it, Zoe' – this was a tic of his that she was starting to find disagreeable; most of the time it was something he really wanted to say – 'but I don't think that's really your responsibility.'

'But she's on her own, and she doesn't have that much money.'

'It was Laura's choice to try and be an artist.'

'Oh, come on!'

'What?'

'"Poor people just make bad choices", yeah?'

'I'm not talking about poor people. Laura comes from a middle-class family, she could have done any degree that she wanted, and she chose to go to art school and pursue an insecure profession. I'm not saying that makes her a bad person, I'm just saying that there are consequences to that kind of choice.'

'But she's really talented.'

'I'm sure she is. Just personally, I think it's foolish to choose a fine art degree when there are so many practical applications of that talent. Graphic design, product design, fashion, even . . . If I had a child, there's no way I would allow them to go to art school. It's irresponsible.'

She told herself then, as she often did, that she must never have children with him, and let it pass, as she always did, without thinking too closely about what that might mean for them now.

He looked sad. 'Don't be like that with me.'

'Like what?'

'Like you think I'm a bad person. I'm not. Sometimes you act like you don't like me very much.'

She didn't say anything.

*

She went out into the living room to divide her possessions from Laura's. It was easier than she'd thought it would be. Laura was sitting cross-legged on the floor, cutting up bits of fabric for an artwork, and she was pretending to be cheerful at least. Zoe's things had grown into Laura's to form a coherent whole, and they didn't make any sense on their own – what sort of person owned a tea strainer but no bowls? How could she make scrambled eggs when Laura had the best pan? Of course, she and Rob would go to Ikea or Argos and build a new collection of things. She couldn't envision it.

Was it normal to feel this anxious about moving in with someone, if you loved them? She would wake up in the middle of the night, terrified. The idea of someone being there every time you woke up felt intrusive. She worried that they wouldn't have enough forks and she worried she would never masturbate again. If she could just have one more year . . .

Laura got up. 'I'm going to make tea – do you want some?'

'Tea tea or supper tea?'

'"Supper" tea.'

'I'd love some. Are you sure that's OK?'

'Yeah, it's just pasta.'

'I was hoping it would be.'

Laura smiled. 'It's always pasta.'

Zoe went out to get some wine. The wine tumblers, the ones they'd bought when they wanted to pretend they were in a European cafe, were hers and packed, so they used water glasses. As Laura cooked and they drank the wine, they began to talk smoothly and fluidly again. Laura had some damson gin that her mum had made – it was near the end of the bottle and hadn't been strained properly. It was like jam mixed with gin; they drank it anyway.

'I guess I'd better start getting ready then,' Laura said without moving. It was Hallowe'en and she was going to a party; Zoe had said she was going to stay in and pack. But suddenly being alone in the flat seemed too bleak. And she didn't want to be apart from Laura, not when they were like this together.

Laura lent her a black body-con dress. She'd bought a black lipstick from Superdrug and they smeared it on – it was thick and greasy and they needed to press hard to get any kind of effect, but after a few coats, it worked. They looked at themselves in the mirror: they were unrecognizable. Zoe sat on the floor in between Laura's legs while Laura gathered her hair in clumps, backcombed it and pinned it up. Laura had a handmade corset and a mask of a bird's head, white with a long yellow beak and black-rimmed eyes.

They got the bus from Dalston Lane and walked through Hackney Wick. Zoe thought she would always find it desolate: those endless stretches of brick and corrugated iron. Even the rows of terraced houses had a kind of blankness about them.

The party was in a warehouse above a Costcutter. The room was full and hot. Fabric was pinned over the windows and on the ceiling and gathered on the walls: red velvet, brown with pulsing orange flowers, batik silk. There were grey velvet sofas, wicker chairs, pot plants, and everyone was dressed up, with peacock feathers, leather masks and fans. Two women had come dressed as Frida Kahlo. Zoe said hello to Laura's friends and hung around the group for a bit, before wandering off. It normally made her anxious to be alone at a party, but she was enjoying the possibility of being anonymous.

She was sitting by herself on the bottom of the wooden steps that led up to one of the mezzanine bedrooms, when someone came up to her – she knew his face, but not where from. He said his name was Sam and he was at Chelsea with her and Laura, on their foundation course. She only had the vaguest memory of him – he did brown sludgy paintings, she thought, like muddy Rothkos. She was surprised he remembered her, and mildly flattered. He was studying at the Royal College now, and she asked him a lot about his work to avoid the moment when he asked her what she did – his paintings sounded exactly the same as they were at Chelsea but she didn't say that. Eventually, he asked and her voice went flat, as it always did now, when she had to say that she worked in marketing, for a charity. She found it hard to admit she didn't like it – it felt like failing – but she couldn't make herself sound more enthusiastic.

'So you don't do art at all now?'

'No.'

'That's such a shame. You were really talented.'

She looked at him sceptically. 'I bet you can't remember any of my work.'

'I can! There was that big painting, it was really blue, of these rows of houses . . .'

'I never painted rows of houses.'

'Really? Shit, OK, but it was, like, a blue landscape, right? With these . . . rectangles . . .' He'd gone red and she wondered why she was being horrible to him, other than the fact that she knew she'd get away with it. She was impressed that he had half remembered. She said, more kindly:

'They were boats, not houses. But you're right: it was really blue. And the boats were a bit like rectangles.'

'There you go! I told you.' He looked relieved and pleased, and she realized then how much he liked her.

It had been a long time since she'd talked to anyone about painting. Sometimes she'd say she wanted to take it up again, in the same way she said she wanted to leave her job, trying desperately to jumpstart her brain into action. It never happened. Rob would encourage her sometimes, but slightly dutifully, as if he were mimicking good boyfriend behaviour. He'd sometimes talk about going to the art shop together and painting on a Sunday afternoon, in the way he'd suggest they go for a long bike ride or make pasta from scratch – it didn't feel realistic or sustainable. He genuinely wanted to help with her career though – he found brochures on retraining and encouraged her to try and move across at the charity. He tried to find people who did jobs he thought she might like and put her in touch with them. 'You need a vocation, Zo,' he'd say and she knew he was right. He made it seem so easy. The architecture firm he worked for designed solid, useful buildings; he seemed to know exactly what he was doing and who he was. Occasionally, he talked about wanting to do something else, but in an unconvincing, smooth, satisfied way. It was as if he knew that he'd made the right choice really and it felt nice to reassure himself. She'd found it attractive at first, but recently it had started to make her irritable with jealousy.

Sam asked where she lived: she told him about Laura and the flat in London Fields, but not that she would be moving out the next day, and not about Rob. They headed into the kitchen, towards the music, and started dancing. He was moving his face closer and closer to hers and she didn't pull away. She wasn't particularly interested in him, but that was precisely what was so compelling about it. It was so simple, this interaction; there was nothing complicated or beholden woven into it. He moved closer in and she turned her face away by instinct. It felt like something she'd done a hundred times and it got tiring after a while, refusing things. Sam looked disappointed and she panicked that she was losing some chance, some opportunity.

She'd never cheated on Rob because she knew that she wouldn't be able to keep it secret and, however much she had wanted other people, she wanted to preserve what they had more. There had been nights out without him, when tequila turned the evening's edges murky, lips almost touching, but she'd stopped it, protected them, right at the last moment. She felt more vulnerable tonight.

Sam said he needed to go to the bathroom and she was afraid that he'd had enough of her. She said, 'I'll come with you,' and then felt stupid. In the end, there was a long queue, so it didn't feel so stupid, keeping each other company while they waited. Then suddenly, he turned round and kissed her. It was an odd moment to choose and she could have stopped it, said that he'd taken her by surprise, but of course she didn't. She wanted to get lost.

In the bathroom, she looked at herself in the mirror – her face seemed all over the place and she realized how drunk she was. They moved onto a sofa in the kitchen and kissed for a bit before he asked if she wanted to go home with him. She said yes, and went to find Laura to say goodbye. She tried to read Laura's expression when she told her what she was doing: she looked confused and concerned, but also a bit excited – or maybe that was just what Zoe wanted her to feel. 'Are you sure?' she asked. Zoe just nodded, although she felt sure of nothing any more.

They went out into the street. It felt even bleaker than when they'd arrived. A train went past overhead, windows like little beads of light pulled along the line. The moon was a thumbnail. Sam lived nearby, in a new development of flats overlooking the canal, a warren of buildings behind endless gates and security doors. The decor was new and sharp: smooth pale wood and black kitchen cabinets so shiny she could see her reflection in them. He shared it with two couples – their furniture and his artwork seemed uncomfortable in it. 'I didn't expect you to live somewhere like this,' she said and he was defensive: 'I've done my time in shitty warehouses, definitely.' He told her he'd always really liked her at Chelsea and she was flattered, even though she didn't remotely feel the same. He showed her some pictures of his new paintings on his phone and she said she thought they were interesting and his work had really developed, and then she was lying on her back on his futon, and he was trying to pull her dress up over her hips. It was too tight and wouldn't go, so she sat up and started patting the fabric: it was Laura's and she couldn't remember how it came off. She found the zip and took it off over her head. He pulled her tights and knickers off together, and put his mouth on her cunt; she wondered how she could have forgotten this liquid feeling, distinct and hazy, and how she could ever have thought that anything in the world was more important than this. He put his tongue in her arsehole, which she thought was quite a weird thing to do without asking first. The Kirby grips stuck in her scalp when he fucked her, and she never wanted it to end, and then after a few minutes, she got bored and wished it would. He pulled out abruptly; she asked him if he'd come and he said no. She reached towards him and he said defensively, 'I'm just drunk. I don't have an *arousal problem* or anything.' They pretended to go to sleep, although neither of them had come, which she supposed was the definition of bad sex. She thought about Rob only fleetingly. It had turned out to be amazingly easy, after all.

*

She woke up at five and waited for the sun to come up. As soon as it was light, she got dressed, gently touching his shoulder to say goodbye. It was easier when he was half asleep. He asked her to put her number in his phone and she did. She got back to the flat at eight, and made herself a cup of tea. Laura was still asleep. Her phone sprang alive and she saw Rob's name on the screen; she let it go on ringing and sat, jittery, among the boxes. She saw a pair of trousers Rob had left at the flat that she'd folded up and put in one of the boxes last night; she fell forward clutching her stomach, heaving with sadness and fear. He rang again, and again, and she still couldn't answer. Her phone flashed and jerked in front of her, and the screen became littered with text and dots. Each one felt physically painful, but she still couldn't bear to pick it up. The dread intensified. In four hours, Rob would be arriving with a van.

They spent the first night in their new flat crying. They temporarily lost their language and started using other people's: he said, 'I can't believe you would do this to me,' and she said, 'It didn't mean anything.' Nothing made sense and her mouth was full of 'sorry' and 'love'. The next day, they opened their 'Happy New Home' cards. She wanted to tell him that she didn't feel anything for Sam, and that the sex was bad, but then he might ask her why she did it, and she wasn't sure either of them would like the answer. He told her he thought she had psychological problems that meant she was never satisfied – she always needed to create drama.

Two days later, they hadn't unpacked or showered, and they wore the same clothes they had when they'd moved in. They ate takeaways with plastic forks. She worried about the money they were spending, and felt guilty for being concerned with something so mundane. She got a missed call from a number she didn't recognize and got excited despite herself, and then deflated when it was from her mobile phone network.

On the third day, she found a pair of knickers that had belonged to Laura; they'd got mixed up in her laundry once and she'd adopted them without thinking about it. She'd meant to give them back some day and never had. It made her cry. There was a pile of flat cardboard boxes with grease spots and tinfoil cartons smeared with sauce or a limp strand of noodle in the kitchen. It was starting to smell. Sam texted and asked if she wanted to meet up. She didn't reply. On the fourth day, Rob told her he thought they should work on it: he knew it would be tough, but he really wanted to try. She was intensely relieved. She deleted Sam's text. On the fifth day, she cleaned the kitchen. On the sixth day, Rob hung his shirts in the wardrobe.

On the seventh day, they had sex, which was fraught, but different at least.

'Rob,' she whispered as he was going down on her, 'stick your tongue in me. No, not there. The other one. There.'

9

Three weeks after the wedding, Eleanor got a message from Amy, suggesting they meet for a coffee, just the two of them. Amy was her oldest friend, yet something about the suggestion felt novel: it had been years since Eleanor had seen her on her own. Usually, Amy and Dominic came round for dinner or they went to theirs or sometimes they went to a new restaurant together or met for brunch. They had more or less learnt to work as a four and although she missed winding, private, two-person conversations, she had started to like more formal, polite, abstract group discussions too. Sometimes it was more enjoyable to talk about what was in the news or music or house prices; you didn't always have to get mired in the guts of life.

She tried to think back to the last time she'd seen Amy without Richard or Dominic. Amy had come to visit just after Isobel was born and they talked about careers and houses and whether Amy should have a baby too, keeping their conversation malleable, so they could mould it around the demands of Rosie and Isobel. Sometimes, Eleanor didn't care if Amy was going to get a promotion and whether that would make life more difficult for Dominic, because none of it felt as vivid or urgent as keeping her children alive, and she only asked because she hated herself for not caring.

Sometimes, they returned to an ancient fluid intimacy, only to be interrupted again, re-emerging miles apart.

She still enjoyed Amy's company and she didn't think about how it used to be that much, except when she saw schoolgirls on the bus, gasping with laughter, or two women in their twenties outside Dalston Junction station, holding hands and running and screaming. Then it came back with an ache and she missed the way it was: visceral and specific, dense with private jokes, secrets and sharp detail that only they would find telling or funny.

The idea of the meeting buoyed her for the rest of the day. It was startlingly easy: a few messages, getting Richard to agree to take the girls, and then they had a date for next Sunday. Amy even offered to come to a cafe near London Fields. Perhaps it had just been laziness that had let them slide apart. Perhaps Amy had missed her too.

Eleanor began to wonder if she could tell Amy about the house. At first, confiding in anyone was unthinkable: when she imagined herself saying the words – *I think my house is making me ill* – it sounded crazy. It would be disloyal to Richard. But now she knew other people thought there was something wrong with it too. The secret was getting closer to the surface, and it stuck at the back of her throat, ready to spill out. Sometimes, broken down and exhausted, she thought it might emerge in front of the wrong person – someone at work, a mother at nursery.

As soon as she left the house on Sunday, she felt lighter. The novelty of being alone made everything seem new. It was mid-March and the sun was out; she experimented with wearing a jacket instead of a coat. She left a little earlier than she needed to so she could walk past all the new shops that had opened, curious about the beautiful, useless things:

vintage kimonos, oil lamps, coffee beans. Ceramics, earrings and cakes.

Amy was sitting outside the cafe, her face rosy under the peach awning, scrolling on her phone. Eleanor was struck by how ordinary she looked, in her mustard jumper, brogues and expensive glasses. Her hair colour had slowly mellowed over the years, from the peroxide that made the ends brittle and raw, to subtle honey highlights. Her jeans were dark and smart; these days, Eleanor could only see the small hole in her nose where the piercing had been if she was looking.

Seeing her provoked an unexpected surge of sadness, even though she knew that Amy was a woman in her mid-thirties who ran a charity combating human trafficking and she had a husband who worked for the Foreign Office and she sometimes flew business class. Of course, she no longer looked like a teenager, like the most exciting person Eleanor had ever met. And then Amy saw her and waved, delighted, and Eleanor recognized her smile and the happiness returned. She was away from the house, her headache was lifting, and even just ordering a coffee in this delightfully tiny cafe, which would have been impossible with a buggy, felt glorious. She sat down opposite Amy, the sun on her face, feeling charged and new.

'It was such a lovely wedding,' Eleanor said, folding the milk into her coffee.

'Yeah, it was OK in the end, wasn't it? I'm just glad it's over. Honestly, I was this close to killing Dom's mum.'

'Did you not enjoy it?'

'Oh, it was all right. We got through it, didn't we? I just had to accept from the beginning that it was never going to be very me. I suppose that's the whole point, isn't it. "Compromise."'

'I wish I could go back to D staircase and tell you that

you were going to get married in a church, with a veil, and your dad walking you up the aisle . . .'

'To Dominic, more to the point! Jesus Christ, I would have slit my wrists.'

'I can still hear you now: "He's arrogant, Eleanor, he's chauvinistic, he's entitled . . ."'

'Ha, maybe I was protesting too much. I don't know though – he could be a real twat in those days.'

'He was fine! A bit arrogant, maybe. I always thought you were too mean about him.'

Amy leaned back in her chair and pulled her hair back into a ponytail. 'It was different with you and Richard though, wasn't it? You always knew.'

Eleanor played with her spoon, not sure whether to just agree or say what she was thinking. 'Well . . . Remember Wilton Street?'

'Oh my God, I'd forgotten all about that! "I'm going to break up with him – honestly, Amy, this weekend, I'm going to do it."'

They were laughing and Eleanor was suddenly giddy with honesty. It was delightful to be liberated from the usual fiction about their relationship. 'At university! That's so romantic!' people said when she told them how she and Richard met and most of the time, she didn't mind going along with the story: she knew its grooves and corners and she found her way around it effortlessly. It was only some-times that she wanted to tell them it wasn't like that. But all the words in the world were inadequate to describe this unique, private, flawed thing she and Richard had created. With Amy, there was no need for words; she'd been there.

'Still,' Amy said, 'it's not like I was that great when I was nineteen.'

'You were pretty great, Amy.'

'I was kind of self-righteous. And stupid. Whenever I look back on that time, I just feel like we were all . . . a bit unformed basically. Don't you think? It was amazing in one way – everything being all intense and spiky and raw, but you have to start moulding yourself into the world a bit, don't you? I mean, can you imagine you, me, Richard and Dom having brunch when we were nineteen? It just wouldn't have happened.'

Eleanor felt intensely sad.

'So, how are you anyway?' Amy said.

Eleanor steadied herself. 'Actually, I'm still not feeling so good.'

'What, you mean the headache/sicky thing? God, Eleanor, it's been months – you should go and see someone.'

'I have. The doctors have done all sorts of tests. Apparently there's nothing wrong with me.'

'Couldn't your mum recommend some magic herbal remedy?'

'Oh, I tried all that too. Richard wants to go private, but we can't really afford it. And also, I don't think it would help.'

'It'd be worth a go, wouldn't it?'

Eleanor sat up straighter and put down her cup. 'Amy, can I tell you something? I know how this sounds, OK? But I think it's something to do with the house.'

'What do you mean?'

'I think there's something in the house that's making me ill. I feel ill when I'm in the house and better when I'm outside it.'

'What, like damp or something in the wiring or . . . ?'

'I don't know! I don't know what it is! I've taken the house apart trying to find it, but I still don't know. I'm still trying. I know it doesn't make any sense. But it's happening.'

Amy started to say something and then stopped, leaving her mouth half open. The expression was familiar: Eleanor knew that she wouldn't like the thing that Amy was about to say, but that she was obliged to invite it in anyway. It could be infuriating, knowing someone so well.

'What? What is it?'

'Have you thought about seeing a psychotherapist?'

Eleanor sometimes envied and admired Amy's bluntness; she didn't today.

'Why would I do that?'

'I just think – Eleanor, don't take this the wrong way, but you just seem a bit run-down and unhappy and you've been like that for a while now . . .'

'Because I'm ill!'

'Sure, but have you ever thought it might be the other way round? That you're ill because you're unhappy? Head-aches are brought on by stress, right?'

'You think it's all in my head?'

'No! Well, I wouldn't put it like that. I just think the mind and body are more connected than we realize.'

'That sounds like the kind of thing my mum would say.'

'I'm not being like your mum. There's whole studies on this: people who have heart attacks on the anniversary of their father's death, say. And they didn't remember it was the anniversary. The body remembered. It was the unconscious acting through the body.'

'Don't armchair psychoanalyse me, Amy! I can't explain how I know it, but I do. It's connected to the house.'

'See, to me, that just sounds like you don't like the house.'

'That's ridiculous. Why wouldn't I like it? We were so lucky to buy it. It's our dream home.'

There was a small, mutinous pause, before Amy said quietly, 'Richard's dream home.'

'What does that mean?'

'You can't shut him up about it, all his plans for extensions and stuff – I'm not being mean, I think it's endearing – but you never seem that excited about it.'

'I'm not as interested in that side of things as Richard is. And why do I have to be excited about it anyway? It's just a house; we've got to live somewhere. And we don't know what's going to happen with Richard's job . . . we had to make a good investment.'

'I just think . . . This is a really difficult time. It's hard work being married – well, so they say – you've got two small children, you're working full-time— Oh come on, it's *practically* full-time! Have you thought about post-natal depression?'

'Amy, stop trying to pathologize everything – it's really annoying me!'

'Well, what do *you* think it is then?'

Eleanor had thought she might tell her about Emily and the Ashworths, but it seemed impossible and ridiculous now. It was too late. She decided to shut down the conversation, and with it, any kind of goodwill.

'It is a difficult time, but you just manage. I love the house, I love being married, I love being a mother. It's hard work and you have to sacrifice things, but it's worth it. I don't think it's something you can properly understand if you haven't experienced it. I think when you have kids, you'll look back and you'll know what I mean.'

Amy turned her face to the side and looked down. 'Well, luckily, I'm not going to have long to wait. To experience this great level of understanding.'

'What—? Oh, Amy – really? You should have said! I was going on about my stupid headaches and—'

'I didn't want to make it all about me.'

'Oh, congratulations – I'm so sorry to ruin it, this is such great news . . .'

Eleanor half stood up and leaned across the table to hug her. It was awkward and she couldn't quite reach; she immediately regretted not walking round the table to hug her properly. She proceeded through the questions – due date, scans, the sex, morning sickness, maternity leave – and talked about Amy's plans and fears and whether anyone had guessed at the wedding, but she sensed they were both slightly bored.

Eleanor imagined being back in D staircase kitchen, showing Amy how to chop an onion, and someone explaining to her that when Amy told her she was having her first child, they would be having an argument, and how aghast she would be at the thought. And that she wouldn't really be happy for Amy, because she would be thinking about herself and how they had just been pulled apart again, and they might never get back to that sweet, unvarnished closeness she missed so much. She tried to engage with Amy over names and what Dominic's mum had said, but all the time she was grappling with the intense disappointment of having tried something else and it not having worked. She was on her own again.

*

The next day, she woke up, more defeated than she'd felt before. She got the children ready to go out, feeling slightly less patient, slightly more stretched and limited. She opened the front door and started. The pebbles were no longer at the bottom of the steps, but just outside the door. They were almost inside the house.

10

Zoe heard herself make a kind of groaning noise, and realized she was standing at the foot of her bed. She had no idea why she was there. She saw that it was dark outside; she was confused and panicked, and then all at once she understood. She sat at the end of the bed, shaking. It was the third time this had happened.

She had almost got used to waking up paralysed. It was particularly horrible if it came with a vision: sometimes she saw the girl she dreamt about sitting in the corner of the room and would want to cry out or wave her arms to ward her off, but find herself unable to move. But often there was another part of her that knew what was happening and that she was dreaming, and she could tell herself not to panic, that it would be over soon. The sleepwalking was new and potentially more dangerous.

It was another reason she liked staying with Adam. She knew – she wasn't sure how – that it wouldn't happen when she was with him. It wasn't just about having another person there, though she acknowledged that it made things safer, an irritating truth she didn't like to think too much about. She never even slept particularly well in the warehouse: the bed was uncomfortable, there wasn't room for both of them and she was usually wired on drink and lust.

It was that the conditions weren't right. It only happened in Litchfield Road.

She looked at her phone: it was 2 a.m. The screen was still covered with reproachful red dots from earlier in the evening. She hadn't picked up her mum's calls for weeks and now Peter had started trying, both of them leaving a procession of kind, neutral voicemails. She tried to fob them off with brief text messages, carefully constructed to give the impression she was very busy. She knew if she spoke to them they would ask about how it was going in the house or with her job, and she couldn't bear to answer.

She went into the living room and poured herself some warm white wine in a mug. She opened up her laptop and scrolled through Facebook. It was soothing to remember that the world was full of people doing ordinary things like eating brunch and attending hen parties, and comforting that people were communicating with her at two in the morning, even in the most abstract way. The wine and lack of sleep made her feel hazy and her heartbeat was starting to slow. Then, it appeared on her screen like a punch in the face: a photo of Adam with someone tagged as 'Kathryn Slater'.

She'd known that he was going to the wedding, and something about it had made her uncomfortable – maybe just the association of them and matrimony. But it was the first time she'd seen a photo of Kathryn. She had promised herself that she wouldn't try to find her online and she'd stuck to it: not because she was particularly self-disciplined but because she was afraid of how it might make her feel. Zoe realized she'd unconsciously built up an image of her, as thin, brittle, with straight dark hair. She was serious, an artist; not beautiful but striking. Sometimes she thought she saw her, or an image of her, in the girls who cycled in front of her through Shacklewell on continental bicycles, wearing complicated trousers.

In fact, Kathryn was not striking, but she was pretty. She had a round face, dirty blonde hair pulled back in a messy ponytail and a huge, open smile. She looked charming and accommodating, not ruthless or single-minded as Adam had said. Zoe immediately felt viscerally jealous and then furious with Adam for putting her through this, and furious with herself because she had no right to feel that way. He had only ever been honest with her, after all.

She clicked on the name 'Kathryn Slater', both disappointed and relieved to find she had privacy settings. The pictures that were visible were unrewarding: a photograph of her feet, her face in silhouette, smoking a cigarette. Still, she examined them closely, mining them for clues.

Zoe was itching to do something – send her a message, write something cryptic yet incriminating on Adam's wall. Lately, she'd found herself thinking, a bit too often: *this is what I'd do if I were completely mad*. She wanted to keep things exactly as they were and she hated confrontation, but another part of her wanted to make the whole thing explode spectacularly.

She had thought about going to his private view on Thursday, just to see what he would do. She liked the idea of unsettling him, getting some kind of revenge for the way he'd disrupted her life. She'd thought more seriously about walking past, in case she could see him there with Kathryn. But he might catch her, and it would be humiliating.

She clicked on the 'About' section of Kathryn's Facebook page and scanned the list of things she liked. They were mainly arts organizations, and a reflexology clinic and then she saw the words 'Triangle Dance Centre'. Zoe remembered something Adam had said last week: 'So she said she was coming for the exhibition, but then of course I find out there's actually some dance class she wants to go to.'

'She's a dancer?'

'It's just something she's got into. She's started to do a lot more performance stuff, and use her body in her work, and I think she wants to add some kind of dance element. It's not really my kind of thing, and actually I don't even think the performance side of her work is the stuff she should be concentrating on right now. Her tutors are really pushing it, but – well, anyway, like she's ever going to listen to what I think. But if she's doing that, maybe we could see each other on Wednesday?'

'Adam, I can't see you while she's staying with you – that's mad.'

'I just feel bad – it's going to end up being, like, five days or something. Will you be OK?'

'Yes! Don't be stupid. I'll do other things.'

'Like what?'

I don't know, she thought. 'Stuff – see friends, go out.'

She clicked on the name of the dance school and found herself on its website. There was a timetable promising classes with the word 'flow' and 'untamed' in them. She clicked on the name of the class on Wednesday. The studio was a bike ride away from Litchfield Road and the class started after she'd finished work. It was a 'Level 1' class and it promised to 'free your body' and 'unlock your movement'. It said, 'Beginners welcome'.

11

Eleanor picked an upended water glass out of the dirty linen basket. Her clothes were damp; she supposed it didn't matter, since they were dirty anyway. It was just that she had no idea how the glass had got there.

She'd found an earplug in a tea cup; a glove in a mixing bowl; a pair of tweezers in the egg drawer of the fridge. She didn't tell Richard about it any more. His rational explanations were impossible to refute: Rosie being naughty, Zoe using their things, Eleanor being absent-minded. She just didn't believe any of them.

She put the glass back on their bedside table and abandoned the washing. She was supposed to be resting anyway. She lay on her back on their bed, feeling her headache enlarge and recede, paying attention to its textures, as it moved around her skull. There was a moment of stillness and she thought, *maybe this is it, maybe it's over* before it crested again worse than before. She tried not to think about the fact that their bedroom was under Emily's room, but she could never quite get the thought out of her head. She sometimes wondered if she could feel the energy being transmitted through the ceiling, in some subtle, accumulative way, the walls of the room gently vibrating.

Rest was the only thing she and Richard could agree on.

Richard insisted it would make her better; she didn't think it would, but after a day of pretending not to be ill, it was luxurious to give in to it.

They were starting to separate earlier and earlier now. The meals she prepared got simpler: things she'd never have considered before, like pasta sauce out of a jar, beans on toast or the fish fingers she'd bought for the children. She stopped caring about vegetables or wholegrains or using up leftovers; she started buying ready meals for the first time in her life. As soon as they'd eaten, she went upstairs to bed and Richard went to his study. She knew it wasn't right; she would start trying again, soon. She was just so tired.

Sometimes, lying on the bed, she had conversations with him in her head, trying to make him understand about the house, wondering if there was a way she could make him see. Even in her imagination, she was left crying with frustration, at his stubbornness, his dismissiveness. She used to look back and marvel at the ways they'd grown up. Now, even more so after that conversation with Amy, she'd started inhabiting the queer false starts of their relationship. Lately, she wondered if they hadn't changed that much after all.

*

After they graduated, she and Richard retreated home for a peculiar, anxious summer. She felt lucky that home was in London, while he had to be in Oxfordshire, though she had to endure Carolyn's disappointment and the unappealing options she flung at her: 'Take off! Go backpacking! Go to art school in Paris! God, when I was your age, I couldn't leave home quick enough. I was living in a squat off the King's Road.' *Yes, for* four months *before you married a lawyer*, Eleanor thought. She had no idea what to do: the options were both too wide and too narrow. She could do anything she wanted, but in the short term, she was desperate to leave home, and she needed to have something to say when people asked what she was up to.

In the end, she was offered her first job in September – an internship at a publishing company. It was badly paid and the work was menial, but it was easy: she created a spreadsheet or made a cup of tea and everyone was delighted. More importantly, when people asked her what she did, she felt like she had the right answer. Working in publishing suited her; it summed her up. It was creative, but not in an unstable, unsettling way: she wasn't going to threaten to jump out of a window or smear menstrual blood on her lips. It was badly paid enough to feel self-righteous, but the editors she worked for could afford expensive tights. Amy knew people who were moving out of a three-bedroom flat in Stepney Green and they moved in together with another friend from Cambridge. She left home, commuted, paid council tax, went to housewarming parties and the Tate Modern at the weekend, quietly marvelling at how well things had worked out. She'd got far, far more than she'd ever expected.

Richard had got far less. He wanted to study more, but couldn't get funding, and his parents refused to help him with something they saw as frivolous. He applied for competitive scholarships and wasn't accepted, each rejection plunging him into a gloom so dramatic and self-absorbed that Eleanor found herself disagreeably unsympathetic. He told her he wanted to be a writer and through his parents' connections, he managed to take on bits and pieces of journalism, but it was never close to an income. He said he was writing a play, but got defensive when Eleanor asked him about it. He became sulky, depressed; the mechanics of their relationship became stiff and uneasy.

She'd go and see him in Oxfordshire every other weekend, resenting the fare and the time away from London. She was afraid that her new life would disappear if she didn't tend to it and felt jealous when Amy went to parties without her. Richard couldn't afford to come to London and although she complained about that, she didn't know if she wanted him to. She was enjoying Amy's company much more than his these days.

Richard's family home was large and austere and full of things that were unfamiliar to her: family silver, nineteenth-century oil paintings, a utility room and parents who were still married. He'd complained about his parents at Cambridge, in a way she thought was needlessly self-pitying; she was more sympathetic after she'd met them. Hugh was dominating and full of 'jokes' at her expense, usually about the *Guardian* or the public sector or people who worked in the arts. He was quick to inform her of the many things he disagreed with Mr Blair about. She hated the way he assumed the family would operate around him; she never saw him clear the table or make a cup of tea or even say thank you when Richard's mother did.

But it was even less easy to be fond of Lorna, who constantly delivered little challenges in an easy, pugnacious tone. 'And your job doesn't feel like rather a waste of a Cambridge degree?' she asked Eleanor, as graciously as if she'd asked her if she wanted more soup. Amy suggested that she thought Eleanor wasn't good enough, but in fact, nothing was good enough: Richard, Hugh, their house, the town, the University of Cambridge, Mr Blair, the quality of supermarket smoked salmon. It was all inherently disappointing. Everything was ghastly or horrid or common, even things that Eleanor had previously thought were innocuous: microwaves, Santa, red front doors.

Once, she came down to the kitchen by herself and overheard Lorna on the phone. 'We have Richard's "girlfriend" staying . . .' Eleanor could hear the inverted commas, as though Richard were a six-year-old. 'Oh, she's *fine*, I mean, perfectly all right. She's a fellow English student. Not particularly pretty.' Eleanor turned away, mortified, not really surprised that Lorna thought that, only that it had been communicated so directly.

She and Richard fought every weekend, worse than they ever had before. They were raw, undulating rows that quickly lost their borders or sense of meaning. They were cruel to each other. She abandoned him in a cafe, crying in frustration; he told her he missed being surrounded by people as intelligent as him. Even now, thirty-seven years old and untangling his socks from their daughter's babygrow, remembering that remark made her furious.

The relationship was slowly being ground into the earth. She fully expected to find one day that there was nothing left, just an imprint where it had been. She would mourn it, but she didn't feel especially sad about it, because there was so little to lose. She carried on: shuttling back and forth between Oxford and London, enduring Hugh and Lorna, feeling her spirits sink when she saw Richard's number on the phone every night. She told Amy that she would do something about it, but she was so sure it would run its course, there was no impetus to act. All she had to do was wait, calmly, patiently, for the end.

*

The February after they left university, Richard decided to give up on writing and academia: he applied for a law conversion course and was accepted, his parents agreed to pay the fees and he made plans to move to London in September. It ought to have been good news – there was hope for them at least – but Eleanor didn't think they would last another six months.

But they did. They began to argue less – they mellowed deliberately: bit tongues, withdrew, put a patina over things. Richard put a huge amount of energy into his course and the internships his father secured for him. It was the first time Eleanor had seen him happy for months, and some of the energy transferred to her. Two years later, Eleanor had a permanent job in publishing and a boyfriend who was a trainee solicitor in a mid-tier London law firm. She didn't recognize herself in that description. 'I live with my partner in Islington,' she told herself. She felt like she was playing a part in a film about career girls. It felt adult and exciting, just not quite true.

Even though they lived together, Richard's life still felt very separate from hers. She tried: she went for drinks with his colleagues and was polite, although she always felt like she'd got it wrong somehow. Her clothes were too scruffy or when she remembered to make an effort, they were smart in the wrong way. She often found herself zoning out, letting the conversations wash over her: 'I've been totally beasted this week', 'I said, come on guys, it's time to put your cock on the block now', 'I told him: I am *not* going to Kuala Lumpur for forty-eight hours.'

Richard was aggressively generous with his new income, buying her lavish gifts she didn't particularly want – Eleanor sometimes wondered if he knew her at all when she opened a shoebox to find something shiny, high and taupe. She found the opulence of the law firm unnerving and vaguely distasteful. But she also liked their Zone 1 flat, which Richard paid more than half the rent on, and taxis on expenses. She refused a credit card and access to his account, but occasionally, if she saw something she liked and it was towards the end of the month, she would tell him about it and the money would appear in her account the next day. It was always slightly more than she'd mentioned. 'Oh, I just got it wrong,' he said. 'Buy me a drink or something.' But she never did and he never underpaid. She would collect parcels from the sorting office – sandals, underwear, bedsheets – feeling like she'd cheated, ashamed and thrilled.

Even from the beginning, Richard had doubts. 'I don't know if I'll do it forever' turned into 'I'm not going to do this forever.' The doubts intensified, and for two years, he was twitchy, on edge, looking for a concrete answer to an open question. He looked into teaching, VSO, becoming a psychoanalyst. After he hurt his knee running, he wanted to train as a physiotherapist. He grew a beard. He bought a flamboyant coat. He developed his own yeast for making sourdough bread and it sat in the fridge, a mushy brain. He had the idea of buying a disused mill in Cumbria and starting an organic flour business. He wrote out a business plan for a stationery shop in Victoria Park village, cut out an advert for a bookshop for sale in the south of France. Nothing changed.

When they talked about Richard's future, dissecting his life and mining it for potential, Eleanor couldn't help noticing that they never talked about hers. It simply seemed to matter less. It was true, she was happier in her job than he was and she sometimes found it satisfying, but she cared about it less than she had at the beginning. Sometimes Richard found her lack of enthusiasm convenient, because then he could give her a role: milling the flour, bringing up their children, doing the accounts in the stationery shop.

Sometimes, she wanted to tell him that she wanted more too. She was now an assistant editor, but she often felt that her job was simply to placate middle-aged men. She sat with authors (mostly older, mostly male) and listened patiently, advising on creative insecurity, footnotes, marital disputes, chapter breaks, health problems, plate sections, plot, structure, punctuation, the nature of love. And it was fine for the most part and she was good at it, but sometimes she wanted someone to help *her*, to listen to her problems and reorder her footnotes. When a colleague, younger and more senior, had come in to ask for Eleanor's help with a piece of software and declared, 'I'm just so shit at all this,' Eleanor knew what she really meant was: *I don't want to do it and I think it's beneath me.* It was said in the same way Richard claimed to be terrible at housework. *I don't want to be good at this either*, she wanted to say. *It's just that I have to be.* But it didn't torment her in the way it did Richard, and she was often glad she'd never expected to be exceptional. She was basically OK; it was just that sometimes she'd catch herself standing by the photocopier in a patch of sunlight, staring out of the window. The copies spun out behind her, sleek as silk, and she would long for a paper jam.

Then, suddenly, Richard told her that he'd applied for a job 'in house', at a commercial property developer. Much better hours. There was less chance of advancement: he would have to give up the idea of a heady rise to the top, of being made partner, of wealth and prestige. It was a step back; his parents would be disappointed. But they could still lead a relatively secure life and he would have more space to decide what he really wanted to do. There was even the option of going part-time eventually.

'I'll also have time for us. I want us to be together properly. I want to make proper meals and watch box sets with you. I don't want you to keep going to parties on your own. I want us to think about starting a family.'

Eleanor was struck by a kind of dread, a fear that she might not really want those things too. But there was no way to consent, only to opt out, and then, all at once, it was happening.

*

When Eleanor turned twenty-nine, she noticed something had shifted. The hunger she'd had for a career in her early twenties now seemed outdated, slightly embarrassing. She and her friends had other considerations: houses and partners. She watched the twenty-four-year-olds in the office, eager and lively, and felt like she lived in another country. Her job was boring her – she seemed stuck at assistant editor level – but she couldn't see a way out. In the end, she took a position as a managing editor, with more money, less contact with authors. It was not as interesting, but it was different and it made more sense, particularly since Richard had started talking about applying for a Master's. They would need the money.

She'd outgrown the role of a career girl, but another role was emerging and she embraced it slowly. The older she got and the longer she and Richard were together, the more responsibilities presented themselves. She had always done more household tasks than Richard, because he worked longer hours and earned more, so it seemed fair. Their homes grew and the work became more demanding. She planned thrifty, nutritious meals for them both and learnt to cook elaborate, expensive meals for when they had people over, which she arranged with the partners of his male friends. She knew exactly what they had in the cupboard and how much, of chickpeas, oven cleaner, toothpaste, mouthwash.

She defrosted the freezer, descaled the kettle and scrubbed mould off the bathroom tiles. She sent birthday, Christmas and thank-you cards from both of them, lit scented candles in the guest room for his parents, and corresponded with Richard's godmother on Facebook. She researched places to stay on holiday, makes of vacuum cleaner and the best method of contraception.

She knew all these things were trivial, but they were also time-consuming and necessary. She didn't hate doing any of it. And if she ever did feel resentful, she remembered that neglecting it would cause collateral damage: it would not just affect Richard, but their family and friends. In the end, it would reflect badly on her, and she didn't want to upset anyone.

There was a sharp increase in the number of duties involving craft: she cut bunting triangles for people's weddings, made mobile ornaments out of felt for baby showers and cakes for family birthdays. Eleanor had never thought of herself as artistic, and at first she was daunted, but then she realized it was fine, as long as you put some time and effort in and then disowned it by telling everyone how awful it was, in a giggly and apologetic way. It was sort of the opposite of being an artist: no talent or ego had to be involved.

Her female friends started talking about how they could make their careers fit around motherhood, and she joined in. They were conversations with no resolution. Sometimes, someone would point out that men never had these conversations, but in an amused, rueful way, and it always struck Eleanor as a pointless observation. What could she do about it? It seemed more practical to prepare for lives they were actually leading, than talk about how things ought to be.

She would never say that she thought men's careers were more important than women's or that childcare was a woman's job; but Richard was the main breadwinner and she was the one who remembered to Rinse Aid the dishwasher. It was just the way their relationship – and that of every other woman she knew – had evolved, but you could only spend so much time sorting the hundred, tiny individual reasons from any broader implications. Her job was dissatisfying, but there didn't seem much point in pushing her career when this potential disruption loomed. It had been cultivating in her for years: this sense that her time, money and freedom were limited. One day, she would have to give all this up. She was unconsciously preparing for motherhood.

*

Through the haze of her headache, she saw that it was half past nine – it was acceptable to start getting ready for bed. She hauled herself up and as she opened the door, she felt a tiny, metallic discomfort under her bare feet. She bent down and found the necklace Richard had given her for her thirtieth birthday stretched out in a line just inside their bedroom door. It made her feel sick. She put it back in her jewellery box and brushed her teeth, all at once horribly alert.

12

The dance studio was smaller than Zoe expected: just one narrow room, two or three floors above a corner shop. On the shelves at one end, there were logs of green yoga mats, half-deflated pink balls, and a huge variety of coloured foam blocks. It smelt of rubber and incense. She was early – the first one there – and after she'd paid, she retreated into a small changing room off the studio. She took her clothes off slowly, easing on her leggings, folding her jeans. When she came out into the studio, two girls had arrived and were warming up. One was face down on the floor, writhing. She turned over onto her back and kicked her legs in the air. The other girl was just moving her arms, but in such a fluid and accurate way that Zoe could tell she was good at this.

Zoe turned away from them and started doing self-conscious, half-hearted stretches in a different corner. The room began to fill up. She looked round tentatively when someone new came into the room, and then quickly turned away. Then, with a sickening feeling, Zoe thought she recognized Kathryn: pale skin, a flippy, mousy ponytail, thin and angular, in leopard-print leggings and a tight vest. Zoe turned her back to her. She had come with the precise intention of this happening and now that it had, she felt incredibly vulnerable. What if she gave herself away? Possessing information that would make such a difference to someone else's life made her feel frighteningly powerful, and dirty.

The teacher arrived. Zoe was mesmerized by her body and the way she moved, so smooth it looked almost involuntary. They began with a warm-up exercise: everyone had to start walking around the room in any direction they liked but if one person stopped, everyone else had to stop too. It involved a curious combination of self-possession and an almost unbearably acute awareness of everyone else in the room. She began to sneak looks at the other dancers. They were almost all women and mostly, they looked right: tall and thin and young and pretty. She began to distinguish them: the girl who had writhed on the floor at the beginning; the tall, slim black girl with an afro and a headband. Kathryn. The only man. She noticed a small, curvy woman with a round, open face, in a large T-shirt and leggings. Unlike the rest of the class, she was deliberately non-intimidating, smiling and laughing every time she nearly bumped into someone. Zoe warmed to her. The movement increased: they had to run, jump, touch the walls. If one person went down on the ground, they all had to get on the floor 'in whatever way you feel'. Zoe started to feel ungainly and creaky: some of them could be sprawling on their front in seconds flat, while Zoe barely managed to crouch, and then they were up again, whirling round the room. She tried to concentrate on what she was doing, keep Kathryn in her vision and not stare at her too much.

The next exercise was called 'the triangle'. The teacher demonstrated it with the writhing girl and another girl she clearly knew. They formed a triangle and the three of them had to keep the same distance between them at all times. If one person drew in, they all did; if someone pulled away, the other two did as well. The triangle expanded and contracted regularly according to the whims of its points. But they were not allocated groups of three: you had to choose the people you formed a triangle with silently – and someone else could have picked you for part of a different triangle.

Zoe wasn't really sure how it was going to work, but the music started, and she picked the two people nearest her: the only man in the group and a girl near him. The man was easy to keep track of, but she lost the girl; she'd never properly distinguished her from the others. For a while, it felt a bit like she was just chasing the man around the room. She tried to be subtle: it seemed somehow unsavoury to let him know that she'd picked him as one of her 'points', when he could be following someone else. And what if someone was following her? The whole exercise was designed to induce social paranoia. Then she became aware of the smiley girl following her. It was reassuring, but odd, the thought that someone had been reacting to her without her knowing it. It was embarrassingly intimate, and Zoe tried not to make eye contact, just be aware of their bodies ebbing and flowing. But then it was working, they were dancing: the three of them were a triangle, pulling in together and then all moving away.

The exercise finished and they stood around in a circle. She allowed herself to look at Kathryn directly, to take her in, and realized, with intense relief, that it wasn't her. Her face was too angular, her mouth too wide. Zoe conjured up the photo she'd seen, and the more she stared at her, the more she was convinced that it was not the same woman. She felt as though she could look round the class directly, now she had nothing to hide, and she caught the eye of the smiley girl in the big T-shirt. The girl beamed back at her directly; something about it was familiar, and then the realization hit. *She* was Kathryn. Kathryn had been following her. Zoe had liked her.

The main part of the class began, where they learnt a choreographed routine. Zoe tried to steal glances at Kathryn while pivoting, crouching, kicking, lying face down on the floor and swinging her arms and legs about. There was something appealingly youthful about her. Her T-shirt had underarm holes and it was the sort of off-white that suggested it had been around a long time. She was unshowy and engaging, laughing at herself when she got things wrong. She had a bird tattooed on the inside of her wrist. Kathryn's smile, her scruffiness, her confidence began to enrage Zoe. She was nothing like she'd imagined. She was *nice*. What could Adam possibly dislike about her?

Zoe longed for the class to end. It was agony; why had she put herself through this? When it finished, Kathryn got to the changing room first and pulled off her T-shirt; she wasn't wearing a bra underneath. Zoe grabbed her clothes and left, running down the stairs two at a time, trying to work out if she'd got what she wanted. She had no idea.

13

Slowly, Eleanor began to abandon her campaign against the house. Once or twice, she'd rung the door of the woman at number 50, but she hadn't been in, and Eleanor had been partly relieved – she was afraid of looking foolish or of Richard finding out. She'd seen Jamie in the street, and he'd waved cheerfully – she was on the verge of starting another conversation, seeing if she could speak to Luke, perhaps, but she always left it just a second too late and then he was gone.

There was very little left to try. Any other idea she had was too much: too outlandish, too destabilizing. She found herself thinking about exorcisms and séances. She wasn't even sure whether she believed the house was haunted – she still didn't know if Emily was dead or alive. She just liked the idea of a purging, a catharsis, the badness in the house leached out all at once. But it was dangerously far from her idea of herself.

There was only one thing she hadn't done. She had turned the rest of the house upside down, but she had resisted touching the upstairs room, afraid of disturbing it. The suitcase was still in the corner. She decided she had to get rid of it. She wouldn't open it, just throw it away as it was.

The next Saturday, when she had time alone in the house, she made her way upstairs, clutching bin bags. When she opened the door to the upstairs room, feeling it push back against her in that peculiar, familiar way, she started. Something had happened in this room. The suitcase had been opened. The objects had been taken off it and now stood on the floor next to it, in front of the pile of quilts. The lid was shut, but the buckles were loose.

Eleanor felt dizzy. The house was getting less and less stable – things continued to shift and move, but it was impossible to prove that it wasn't the children, or Richard, or Zoe, or her. This was different. She approached the suitcase cautiously. She stared at the buckles, trying to bore the image into her mind, the way she did now when she double-locked the door or switched the oven off. She wanted to be certain what she had seen.

Eleanor lifted the lid. At the sight of the mess of paper, her stomach jolted – she thought of the notepad she'd found and imagined intimacies spilling out, whole, horrible stories, sprawled out in letters or diaries. But they were just drawings. As she leafed through, she became more disturbed by what she saw – birds and figures and faces – but also drawn in.

While they were crude in some ways, there was a sophistication to them that was admirable and unnerving. They did not quite look like children's drawings. Although the suitcase was full, the drawings didn't seem to show any development or span years of Emily's life. She must have worked furiously, continuously. And someone had left them behind.

She knew that they would be easy to get rid of but it made her feel uncomfortable. The more she looked, the closer she felt to Emily. She felt a kind of sympathy for her.

It was her work, and it had just been shut up in a suitcase, like she had been shut in her room. It felt cruel to throw them away. She would be putting the contents of someone's mind in a bin bag.

Still, she knew she couldn't keep them. The house was theirs now and so was the room; it couldn't be Emily's for ever. In desperation, she thought again about trying to find the previous owners – handing the suitcase back to them, letting them deal with it. But she had tried everything and they remained elusive. She'd never had a reply to the letters she'd asked the solicitor to forward. She grabbed a bin bag and shoved the paper inside it. The empty suitcase was soft and pliable; she put it into a bin bag too. She gathered up the objects and threw them in next. Then she looked at the quilts with the doll's dress on top and hesitated, thinking about her own collection of Isobel and Rosie's newborn clothes that she couldn't face getting rid of. She resolved to be braver and clear them out next time; she was pleased with the work she had done today.

The rubbish wouldn't be collected until next week and she didn't want it anywhere near the house. She wandered the streets, carrying a bag in each hand, searching for a skip. Eventually, she found one. She lifted the bags with the drawings up and stopped, suspended for a moment. Strange, irrational thoughts spun through her mind: what if the drawings needed to stay in the house? Then she dropped them in, swung the bag with the suitcase in too and walked away.

She was unsettled for the rest of the day, unable to shake off the feeling that she had stirred something up. It would clearly upset Emily, and it felt as though a part of Emily was still in the house.

Eleanor spent the next week on edge, feeling that the

house was about to turn, wondering what she had unearthed. It was impossible to speak about, so she harboured the fear alone, watching the children for signs, asking the nursery to keep a closer eye on them, looking out for any misplaced cutlery or cushions. But the house was unusually quiet. There were no more queer little messages; there weren't even any stones on the step. As the week went on, Eleanor began to calm down, even start to feel hopeful. Perhaps she had not initiated anything. Perhaps she had, in fact, let Emily go.

It happened the weekend after she'd cleared the upstairs room. It was a Saturday afternoon; Richard had taken Rosie and Isobel to the playground. She'd heard Zoe go out earlier; she was alone in the house. She had a slight headache and small tugs of nausea, but it was manageable. Still, Eleanor didn't want to risk a whole day indoors. She wasn't sure where she would go – to the supermarket maybe, under the guise of doing something productive, or to walk round London Fields. She might only need half an hour. She stepped out of the front door and stopped on the top step, unable to move.

A small figure, a girl, wearing a black duffel coat, stood on the other side of the road, watching the house. She began walking round and round in frantic small circles. It seemed as if some force was compelling her to turn inwards. The movements were disjointed and uncomfortable; her feet were splayed out. She wasn't moving because she wanted to, but because she had to. It was not a game. Then the girl suddenly dropped to the ground and started walking on all fours. She was growling – it was unnervingly realistic. Eleanor flinched.

She wondered why the girl was alone. Then she reared up and for a moment, Eleanor saw her face. The girl dashed down the road.

Eleanor was shaking. She was weak, she was vulnerable, she was exhausted – was it any wonder her mind would play tricks on her? But the child had stopped outside the house. It looked like the house was having some effect on her. Perhaps she had imagined it. Perhaps she was going mad. She didn't know which she'd prefer.

The adrenaline was the kind that would linger, she knew, for hours. She turned round and saw another perfect line of small pebbles on the step, in size order. She cried out and picked them up clumsily, not sure what she was doing, just needing to destroy that perfect line. Tomorrow, she would start looking for mediums.

THREE

THREE

1

Eleanor had no idea how to find a psychic. She wanted one who came with a stamp of authenticity but didn't know what criteria to apply. She supposed if she moved in different circles, she would know people who would recommend one, like an acupuncturist or a therapist. Instead, she started with the internet. Late on Sunday evening, after she'd retreated to her bedroom to rest and heard Richard go upstairs to his study, she went downstairs to get her laptop and took it back up to their bedroom. She sat with it on her knees on the edge of the bed, tentatively typing in searches, half afraid of what she might conjure up.

The internet was a dark and unforgiving place for this kind of search. She kept finding things that disturbed her – something unsavoury, ghoulish or unconvincing – and having to hurriedly shut down the lid of her laptop before gathering the strength to begin again. The patent falseness of some of the sites, and the air of duped, desperate people that accompanied them, made Eleanor sad and afraid. She scrolled through acres of dark purple, constellations, butter-flies, gothic script and headshots. Some of the head shots were unnerving – bald women, leather trench coats, blank stares and bad moustaches – while others looked as polished and bland as television presenters.

But as the same phrases recurred again and again, a kind of logic started to emerge – a story that made sense to her. 'Does your house make you feel uncomfortable?' 'I feel unhappy every time I walk into my house.' 'Houses can hold on to negative energy.' 'Emotional events can leave imprints in buildings.' When she read the line 'Stop wondering if it's just you', Eleanor was on the verge of tears. She wanted, more than anything, for it not to be just her.

She settled on an organization that looked more corporate and formal than the others – it was an aggregate of mediums that claimed to work only with the most ethical psychics, which she found reassuring. She rang them the next day, during Isobel's nap, explaining her situation, her voice guarded and low. The woman on the end of the line behaved as if Eleanor's story was the most normal thing she'd ever heard. Something inside her collapsed – it was so lovely to be believed.

She was put through to Sarah, a medium who dealt with 'house clearances'. Sarah claimed she could feel tension in the house even from their telephone conversation, and said she could come and visit the next day at two. Eleanor agreed, while rapidly making plans: she would email her manager and say she had to wait in for an engineer. She would not tell Richard. As she hung up, she told herself this was just another thing to try. She would remain sceptical. But a grain of excitement was beginning to form.

The next day, Eleanor took the children to nursery and then, instead of going to work, went to a cafe. It felt pleasingly audacious having a coffee and reading a newspaper by herself. The excitement mounted. She waited until she was sure Richard and Zoe would have left the house before going home. She got on with household tasks, enjoying the anticipatory jumpy feeling, which curdled to anxiety as it got closer to 2 p.m. Sarah was fifteen minutes late, and Eleanor started to get more and more nervous: she had no idea how long this would take and they would both have to be out of the house before Zoe got home. Her stomach clutched when the doorbell rang; for a second, she thought about ignoring it.

Sarah was overweight, with inexpertly dyed black hair, pale at the roots. It hung down her back, almost touching her waist. A fringe of thin gelled strands arched over her forehead and her eyebrows were painted on. Her white foundation was cakey and uneven; her face looked greasy. She wore a deep purple sheer top with a velvet pattern imposed on it, a long black skirt and surprisingly functional trainers.

'Oh my God, where *is* this place!' she said as she wiped her feet on the mat. She complained about the Overground service and the walk from the station in such a way that Eleanor understood she was to be held responsible. She set her backpack down in the hall. It was childishly small, with a print of the sky: constellations of tiny indistinct stars set against a background of lurid turquoise, purple and pink. It looked incongruous against their skirting boards, next to the buggy; for a moment, Eleanor wanted to ask her to leave. But she waited politely, while Sarah went into the living room and paced slowly round, muttering under her breath. Eventually, she said, 'This is a bad place. A very bad place.'

Eleanor felt afraid, despite herself. Sarah walked into the kitchen, while Eleanor hovered in the living room, watching from the double doors, unsure if she should follow. Sarah stopped in front of the fridge-freezer and muttered something else, running a strand of hair between her fingers. Then she turned to Eleanor and said, 'You have a portal in the house.'

'A what?'

She smiled benevolently, arranging her hair around her shoulders like a cloak. 'A portal: an entrance place for spirits, from the other side. Not all mediums believe in their existence but I've certainly felt them in my time. You may have heard that when people begin to cross over to the other side they talk about a tunnel, a light tunnel? It's my belief that they're talking about the pathway between their world and ours, which the spirits use to visit us. And the portal is the entrance to that tunnel – that's what you have here. It isn't surprising you've been disturbed, with all this traffic. Oh yes, it's like Piccadilly Circus in here!'

'And the portal is – here?'

'That's right.'

'Next to the fridge?'

She smiled again. 'That's right.'

She walked back through to the living room. 'I'm feeling good energy here too. Some good spirits have come, come to look after you. I think I'm receiving messages from your father's mother? Is that possible? Has she passed over?'

'She . . . yes.'

'She's with us now. I'm getting an "A". Anne? Anna? Alison?'

'Her name was Marianne.'

'Ah, there you are, that's how I heard Anne.'

'I never met her.'

'Well, she's here all right. Here to look after you.' There was a false kindness in her voice and Eleanor suddenly felt angry, with Sarah for being so unconvincing and with herself for allowing this to happen.

'So, what do you suggest we do?' she asked, to conclude it politely.

'Well, I could do some cleansing spells, but I can't say

they'd do much good unless we closed the portal. I don't believe anyone could live here with it open.'

'So can you close it?'

'I would try.'

'How much will it cost?'

'That's something I'll have to ask the spirits.'

'What – really?'

'I ask the spirits to guide me on everything.'

Eleanor let Sarah out with the same meaningless place-holders she used in shops – 'I'll have to think about it, talk to my husband, thank you so much for all your help!' – and then sat down at the kitchen table. Her latent headache suddenly mushroomed in her skull and she started to feel shaky. She would have to go out. First, she cleared the browsing history on her laptop and deleted the calls she'd made from her phone, pressing her fingers into her temples. She would have to think of something else.

2

Richard decided to start with the living room. He'd managed to put aside a small amount last month and he would put the rest on credit cards, even though he hated the thought of more debt. Eleanor had been even more withdrawn lately in a way he couldn't put his finger on: she was preoccupied, almost secretive. It felt like they hadn't talked for months. He had to do something.

Painting the walls would make enough of a difference, for now. He sat at the kitchen table, surrounded by colour charts, while Eleanor rested upstairs. He had looked at them all a hundred times, but it became instantly less pleasurable now he actually had to make a choice. As soon as he lighted on something, it seemed too strong, too ordinary, too much of a cliché, too much of a statement. He tried to think about what Eleanor would like. He'd asked her and she'd said, 'Just different. Just change them, I don't care.' He tried to think about her favourite colours, her favourite things, and all he could remember was the times he'd got it wrong. The shoes she never wore. The engagement ring he knew wasn't quite right.

She came downstairs carrying a bundle of washing in her arms and for a second, he was shocked at the sight of her: so pale and unhappy. She sat down at the table, still cradling the washing, and he put his arm round her. The novelty of the gesture shocked him; he wondered how long it had been since they'd touched.

'Are you OK?'

'I just don't feel well.'

He took a deep breath, suppressing the panic. 'I know. I'm sorry. Look, leave the washing. You should be resting. I'll do that.'

'It's not . . . it's not about now.' She turned her face towards him and it felt like the first time she'd looked at him directly for years. She spoke quietly and cautiously, but with an undercurrent of firmness that made him dread what would follow. 'I don't think resting helps.'

'You just need to rest properly. Come on, give that to me and go and lie down.' He tried to take the washing out of her hands; she held on to it.

'It's the house, Richard. I don't feel well in the house. I haven't since we've moved in here. There's something in the house that makes me ill.'

He pulled his arms away. He felt like he physically couldn't bear this conversation. He tried to stay calm. 'Eleanor, that's impossible.'

'I really don't care any more! I don't care what's impossible or not. It's what's happening.'

'I'm sorry you're ill. I really am. But it's nothing to do with the house. Look, you're run-down, you're stressed out, I know things haven't been easy.'

She hesitated. 'I want to move.'

'Eleanor, what? Where to? Think how long it took us to find this place. We can't!'

'Let's look somewhere cheaper then, leave London, I don't care! I just don't want to stay here!'

He tried to be rational, though he wanted, more than

anything, to leave the room. 'It doesn't make any sense. We've done nothing to this place – we'd be lucky to get a single offer for it. We have a real opportunity, Eleanor, to shore something up for the future. We need this house.'

He thought about how much simpler things would be if he'd been working full-time, how much freer they'd be with his full salary. They could have started on the house by now; they might not even need Zoe. He thought about his days in the study; how they were now almost less appealing than his days in the office, as the undercurrent of guilt and dissatisfaction that accompanied them grew. He thought about how behind he'd got. The hours he'd spent in Zoe's bedroom when he should have been working.

'It's not just the illness, Richard. It's everything I've heard about the house, everything the neighbours have said. Knowing that something bad happened here. The stones! The stones on the step.'

'The stones are weird, I know. Someone's messing about. Maybe a child. But a few stones – it's harmless, isn't it? And the rest is just – stories, Eleanor! Gossip. I don't know why you've taken it to heart.'

'Richard, things move in the house. Nothing stays where I left it. I opened a cupboard this morning and found my engagement ring in a bowl.'

He tried to sound reassuring, but his heart was beating faster. 'You probably just put it there when you were doing the washing up.'

'I know I didn't! Everything's in the wrong place! I feel like I can't keep hold of anything any more!'

'You just forgot, that's all.' He remembered the open door of the upstairs room, a few months ago now, and the strange feeling he'd had about his desk. It couldn't be true and besides, Eleanor was so run-down. He spoke cautiously, afraid he might be advancing where he shouldn't, unable to let it stay unspoken. 'When you're ill . . . well, it's natural to get confused. And sometimes the mind plays tricks on you.'

She pulled away. 'Richard, it's not me! I'm not going mad, I promise you!'

'I'm not saying you're mad! Just . . . you've been under a lot of pressure lately and . . . Look, I'll do something about the house, and then we won't need to think about moving. I've wasted too much time already, and money, and I'm sorry. I'll make a start, make it nice, choose some paint.'

'It isn't about paint.'

'Well, what's it about then?' He tried to stop the note of desperation in his voice.

She didn't answer. He held her in his arms again, hoping she couldn't feel his hands trembling. She leant against him but it felt more like surrender than reconciliation. Tomorrow, he would choose the paint; it didn't matter what colour. He'd order samples and try them out on the walls.

*

On Friday, after he'd said goodbye to Eleanor and then Zoe, and put off going upstairs as long as he could, he sat at his desk, walled in by piles of unread books. One was open in front of him, but it refused to yield, no matter how many times he stared at its pages. The image he'd had of himself here – absorbed, at peace, his mind working nimbly and energetically – was getting fainter. And he was finding it impossible not to think about what he'd always half known but now knew for certain: Eleanor wanted to leave. They might lose the house.

It used to be so much easier to convince himself that he was doing the right thing. 'It'll be worth it if you're happier,' Eleanor had said, when they talked about his Master's and the sacrifice of time and money. He'd told himself that university was the last time work had meant anything to him, the last time he'd felt any pride or fulfilment in it. He'd thought it would be easy to find his way back to it.

But the side of his mind that was good at all these things had atrophied after years of underuse. Maybe it was irretrievable, maybe that hungry curiosity was lost to him now. His memories were changing too. He'd liked being good – the quick satisfaction of challenging someone's argument or passing an exam. He had wanted to like the rest of it – solitude, library stacks, desks, notebooks – but now he wasn't sure if he ever had. Perhaps he was as bored by it then as he was now. Perhaps it had all just been a means to an end.

The paint charts on the desk reproached him; he'd circled a few squares in biro but still hadn't ordered the samples. His mind turned to Zoe's bedroom as it always did on Friday afternoons. He closed the book, folded the paint charts and went downstairs.

Standing by her bed, he saw there were two empty contact lens sachets on the bedside table, little plastic dishes with a chalky white residue inside. He picked them up one by one, pressing down their unpeeled foil lids so he could read her prescription. Her eyesight was slightly better than his. He didn't know why he could possibly want that information. Her old lenses had been abandoned on the table, two shrivelled translucent petals. He picked one up, feeling queasily electrified at the thought of touching something that had been in her eye.

It slipped out of his fingers and he panicked. He didn't know if she would remember that she had left them by her bed; she might. He saw it glinting on the carpet and carefully picked it up, but as he tried to place it the exact same distance it had been from the other one, he knocked over the glass of water next to it. He watched, sickened, as the water pooled in the contact lens sachets and the other discarded lens regenerated in the liquid, expanding to a full moon. A dark incriminating bloom spread on the carpet. He had a blinding flash of clarity and saw himself through Zoe or Eleanor's eyes. He knew what it looked like, and that what it looked like was essentially what it was: he was spying on their lodger.

He tried to blot the stain with tissue, but little shreds of paper, like grains of rice, got caught in the carpet and he had to pick them out. The dark patch remained. He looked at it from different angles, trying to convince himself it wasn't obvious. He prayed it would fade by the time she got home. He had to stop this. This had to be the last time.

But he went into Zoe's living room anyway, because if it was the last time, then he should at least make the most of it. He went straight for her fold-up writing table, which always seemed to yield the most interesting things. He found a photograph there, of her and another girl sitting on a kitchen table. They looked young – from their faces, he might have guessed twelve or thirteen but they appeared to be in a student kitchen, full of sticky jars and bottles, wine glasses and ashtrays. He was amazed by how ordinary Zoe looked: her hair was straight, shoulder-length and a kind of strawberry blonde. She had no piercings. She wore jeans and a tight, cropped T-shirt but the girl she was with was wearing a ratty black ballgown and elbow-length white gloves, which even from the photograph Richard could tell were grubby. There was something compelling about the delighted way they were looking at each other – Richard guessed that was why Zoe had kept it.

The last time he was there, she had left her laptop open, and he had delicately nudged the trackpad, as if he were brushing it by accident. The screen lit up, and he did a frenzied scan of her email inbox, but it didn't tell him much: it was just a cluster of girls' names and subject headers like 'tomorrow', 'Exhibition' and 'Hello!' Now he deliberately eased the lid up, as if he were prising open a shell. There was a brief email from someone called Liz on the screen, suggesting a time to meet – he scrolled down to read Zoe's email to her.

> So, yeah, Adam, I don't really know what to do. I really like him. But then, I don't know whether I *actually* like him or if I'm just getting off on the situation. I mean, I know it's all kind of pointless. If we don't really want to be together, why am I wasting my time? Then sometimes I think he's kind of . . . showing me how to live. Ugh – I know that sounds sappy.
>
> And then I think maybe I should just enjoy it. He's really good-looking! There's loads of stuff about him online – he's got a website and things with pics. Adam Cunningham, Google him, tell me what you think! Anyway, I'm really sorry for going on about it all the time. How's your new house? How's Ed? Shall we go for a drink next week?
>
> xxx

He saw a bicycle stop at the kerb outside. Someone climbed off: a woman in jeans and plimsolls. It couldn't be Zoe, it was too early, but the jeans and the bike . . . He pushed down the laptop lid and raced up the stairs as quickly and as quietly as he could. He wanted to cocoon himself in his study, but he wouldn't make it all the way to the top of the house. He went into the kitchen and pretended to look in a cupboard, so she wouldn't see his face.

'Oh, hi. How's it going?' Richard heard her say and he emerged from the cupboard, thinking it was going to be OK, though his pulse was still racing.

'You're back early!'

'Yeah, we haven't had any orders in and it's so quiet on a Friday. Duncan said there was no point us both being there.'

'Lucky you! Well, best get back to it.' He tried to walk past her without looking at her.

'Oh, I'm not getting in your way, am I? I was just about to go down—'

'No, it's fine. It's fine,' he said, without turning round.

Upstairs, he thought about the glass of water and the missing contact lenses. He had no idea if she would notice. He felt sick when he heard her footsteps on the stairs down to the basement, braced himself for a cry of outrage or repulsion. Only when it had been quiet for some time did he start to calm down. Maybe it hadn't been a disaster after all. The residue of adrenaline was almost pleasurable. His resolution that he had to stop began to fade.

Later, he put 'Adam Cunningham artist' into Google. His website came up straight away. There were pictures of lumps of metal and plaster, in unrecognizable forms. Sometimes they were squeamishly corporeal and had bits of rusty nail or pipe stuck in them. Some of them were described as being made out of wax and latex, which made him feel a bit sick. His artist's statement was full of incomprehensible jargon and his long CV meant nothing to Richard: he'd been in lots of exhibitions, most of which seemed to take place in a 'project space'. Still, he had given lectures in art institutions

Richard had heard of. He'd won prizes. He had a live/work space in Hackney. He was born when Richard was ten. Richard clicked on 'Media'. There was a video of him speaking, saying things like 'emotional resonance' and 'navigating the inner self'. Zoe was right: he was good-looking.

Richard thought about Adam's talent and assurance, and wondered what his life would be like now if he'd given himself more of a chance. The year after graduating had felt horribly, torturously long, a heavy, sticky mouthful; now, years slipped down without him even noticing. He'd retreated to the law conversion so quickly, afraid of how unboundaried and unjust the real world seemed. He wanted the security of exams, progressions, levels and ladders. He wanted to be good at something. He thought fruitlessly about the life he might have had and the things he could have done if he'd been braver. He shut down his laptop. He potentially had a couple more hours to work, but his appetite had entirely gone.

3

Eleanor had never thought Richard would agree to move, and she was angry with herself for raising it in desperation. But now it was certain: she was stuck. She needed to find a way to live with it. She just wasn't sure how. After Sarah's visit, she'd vowed to stop thinking about mediums – it was idiotic; all nonsense – and yet she still found herself returning to certain websites. If she had a private few minutes with her phone or laptop, she allowed herself to be comforted by familiar sentences, offering some kind of understanding: 'Houses can hold a recording of the past.' 'A previous tenant or event can be left in the fabric of the building.' 'Perhaps your house is haunted or visited by a former resident.'

On Monday afternoon, she was trawling through them at the kitchen table, when she heard Zoe come home. She started at the sound of the key in the lock and tried to shut down her tabs as quickly as possible. Zoe came into the kitchen to make a cup of tea, as she always did. Eleanor was about to get up and out of her way, irritated at the interruption, when she remembered that she had something to tell her.

'Zoe, I've been meaning to say: Richard's parents are visiting next weekend. I just wanted to let you know.'

'Oh, right. Are they staying?'

'No, we're not quite ready for that yet.' She'd meant the house, but Zoe smiled as she said it, and she found herself smiling back.

'They're staying with Richard's sister. But they'll be here on Saturday night. I just thought I'd tell you because . . .' She allowed the unspoken assumption that Zoe would keep out of their way to manifest itself. It was unfair, but she couldn't think of any other way of doing it.

'Sure.' Zoe went to the cupboard and got out her mug. 'How was the wedding, by the way?'

It took Eleanor a moment to grasp what Zoe meant. Amy and Dominic's wedding was weeks ago; she supposed they might not have spoken since then. 'Oh, lovely, you know. They're old friends, so . . . very nice.' Eleanor stared at her screensaver. She wanted the conversation to end. But Zoe was moving so slowly and it felt like something else was required so she said, pointlessly, 'It wasn't too far from where we had our wedding. So it was nice to, you know, be back, I suppose.'

This seemed to pique Zoe's interest; she put down her mug and leant over the kitchen counter. Eleanor's heart sank. Isobel could wake up any moment and Rosie's TV programme would end soon.

'Where did you get married?' Zoe asked.

'In Oxfordshire. Near Richard's parents. We had the ceremony at the parish church where Richard was baptized and the reception at a venue, you know, one of those stately homes that you can hire for that kind of thing.'

'It sounds lovely.'

'It was.'

Zoe stood up again, stretched and opened the cupboard above the kettle. 'How long have you been married?'

'Oh . . . five years? Five and a half? It'll be our sixth anniversary in June.'

'What is that, like, china?' Zoe took the box out of the cupboard and sorted through the teabags before selecting one, even though they were all the same. Eleanor glanced at her computer screen.

'Oh, I don't know, actually.'

'One's paper, isn't it, and five is . . . wood . . . ?'

Eleanor listened to the kettle boiling. 'We don't really keep track . . .'

The tea stewed in the mug. Zoe sauntered to the fridge to get the milk and brought it back to the counter. She paused before unscrewing the lid and then asked, shyly, 'And how . . . how did Richard propose?'

'On holiday, in Venice. We went there for a weekend away and went out for dinner and he gave me a ring.'

'Can I see?'

Eleanor held out her hand obediently, looking again at the trio of diamonds on gold. They were originally from Richard's grandmother's ring and he'd had them reset. However familiar the sight of it on her finger was now, it still sometimes took her by surprise; the stones were just a little too large, a little too ostentatious.

'Wow, it's gorgeous. Was it a surprise?'

'Complete surprise, yes.'

'But you said yes straight away?' Zoe hauled the bag out of the mug and wandered over to the bin.

'Yes. Of course.'

Zoe hesitated. 'How did you . . . Sorry, I shouldn't— I just always wonder . . . I mean: how did you know? It's such a huge thing. I never understand how someone can, you know, be sure.'

251

'I don't know how to explain it. You just are. When it's the right person, you just know.'

Eleanor looked at Zoe curiously. She looked very tired, paler than usual, and she seemed to be getting agitated. Eleanor thought she was about to ask something else, but she just said, 'I'd better let you get on.' Her voice didn't sound quite right. She picked up her mug of tea and went downstairs.

*

The minute he'd suggested Venice, Eleanor had known. Richard had even said to her once, over tea outside the university library, that he wanted to propose to his future wife in Venice. Even at the time, she thought it sounded ridiculous: overblown, indulgent. But then, the idea of getting engaged – at all, to anyone – was fairly ridiculous in itself. She knew it was possible, maybe even likely, but it was too distant to properly comprehend, like getting a mortgage or dying. But it seemed important to Richard, like he was attached to the idea somehow, so she just said it sounded nice.

After Richard changed jobs, their conversations about marriage started to multiply, from airing vague, romantic notions to drafting blueprints for a shared existence. They talked seriously about children, money and property; Richard squeezed her hand during the vows at wedding services. Sometimes she wished they would just be open with each other and decide, instead of endlessly circling the unspoken thing. But she knew that Richard would want to do things properly – and that would mean a formal proposal, in some traditionally romantic location.

So, Venice. It was inevitable. She only had to wait. She marked time until the trip, thinking about it constantly, coursing forward, fingers on the emergency button. She exhausted herself questioning every habit or gesture – *Can I really do this? Can I live with this?* And occasionally: *Can I live without this?* She felt sick walking past bridal shops.

Eleanor had lost her virginity in Venice. (She couldn't remember whether she'd ever told Richard this, but it didn't seem the moment to bring it up.) Her boyfriend, Ian, had suggested they go away after they got their A-level results, to celebrate or to hide from the world, and they'd chosen Venice. It sounded romantic and grand; it felt like a good place to have sex for the first time. Eleanor understood, from magazines and sex education lessons, that her virginity should be taken seriously, and ideas of regret and loss weighed on her. But she was eighteen, she wanted to do it before she went to university, and she hated how young being a virgin made her feel. She had been with Ian for three months, and he was kind and safe and had made her a compilation tape called 'Songs for Eleanor'. He had filled a whole tube with blue Smarties for her after she'd told him they were her favourite.

When they rang their schools in August, she'd got the grades for Cambridge and Ian hadn't. He said he didn't care, but on the flight over he started to gripe about it and by the end of the trip, they were shouting at each other in the hostel bedroom, mortified at the thought of anyone overhearing, unable to stop. Ian's resentment at the terrible hand life had dealt him turned into a resentment of her and as it got closer to October, a long-distance relationship seemed less and less appealing. He descended into a subtle meanness, increasing it slowly and deliberately, until she broke up with him, a fortnight before Freshers' Week.

She still didn't regret having sex with him. It felt like something tangible she could take to Cambridge with her, something to keep close when she felt out of her depth. She hadn't taken a gap year, so she hadn't travelled or worked or seen poverty, but she had at least had sex. She was anxious beforehand, because Ian was a virgin too – she worried they would be too incompetent to actually do it. At first, they were: it felt like there was a solid wall of muscle between her legs, the pain was excruciating and so was the disappointment. She didn't know if it was his fault or hers, if she was too hard or he was too soft. When they did manage it, all she could remember was the feeling of relief at it having finally worked, the satisfaction at having done it properly. And doing it properly included enjoying it, which she did at times, although if she was truly honest, she'd had more vivid sexual experiences by herself on the bathroom floor.

In the end, Ian was eclipsed by Venice. She was entranced by it. It was familiar – she wasn't sure what from exactly; films, she supposed, or postcards – but real, not some dead captured version or a bland mock-up. It was like climbing inside a favourite book. They had chosen entirely the wrong time of year to go – the Venetians were still on holiday, it was thick with tourists and too hot. Their hostel was in the quieter, scruffier northern end and they had to walk a mile or so through twisted streets to see anything in the guide-book. The local cafes, restaurants and shops were shut for the summer, so they either had something overpriced and unsatisfying in the centre or cooked pasta in the hostel's communal kitchen and ate it out in the courtyard, marvelling at how cheap the wine from the supermarket was.

But it was so beautiful. Every time she went round a corner there was some new vision that turned her soul, and sometimes she would just stop, dumb, gaping, almost aching from it. They wandered round darkened churches, climbed bridges and drank espresso standing up. She was hungry to learn; she wanted to understand empire and doges and masterful foreshortening. Everything felt rich, vivid and sublime. She didn't ever want to leave – she would defer Cambridge, take a year out, study, move here.

She never did go back, not until Richard suggested it. They went in November; Richard told her early spring or late autumn was the best time to go. It rained all weekend, the streets were damp and a chill rose up from the water. They went back to St Mark's, Eleanor bracing herself for the thrill, but when the narrow streets gave way to the square, she felt nothing. How had she not seen that the basilica was strange, gaudy, overfull? Had she forgotten the crowds or did she not care about them then? Had she not found it unbearable pushing through sweaty bodies, churning slowly through the streets like treacle, men ramming red roses in her face? The street vendors were selling a toy that made a clicking sound, like a cricket, and it accompanied them wherever they went, a chronic tinnitus. Richard read to her from the guidebook and she dutifully observed the things she was supposed to, but she didn't particularly want to learn any more. There was too much to know and you forgot it all anyway. Richard was explaining the clock tower to her: 'The engineers that made it, after they'd finished, they put their eyes out to stop them making another one anywhere else.'

'That's hideous,' Eleanor said.

'Actually, it says here it's just a myth,' Richard said. 'They gave them an apartment in the clock tower.'

When it got dark, around four, the tourists drained from the city. With just one wrong turn, they would find themselves alone in dimly lit, deserted streets, alleys tapering off into the black, water still as glass. Even the streets with shops were disquieting: they sold furs, lingerie or giant fish, blank-eyed, packed in ice. Eels thick as a rope. And the masks: the long tapering beak of the plague-catcher, cat puppets, alligator heads. She was amazed that she hadn't noticed how grotesque it all was. Canova's heart in a mausoleum. Moors holding up the doge's tomb. Misshapen wooden stakes rearing out of the water.

On their second night, Richard announced that he had booked somewhere for dinner, as a surprise. She put on the dress she had brought specially and the necklace Richard had given her for her thirtieth birthday. She thought again how perfect it was and remembered how arduous it had been, Richard learning to choose something she loved. Eleven years of failed presents, tactfully and not so tactfully discarded. Eleven years of love and labour. It occurred to her that she still had no idea what she would say when he asked.

They took a vaporetto to the restaurant. They'd had red wine with lunch and Eleanor's stomach had felt mildly disagreeable all afternoon; she kept drinking water to quell it. The water slapped the jetty and the smell was thick and briny. Eleanor started to feel worse. When she was younger, she got carsick and she couldn't go more than a mile in a car without vomiting. She tried everything: sitting in the front, staring straight ahead, pills, ginger biscuits, pressure points. In the end, she just got used to it: to mess, strip-washing in service stations, walking around motorway lay-bys feeling dizzy and dreadful, handing her mother full plastic bags. She'd more or less grown out of it, though she still couldn't read on buses. That night, as the boat weaved slowly between the gondolas and they jostled with other tourists for the best view, she felt as terrible as she had when she was nine years old.

The restaurant was sumptuous and ornate, and Richard had booked a table with a view of the water. She could feel he was behaving strangely, but maybe that was because she was behaving strangely – it was now impossible to tell. He ordered a bottle of prosecco. The sickness ought to have subsided by then but in fact it was increasing: she was finding it hard to concentrate on what they were saying to each other. Agitation grew. After the prosecco had come, a thick white napkin wrapped around its neck, and she had touched his glass with hers, she saw his hand go to his jacket pocket. She felt dizzy. He opened the small leather box and she saw the ring. It was pretty, though not what she would have chosen. He was speaking but she couldn't hear because something was happening to her, something horribly familiar. She wanted to get up, but she was afraid that if she moved, something terrible would happen. But it was happening anyway: something was rising up, uncontrollable and dark, too strong and too fierce to suppress. She instinctively put out her hands to stop it, but it was no good, of course: she was sick all over the table. It shot out of her mouth with a force that astonished her and then she was panting, shaking, wet-eyed, her dripping hands in front of her face, staring at the thin red liquid, spattered everywhere. In a crescendo of dismay, she took in the extent of it: the plates, the glasses, the ring box, Richard's suit. There were spots of red in the prosecco. She felt intense horror and perfect relief.

Then Richard was speaking to the waiter and taking her by the arm and carefully leading her down a staircase. He guided her into the small bathroom and whispered that he would wait for her. Kneeling down, her knees cold, she stared into the toilet: the water was pink with blood and there was a rich iron-like smell. She tried putting her fingers down her throat to pre-empt another attack but it didn't work. She focused on the clots in the pale red water and inhaled to take in the smell, but it was no good: she was empty. She washed her hands and face thoroughly, checked her dress for vomit and stood in front of the full-length mirror, slack and shaky, examining her reflection. Her skin was totally white apart from patches of red at the corners of her mouth, as though her lips had overrun their borders. Her eyes were slightly pink. She had the clearest, most resonant thought she'd had for months: *I am not in love with Richard*. She went back out.

*

Richard led her through the streets, back to their hotel. She had entirely lost her bearings and followed him down identical waterways, over tiny bridges, paving stones worn with use, smooth as teeth. She babbled apologetically and he told her it was all right, he just wanted her to be OK. Neither of them spoke about the ring. In the small, dark hotel room, he stroked her hair and offered her water and tea. Eleanor didn't feel ill any more, but she couldn't say that, so she pliantly put on pyjamas and got into bed. She realized she was insurmountably tired, and dropped into a deep, thick sleep, half surfacing a couple of hours later when Richard got into bed beside her, and then drifting into a fitful doze, the scene coming back to her with shame and misery. She tried to sink back to sleep, but by 3 a.m., she was fully awake. She got up and sat in the chair by the window.

I am not in love with Richard. It was an entirely new thought, and yet familiar. *I care deeply for him and he is part of my life, part of me, he is in my heart and my bloodstream and my brain cells, but there is still too much of me that is separate*. It felt truer than anything she'd ever known, yet impossible to know what to do with. She thought about telling Amy, her mum: *Richard proposed and I was sick, so we split up.* It sounded ridiculous. Her mum would love it. She tried out the language of romantic novels: *he just wasn't The One.* It felt childish and false, completely inadequate to describe what she was feeling. Perhaps she just wasn't ready – could she say no to marriage without breaking up with him, convince him she needed more time? More time – after eleven years! She couldn't go back to the waking death of the last three months before the trip, uncommitted, with him and not with him. She had to choose.

What would she be without him? It was impossible to tell. She thought about an argument with Amy, before she'd settled down with Dominic, when Eleanor was trying to console her about being on her own. 'I think you've forgotten how bad it is to be single,' Amy snapped. 'Perhaps you've forgotten how bad it is to be in a relationship,' Eleanor said.

Maybe she had forgotten. She didn't know if she was cut out to be alone. 'Visceral loneliness,' Amy had said; the phrase stayed with her. Instability, insecurity, speed-dating. She thought about the wilful, hideous vandalism it would take to destroy the life they'd planned together, to kill the children they'd spoken about before they'd even existed. They already had names for them.

What did love mean anyway? It was such an overburdened word. She thought of the stoic, imperious way Richard had sorted out the mess she'd made in the restaurant, the way he'd taken her arm and led her down the stairs, and how she loved and hated him for it at the same time. She thought about Ian giving her Smarties and sniping about Cambridge. She thought about her mum, lurching from flat to flat, boyfriend to boyfriend, derailed by infatuation, floored with grief when it went wrong. She thought about all the things she'd always thought she wanted: family, predict-ability, home.

She sat for two hours, imagining each path, dissatisfied with both of them. It was five in the morning when she realized that she had chosen or rather, life had chosen for her. Her experiences had slowly shaped her; she could no more remove the last eleven years from her life than she could redirect her neural pathways. So it was chosen. She considered playing it out, turning it into a grand gesture, a good story, but it was too urgent for that. She knelt beside the bed and shook Richard awake. She would rather marry him than lose him.

'Richard? Richard? Yes. The answer's yes.'

Richard stirred, befuddled, only half there.

'In the restaurant, with the ring . . . You were going to ask me to marry you, weren't you. Well, I'm saying yes. The answer's yes.'

He sat up, readjusting to his surroundings, her kneel-ing fervently beside him, gripping his hand. There was a pause. 'Eleanor, seriously? Are you sure? Because in the restaurant . . .'

'The boat made me sick, I didn't say anything and then – it was a real shock. I wasn't expecting it. But I feel better now and I've thought about it, and: yes. I want to get married.'

'Really? Do you mean it? If you hadn't been sick, you would have said yes?'

'Of course.'

'So, that means . . . we're engaged?'

'Yes. We're engaged.'

4

Zoe woke up to find she had a creature sitting on her chest. It was some kind of large bird, but it had human arms where its legs should have been, splayed-out palms instead of feet. The palms were pressing, increasingly hard, on her chest. She tried to scream and throw it off, but it was no good, she was trapped. She could see the girl sitting in the corner of the room, watching. The pressure intensified. She wondered if this time she wouldn't survive and then suddenly she was crying out and her arms were thrashing and there was no bird-creature and no girl. She sat upright, gasping, and then jumped out of bed.

It was two in the morning and she was frantic, exhaustion pulling at her while she tried to resist, scared of what would happen if she gave in. She went into her living room and switched the light on; immediately, the room was reflected back at her in the window and she was facing a ghost of herself. She pressed her face against the window to make sure there was nothing outside: she made out the narrow walled area, the empty street, and felt calmer. She inspected the interiors of her various mugs, selected the least horrible, washed it out in the bathroom sink and poured herself some wine from the half-empty bottle in her room. There were no curtains or blinds in the living room, so she switched off the light, conscious of how visible she would be from the street if she left it on, and sat in the dark, drinking.

It was getting worse. Something was happening once or twice a week now, either the paralysis or sleepwalking. The dreams about the girl intensified, becoming more horrid, vivid and peculiar. Often, the girl was in the upstairs room, pacing frantically, but sometimes she would be in Zoe's room, coming closer each night, once standing by her bed, next to her face. Her expression was becoming familiar; she looked intent, focused, determined.

The sleepwalking was taking her further and further away. She'd woken up in the living room and, once, on the landing, at the foot of the stairs. Last week, she'd woken up by the window in her bedroom, facing the garden, while the taps ran in the shower room – she must have got up and turned them on in her sleep.

She'd read about sleep disorders online, and she knew they were common and caused by stress. She didn't feel stressed, but she hadn't felt like herself for months. It could just be her state of mind. It was possible.

And yet, on Friday night, just before she'd got into bed, she felt something cold and damp under her bare feet. She stepped away, and noticed a faint stain on the oatmeal carpet. She'd looked up at the ceiling, but there was no evidence of a leak: the plaster was blank and smooth. She wondered if it was coming up through the floorboards but the next day it was gone and it didn't reappear. For weeks, she'd had the uncanny sense that her things had moved when she wasn't there – the papers on her desk never seemed to be where she left them.

And then there were the things she just couldn't articulate at all: an unexplained sense of presence. Last Tuesday, she'd got back from work and was sure someone had been in the house during the day. There were traces of life that hadn't been there that morning – a teaspoon in the sink, Eleanor's laptop on the table, a long thick black hair on the kitchen worktop – and yet she'd heard Eleanor and Richard leave for work. The day Duncan sent her home from work early, she thought she saw something moving in her bedroom, some kind of figure. When she went downstairs, the room was empty. It had just been a shadow, a trick of the light.

She drank the wine and tried to shut her mind down before it started spiralling. But the conversation with Eleanor about engagements appeared unbidden and then it was too late: thoughts were breeding fast, multiplying uncontrollably. She found herself thinking about Adam. It was going wrong. It wasn't supposed to be like this.

All she had wanted was that dizzy obsessive attraction she'd felt when she met him. Everyone said that feeling couldn't last and she understood – it was altogether too much and she didn't want to spend the rest of her life dissolved in a stupid haze, thinking about what Adam might be doing. In some ways, she longed to re-engage with the world. But it was so exciting, that feeling, so marvellously obliterative. When she talked to her friends about it, they subtly pushed for her to do something with it: try and oust Kathryn, turn it into something else. Every film she'd seen, book she'd read or conversation she'd had suggested that if someone made you feel that wonderful, you ought to be with them. But that meant neutering the feeling, with familiarity and gas bills and compromise, and then you had to promise never to feel that way about anyone ever again. It didn't make any sense.

Her plan with Adam was to preserve the feeling as long as possible, and if it ended, move away, find someone else.

But it wasn't working out like that. She was starting to notice unwelcome things. She used to like hearing him talk about his art – it sounded profound and sexy. It was only recently she realized that either she didn't properly listen or she didn't understand him – it was as though he was just arranging words in pleasing patterns. She tried to engage with it, but on some level she found it boring. Sometimes she would say something in return and he would say, 'That's so interesting, Zoe,' and she would be pleased, but they never really connected: they were just talking at each other. It shouldn't matter, yet it became dissatisfying after a while. When they'd met, she'd thought he would encourage her to be more creative, but she found they talked about Adam's hopes and ambitions a lot more than they talked about hers. She liked sex and she liked being in his flat more than in her own and she liked the way he touched her hair. She just wouldn't particularly want to go on a long train journey with him.

When she said she didn't want anything more from him, her friends who had partners looked concerned and consoling, as though she was deluding herself. She reacted by emphasizing how much the arrangement satisfied her – it wasn't entirely true, but then whose relationship did satisfy them? It seemed an utter fiction that being in a relationship made you happy, but no one ever challenged it.

But the days alone in the shop were slowly becoming harder. Having to hoard and protect her small salary, obsessively counting and rearranging, just to get to the end of the week was exhausting, as was waking up in the middle of the night worrying about student debt. Then it would all be punctuated by ecstasy and intrigue, but it was impossible to know if that made it worthwhile. She reminded herself that it was her choice, but in certain lights, that made her feel worse; she had done something irrational and destructive, and it was all self-inflicted. Particularly in the unforgiving light of the small hours, when she worried that she had chosen the wrong thing.

*

When it ended, she was surprised at how quick it was. It was New Year's Eve, the year before she'd moved to Litch-field Road, and she'd been unpacking the shoebox on the bed, in the one-bedroom flat in Homerton she shared with Rob. She was resentful at having to go out. She disliked New Year's Eve for the same reasons everyone else did – the expense and the crowds and the pressure – but it used to excite her too, in a childish, auspicious way. A whole year, full and heavy, suddenly extinguished, a new one in its place. A revolution in less than a second.

That year, she felt something else: a kind of dread that had become increasingly familiar. It was slowly intensifying, making itself known at birthdays and anniversaries, and it had started to infect everything: she could barely move without feeling it. This New Year's Eve was the fifth she'd spent with Rob. And it would be their anniversary in March – there was something ill-fitting and wrong about that. Six years. It didn't suit them.

Her dress didn't look the way it had in her head, when she'd decided what to wear: maybe she'd put on weight or it just hadn't been right in the first place. She opened the Ikea wardrobe and stared blankly at her clothes. The ward-robe was too small, like everything in the flat, and her clothes were compressed so tightly against Rob's shirts that she couldn't really see what was in there. She didn't have the energy to look properly so she shut the door again. She took her new boots out of the box and eased her feet into them, the leather cold and stiff as card. They were too shiny and made her feel curiously raised. She might as well start breaking them in tonight.

Rob was pacing around the room, getting in her way. It was a tiny flat above a shop, which cost more than half their salaries, but talking about moving never went well, so they tried to contain themselves, jamming their things in cupboards. They couldn't agree on where they would move to: Zoe didn't want to move further out of London; Rob wanted a house with a garden. He had plans to make fortunes, involving mortgages, up-and-coming areas and transport links. He became an authority on Crossrail. The whole idea seemed absurd to Zoe, but she was beginning to find this sort of thing genuinely impossible. If one person wanted one thing and the other wanted something else, how did you choose, without one of you feeling resentful and diminished? She knew couples managed it all the time, fluidly and effortlessly, but she had no idea how.

Rob was hurrying her and she had to stop herself snapping at him. She had been trying so hard lately. She kept remembering something her brother had said, aged thirteen, about a friend he went camping with: 'It's not his fault he annoys me.' It wasn't Rob's fault he annoyed her, but it was exhausting, clamping down on irritation all the time. It left no room for anything else and it made her feel constantly guilty.

She knew that he was trying too. They'd talked about how they needed to work harder at the relationship, and she was; she just couldn't tell him that all her energy was going into not snapping at him. She was tired all the time – too tired to go to late-night exhibitions, have sex or cook a proper meal. Rob kept wanting to do things like go to the theatre and they did a couple of times, but it really fucked up your evening, the theatre – there was no time to eat or drink properly, so you ended up roaming around London at half past ten, ravenous and light-headed from interval wine, and then you'd eat some expensive and disappointing noodles. Better to stay at home and have pasta. At the same time, she loved the way he wanted to make their lives better; there was a resourcefulness about him she found very attractive. He was a good person. He would be a good person to marry. She tried to nurture this wave of fondness. She kissed his cheek and stroked his hair.

They were going to a party at Rob's friend Simon's house, just off Mare Street. Simon was a friend from Rob's art foundation course, his gap year, the last frivolity he'd allowed himself before he started studying architecture. Simon now worked for a company that made things out of neon tubing and had produced work for artists Zoe had heard of. Zoe liked him, when she could be bothered.

She thought they were getting there too early – it was seven thirty and all she could think about was that they wouldn't be able to go home for at least another five hours – but Rob insisted. Simon answered the door and gave Rob a lengthy and emotional hug, while Zoe stood awkwardly in the doorway. The house was a large Victorian terrace, shared with five or six others. Jess, Simon's housemate, appeared in a green silk dress that didn't fit properly, vertical creases scored across her chest. She had an imposingly square build, with a nose ring and tattoos, offset by long blonde hair and red lipstick. Zoe had never quite been sure about Jess and she couldn't work out whether it was because Jess wasn't sure about her – which one of them was manu-facturing the doubt. Tonight though, she seemed strangely excited to see Zoe, squealing and kissing her. Zoe wondered if they were already drunk.

Very few people were there, and Zoe felt a private, righteous flare of anger: they were definitely too early. They stood around in the grubby kitchen, drinking warm prosecco out of plastic cups, and eating a chocolate cake that Jess had made. Zoe had no desire to eat cake at half past seven in the evening, but she did it anyway. Rob and Simon were conferring about something and kept disappearing. Other housemates and their boyfriends and girlfriends faded in and out, were introduced and forgotten.

Zoe felt Rob put his hand on her back. 'Come here, I want to show you something.' She let herself be dragged out of the kitchen and up the stairs. 'What's going on? Are we even allowed up here?' 'It's fine, you'll see.' He led her right to the top of the house and opened the door into a small attic room, which Zoe guessed was Simon's. It was fastidiously neat, and dark, apart from candles and a strand of fairy lights, so she supposed the room was part of the party, even though it was so far away from the kitchen and the living room. Rob shut the door behind them and suddenly she felt nervous. She thought of the first time she'd had sex, aged fourteen, in someone's parents' bedroom at a house party. She hadn't felt entirely in control of what was happening, but embraced it hungrily anyway.

Something was wrong. Rob had started to cry and was telling her that he loved her. She told him that she loved him too, quizzically, reassuringly, but that made him cry even more and he started saying her name over and over again. Zoe looked at him, trying to read his face for clues, while he gulped words at her. She wondered if this was it for them, if this was how it was going to end. She felt a tiny shot of fear. He was staring at her intensely, searching her face for a reaction. She started to panic. She had no idea what she was supposed to do.

He said, 'Right, OK,' and crouched down on the floor in the corner, fiddling with something. There was a flash of white light and neon tubes lit up the corner of the room. It must be something Simon had made – why was Rob showing it to her? He was crying harder than ever. In large, plain, white capitals, it said, 'MARRY ME'. But Simon wasn't going out with anyone. She looked back at Rob and the realization came cold and quick: this was happening to her.

For a moment, they were suspended, standing, listening to Rob crying. It was not normal crying. He was making noises she hadn't heard before, strangely high-pitched moans. She had no idea what to say; only what she couldn't. Her panic threatened to edge into hysteria.

'We need to go out,' she told him, and took his hand and ran down the stairs, through the hall, only half aware of some kind of stir in the kitchen as she opened the front door. She ran down the road, towards Mare Street.

It was New Year's Eve. It was fucking freezing. The wind was aggressive, litter was hurtling at their feet. The shops were shutting, the restaurants were full, the pubs would be charging for entry; they were locked out of the city. Zoe reeled around, wondering what was going to happen next, when she saw a sign glowing and familiar, and shouted, 'Quick, run!' She set off down the pavement, her new boots feeling heavy and stiff, concentrating on weaving between the crowds without letting them slow her down, not even turning round to check Rob was following her, half hoping he wasn't. Then suddenly she saw a clear path ahead of her, pavement stretched out like a dirty grey ribbon, and she let go, accelerating until her legs felt long and loose and her chest burned and she was dancing, flying. The bus stop was empty. She prayed for someone to want to get off, or for the driver to see her and take pity on her; the bus slowed down teasingly before drawing away. She doubled over, heaving breath from the pit of her stomach. She realized Rob was standing next to her.

'Sorry,' she said, when she could speak. 'I thought it would take us home.'

They sat next to each other on the narrow red bench. She could see people walking past them, but she was entirely submerged – they may as well have been in another country. Rob had started to cry again, in little involuntary yelps, like hiccups. She stared straight ahead, waiting for him to stop. 'I love you,' he kept saying, as if it would help.

Zoe leant back and felt the cold glass at the back of her head. Of course she had thought about marriage. People asked her about it all the time and Rob had made enough hints that it was what he wanted; she'd just ignored them. She had tried, of course she had, to imagine a life together, but it never felt real or close. She had been waiting for the vision to draw a little nearer but it had kept its distance. It was only in the past year that it dawned on her this might not change. She'd told Laura that she was terribly conflicted about their future, but she wasn't really. She knew what the answer was. She just didn't like it.

She clung to the least relevant thing. 'I suppose Simon and Jess knew about this.'

'Yeah. I got Simon to make the lettering.'

'I can't believe they were all in on it. That you would tell *Jess* before you told me.'

'Well, it is their house, Zoe. I did have to tell them. And I wanted it to be on New Year's because . . . Oh, never mind.'

She looked down. 'It's just so humiliating.'

'*You're* humiliated. Right.'

'Why would you do this without asking me first?'

'What do you mean, ask you first? That was me asking you! I can't ask you if you want to marry me before I ask you to marry me!'

'I mean – why did you have to ask like that, why didn't we talk about it or – something? Why would you just spring it on me like that? In public?'

'I didn't think it was going to pan out like this, OK?' Then his tone changed and his voice was small. 'I thought it was romantic. I thought I was doing what I was supposed to do.'

They sat in silence a bit longer.

'I meant it, Zoe. I want to get married. I know I kind of fucked things up tonight – it was probably a shock for you – but it is what I want.'

She looked down at her new boots. 'I don't feel ready.'

'I don't understand. How can you not be ready?'

'Rob, I haven't been particularly happy recently . . . I need more time to think.'

'I know you don't like your job, but that's not anything to do with us. If you just wait till I'm earning a bit more, you can leave, I'll support you. We can live wherever you like. You don't have to take my name. You don't have to do anything. Just say yes.'

She didn't speak.

'I'm going to be thirty soon, Zoe. It's been six years.'

'I'm only twenty-six!'

Did it have to end, because of this? The thought was agony. Maybe they could just put it away, not think about it, go back to how things were, wait for something to happen. But something was happening. And could she really sustain another year or two, testing each other out, getting on each other's nerves, only to find themselves here again, older and more tired?

KATE MURRAY-BROWNE

'So, when do you think you will be ready?'

When she imagined being married, she was filled with an overwhelming sense of dread. How could she explain that? How do you tell someone that you love them, but that your love is insufficient? She imagined the two of them, paired up and isolated from the world. It would be so lonely.

His tone changed. 'Do you really want to be on your own? Don't you want children?'

He was trying to manipulate her now and she hated him, but at least that made it easier. She didn't say anything.

'For God's sake, what is *wrong* with you?'

What *was* wrong with her? Wasn't this what she was supposed to want? Wouldn't she be desperate for this moment eventually, on the shelf, biological clock ticking? What made her think she was any different?

'Zoe, we have to do something. It's not working at the moment, you know it isn't.' He gripped her arm. 'Please. Let's just do it. Let's just be together and be happy.'

Suddenly, it was unbearable. 'I've got to go, Rob; I'm sorry.' She pulled away from him and ran off down the street. She didn't know it was over; she felt it, like a change in weather. She felt a detached sense of curiosity: *so this is how it ends*. She realized that somehow, maybe even from the day they'd met, she'd been waiting for the end.

Her run turned into a fast walk. She took the first turning she came to and the next, in case he decided to come after her. She wanted to lose him. She had a memory of being five or six, telling her mum she was leaving home, packing a bag, even opening the front door, all the time her mum calmly asking her to stay. It was a performance; they both knew that. Her mum would never let her go too far.

She could sense Rob just behind her and she was furious

272

– she wanted to leave, why wouldn't he let her? She'd seen a way out, for both of them, and she was following it – *please, please don't take this away from me*. But when she turned round, he wasn't there.

5

Eleanor sometimes thought she might have found a way to live with her illness, if it hadn't been for Rosie and Isobel. She'd long since given up on the idea of doing anything properly or well – her health was just something else, like the dishwasher or the bin lid, which would never work properly and never get fixed. And she had nearly got used to it – the way every day felt suppressed, not quite right, not quite there. And while there were times when she thought, *This is intolerable, I cannot do this*, there were days when she calibrated things perfectly: spent enough time out of the house, vomited neatly, distracted herself, talked over the headache. It was almost satisfying.

She could manage what the house was doing to her, but she couldn't bear the thought of it doing something to Rosie. She was still biting and kicking and pinching, and Eleanor wondered when something stopped being a phase and just became character. Rosie still woke up in the night, howling and shaking. Once, she got out of bed and ran to the window, pummelling the glass until Eleanor pulled her away, terrified it would shatter and hurt her. In the mornings, she tried to ask Rosie, tentatively, trying not to scare her, if she remembered getting up in the night, if she'd had a nightmare, if she'd seen anything in the room. Rosie had no idea what she was talking about.

In the last few weeks, Rosie had invented an imaginary friend, who she called 'Girl' or 'Little Girl'. Eleanor had consulted the books and the internet and again, it was perfectly normal behaviour. She was company for Rosie and occasionally Rosie would use Girl as a foil, blaming anything naughty she did on her. But sometimes, Rosie was so convincing, Eleanor found herself believing there was another person in the house. She came to half believe in Girl, resenting her when Rosie said Girl had stolen Isobel's toy or thrown her food on the floor. She noticed that Girl never followed them outside the house, that Rosie never spoke to her in the car or in the shops. She tried not to think about it.

*

On Saturday, Eleanor spent the day preparing for Richard's parents. Her head raged and her stomach grew increasingly unsettled. She'd hoped to get out, even just for half an hour or so, but Richard was already tense and she knew it would make things worse if she tried to leave.

She put Rosie and Isobel to bed, praying they would go to sleep before Hugh and Lorna arrived. She couldn't countenance the idea of Rosie having a night terror if Richard's parents were there; how exposing it would be. She finished the story and put the book down.

'OK, time to go to sleep now, Rosie.'

'Is it nursery tomorrow?'

'No, tomorrow's Sunday. Tomorrow you're going swimming with Daddy.'

'No, I'm not, Girl says I'm not allowed. I'm going to stay here and play with her.'

'Well, we'll see, OK? But it's time to go to sleep now.'

'I can't sleep.'

'You haven't tried, darling.'

'Girl keeps me awake.'

'Well, she shouldn't!' Eleanor said, immediately regretting how panicked she sounded. She put her hand on the duvet and tried to speak more calmly. 'Girl's going to sleep now too, Rosie. Come on, you can both go to sleep together.'

Rosie pointed at the ceiling. 'That's where Little Girl sleeps,' she said. 'She lives upstairs.'

'No, she doesn't!' Eleanor said, pulling her hand away from the bedcover. Genuine hurt crossed Rosie's face.

'Sorry, Rosie, sorry,' she said. 'I'm sorry; I didn't mean to snap.' She stroked Rosie's hair and tried to stop her hand trembling.

She was still rattled when Lorna and Hugh arrived. Lorna had only got more imposing with age; her hair was a perfect, even silver now and she wore it in a thick crop. Her skin creased beautifully, as though it was intended to, like textured silk, and even the deep hollows in her neck formed a refined landscape. Hugh got rounder and redder every time she saw him and showed no signs of minding. She sometimes wondered if they still had sex – it seemed almost physically impossible – and whether Lorna had sex with anyone else, and then stopped herself. They embraced her formally, as they always did, and she took their coats upstairs, while Richard showed them into the living room. As she walked past the bathroom, she wondered if she ought to make herself sick now, to get it out of the way, so she could have a brief period of relief before they ate. She wasn't sure if she could do it without anyone hearing, but she didn't know if she would be able to stomach the meal if she didn't.

'How's Jessica?' Richard was saying as she came back in.

'Bloody miles away,' Hugh said. 'You'd have thought you two could have worked it out so we didn't have to spend over an hour on the tube every time we come.'

'It's just beastly. I don't know how you can live in London,' Lorna said.

'Crazy place,' Hugh confirmed. He looked around. 'Not much point in having a four-bedroom house if we can't stay with you, is there.'

Eleanor smiled. 'We just haven't had time to do up the spare room, I'm afraid. But when we do . . .'

'Hugh, darling, I think this house is in need of rather more pressing things than a spare room, don't you?' Lorna cast her eye over the room. It was unchanged, apart from five small squares of paint on the living-room walls. Richard wanted them to live with the colours for a while before choosing one. 'I suppose you're no further on with the basement?'

They talked more about the amount of work they needed to do on the house, how much it would cost, how long it would take, how they could possibly manage to save while they lived in London, whether they would have to move out when the major work was taking place, where on earth they would move to, whether that would unsettle the children. Eleanor could feel Richard getting tighter and tenser, while she tried to suppress quick, sudden surges of nausea.

When it was time to eat, Eleanor led them through into the kitchen. It was still as a showroom and the table was laid. She'd prepared everything during the day, compulsively tidying as she went along. The last time she had cooked in front of Richard's parents, Lorna had come up behind her, looked in the pan and said, 'Gosh, how interesting.'

'I don't know how you do it, Eleanor,' Lorna said. 'Putting all this on when you've been working all week.'

'Well, I'm part-time.'

'Oh, four days a week isn't part-time!'

'You worked too, Mum,' Richard said.

'Not when you were as little as this! I had ten years at home and I wouldn't have given it up for anything. Of course, I was terribly lucky – I know some mothers don't have a choice.'

'Perhaps if you worked full-time, Richard, Eleanor wouldn't need to work,' Hugh said. 'And perhaps you wouldn't need to have a lodger. I don't see how this Master's of yours is going to pay the bills.'

Eleanor hated the way Richard was demolished by his parents; she wished he would fight back. Instead, he turned away from them and muttered sulkily, 'Yes, I'm sure Simon Schama has a lot of trouble paying his bills.'

'Oh well, if you're going to be Simon Schama . . . !' Lorna hooted. 'Why didn't you tell us?'

They ate the meal Eleanor cooked, goodwill draining out of the room. Just as she'd got up to clear the plates, Isobel woke up and tinny howling came through the baby monitor. As Eleanor ran up the stairs, she remembered how naively delighted she was when she'd first heard Rosie cry: light and delicate little squalls, barely more than exclaiming. In the first few weeks, she was easily soothed and Eleanor wondered, privately, why people complained. It was only as Rosie got bigger and her capacity grew that the crying turned to bellowing and became distressing, debilitating, and suddenly she understood what people meant when they said it could fray your nerves to the point of destruction.

The noise Isobel was making was painful. Eleanor picked her up and she wrenched away. Eleanor felt her grip loosen. She knew, rationally, that all babies cried, and yet it still felt personal. *Why are you doing this to me? What have I done?*

She took Isobel into their bedroom, while she struggled and bawled. Eleanor rocked and soothed, conscious that every minute away from the table revealed her incompetence. Eventually Richard appeared; they spoke in tense, low voices.

'Bring her down – that sometimes works.'

'I can't, not when she's like this.'

'It'll look stranger if you stay up here all night. And we don't want Rosie to wake up properly.'

'Could I take her to your study?' Eleanor said weakly, although she knew that there would be nothing bleaker than being alone with a crying baby on the top floor of the house.

'Come on, just bring her down. It'll be OK.'

'Ah, my delightful granddaughter!' Hugh said, when she appeared with Isobel roaring. 'This isn't very ladylike behaviour, Isobel.'

'Oh poor child, she's clearly overtired,' Lorna said. 'Give her to me.'

Eleanor handed her over. She felt a mixture of satisfaction and embarrassment as Isobel howled in Lorna's arms, pressing her little hands into her neck.

'Of course, we would never have brought children to the table when they were this young, would we,' Hugh said. 'We kept that sort of thing private. I don't agree with all this modern parenting, nappy-changing on the sofa, breastfeeding in public.'

Eleanor took Isobel back from Lorna. She screamed even louder. 'Ah, the mother's touch,' Hugh said drily and Eleanor really hated him. She sat down at the table with Isobel on her lap. Richard put the cafetière and mugs on the table and poured the coffee. He put a mug in front of Eleanor and added some milk for her. It was slightly too much; she thought about saying something and then changed her mind.

Eleanor didn't know what happened next except that she was too fast and then too slow: too fast reaching across the table, while Isobel struggled in her arms, sending her off balance, and too slow to stop the mug tipping and scalding liquid gushing. 'My God!' Hugh shouted and Isobel shrieked. It was the worst sound Eleanor had ever heard. Then slow again: too slow to get off Isobel's sodden hot babygrow and the utter horror of her arm, the skin peeling off in great white sheets, revealing scarlet below. Reaching for her phone, only to have her hand covered by Lorna's, too slow to realize that Richard was already saying 'ambulance' and giving their address. Everyone in the room became active and busy: Hugh took Isobel away, wrapped her in a tea towel and held her arm under the tap, Lorna was asking Richard where they kept the clingfilm. All she could do was watch and listen to Isobel making anguished sounds that she'd never heard before, and listen to herself crying, saying, 'My baby, my baby, I've hurt my baby,' over and over again as if it would make any difference. Lorna gripped her shoulder, telling her it would be all right: 'It's worse for you than it is for her.'

She remembered the first few weeks of Rosie's life, when she was half crazed with fear, every object in the house taking on a new sinister shape, enlarging and expanding, as she imagined the ways it could do harm. Eleanor had realized that she would have to learn to manage this intolerable anxiety because if she didn't, she would never do anything ever again, just spend every waking moment holding Rosie and staring at her. She had to tell herself it would never happen, to pretend that they would somehow always be all right, but now it had happened and it was as if she'd always known it would. The reality was far, far worse than she could ever have imagined.

The madness was not the hypervigilance – it was thinking that they would be OK. She should have given up everything, devoted her entire life, every waking minute, to preventing this. And then, shamefully, the headache pressed into her, and the sickness rose and she couldn't bear the fact that even here, even now, she was remembering herself, brought back to her body, when all she wanted to be was lost.

Then the siren, the doorbell, and although all Eleanor wanted was to make Isobel safe, she could hear Jamie's voice in her head too, crowding everything out. *Didn't he think there'd been some kind of accident there? Didn't he say he saw an ambulance?* Hugh speaking to the paramedics in a voice she'd never heard before, quiet and competent, and still she couldn't do anything, except grip Isobel and uselessly try to comfort her. *And Luke was all like, oh my God, the house is definitely haunted, the girl's spirit is coming back.* She climbed in the ambulance and a thought of her own formed, perfectly clear and intact: *If we survive this, I'll do something. I'll do something about the house.*

6

It was the first time Zoe had seen Adam since Kathryn's visit and she was nervous. She'd been round to Laura's the night before to avoid Richard's parents and ended up staying on the sofa, piqued that Nick had come over, so she couldn't sleep in Laura's bed. She was tired and didn't particularly feel like going out, but this meeting felt significant, charged. She needed to know if anything had changed between Adam and Kathryn, because that would mean something would have changed for her too. The foolishness of her going to the dance class would occasionally swell up and she was terrified Adam would find out somehow. Her hands shook as she put on her eyeliner.

She heard her phone and swooped towards it, thinking about Adam or Laura. It was Alice; she never rang Zoe. Zoe guessed Peter had asked her to do it; maybe he thought it was more likely Zoe would take her call. She felt guilty as she watched the phone dance on her bed but couldn't make herself answer. The voicemail alert was like a little jab in the ribs; she put her phone into her bag. She would listen to it later.

She met Adam, where they always met: the pub just behind the warehouse. He kissed her on the cheek the way he always did, affectionately and discreetly. They were cautious at first, feeling their way, but there was no 'I've got something to tell you' or 'we need to talk'. They began to soften into each other again. After they'd had three drinks, he looked around the pub and kissed her on the mouth. The furtiveness with which he did it was beginning to irritate her, even though she couldn't expect anything else.

They walked back to the warehouse together. It was crowded: Oscar was finishing supper at the kitchen table with Katy, Ursula was on the sofa with one of her friends, and Cora was making a stew. Adam took two glasses from the cupboard and they retreated into his room. She sat on his bed, while he poured her some whisky from the bottle on his shelf and as he handed it to her, he said, 'I've actually got some good news: I sold a piece at the private view. The copper pipe one?'

'Oh, that's great! Congratulations.'

'Yeah, thanks. It was amazing to have a sale on the first night, but I was sad about it in some ways. I lived with that piece for ages. But you've got to let go. You know, when Ai Weiwei was in New York in the eighties, he would make work and just throw it away? He said the process was the most important thing.'

You've told me that before, she thought. But she smiled politely and said, 'Amazing.'

He sat down next to her. 'And anyway, that's my rent paid for a couple of months.'

They'd avoided talking about money in any concrete way. Zoe was always curious about how it all worked – how he made a living. She supposed his rent was cheap, and she knew he gave lectures and ran workshops and wrote articles for online art magazines, but she was surprised it added up to an income. He never seemed to have problems with money, but then, they never went out anywhere – she didn't know if that was because he couldn't afford to or because they weren't properly seeing each other. She told herself not to try to find out; it was more romantic not to know. But now she was asking.

'How often do you sell work?'

'I don't know – a couple of pieces a year maybe? It's not really about that though.'

'No, I know. But you've got to make a living.'

He spoke as if he'd explained this many times before. 'I don't make much money from selling work. The majority of practising artists have another income stream. Making art's expensive. I mean, yeah, I do know artists who scrape by on nothing and just spend twenty-four hours a day in the studio, but I don't think it's that healthy, you know? It's not for me, anyway.'

'But what's the other income stream; what do you actually do?'

She wasn't asking gently or sympathetically. She was starting to dislike herself.

'You know, lectures and stuff. Like the one I did today. Professional practice. Teaching people how to have a career as an artist.'

'You make money teaching people how to make money as an artist? Isn't that a bit meta?'

'No, it's just – look, I've been in the art world for a few years now. I understand it. And if someone's just graduated from art school, the stuff I've got to say is useful.'

He was getting defensive. *You should stop now*, she thought. *Leave it, get it back to before again. You can still get back to before if you stop.* Instead, she said, 'OK, sure, but I still don't see how that makes enough money for you to live on.'

He gave a forced smile. 'What, do you want to see my bank statements? I don't get what you're accusing me of.'

'I'm not accusing you of anything. I'm surprised doing the lectures makes enough for you to live on. That's all.'

'OK, well, I also have a bit of help from my parents.'

'Your parents give you money?'

'Just a bit every month. It's not like a salary or anything, it's just enough to, you know, stop me going under.'

She laughed unkindly.

'What?'

'I didn't know you had a trust fund.'

'It's not a trust fund. That's ridiculous. I still have to work. Look, it's really fucking hard to have any sort of career as an artist, OK? So what if I have help?'

'But you told me your parents don't get your art.' She'd imagined a couple, with working-class roots and staunch, useful careers, bemused by the London art scene, unable to comprehend why their son had chosen to bang nails into things as a vocation. She didn't know where that image had come from, but she didn't think she'd reached it independently.

'They don't. That's why they don't come to my shows.'

'But they get it enough to fund it.'

Something was starting to shift, already. Everything looked different now. His career stopped being glamorous, the warehouse was no longer exotic and marvellous. It was just a playpen for rich kids. It was irrational, it shouldn't matter, she should just shut up and yet:

'I mean, why don't you just get a job, like everyone else?'

'I do have a job! I earn money—'

'Just not enough to live on. Pocket money.'

'Jesus Christ, at least I'm actually doing something! You think you've got such integrity because you work in a shop, but you never actually do anything. Why don't *you* get a proper job?'

'Because of my . . . stuff, my writing!'

'Yeah, whatever.' He sank back against the wall.

'What do you mean?'

'Just . . . I don't want to get into this.'

'No, tell me.'

'Well, you're not a writer, are you? You work in a shop. You just write sometimes. Everyone writes sometimes.'

'No, I—'

'If you want to be a writer, you should be a writer. But you never talk about it. I think you like hanging around with me and the others and working in the shop, but you don't mean it. I think if you were a real writer, you would – I don't know, talk about it more, be serious about it, try and get stuff published, or something.'

'Oh, fuck off!'

She really wanted another drink. Without saying anything, she got up and poured herself more whisky. She sat back down on the bed. Everything was moving too fast; she couldn't make sense of it. All she knew was that this wasn't supposed to be happening – she'd chosen Adam because he said she was beautiful and irresistible. She didn't want to hear all this. They were quiet for a moment.

'Zoe, is this really working?'

She didn't say anything. It cut her that he was asking, even though she knew the answer.

'I mean, between us,' he said, unnecessarily.

'I know.' She curled back against the wall.

'I don't know what to do. Maybe it's not the right thing any more.'

'Maybe not.'

They sat in silence a little longer. She looked down at her

hands in her lap; it was as if she'd never seen them before. Then she asked, 'What about Kathryn?'

'I don't know. I need to think about things with Kat properly. It was probably stupid of me to think that I could do that when I was seeing you.'

She downed her drink. She felt exactly as she had when she'd found out about Kathryn at the party. Mistaken. She'd got him wrong. And now nearly six months later, she was back in the same place, only a small amount of dislike had grown between them. She would never get that time back.

Adam started violently jolting his head back.

'What—? What are you doing?'

His neck was arched back, his face strained. 'I'm having a nose bleed.' She saw red forming in his nostrils and starting to run towards his mouth. He was looking up at the ceiling, jerking uselessly.

'Zoe, can you fucking do something?'

'Oh, OK – sorry! What do you want me to do?'

'Do you not have any tissues in your bag?'

She laughed. 'I'm not your mum!'

'OK, fine – can you go to the bathroom? I don't want all of them to see.'

She leapt up and ran into the living room, avoiding his flatmates' eyes, muttering something about spilling a drink. She came back with a cloud of loo roll. He leant forward gratefully, holding the tissue with one hand and pinching the bridge of his nose with the other. She watched in fascination as the scarlet bloomed on the rough white paper, soaking it.

'Can I . . . do you need anything else?'

He said something muffled through the tissue paper. They waited. Then he said, 'It's OK. I think it's over. Sorry.'

He pulled the tissue away from his face and a huge dark

shining clot pulled out of his nostril. It was repulsive but strangely cathartic to watch.

He looked up at her. 'Is my face OK?'

'Not really.' She went back out and ran the tap over some more tissue. She came back, knelt in front of him on the bed and washed his face. Sitting back down, she saw there were tiny shreds of tissue around his nose, and decided not to say anything.

'I didn't know you got nosebleeds.'

'When I'm stressed.'

'Right.'

'Oh, Zoe, I'm sorry. I'm sorry I said all that stuff just then, about you not being a writer. I was just annoyed with you.'

'It's OK. I wasn't being particularly great either.'

'I don't know why I had a go at you about it because it's always been one of the things I liked about you. You seem really laid-back and kind of easy-going about life. Don't get me wrong, I love what I do, but sometimes it feels like everyone I meet is networking and ambitious and trying so hard to be something, and I just get tired of it.'

He was still furtively touching his nose.

'And with Kathryn, it's like she's got this *drive* – it's exhausting to be around.'

Zoe ached with jealousy.

'I used to feel really lucky that I was with someone whose art I respected. And then I just thought, is this actually ever going to work? Are we really going to both be able to have our own careers? And you know, art is the most important thing in the world to me, so at the end of the day, I need someone who can support me.'

He turned to look at her.

'It's funny cos, lately, before this evening – well, I'd been thinking that I might need someone more like you.'

She wondered if, six months ago, she would have found this appealing. She imagined herself folding into him gratefully, happy to be needed. But now she felt herself resisting.

Still, she was polite when she said, 'I'm not sure you do.' And she didn't say what she was thinking: *I don't think I need someone like you.*

7

The night after the accident, Richard was at home with Rosie, while Eleanor stayed with Isobel at the hospital. He got Rosie ready for bed, struggling with the feeling that he was performing the task inadequately. She fell asleep quickly, but he didn't think it would last long. They'd tried to keep her occupied and protect her from their anxiety, but he was sure she'd picked up on it. He settled in his study with the baby monitor. He just hoped she wouldn't have another terror; he didn't think he could cope with it on his own.

He couldn't stop thinking about the scalding. He told Eleanor compulsively and strenuously that it was just an accident, that it couldn't have been prevented, and his parents had supported him. At the hospital, Lorna complained about the nurses and the waiting room, but she made a point of telling Eleanor jolly stories about the time Jessica rolled off the sofa or Richard touched a hot iron. 'These things happen, Eleanor,' Hugh said. 'I've seen much worse in clinic.' Eleanor had just smiled weakly and stared straight ahead.

He couldn't understand why she would have reached for the coffee when Isobel was struggling in her arms. He remembered Eleanor describing her illness: *I feel like there's a screen between me and the world. I feel like I'm doing everything on a slight delay.* He hadn't properly taken it in: he felt sorry for her, but he'd never imagined that something like this would happen. He thought about when she'd said she wanted to move; how he'd shut it down in a panic. Maybe if he'd listened . . . He replayed the accident in his head until it became less like a memory and more like a nightmare: the table sliding, coffee cups live and swarming. Nothing felt safe any more.

It was ten o'clock and the house was empty. He knew, because Zoe had left her laptop open on Friday and he had read her emails, that she was meeting Adam tonight; she wouldn't be home. He thought about going to look round the basement. He wanted something to soothe him and thoughts of paint colours or door handles only provoked panic these days. He wanted to spend some time in someone else's world. He picked up the baby monitor and went downstairs.

He went into her living room first. It was dark; he switched the light on and surveyed the room. There was a pile of her clothes on the armchair and from the arrangement, he could tell she had peeled them off and left them there. She did this sometimes; he never understood why. Getting undressed in the living room – it seemed perverse. There was a bowl with the sediment of cereal gathered at the bottom and an empty crisp packet on the sofa. He moved towards the writing desk.

Then he heard the door go and feet in the hall. He was temporarily paralysed. There was no time to get upstairs. Besides, the room would be lit up like a stage set; he was visible from the street. He heard Zoe's footsteps on the stairs, slow and cautious. There was an interminable wait, when he could hear her breathing, rapid and frightened, outside the door. Then it opened and she yelped.

'Oh God! Sorry, sorry! I didn't know it was you. I just saw this person through the window and . . . I freaked out. I'm really sorry.'

'Zoe, no, I'm sorry – I shouldn't have come down here, it's just there's been this leak . . .' His tongue had gone thick; he had no idea what he was saying.

'A leak?'

'From the dishwasher . . . And I just worried it had come down here, so I wanted to check, but I should have asked, I'm so sorry.' Was he apologizing too much? She was looking confused. 'I just didn't want it to damage your things . . .' he said, weakly.

'Oh, right, thanks. That's nice of you,' she said, distracted. She was looking round the room, trying to work something out. There was something different about her; he wasn't sure what. Her face seemed more fluid and malleable; she was jumpy, animated.

There was a pause, while she kept staring at the room. He tried again, desperate to get them back on safe ground.

'I should have waited till you got home and asked you. This is your room; it's unforgivable.'

She seemed to pull herself together. 'Don't be silly, it's your house,' she said, vigorously. She smiled. 'It's just funny seeing you down here.'

He allowed himself to smile back. It was as if he'd forgotten how to – his mouth felt wide and horrible and he left it in place too long. 'It's funny being here,' he said.

He knew he should go back upstairs. He just couldn't leave the situation alone; he wanted some assurance that he was safe. He had already realized that the dishwasher was above her bedroom, not her living room. He wondered whether Zoe would work this out too and if she did, when.

He didn't know whether to embellish the story, try and make it more convincing, or leave it opaque.

'I was actually going to make myself a nightcap,' she said. 'Do you want one?'

'I don't want to disturb you . . .'

'No! It would be great!' She walked over to the mantelpiece. He watched her pick up each of the wine bottles and peer at them before she selected one. She lifted up one of her water glasses and held it in front of her face, looking at the red grains stuck at the bottom for slightly too long, and then took two glasses into the bathroom. Every movement was slow and effortful and slightly uncoordinated. He realized she was drunk. He was relieved – maybe she wouldn't remember this – and then fearful: perhaps when sobriety set in, she would start to suspect, talk to Eleanor . . .

She came back, drying the glasses with a bath towel, and poured Richard some wine. There was a red hair clinging to the top of the glass she handed him. He wanted to remove it, but didn't know how to do it inconspicuously, so he turned the glass round and took a sip from the other side. The hair made him feel sick. He didn't know if he should wait to be asked to sit down; it was his house, as Zoe said, but also her room. There was an awkward pause while they both stood facing each other.

'Sorry, sorry! Sit down!' she said, bundling up her clothes on the armchair and throwing them onto the floor. She picked up the cereal bowl and stood indecisive for a moment before putting it down on top of her papers on the writing table. She shunted the crisp packet down to the other end of the sofa and sat opposite him. She took a big gulp from her glass.

'Is everything OK then?' she asked.

'Sorry?'

'With the leak? Is it all OK?'

'I think it's fine. It hasn't come through the floor.'

'Cos actually I just thought: I found this damp patch on the carpet the other day, by my bed, so I thought that could be something to do with this, maybe . . .'

Richard buckled inside.

'But the ceiling looked OK and it was a few days ago, or maybe a week . . . or two, I can't remember . . .' She looked strained and then seemed to give up on the train of thought. 'I don't know.'

'I'll— That's not good. I'll look into it. I'm sorry you had to deal with it.'

'It's OK – I just didn't know what it was. Thanks for checking things out tonight.'

'No problem,' he said. They sat in silence for a moment.

'Have you had a nice weekend?' she asked, careful and polite.

He thought about not saying anything; if he told her about Isobel, she would feel sorry for him, and the idea of using it to distract her or get her back on side felt horribly low. But it seemed stranger to avoid it. 'Well, actually, I was going to say – there was an accident last night. Eleanor— Well, we don't know how it happened, but some coffee got spilt and Isobel got burned. She's in hospital.'

Zoe looked genuinely upset. 'Oh my God! I'm so sorry! Is she OK?'

'We were lucky in all sorts of ways: there was milk in the coffee, my mum and dad were there and knew what to do . . . There's every chance it'll heal completely. And the worst of it was at the top of her arm. She could wear sleeves when she's older . . .' He felt his voice catch and then he recovered. 'They're keeping her in the burns unit tonight, but she'll be home tomorrow. It was just a shock for all of us. Eleanor's staying with her, so I'm manning the fort.'

'Oh well, look, if there's anything I can do . . .' She looked down at her glass. It was particularly unconvincing.

'Thank you, thank you. We'll manage.'

He took a sip of the wine. It was horrible – cheap or off or both – but in some ways, the harshness was pleasing. He looked around the room. Now that he was inhabiting it, rather than mining it for clues, it seemed squalid and cold: the springs in the chair had gone and it tipped him back uncomfortably. Zoe actually lived here. There was a rustling sound and a little moan, and he jumped and then remembered the baby monitor. Zoe looked round, alarmed, and then saw what it was.

'Sorry. I just have to keep it with me,' he said.

'Sure.' They listened to Rosie murmur, Richard on tenterhooks, but then the noise tailed off. He sagged with relief. There was another pause. He couldn't think what to say. Most of what he knew about her, he'd found out through deceit. She was looking at her wine glass, pensive. She'd probably only offered him a drink to be polite; it was stupid of him to say yes. But now he was here, he didn't see how he could go.

'You're home early,' he said, for something to say.

'Am I?' She looked puzzled and he remembered that he wasn't supposed to know where she had gone.

'I just meant, it's only ten, Saturday night – Sunday! Sunday night. The weekend, anyway, and you're young, so . . .'

'Yeah,' she said, still staring at her glass. Then her head snapped up. 'Sorry if I'm being weird,' she said. 'I'm a bit drunk. Sorry.'

'No, no—'

'And I was with someone tonight . . . Well, someone I was kind of seeing. And we just broke up.'

Richard pulled himself forward in the chair. She'd broken up with Adam. This was amazing. It was like spying but in real time.

'I'm sorry to hear that.' He wondered why he was speaking like this: over-formal, condescending.

'No, don't worry. It was doomed from the start really. He had a girlfriend. That wasn't me, I mean. Another girlfriend. It was a bit complicated.'

She tipped her glass back and drained it. She picked up the bottle and held it out towards his glass; it was still full. She filled hers anyway.

'I feel like such an idiot. I knew, all the way through, that it wouldn't last. But you just carry on, don't you. Stupid.'

'Yes,' Richard said, carefully. He paused. 'Why— How did it end?'

She drained her second glass and lay on her back on the sofa, with her knees up, her head on the arm, hair falling down the side. Her denim skirt was riding up. There was a hole in the top of her tights.

She began to talk, about how Adam had let her down by not being who she thought he was, how he had lied to her about what his girlfriend was like. She said how upset she was that it had ended and how good it was that it had because it would never have worked out anyway. Then she began to talk about someone called Rob, who she'd been with for six years.

This was new information and it was surprisingly disappointing. Six years. She said she'd met Rob at university. He'd just assumed she'd always had an entirely different existence to him: a round of drunkenness and casual sex with artists.

He felt pressure to respond, but he couldn't think what to say; he reached for a cliché. 'Perhaps you just haven't met the right person yet.'

She sat up and looked perplexed. 'Oh, I don't think it's *that*. I mean, it's got to be more complicated than that, right?'

'I don't know. I just think if he was with someone else, he can't have been giving you everything. And I think you – you deserve more than that.' He was still repeating platitudes, but the conversation had turned without him realizing. They looked at each other, confused.

'It's just so, so disappointing.'

Her face started to shift: her lips wobbled and her eyes were shiny. Richard grew fearful.

'I know everyone feels like this after a break-up – "I'll never love again" and all that – but I really don't think I will find someone else.'

I'm sure you will. Should he say that? Richard saw another version of himself go and sit next to her on the sofa. *I'm sure you will*, he'd say and touch her hair; she'd turn her face towards him and he'd kiss her. It would be stupid and destructive, and almost repellent, but it would be brave. It would disrupt everything, and he had been longing for something to change for fifteen years. Richard watched himself do it, the way every morning at Dalston Junction station, he watched himself jump in front of the oncoming train. It would never happen, but he would never quite be rid of the image either.

Then she started to cry. Loudly, unattractively.

'I just don't think I believe in love any more.'

Richard got up, searching the room for something he could give her. He knew he ought to comfort her, but he had no desire to be in this room any more. All at once, he was tired: he had seen enough.

He suddenly missed Eleanor acutely. He saw how stupid he had been. If Eleanor came back now and found him in Zoe's room, her drunk and lying on the sofa, she would misunderstand. He still had no idea if Zoe would wake up tomorrow morning, wonder what he'd been doing in her room, start to interrogate his story . . . He didn't want to disrupt his life any more. He wanted one more chance at it.

He remembered lying in his single bed in Cambridge, towards the end of their third year, holding Eleanor, and becoming intensely afraid of dying. He thought about death a lot, sometimes making himself incapable with fear imagining the few seconds before you died, trapped in the awful circle of trying to comprehend being nothing. But in that moment, the fear was different: he was afraid because mortality meant that one day he would have to see Eleanor for the last time and the idea was almost physically painful. And when he was dead he would lose access to this – this particular mixture of joy and contentment that came from feeling the skin of her back against his cheek.

The baby monitor jerked into life and he could hear Rosie calling out. He turned round. 'Zoe, I'm sorry, I've got to—' he started, but she was asleep, foetal, on the sofa. Richard had never felt such relief. He ran upstairs to his daughter.

8

Zoe didn't know where she was or what time it was. Her stomach yawned wretchedly and her face was hot. She could feel upholstery against her face and a cold mist at her hair-line. Her head was hollow and light, a thin layer of pain around the skull. She realized she was on her sofa; she just didn't know why. Then it came, in a hurtling succession of images – the pub, Adam, whisky, wine, Richard. Her memories were muffled and fragmented, but certain parts surfaced, hideously acute. Things she'd only half registered at the time were now painfully vivid. Her skirt at her waist, the holes in her tights. Richard's face when she started crying. 'I just don't think I believe in love any more.'

She assumed it was about four in the morning, but it was only one. She was slightly too aware of the contents of her stomach: there was something heavy and awkward there. She heaved experimentally over the toilet and her chest started to burn. It wouldn't come. She stayed there in a dizzy haze, unsure if she was going forward or back, and then her stomach subsided, and she took off her skirt and tights and got into bed in her underwear. The sheets felt cold on her skin. She tried desperately to get back to sleep, but she was horrifically awake.

She began to replay the evening, wondering if it would

somehow improve with familiarity, if she could find an interpretation that wasn't terrible. In fact, it got worse. It dawned on her that Richard might have thought she was coming on to him. What if he told Eleanor and they threw her out? He'd seemed so embarrassed. Should she talk to him, try to explain? She remembered thinking what a marvellous idea it was to confide in him about Adam, that from someone older, with experience of marriage and relationships, she would get a new, better perspective. But now she saw that it was grossly inappropriate.

She managed to sleep for a few hours and her alarm went off at eight. She couldn't imagine a worse start to the week. As she got out of the shower, she heard footsteps on the stairs and went cold. There was a knock at her door. She cast around for a dressing gown, remembered that she didn't own one, and then opened the door in her towel. Richard was standing there. Zoe was immediately aware of the make-up smudged under her eyes, the exposed skin across her shoulders and the cold drops of water on them, the looseness of the towel. This could only be something bad. They must want to evict her.

'Hi, Zoe. Sorry to disturb you so early.' He looked uncomfortable; her stomach dropped.

'No, no problem. I'm sorry about last night.' She shuddered internally; that made it sound even worse.

'No, no, don't be silly. It was nice to— And I should never have— Look, Zoe, I'm sorry to have to ask you this, but the thing is, we're in a bit of a mess. I need to go and pick Eleanor and Isobel up from the hospital later today and Rosie's being . . . Well, she's a bit unsettled and we don't think it's a good idea for her to go back there. Our usual people have let us down and . . . I don't suppose you could keep an eye on her?'

Zoe was submerged in relief. 'Oh God, yes of course! I'd *love* to. No problem.'

He seemed relieved too. 'Really? That's very kind of you. I can stay with her until five thirty – you'll be home by then, won't you? It'll only be an hour or so.'

She agreed and he thanked her profusely. High from the averted disaster, she lied enthusiastically about how much fun it would be and how she'd love to get to know Rosie better. As he was about to go, he said, 'I expect you've got little . . . cousins or nieces or nephews, have you? I mean, you've looked after small children before?'

'I don't have . . . those things,' Zoe said. 'But I have looked after children before. I mean, a while ago. But yes.'

Richard looked at her uncertainly. She wondered if he was going to change his mind. 'You'll be fine,' he said and went back upstairs.

*

Zoe hoped she would feel better by the time she got home, but when the time came to look after Rosie, she felt low and flat. It had been a miserable day – a hangover at the shop was a kind of torture: having to stay in one place with nothing to do. She was worried that Duncan would get fed up with her; it was getting harder and harder to match his enthusiasm. She didn't know what she would do if she lost the job. Richard left for the hospital and she tried not to panic as she shut the door behind him. It was only an hour, after all.

She watched Rosie drawing at the kitchen table. She was struck again by how unchildlike she was: she was not round or chubby or cute, but elfin and angular. Her brown hair hung in hanks around her pale face, which seemed to hold a thousand expressions Zoe couldn't read. She sat down next to her, feeling a new and acute kind of social anxiety; she wanted to impress Rosie, she realized, but had no idea how. She saw dried snot on Rosie's upper lip. It made her feel sick and she didn't know what to do about it.

Rosie began to tell her to draw things, and she was relieved to have instructions, although she was surprised at how wilful Rosie was. Zoe obediently drew cats and monkeys, grateful to have a task, until Rosie sprang off the chair and onto the floor, rolling around grotesquely, making gibberish noises.

'Rosie?'

'I'm not Rosie!' She writhed on the floor.

'Oh, OK. Um, who are you then?'

'I'm the baby!'

'Isobel?'

'No, the baby!'

'Which baby?'

She abruptly got up. 'I want to play hide and seek!'

They began to play: Rosie hiding, Zoe seeking. Rosie always chose somewhere obvious – behind the sofa or under the kitchen table – and often the same place again and again. It was a game that lacked suspense, but Rosie seemed to be enjoying it, so Zoe carried on. She learnt that the more elaborate she made her seeking and the more she talked about not being able to find Rosie, the more delighted Rosie was, and she started to perform stagily, craven for approval. 'I can't find Rosie *anywhere*!' she said loudly and heard giggling from behind the sofa. She started to relax, tentatively enjoying herself. Maybe she wasn't so bad at this after all.

She put her hands over her face and started to count, for the seventh or eighth time. She heard Rosie go upstairs. She accelerated her counting and ran up after her.

She went into Rosie and Isobel's bedroom. It was empty

and still. Then she heard loud breathing; she couldn't tell where from. Zoe looked under the bed and in the cot. A note of panic crept in; she tried to quash it.

'Where's Rosie? I can't find Rosie anywhere!' She tried to speak as falsely as she had before, but this time it was true.

'Rosie's not here.' The voice was detached; she couldn't hear where it was coming from.

'Oh. OK. Who am I talking to then?'

'Girl.'

'Rosie, I don't understand. Come on, I need to find you. Give me a clue.'

'I'm *not* Rosie!'

'Who are you then? Are you the baby?'

'I'm Emily.'

Zoe froze. 'Rosie! Don't be silly.'

'Rosie's not here. This is Emily. Rosie's upstairs.'

'No, she's not!' Zoe wrenched open the wardrobe door. Rosie pushed her, hard, and she stumbled back.

'You can't see me!'

'Rosie, I want to play something else. I don't like this game.'

Rosie sounded normal again. 'Isobel did a poo in here.'

'OK, Rosie, let's do something else. What do you want to do? Do you want me to read to you? More drawing?'

'I'm not Rosie! I want to play again. Go downstairs!'

Without knowing quite why, Zoe turned round and went downstairs. She stayed at the foot of the stairs for a few seconds and then went back up.

'Do it properly! Count properly!' Rosie shouted at her. Zoe went downstairs again and covered her face; her hands were shaking. She counted to ten loudly and rapidly.

'That's not proper counting! Do proper counting!' Rosie

ran downstairs and pressed her hands into Zoe's legs, propelling her into the living room, shutting the door behind her. Zoe forced herself to count slowly, trying to listen out for Rosie's footsteps.

As soon as she got to ten, Zoe ran up the stairs. The children's room was still and this time, she couldn't even hear Rosie breathing. She checked under the bed and in the wardrobe. She called Rosie's name; nothing. She went into Richard and Eleanor's room and did the same. She stood on the landing, looking up the stairs to the top floor.

'Rosie? Rosie, if you're up there, you need to come down.'

There was no answer. She steeled herself, and went up one more flight of stairs.

'Rosie . . . ?' She opened the door to Richard's study, and looked under the desk. She stopped outside the upstairs room. 'Rosie, this isn't funny! You shouldn't be up here.'

'Rosie's not here.'

Zoe went to open the door and someone was pushing against it.

'Rosie! Let me in! This isn't funny!' She pushed and pushed in desperation until it finally gave and Rosie was standing in the middle of the room, on her own.

'I don't like this room,' she said, quietly.

'No, I don't like it either, Rosie. Let's go downstairs, shall we?'

'I've seen a little girl,' Rosie said. 'She's called Emily.'

Zoe grabbed Rosie by the shoulders and marched her downstairs. Rosie started crying, 'Don't want to! I want to play!'

'Rosie, please don't go up there again. Let's play down here. Look, we can play whatever you want. Any toys you want! But please, let's play down here, OK?' She pulled the paper over and the felt-tips. 'What do you want me to draw? I can draw anything you like! Another cat?'

Rosie sat down beside her.

'A cat.'

'OK.' Zoe felt her heartbeat begin to calm, as she started drawing. A cat. A monkey. Draw spots on the cat. Not that one, this one. Not like that. Make the monkey stripy. Like this. In red. That's not red. Zoe drew ferociously, grateful for every minute that Rosie was here next to her, determined not to let her out of her sight again.

'The monkey's called Sophie,' Rosie said.

'Is she?'

'He. The monkey's a he.'

'But Sophie's a . . . Well, OK.'

'And the cat's called Julia and Julia and Sophie are friends and they live in London Fields and one day, when I was with Mummy, I saw them, but Mummy couldn't see them. Only I could see them.'

Zoe nodded encouragingly and started to feel better. Children obviously talked a lot of shit. Rosie could have picked up the name Emily from anywhere. It was silly of her to have thought it meant anything.

Her phone started ringing. She craned over to see the name on the screen; it was Laura. She wanted to speak to her so badly, to tell her about Adam, and even though she knew she couldn't do it now, she answered.

'Laura? Hi! I'm babysitting. Yeah, I know! For them, yeah. Look, can I call you later? Or could we go for a drink? I really want to talk to you.'

Rosie got down from the table and wandered into the living room. Zoe watched her through the double doors. She didn't leave the room, only sat down by the door into the hallway.

'What about tomorrow? Can you— Oh God, hang on, Laura, I've got to go!'

Rosie was writing on the wall. Zoe rushed over. 'Don't do that! That's not allowed.' She tried to wrench the felt-tip out of her hand, but her grip was surprisingly strong. Rosie stood up and pushed Zoe.

'Go away!'

'I can't, I've got to look after you. But Mummy and Daddy'll be home soon.'

'Go away! Go back home! You don't live here!'

Zoe started to cry. She had no idea what to do. 'Rosie, please, please can we just do some more drawing? A book? Can I read to you?'

'No!' Rosie pushed her again, hard. Zoe saw Eleanor and Richard out of the window and was simultaneously relieved and mortified. She heard the front door open; Rosie shouted, 'Mummy!' and ran into the hall. Zoe stayed where she was, wiping the tears off her face.

Eleanor came into the living room, carrying Rosie on her hip. 'Has everything been OK?'

'It's been fine.' Zoe thought about not saying anything, but it might make it worse. 'She just—' Zoe pointed at the wall. 'I'm sorry – I couldn't stop her.'

The mark Rosie had made was a kind of squared curve. It could have been anything, Zoe knew, any shape at all. It looked very much like the beginnings of an 'E'.

'Rosie did that?'

Rosie buried her face in Eleanor's shoulder; her voice was muffled. 'Wasn't Rosie. It was Little Girl.' Tears started to run down Eleanor's face. Zoe looked away; it was unbearably intimate and there was nothing she could say.

'I'm sorry, I tried to stop her,' she said, though she knew Eleanor wasn't worried about the walls.

'It's OK – it'll come off. It's just been a difficult few days, that's all.'

Rosie moved her face away from Eleanor's shoulder and kissed her tenderly on the cheek. Zoe saw something forceful and primal cross Eleanor's face, as if she'd been swamped in love. She saw Rosie lean over and whisper something in Eleanor's ear.

'Thank you, Rosie. Thank you, that's lovely.'

'Is everything OK, then, if I . . . ?' Zoe asked. Eleanor didn't answer. She was staring at the mark on the wall.

9

Eleanor sat in the bay window of the living room, her head-ache circling her skull, half listening to Richard playing with the children in the kitchen. It was the first weekend since Isobel's accident and she still felt as though she were living underwater. They knew now they'd been lucky: it looked like Isobel's arm would heal completely. They could forget about the accident; Richard said that they should. But they might not be lucky next time. Eleanor had promised herself she would do something about the house. She just had no idea what.

She pressed her forehead against the cold glass. The change in sensation made her feel better temporarily. Her vision was focused on her reflection; the street outside was blurred. She was submerged in her headache, barely noticing a slight rustling sound outside the front door.

Then something caught her eye: some movement, some-thing not right outside the house. She pulled her face away and looked. There was someone walking away from the front of the house. It was the girl again. The girl in the black duffel coat. She crossed the road and sat down opposite the house on the pavement, staring up at it. Eleanor was half frightened, half thrilled: the thing in her head was made manifest. She looked at the girl and they made eye contact.

Eleanor was still for a moment. Her overwhelming instinct was to go outside, but propriety stopped her – what would she say? What would she do? Then a woman ran towards the girl. She was out of breath, and she tried to pull the girl roughly up from the pavement. There was a brief struggle. She heard the woman say, 'Come *on*, Emily!' Eleanor reeled back. The woman looked up at the house and their eyes met. Eleanor was certain that she saw something there: recognition.

The woman knew who she was. Eleanor ran into the hall and out of the house, slamming the front door behind her. She registered a fresh line of stones outside the door. The girl must have put them there; her stomach turned. She cantered down the steps and ran across the road but the girl and the woman were no longer there.

She whirled round and saw them walking away, towards London Fields. Eleanor was paralysed for a second. Richard was at the front door, calling her name and for a moment, she wanted to go back inside. Maybe she was wrong. Emily was a common name. Maybe it was better not to know. Then she turned and went after them.

The woman glanced back furtively and quickened her pace; she yanked at the girl's arm to get her to keep up. They crossed the road and before Eleanor could follow, her vision was obscured by a lorry cutting in front of her. Helpless with frustration, she waited for a break in the traffic and started to run, across the road and into the fields.

She ran up the short hill past the tennis courts and the paddling pool, through the trees, heavy and full with purple leaves. She was gaining on them. The woman's steps were brisk and short, but she did not run, as though she was refusing to indulge in the madness of being chased. Eleanor picked up speed, navigating the prams and cyclists, getting steadily closer.

'Mrs Ashworth?' she called out before she had time to think. There was no reply; they walked faster.

'Mrs Ashworth? Emily?'

She was close now, right behind them. Eleanor knew the woman could hear her; one or two other passersby had turned their heads when she spoke. If she was wrong, and they were not who she thought they were, the woman would look round. But she was deliberately ignoring her. Eleanor was close now, inches from the back of her head. Her hair was thin; there was a tangled greasy knot forming and Eleanor could see patches of scalp. Then abruptly, in the middle of the path, the woman halted. Eleanor was slightly too slow to stop, so when the woman turned, her face was unnaturally close.

'Look, I'm sorry, OK?' the woman said, and her voice was not quite right: a little strained, a little hoarse, sup-pressed. 'Please don't make a scene. Please. I'm sorry she keeps coming back. But it's not my fault. It's the house!'

Eleanor was briefly stunned. For a moment, everything seemed hyper-real: the faded red jumper hanging from the woman's frame, as if she'd shrunk inside it; the green grass; the woman's arm yanked back from her shoulder as the girl in the duffel coat, Emily, tried to pull away. The prominence of her bones, the way her face seemed to have sunk under-neath its structure, the cross-hatching on her skin, and the hundred things scrawled on her face: exhaustion, fear, grief. Emily finally wrenched away and ran out onto the grass. The woman opened her mouth, then she closed her eyes and sighed. Emily was crawling on her hands, picking up leaves, examining each one intently, judging it before discarding it or keeping hold of it.

The woman was breathing loudly and shortly; with some effort, she brought it under control. 'I'm sorry,' she said. Her tone was more even now; quiet, defiant. 'I'm sorry if you've been having problems too. I'm sorry we sold it to you, but we didn't have any choice. We couldn't live there any more. It's not us. It's the house!'

'What's the house?' Eleanor asked, dumbly.

'I don't know! I don't know what it is and I don't want to know any more! We just couldn't live there and I'm sorry if you can't either, but there's nothing I can do.'

Eleanor felt her breath grow rapid, some sort of dark energy returning. 'What sort of problems did you have?'

'Just . . . the . . . oh, look, I don't want to go over it all! I try and stop her coming back, but I can't always control . . . She's not always . . .' She looked at Emily on the grass, absorbed in the leaves.

'You left your things . . . your quilts, blankets. I kept them. You can have them back.'

Mrs Ashworth flinched. 'I don't want them! Get rid of it all, burn them, I don't care. I don't want anything more to do with that place. I've tried to keep her away, I promise, I've tried, but she just goes back! I wish to God we'd moved further away. I didn't know it had some kind of – hold over her! That house!'

'Please, can you just tell me what was wrong with the house? Was it illness or Emily or . . .'

The woman's voice broke. 'We were all right before we moved, *she* was all right, but then the bad things started and now this is just what she's like!' She was starting to lose control, squeaks setting in. 'I've said to her, we were all unhappy, we were all sad when the baby – went. Her father lost his mind, did some stupid things, and then he took off when he couldn't deal with *her* any more. And with me

311

being . . . poorly for so long after he left . . . She saw things a child shouldn't see and I'm sorry for that, but it's hard for all of us and we get on with it! We don't behave like this.'

'I'm sorry,' Eleanor said.

The expression of sympathy caused a sudden reaction: Mrs Ashworth immediately stiffened, galvanized. 'Well, thank you, but we keep going in our family. I'm sorry for those stones she's been leaving, but this is just what she's like—! Bringing things into the house, birds, stones, hoarding. I tell her, she should have grown out of this by now, but she's got worse, if anything. And then the accident – I couldn't take it any more, I wasn't going to wait to sell it! We just had to get out.'

'What was the accident?'

She closed her eyes. 'The accident, the burning – I – I don't . . .'

'I'm sorry,' Eleanor said again and reached out her hand. Mrs Ashworth opened her eyes and pulled away.

'Look, what do you want me to say? What else was I going to do? We couldn't stay there! We're good people, a good family, I promise you – there's just something wrong with the house!'

She looked over at Emily, who was sitting cross-legged on the grass, arranging the leaves in a line. 'Come on, you. We're going home. And you're not taking those with you.'

Emily looked up and Eleanor looked directly at her for the first time. She must have been about seven or eight. There was a sadness in her face, and a kind of defiance. For a moment, Eleanor wanted to take her in her arms. Then Emily's expression changed and she snarled, 'No!' at her mother, the noise loud and distorted enough for Mrs Ashworth to glance behind her fearfully, in case anyone was looking. Eleanor felt a curious flash of sympathy for Emily, perhaps envy, and then, too self-conscious to watch them argue, she turned around and walked home.

*

She walked back slowly along Litchfield Road and put her key in the door, dazed. Richard was in the hall, waiting for her.

'Eleanor! Where did you go? You have to stop running out of the house like that! I was worried about you!'

'I saw the people that used to live here. They were just outside the house.' She shrugged off her coat limply and walked into the living room, where Rosie and Isobel were watching television. She sat down at the kitchen table, sinking her chin into her hands. Richard followed, shutting the double doors behind him, and sat down opposite her.

'How did you know it was them?'

'The way they looked at the house . . . I don't know. I just did! I went after them and I spoke to them.' She repeated the conversation to Richard, her voice thin and halting, trying to process it as she spoke.

'God, Eleanor,' he said. 'That sounds really upsetting. But doesn't it make you feel better? Now we know.'

'How could it possibly make me feel better? To know that they feel like that about our house?'

'To know there's nothing sinister about them, that Emily's not a . . . ghost-child or something. She's just a little girl who's had a bad time. It sounds like they had an awful run of things, but it's not anything . . . supernatural. It's just bad luck.'

'But she said it started when they moved house! They were fine before they moved here.'

'Eleanor, love . . . Bad things happen in any house. And what did she say exactly? Someone died? Illness? They're ordinary things, Eleanor – horrible, I agree, but these things happen to people.'

Eleanor looked up. 'She said there's something in the house.'

'But she doesn't sound . . . She sounds quite . . . damaged.'

She lowered her voice. 'I could live with it, Richard, I would live with it, but Rosie! I can't bear what it's doing to her! The night terrors, Girl . . . She's picking up on something!'

'She's behaving like a typical toddler! We know this. Tantrums, night terrors, imaginary friends: it's all normal stuff. She'll grow out of it. And remember, you've not been well either, Eleanor: if she's picking up on anything, it'll be that. She's not going to like the house if you don't.'

'Mrs Ashworth . . . she said something about a burning.'

'Well, that sounds nasty, but like I said—'

'But Isobel! Isobel got burnt, Richard! What if it was the house?'

He got up and walked away from her. He put his hands on the worktop and lowered his head. When he turned round, his expression was gentle, sympathetic. For a moment, she thought he'd finally heard her.

'Eleanor . . . I don't think it was the house.'

'What do you mean? Why are you looking at me like that?'

'It wasn't your fault. I understand why you feel guilty, but it was an accident, bad luck, like whatever happened to the Ashworths was bad luck. We don't have to . . . make up a story about it.'

Her breath was hoarse and ragged. 'You think I'm making things up?'

'I think you're unwell. And it's hard to think straight when you're unwell.'

She sat in silence, head bowed, staring at her hands lying in her lap. He kissed the top of her head.

'You just need to rest.'

10

It was near closing at the shop and Zoe was exhausted. She hadn't showered and her armpits smelt goaty. She'd spent all morning trying not to be sick. Then the nausea lifted, but was replaced by something worse: a kind of depression that was becoming too familiar.

It was Monday and she had spent the day before in Litchfield Road. She hadn't wanted to be there: something was obviously going on between Eleanor and Richard. Whenever she emerged upstairs, they were polite and tense. She supposed they were still upset about Isobel's accident. But Laura had cancelled on her and she had nowhere else to go.

By the afternoon, she could feel herself turning inwards. She knew she should go out, just for a walk, anywhere, but instead she reached for her phone. She was amazed that Adam picked up and even more so at how joyful he sounded to hear her voice.

When she went round to the warehouse, she felt a charge that she hadn't felt for a long time. She hadn't even missed it, until she felt it again. They had a drink together in his room and although she was almost certain they were going to have sex, there was always the possibility that they wouldn't. They talked about how his art was going and the shop; their whole conversation lit up with the question of whether she would stay the night or not. Then, he took hold of her wrists and pushed her back on the bed. He was inside her, pulling at her top, and she made a half-hearted gesture towards propriety – 'Maybe this isn't such a good idea' – and he said, 'Zoe, I think it's a bit late for that now.' It was exciting and abnormal. When she came, it was unfamiliar, as if the orgasm had its own character.

She stayed the night, but didn't sleep; just lay awake next to him waiting for morning. He woke up early too and they had queasy, hungover sex and agreed it wouldn't happen again. Knowing this was the last time she would be in his bed, she tried to put off getting out; she climbed on top of him and he pushed her off. She got up and got dressed, and told him she had to go to work. He pushed her back down on the bed, pinning her hands above her head, and she was surprised because she didn't think he wanted more sex. But he just held her where she was. She used all her strength to push against him, but it was no good, she couldn't move. Finally, he let her up and they said goodbye.

It was a chilly spring day and the shop was cold. She was hunched on a stool behind the counter; she hadn't moved for hours and thought she could feel her bones stiffening. She thought of her old desk at the office – warm, busy, bathed in the sterile comfort of electric strip lights – and her old salary, which now seemed lavish. Her flat with Rob was cosy and filled, at least, with some kind of love, even if it wasn't always full or proper. She could feel the allure of printers, staplers, cushions and cafetière. How could she have given all that up? She didn't care about euphoria or intoxication any more – she just wanted something constant, neutral and bland.

With five minutes to go, she heard the door open. Zoe was hoping that it would be someone she could get rid of quickly or pass to Duncan, because she didn't want to stay a minute later than she had to. She looked up. It took Zoe a split second to recognize Kathryn and then another to realize that this was not a coincidence: she was coming towards her and saying, 'Zoe?'

Zoe nodded. Kathryn's hair was loose today: it was wavy and shoulder-length and her fringe was too long. She was wearing a navy forties-style tea dress with a constellation of white dots on it. Zoe admired it, in spite of herself.

'You're Adam's girlfriend, aren't you?' she said.

'No,' Zoe said, weakly.

'OK, but you've been seeing him.'

Zoe said nothing.

'Zoe, I'm not angry, I promise.' She laughed and reached over the counter to touch Zoe's arm. It took all of Zoe's resources not to pull her arm away. 'I just want to talk to you. Would you come for a drink with me?'

'I have to close up, so . . .'

'I don't mind waiting,' Kathryn said.

It wasn't true anyway; Duncan closed up on Mondays. She went to the studio at the back to say goodbye to him and got her bag and coat from the stand in the kitchen. She washed up a mug in the sink, trying to put off leaving for as long as possible, her mind working wildly and unrealistically: could she just not go back out? Might Kathryn just leave? When she finally emerged, Kathryn was waiting patiently by the counter. She suggested a place to go and Zoe agreed, approving of her choice involuntarily. Kathryn was friendly as they walked there – she told Zoe she'd got in from Edinburgh that morning and chatted happily about the sleeper train. All Zoe could think about was whether Kathryn had seen Adam already and the hideous proximity of her saying goodbye to him and Kathryn arriving.

The bar that Kathryn had chosen was part of another warehouse, glass-fronted. Zoe wondered if she'd ever get warm. They stood awkwardly together at the bar and Zoe wasn't sure who ought to buy the drinks – she didn't get paid for another week and also it might seem as if she were trying to compensate somehow. In the end, Kathryn took charge and bought herself a pint of pale ale and Zoe a glass of white wine.

Kathryn chose a table and they sat on chairs upholstered in a seventies floral print. There was a silence, which felt horrific. Kathryn groaned loudly, flung her head back and put her hands over her face. Then she looked at Zoe directly. 'I know. I know how weird this is. I'm sorry. I really appreciate you meeting me. And Adam doesn't know, I swear – he'd kill me if he knew I was doing this. He didn't want to tell me anything about you – he wouldn't even tell me your name! But I got it out of him eventually and he told me how you met, and then I looked you up on Facebook, so . . .'

'Adam told you that we were . . . ?'

She nodded. 'A few weeks ago, yeah. I didn't know if you knew I knew, if you see what I mean.'

Zoe shook her head.

Kathryn leant forward, pressing her arms flat on the table. 'Oh, Zoe. I don't really know what I'm doing. The thing is, Adam and I are going through a really tough time – as you know, I guess – and I thought if I met you face to face and could talk to you about this, this whole thing, what was going on with you guys . . . I don't know, it might make things clearer. Adam won't tell me anything, just said it was over between you, but . . .'

Zoe drew back in discomfort. 'There isn't much to say, really, I—'

'Oh, I'm not angry! You know what the deal is with me and Adam, right? He told you about us? It's been going on since forever, but it's hardly been, like, love's young dream the entire time. It's just that we can't seem to let go . . . I mean, you know we met at boarding school, right?'

'He said you met at school . . .'

'Oh, what, did he tell you he went to the local comp? I swear, Adam has so much middle-class guilt – he's *still* going on about his music scholarship. It was like twenty-five per cent of the fees or something. But anyway, yeah, that was where we met. We got together when we were sixteen and it was, like, *bam*, you know, totally intense. We just had this *connection*. It was so special, I can't really explain it. We thought we were going to get married.' She said it as though it was the most radical idea anyone had ever had.

'So we did our foundation together in London and that was just the best, like, maybe the happiest I've ever been. But then I got into Edinburgh and he didn't, and he wanted me to stay in London, but I was like *no way*. And so we were long-distance for four years, which wasn't great at that age, plus I found it literally impossible not to have sex with other people. So sometimes Adam would find out about these other guys or sometimes I'd tell him – and God, there's still a *lot* he doesn't know about – and he couldn't take it. Which I understand a bit more now, but at the time, I was like, come on, we're young, we're artists, we're not *fifty*. But he'd break up with me and then I couldn't live without him, so we'd get back together and I'd promise I'd try to be faithful this time, but I just *physically couldn't do it*. And one time, I broke up with him because I was watching him chop an onion and I just got so *irritated* by the way he was doing it that it scared me: I thought, is this what the rest of my life is going to be like? Getting annoyed at the way someone chops onions? And you get to a stage with someone, you know, where you love them, you definitely, really love them, but you think, "Is this really the only person I'm going to have sex with for the rest of my life?" And then you think, "Is this how *frequently* I'm going to have sex for the rest of my life?" And maybe you do have to accept that eventually it isn't going to be as exciting as it was at the beginning. You know what I mean?'

'I think so,' Zoe said. She was still recoiling, dizzied. But she wanted Kathryn to keep talking, to put off the moment she had to say anything herself. 'So, what . . . then you went away for your Master's?'

'Yeah! We were doing OK, I thought, until then – of course, I get onto the MA course and it's the exact moment that Adam's got this whole quarter-life crisis thing going on and he wants to settle down and says I'm not trying hard enough, but you know, this is so obviously the best thing for my career right now, like, do you *know* how many people apply for that thing? I can't give that up just cos he's gone all broody. And I'm *trying*, I'm coming back weekends, I let him come and visit me, but every time I see him, he's getting at me in some way and I'm a bit like, OK, so I just spent ninety quid on a train journey for you to tell me how shit a girlfriend I am? But then he tells me he's met you and I'm like, whoa, OK, I didn't know you were going to do *that*.'

Zoe started an apology. Kathryn waved her hand dismissively.

'You know, in one way I was pleased! Because it felt more equal. It was, like, the first time he cheated on me and I've cheated on him – God, I don't even want to think about how many times. And yeah, I was furious – I mean, I cried half the night and I hit him, really hard, but also, like, suddenly I really wanted him. So I came to London for his show, which I wasn't going to do, and we had the most amazing weekend, totally intense, it was like we were sixteen again. And I go back to Edinburgh all loved up, and he tells me he's stopped seeing you! And yeah, I was glad – I mean, I feel *physically sick* when I think about the two of you together and a lot of the time I just wanted to stab you in the face – no offence – but it was kind of a turn-off too, because then he was all like, let's get married and go and live in the country and I was like, oh God, not this again.'

Zoe started involuntarily. Kathryn paused.

'Adam said you were fine with all this. I mean, with him being in a relationship. He said you'd broken up with someone long-term and you wanted something really casual.'

'I did,' Zoe said, 'but this doesn't feel very casual.'

'No, I guess not,' Kathryn said and she was quiet for a moment.

Rob had told Zoe that she liked to pick at things, to seek out drama where there wasn't any, to live life at too high an intensity. She wished there was some way she could introduce him to Kathryn.

'So I guess what I really wanted to know was: was it serious with you two?'

Zoe shook her head. 'No. It wasn't at all.'

'Because Adam said something once, when we were fighting, about you being the kind of person he should end up with. He said he didn't mean it and he took it back, but it really hurt me. I've had doubts about our relationship, sure, all the time, but I never seriously thought we wouldn't end up together. I thought it would always be us.'

She looked genuinely sad. 'We've just been through so much and he's still my favourite person in the world. I used to think that the fact we'd stayed together through all this proved something – you're know, that we're strong, it's meant to be. And now I'm wondering if all it means is that we should have broken up ages ago.'

She looked Zoe in the eye. It was unsettling; Zoe thought she meant it to be. She felt a surge of envy – for Kathryn's confidence, her dynamism, her frankness – and she wondered if she could try and take her place, insert herself between the two of them. Then Kathryn slumped back in her chair and the feeling subsided.

She thought about the early days, when Adam would kiss her goodbye and it felt like an explosion of stars in her brain. That hadn't happened for a while now. She thought about lying in bed next to Adam, watching him, slightly curious, as he got worked up about the way Kathryn didn't call enough or hadn't taken his advice about her course or left her shoes in the middle of the room. She remembered the last months of her relationship with Rob: how depleted she'd felt, how soporific it had been.

Without thinking about it, she reached her hand across the table. 'Look, there's nothing between Adam and me. Really. It was only ever about the two of you, for him. I think if you still have some energy – you should go for it. If you don't and you're tired all the time and you've got nothing left for each other, then maybe you should break up. But if you think you can see a way to make it better – you should try?'

Kathryn looked at her hand, but didn't take it. For a second, Zoe thought Kathryn might cry. Instead she moved the conversation on, to how Adam really wanted a family and she wasn't sure. Zoe asked her what she thought about having children and she gave a long complicated answer, which was essentially how she thought their lives were too interesting for them to become parents.

'I mean, I'm an artist! I don't want to end up just some stay-at-home mum going to pottery classes. And that's what I would be, you know, in Adam's fantasy. He always wants to pack it all in and move to the seaside. I'm like, you're *insane* – this is where our careers are, what, you think you're going to be happy showing in some little gallery in Whitstable with a load of old lady watercolourists? Like, why don't you just start painting cheese and bottles of wine and sell your stuff outside Green Park tube? But there's this part of him that just *craves* normality: he wants, like, a three-bedroom house, with, I don't know, a dog or something . . . What? You're smiling?'

'Nothing – I just didn't know that about him. I mean, he said stuff like that to me sometimes, but I . . . didn't see it.'

'Adam's basically pretty conservative,' Kathryn said. 'He likes to pretend he's more complicated than he is.' She spoke with the mixture of affection and irritation that came with really knowing someone and Zoe decided that she'd had enough. She had no reason to stay. She told Kathryn she had to get going and as they were standing up, Kathryn grabbed her arm.

'Wait, I *know* you!'

'What do you mean?'

'I thought I recognized you! I mean, I knew what you looked like obviously, because: Facebook, but there's something else too! I've been trying to work it out the whole time we've been talking! It's the dance class, isn't it? You go to Triangle.'

Zoe had no idea whether to lie or not. 'I've been a couple of times.'

'Oh my God, this is the *weirdest thing*! I love that place. I remembered you from that class because I was so relieved there was someone there who wasn't totally professional – oh my God, I don't mean, like, you're really crap or anything! Don't you think Sofia is the most amazing teacher? It's one of the things that makes me *really* regret leaving London – I just can't find anything that good in Edinburgh.'

'It is really good,' Zoe said unconvincingly.

Kathryn hugged her and Zoe hated it. 'I'm so pleased you're so great! I knew you would be. I knew Adam would have chosen someone special. Hey, maybe we could go to a class together some time? When I'm back in London?'

'Yeah, maybe!' Zoe said, knowing she would never go near the dance studio again. She was suddenly tired of all this: working in someone else's shop, living in someone else's house, fucking someone else's boyfriend. She went home and deleted Adam's number from her phone. It was time for something of her own.

11

All weekend, Eleanor thought about Mrs Ashworth and Emily. She thought about what Richard had said: they were just an ordinary family, damaged by what had happened to them. But Mrs Ashworth's words played in her mind: *when the baby – went, me being poorly*. When she dressed Isobel's burns, she remembered *the accident, the burning*. So bad it had forced them to leave. Rosie bit her hand and she wondered if she could see something of Emily's expression in her face. *She saw things a child shouldn't see*. She thought about how hunched and diminished Mrs Ashworth was, Emily's wildness, and she wondered if they would ever recover. Her wallet went missing until she found it underneath a cushion on the sofa. *It's the house*. She tried to stay rational, but something stronger and more instinctive took over: she had to stop the same thing happening to them.

On Monday, she did another internet search and the familiar link came up; her computer reminded her: 'you've visited this page many times.' Rebecca lived in Surrey and her photograph was professional: she emerged from the plain white background, face forward, her shoulders angled away from the camera. She looked attractive and confident. Eleanor guessed she was in her fifties; she had thick shoulder-length brown hair, traced with grey. Her website was simple, elegant and convincing. She was reliable and discreet; she was fully insured and had references available. Eleanor ignored the tabs about readings or healings and went straight to house clearances. Rebecca said that she would discern whether spirit activity in the house was causing problems for its inhabitants. She would clear the house of negative energy and speak to the spirit visitors to try to understand why they were returning. She would help them cross over peacefully to the other side. Eleanor liked that idea, in spite of herself.

Sarah's ghost portal held no resonance for her. But neither did any of the other possibilities: ley lines, spores, mites, viruses or post-natal depression. She had no words for what was happening to her. But it was real. Her sickness was real; the burns on Isobel's arm; Rosie's writing on the wall. Mrs Ashworth's broken expression. There was no explanation, but still, it was happening.

She emailed Rebecca and arranged for her to come and visit the house the next day. Rebecca was polite and formal, and the blandness of the exchange – arranging the fee, plus travel expenses, and explaining transport links – soothed Eleanor. It felt like any other transaction. The next morning, she took the children to nursery and called in sick.

In person, Rebecca was every bit as impressive as her website. Her clothes were smart and sober, and she exuded pleasant capability. After she'd been invited in, she stopped in the hall, looking intent and serious. Then she smiled and said brightly, 'Well, I can certainly see why you've been having problems!' as if she were talking about the drains. Eleanor started to cry.

Rebecca stayed calm and followed Eleanor into the kitchen. They sat at the table together and Eleanor talked, in a jagged, unformed way, about her illness and how things had been moving, and everything Mrs Ashworth had said. Rebecca put her hand on Eleanor's and listened carefully. Eleanor suddenly couldn't stop talking. Still crying, she took Rebecca to see the upstairs room.

Rebecca walked confidently into the centre of the room and stood very still. Eleanor watched her take in the drawings and writing on the wall. She took a sharp breath and said, 'There's something here.' Eleanor felt fear and relief.

'The minute I walked in the front door, I knew it,' Rebecca said, patrolling the room. 'I felt it pulling at me here.' She put a hand to her chest. 'Pulling me upstairs. There's very, very bad energy up here. The air's different – can you feel it? It's denser, viscous.' She smiled at Eleanor. 'It makes *me* want to be sick.'

She walked around the room. 'A very strong, bad energy – a spirit that won't rest. It's moving your things and causing you illness.'

'Why?'

'It doesn't want you in the house. But don't be alarmed – it's quite common for spirits who are troubled in some way to have difficulty crossing over. They deserve our sympathy. Some mediums just banish spirits, but that isn't my way – I try to be gentle with them. If they can cross over calmly, so much the better. Is it affecting anyone else who lives here, apart from you and Rosie?'

Eleanor shook her head. 'Not my husband. We have a lodger and we don't know her very well, but she seems fine.'

'I'm not too surprised that they're not sensing it; some people simply aren't attuned to it. Rosie's behaviour, on the other hand . . . children that age are highly sensitive; they can pick up on spirit activity where we can't. Rosie doesn't have an imaginary friend, does she?'

Eleanor nodded, her heart sinking.

'Children can't tell the difference between spirits and people. What they call imaginary friends are usually spirits communicating with them. And this was Emily's bedroom? No wonder she's troubled, poor child.'

'And do you think . . .' Eleanor said. 'Do you think the spirits caused the bad things that happened to them, this family?'

Rebecca smiled. 'Negative energy comes from the living too. Most of the time, people prefer to think it's the dead; no one wants to believe it's coming from them. They'd obviously suffered great trauma as a family and that might be nothing to do with the house . . . But there are spirits here, that's certain. Who knows how much worse they were making things? I don't believe anyone sensitive can live in this house and be at peace.'

Eleanor started to cry again. 'Do you think . . . I mean, if we do a clearance and it goes well, do you think we can be happy here? Do you think we'll be OK?'

Rebecca put an arm around her. 'Absolutely,' she said. 'You'll feel completely different when you walk in here. It'll be like a new house. You can start all over again.'

*

Eleanor decided to tell Richard about Rebecca that evening. She had no choice if she wanted to go ahead. After they'd eaten, instead of going upstairs to rest, she told him about her visit, bracing herself for scorn and disbelief.

'No way, Eleanor. No way. This has gone too far now – you have to stop.'

Eleanor made an effort to stay calm. She didn't think Zoe was at home, but she got up and shut the door to the living room anyway.

'Please, Richard. I just want to try it.'

'A séance? In our house?'

'It's not a séance. It's called a house clearance.'

'Whatever it's called, we're not doing it. She's a con artist. She's scamming you.'

'So what if she is? We'll try it and if it doesn't work, at least then we'll know.'

Richard sighed. 'How much does it cost?'

'Four hundred pounds.'

'Four hundred pounds! Eleanor, four hundred pounds could be a new carpet or wallpaper. That's going to mean so much more to us than a . . . house clearance.'

Eleanor's head was raging. 'Richard, she can feel something in the house. She said it's full of bad energy.'

'Oh, and you honestly thought you'd invite a medium into the house and she'd say, "Actually everything's fine, you don't have to do anything."'

'I just want to try and get rid of it! Whatever caused problems for the Ashworths, whatever it is that's making me feel ill . . .'

'The Ashworths caused problems for the Ashworths! And we'll see a private doctor for your illness. We'll book an appointment next week.'

She laughed. 'A minute ago, we didn't have four hundred pounds.'

'But that's something worth trying! You've seen, what, one doctor? A couple of other quacks? We'll keep trying until we find out what it is. But it will be something physical.'

They were quiet for a moment. He sat back down at the kitchen table, took off his glasses and rubbed his eyes. He put them back on and looked directly at her. 'Do you really believe this? That the house is haunted? You're saying you believe in ghosts?'

'I know it sounds ridiculous. I know. But there's something wrong and I need to find out what it is.'

'Please let's just leave it, Eleanor. I don't like it either, thinking about this other family, that there was so much unhappiness here. But can't we just . . . let it go? What's the point of digging things up? They lived in this house. We're never going to change that. But we can . . . paper over it. Not think about it. If you obsess like this, you're just going to make things worse.'

She floundered; she was running dry. Her head hurt and she felt sick. Richard stood up and put his arms around her.

12

It was only Thursday morning, but Richard had given up on work. He was getting behind, and he couldn't make himself care. It was becoming clear that he was not going to complete his Master's. He knew that he would have to admit it, but he wasn't sure how. The waste of time and money was horrible, but the disappointment was worse: so it was the wrong thing, after all. And he wasn't any closer to finding the right thing, the thing that would complete him. Perhaps he was even further away. He didn't know what, without the prospect of the PhD and the academic career, would be left for him: just a part-time job that he had never liked. At another time, he would have unburdened himself to Eleanor, and let her help him. The idea seemed wildly inappropriate now.

He was at his desk, making calculations. It was no good. He couldn't do it. He wanted to make a start on the house in earnest, do as much as he could, try to get the thoughts of ghosts and mediums out of Eleanor's head. But there was simply not enough money there. And he didn't see how that would change.

They couldn't sell the house. He'd boasted about how they'd been the only people to offer on it – he'd seen it as a sign of their vision and insight – but now the fact was terrible, ominous. And even if they could find someone to buy it, where would they find the money to move, for the lawyers and surveyors and estate agents? They were stuck.

Something dropped onto his desk. He started. He didn't know what had happened: he was only aware of something falling and a tiny wet sound. It happened again. He pushed back his chair. Something was moving. Then he saw it: three white maggots crawling over the black keys of his laptop. Another one dropped to join them.

He looked up at the ceiling. Above his desk was a hatch that led to the attic. He'd noticed that the wood was starting to rot in the centre; it was on one of his many lists of things to do to the house. Another maggot dropped. He pulled away from the desk, repulsed. He stood on his chair and gingerly looked upwards. The rotten patch of wood had almost entirely disintegrated and its centre squirmed. He felt sick. He slid back the lock and started to ease the hatch down. It was heavier than he thought it would be and his hands gave; something slid off it and softly thumped onto his desk. It was the corpse of a bird, covered in maggots. Its surface was live and crawling.

He stood suspended for a moment. Then he went downstairs and got an old tea towel and a torch. Shaking, he wrapped the bird up and stood on his chair, shining the torch into the attic. All he saw was boxes and rafters. He supposed the bird must have come in through the roof, although he couldn't see how that could have happened. They'd had intensive surveys; the roof was in good condition. Then he saw that rows of pebbles were lining the opening of the hatch, a perfect square. It looked as if they had been deliberately placed there.

Richard sat back down. He was rational; he knew this about himself. If he didn't understand how this bird had got in the roof, then he should find out. It could indicate serious problems. But the bird was directly in the centre of the hatch, in the centre of the square of pebbles. It was so unlikely that it would have fallen there. There were two entrances to the attic – one in his study and the other in the room next door, Emily's room. An image came into his head of someone crawling about in the roof. He sat for a few moments with the hole gaping above his head, maggots wriggling on his keyboard.

He picked up the corpse and, after a moment's hesitation, carried it out into the garden. He forced himself to take care on the stairs, to resist the fierce compulsion to hurry and get rid of the thing in his hands. He thought he could feel the movements of the maggots through the cloth. It was all he could do not to hurl it away from him.

He had not been out to the garden since they'd moved in and the grass was wild and long. The soil was becoming overgrown with weeds – clearly no one had cared for it for a long time. It was a cold, grey day and he hadn't taken a coat out with him. He carried the corpse right to the end of the garden, where a flowerbed ran along the back wall. He was shivering as he knelt down, tipping the corpse out of the cloth, onto the soil.

Richard realized that the flowerbed was covered with different arrangements of pebbles: sometimes little rows in size order, sometimes circles, sometimes pentagons. The most elaborate was a large spiral, in perfect size order, the smallest pebble on the outside, gradually getting larger as they wound in. The one in the centre was the size of a small fist. Richard wasn't sure what instinct made him dismantle it, but he pushed the pebbles to one side and started clawing at the earth, his heart beating faster. His hands hit something unexpectedly soft. He pulled back the soil more carefully.

He saw feathers, sensed something white and undulating. His stomach lurched. Another bird corpse.

He roughly covered it in soil and rocked back into a squat. He looked at the other strange shapes and pebbles with dread. He remembered the birds drawn on the walls of the upstairs room. Emily.

Richard went back inside and scoured his desk and the wooden panel, taking care to stop it disintegrating completely. By the end, it was impossible to tell if the tiny movements he saw were maggots or a trick of the light. His whole body was itching. He shut and locked the hatch and had a scalding shower.

He sat back down at his desk. It must have come from Emily. She was traumatized; they knew that for sure now. The family was bereaved; this was just her reaction. Could a corpse survive a year? It was big, perhaps a pigeon, and he hadn't got a close look at it. It was just another horrible remnant of the Ashworth family. They would clear them out, get rid of it all, start again.

Still, he found himself getting up from his desk and opening the door of Emily's room. How much had come from Emily and how much was there already? The air felt viscous here, like wading through cobwebs. He thought about Eleanor telling him that things moved in the house and the memory he'd been trying to suppress, the door to the upstairs room wide open, surfaced again. He remembered what Eleanor had said about the medium: *she says it doesn't want us in the house*. He looked at the faint images of birds on the wall.

13

By Thursday night, Eleanor had exhausted herself, thinking about the house clearance. She couldn't let go of the idea, yet it seemed impossible. She would never say it to Richard, but it made her uncomfortable too: the thought of summoning spirits in their home. She had no idea where they would find the money, what they would do with the children, how they would tell Zoe. How she would ever convince Richard. She wasn't even sure she believed it would work. But now when her head ached and her stomach lurched, it felt different, personal. *It doesn't want you in the house.* They had to do something. She went to bed early and dropped into a thick, black sleep.

She was woken by footsteps outside their bedroom. She picked up her phone by the side of the bed; it was two in the morning. 'Rosie?' she called out. 'Is that you?' There was no answer and panic hit her; she prayed she'd made a mistake or it was part of a dream. She lay there, rigid, alert – and then she heard it again. It was real, distinct: footsteps on the stairs leading up to the top floor. They had been outside Rosie and Isobel's bedroom. She was out of bed in an instant, opening the door to the children's room, as quickly and gently as she could, the same way she had every night in the months after they were born. They were both asleep, looking so peaceful. She slumped against the door frame, felled by relief.

But she could still hear footsteps. They were above her now, outside the upstairs room. Something was in the house. The footsteps were light, like a child's.

She felt dizzy. Perhaps she *was* going mad. She thought about how it would look if she woke Richard and he couldn't hear it or if she called the police and there was nothing there. She heard Richard, muffled, in their room: 'Eleanor, is everything OK?' She put her head round the door. 'It's fine; I just thought I heard Isobel.' He murmured and rolled over; he had barely woken up.

She shut the door and stood on the landing. Again, a floorboard creaked. She was certain: there was someone in the upstairs room. She began to make her way up the stairs. If there was no one there, that would prove there was something wrong with the house. Maybe no one would believe her but she would know.

She stopped outside the door to the upstairs room. She could hear an almost imperceptible rustling, the sound of someone's presence. The door put up its usual resistance, before giving way and swinging open. She saw a figure in the half-light, a girl, with long hair over her face. The girl turned towards her and Eleanor wondered if she might pass out with fear. Her breath became shallow and her hands were shaking. She reached for the light switch.

'Zoe!' There was nothing reassuring about the scene. Zoe was half naked, wearing a T-shirt and pants, and she was staring at Eleanor blankly.

'There are things in here,' she said.

'What things?'

'There are . . .' She tailed off and made a noise, a groan that came from the back of her throat.

'Zoe . . .'

She said something else, the words indistinct. Then, more clearly:

'There's something here.'

'Zoe, are you awake?'

'Yes!' she said, impatiently.

'I don't think you are,' Eleanor said.

'No!' Zoe said, getting agitated. 'There's something here, I can see her . . .' She trailed off again, looking blank.

Eleanor moved towards her and Zoe made the same guttural sound. Then she looked around and her expression changed to terror. She spoke rapidly: 'What? What's happening?'

'You're OK, Zoe, you're fine – I think you were sleep-walking.'

'I wasn't!'

There was a pause.

'Oh . . . Oh God. Oh, Eleanor, I'm so sorry.'

'It's OK, you don't need to worry—'

'I'm so sorry, this is so embarrassing . . .'

Eleanor put an arm around her and led her downstairs.

*

Zoe sat at the kitchen table. She was still bare-legged and on the verge of tears. Eleanor wondered if she ought to offer to get her a dressing gown, but she didn't want to embarrass her and she felt oddly calm about this peculiar scene unfolding, as though Zoe had absorbed her agitation and drained it from her. She put the kettle on.

'It's never been this bad, Eleanor, I promise, I would have warned you if I'd ever thought this would happen . . . I can't believe I woke you up, I'm so ashamed – please, please go back to bed.'

'It's fine – there's no need to worry.' She took two mugs out of the cupboard and put them on the worktop. 'Do you remember what you were dreaming about? Upstairs? You said you could see something?'

Zoe shook her head. She still seemed very upset. 'I can't. I can't remember anything. Sometimes I can, but . . . I just have no idea what I was doing up there. I'm so sorry.'

'Is this something that happens to you a lot?'

Zoe shook her head. 'Not like this. I'm a bad sleeper, I talk in my sleep, but this is something else. It's been terrible since I moved in. I don't know what it is, sometimes I think it's something to do with this house—'

Eleanor put down the mug she was holding and stared at her.

'Oh, I didn't mean it like that!' Zoe paused. 'It's a really lovely house.' Eleanor sensed they were both unconvinced.

'But the sleepwalking is something that started when you came here?'

'Yes, but—'

'Has it happened anywhere else?'

'No.'

Eleanor came out from behind the kitchen counter and sat opposite Zoe. Excitement was threatening; she tried to speak calmly. 'Zoe, have you noticed anything strange about the house? Do you think it's had an effect on you?'

Zoe looked as though she were about to say something, and then stopped. Eleanor realized that if she wanted honesty, she would have to be honest herself. She looked her in the eye and said, 'I sometimes think it might be haunted.'

Zoe looked startled. 'What, really?'

'Maybe not in the conventional sense – I don't know if there are ghosts floating round or anything like that. But I think there's a kind of . . . bad energy.'

'I know what you mean,' Zoe said.

The relief was almost painful. Eleanor felt her whole body slacken.

'I haven't felt quite right since I moved here,' Zoe said. 'I've never had a problem with sleepwalking or had dreams like the ones I've had here. And sometimes, I do get this sense of a presence. Something else here. Maybe you could call it an energy.'

'Zoe, it makes me ill. The house makes me ill. I'm OK when I'm not here but when I'm inside it, I get sick and have headaches. I can't explain it to anyone, but I know it's something to do with the house. I just know. Maybe it's the same thing that's affecting you.'

Zoe was looking at her with real sympathy; Eleanor thought she might collapse. It had been so long. 'It's so awful, Zoe. I don't trust myself with the children any more – Rosie's obviously stirred up by something, Isobel would never have had her accident if we hadn't moved. I don't think we can ever be happy here.'

'What are you going to do? Are you going to sell it?'

'We can't. We can't afford to. And it would break Richard's heart. I've been – trying to find a way to make the house habitable. I've even contacted mediums. There's one – believe me, I know how this sounds – who wants to try a house clearance to, you know, get rid of the spirits.'

Zoe looked intrigued. 'Do you think that would work?'

Eleanor laughed. 'Actually, I have no idea. I just need to do something. We can't live here otherwise.' She spoke hesitantly, afraid of breaking this spell of intimacy. 'One of the things that made me unsure was that she wants everyone who lives in the house to be present. I had no idea how I would ask you.'

'What, you mean me? She'd want me to come too?'

'Would you do it?'

Zoe looked alarmed. Eleanor saw that she had gone too far. She had got drunk on compassion, the heady strangeness of the small hours.

'I'm sorry – you don't have to answer. You must want to go back to bed.' Eleanor got up and started to put the cups and the tea tin back in the cupboard. Zoe didn't move.

'That thing you said – about the energy in the house. I mean, I haven't been having that good a time lately.'

Eleanor shut the cupboards and leant forward on the worktop.

'When I started sleeping strangely, I thought it was something to do with me. I wasn't depressed – I wouldn't even call it unhappy really – but it's been a strange time for me. I broke up with someone, left my job and I just – haven't been myself, I suppose. I wondered about you and Richard . . . were you happy when you moved in?'

Eleanor didn't know how to answer.

'Oh God. I didn't mean to get personal or anything – I mean, you seem happy. You seem like a lovely family. Maybe I'm being silly.'

Eleanor sat back down at the table. She thought about something Rebecca had said, something she hadn't particularly wanted to think about – *negative energy comes from the living too*. Tantrums, sickness, accidents. The closeness she and Richard had lost. Ordinary bad luck. Ordinary sadness.

'The thing that's wrong – you think it's coming from us?'

'Or me. Or all of us. I don't know. It was just one of the things I thought about.'

Eleanor paused. Maybe it was just them, after all. She wasn't sure if she could believe it; she wasn't sure if she wanted to believe it. It felt like so much more, more than three people could create.

Zoe reached across the table and held her hand towards Eleanor. 'I do know what you mean,' she said. 'About the house. It does feel like there's something else here too. I've always felt that. And if you want to go ahead with the exorcism or whatever it is, I'll help. Definitely. Maybe it would help me too.'

Eleanor smiled. 'Thank you,' she said, taking Zoe's hand.

14

The house clearance was arranged for the following week. At first, Zoe had liked the idea – she imagined it as a kind of release, for her as well as Eleanor and Richard – but as the date got closer, she began to worry. Her nerves became more pronounced, until the feeling was actively unpleasant. She hadn't told anyone that she was going to do it, because even colluding in something so irrational made her feel silly, but the secrecy made it darker. She didn't seriously believe this woman would communicate with spirits in the house. So, what was she afraid of?

She remembered being thirteen or fourteen and doing Ouija boards with friends. It was always half-hearted – they used to do it in the girls' changing rooms at break and someone would always accuse someone else of cheating and it would dissolve into an argument. It still scared her though. And when Natalie Flynn said they should do it 'properly', she never wanted to. She believed in it enough to want to leave it alone.

She wanted, many times, to tell Eleanor that she'd changed her mind. She'd given up on the idea of being happy at Litchfield Road. Since that awful night in the upstairs room, she'd been too afraid to sleep. Every time she remembered the humiliation of talking to Eleanor in her

T-shirt and underwear, she grimaced and had to suppress a small moan. She purposely stayed up as late as she could and then slept lightly and fitfully for a few hours, jerking awake if she threatened to go under.

The day before the house clearance, Zoe's mobile rang and she saw the word 'Home' on the screen. She kept meaning to change it to 'Mum', but she hadn't. For the first time in weeks, she wanted to answer and all it took was her mother saying, 'I was just wondering if you were all right,' for her to start crying. She told her about the sleepwalking, and how her job bored her, and a little bit about Adam. She gave few details, but even telling the stories in the barest, most abstract form gave them a new power.

'Are you missing Rob?' her mother asked. Zoe was surprised; they hadn't spoken about him since the separation. Her mother liked Rob – Zoe had always privately worried she'd let her down by breaking up with him – but she was possessed by honesty now.

'Sometimes. Not as much as I thought I would. Sometimes I'm really happy.' She started to cry again. 'Actually, the worst thing is not understanding myself. I still don't know why I didn't marry him. I mean, apart from the fact I just didn't really want to.'

'Well, if that's true, Zoe, I wouldn't bother thinking about it any more,' her mother said briskly. 'Entering a marriage when one person doesn't really want to is madness.'

Zoe felt something change inside her. The idea that not wanting to was enough had never occurred to her; nor had just not thinking about it. Later, she would look back on that conversation as the moment she'd finally let go.

'And what about the house?' her mother asked. 'Is it working out for you there?'

'No,' Zoe said, with a clarity that surprised her. 'It isn't. I want to come home.'

They talked about how much notice she ought to give and when her mother could come and get her. She felt stupid, childish, a failure, but inordinately grateful. It wasn't a real solution: she knew they would begin to irritate each other and she had only initiated the awful problem of finding somewhere else to live. But it was counteracted by the sheer, hungry joy at not having to live in Litchfield Road, as well as the possibility of starting again: something new.

There was no reason to go through with the house clearance now, except that she was afraid to let Eleanor down. They'd been warmer to each other since the sleepwalking; there was a quiet affinity between them now that made interactions in the house smoother and kinder. And certain details from that night wouldn't leave her. Eleanor's pyjamas were not how she would have imagined them; they were faded and stained, and her stomach showed through the missing buttons. When Eleanor had held her hand, Zoe had seen that the skin around her nails was red and raw. It was the first time she had thought of Eleanor as anything other than together, composed. When Eleanor knocked on her door later, to confirm the details of the house clearance the next day, she couldn't bear to tell her that she wouldn't do it. She couldn't even say she was planning to move out.

*

Eleanor told her that the medium would be arriving at nine, after it had got dark. Zoe came upstairs when she heard the doorbell ring. Rebecca didn't look how she expected: she didn't wear black or have long hair. She looked like a life coach or a lecturer in economics. The only sign that she had any connection to the supernatural world was the large crystal round her neck – in other circumstances, it might have passed for contemporary jewellery, though it was slightly too unwieldy and crude for that. Eleanor introduced her to Zoe and Richard, and Rebecca asked, 'Are the children here?'

'They're staying at their grandmother's,' Richard said, barely on the cusp of civility.

'But Eleanor, we discussed this: everyone who lives in the house ought to be here, particularly if Rosie has some connection—'

'I'm not having them here while this goes on,' Richard said. 'I'll be here, I'll give you the money, we'll do whatever you need to do, but I'm not having our children mixed up in this.'

'I'm sorry, Rebecca, we just thought it would be too much for them,' Eleanor said. Rebecca and Richard were looking at each other intently.

'Very well!' Rebecca began to prepare the living room, lighting candles. She turned off the lights, opened all the doors, including the kitchen cabinets, and switched the toaster, the kettle and the television off at the wall. She lit bundles of white sage and placed them by the windows. Zoe asked her what she was doing, partly because she was curious and partly because she wanted to puncture the tense silence. Rebecca explained that the sage was a way of getting rid of negative energy and it was a ritual that had roots in Native American culture. She seemed pleased by Zoe's interest: 'You can do this yourself, in any space,' she said encouragingly. 'You can buy the sage sticks on Amazon.'

She sprinkled salt crystals in the doorways. Zoe couldn't help wondering how they were going to get it out of the carpets. Richard was watching Rebecca with a look of disgust; she guessed he was thinking the same thing.

Rebecca walked away from them and stood in the corner of the living room with her back to them, her head bowed. 'I wish to take away negative energy,' she announced and then said some words Zoe didn't understand in a rhythmic chant. She repeated the ritual at every corner, and then at each window and door. Zoe stood in a line with Eleanor and Richard, watching, fidgeting. She couldn't bear to make eye contact with them.

Rebecca turned to them. 'Now,' she said. 'That will clear some of the energy at least. Let's go upstairs and see if I can make contact with the spirits.'

'Do we need to come?' Richard asked. 'I mean, can't we just wait here while you talk to them or whatever it is you're going to do?'

'I need to show them that this is your house,' Rebecca said. 'They need to see that you're the new inhabitants now.' She turned to the doorway and Eleanor started to follow her.

'Is it safe to leave these sticks burning down here?' Richard asked.

Rebecca looked at him.

'I really think it would be better if we put them out before we went upstairs,' Richard said.

'It'll be fine,' Eleanor said.

They processed up the stairs in the dark, carrying candles. They gathered in the upstairs room, in an unformed circle. In the flickering half-light, Emily's drawings took on a new sinister form. Zoe thought she could see the faces moving, the letters enlarging and expanding; she was aware that her breath was getting short. She saw herself on the floor, with Adam on top of her, and remembered that she would not see him again. Rebecca lit more sage and sprinkled salt crystals in the corners. She repeated her ritual in each corner of the room and at the windows, silhouetted against the glass.

Rebecca asked them to hold hands. Zoe reached out reluctantly. She had to stretch to reach Richard and the unearned intimacy of his hand in hers made her deeply uncomfortable. Eleanor's hand was cold. Zoe glanced at her face; her eyes were frightened. Rebecca gestured for them to draw slightly closer in. Then she took a deep breath and closed her eyes.

Rebecca frowned slightly as if she were concentrating. Then she spoke and her voice was lower, more authoritative. 'It's safe to cross over now,' she said. 'It's safe to go.'

Zoe felt Eleanor's hand start to shake. They waited, watching. Rebecca spoke again, explaining that it was safe to leave the house.

She waited, then said, 'I knew it! I'm sensing something! There's a spirit here with us.'

She paused. 'It's a little girl.'

Zoe felt Eleanor's hand twitch violently in hers. The face of the girl in her dreams appeared; she tried to shut it out. It was only a dream. She started to shake too.

Rebecca sounded intrigued. 'She doesn't want to move on, but she won't say why.'

Then she started speaking in a child's voice. It was a high-pitched and clear voice and seemed entirely detached from her body.

'I won't leave,' the voice said.

'Can you hear me? Can you hear me?' Rebecca said. 'It's time for you to cross over. It's safe now, you can pass.'

The child's voice again: 'I won't go!'

Rebecca spoke more gently. 'Tell me why you can't cross over. I may be able to help.'

There was a silence.

Rebecca's tone became firm. 'You are frightening the inhabitants of this house. This is their home now. I will ask you to leave.'

Zoe reminded herself that it was just Rebecca, just Rebecca speaking to herself. But the voices were so distinct. She couldn't believe they were alone in the room.

Then Rebecca broke away from the circle, ducking slightly as if something had flown towards her. She held out her hand and opened her fingers. Zoe peered at her hand: a small stone sat in the centre of her palm.

'An apport!' she said happily. 'The spirits have brought this to me! We're getting somewhere.'

'Oh, for God's sake,' Richard said.

Rebecca seemed visibly taken aback by something. The voice that came through her changed. It was still childish, but harsher, stronger, more determined.

'You don't live here,' it said. 'This is not your home.'

Zoe started to feel dizzy. Images were surfacing, too bright and sharp: she could see the blood clot pulling out of Adam's nose, feel Kathryn's hand on her arm. She saw Rob's face at the bus stop. She didn't care if this was real or not – she had to get out of this room.

Later, Zoe would try to remember what had happened: whether she actually saw it or whether it was just Rebecca ducking, this time faster and lower, crying out, her fear chillingly genuine. Rebecca said something about a bird; Zoe was frightened and distressed; in the flickering light, the whole room seemed animistic and unsafe. But the memory stayed with her, the image a distinct print on her mind: the dark shape swooping towards Rebecca's face, wings outstretched. Rebecca cowering, hands covering her face; a muffled, chaotic collision. Eleanor in the candlelight, looking terrified.

Zoe turned her head away involuntarily. She was about to leave, when Eleanor bent over suddenly and vomited on the floor. Richard shouted 'Oh, fuck!' and Rebecca was saying, 'It's ectoplasm. The spirits have chosen to communicate through ectoplasm.'

Zoe started to feel dizzy, in a way that was familiar, but that she couldn't quite identify. Her vision blurred; the room was getting darker. In a minute, she wouldn't be able to see anything at all. 'I'm really sorry,' she managed to say, and then she was on the floor, and Rebecca and Richard were standing over her. She could feel something warm on her jeans, and realized that in the seconds she'd lost control of her body, she'd wet herself.

'Right, that's enough,' Richard said and switched on the lights. He started to blow out the candles. Zoe sat up. There was no bird. Eleanor had gone over to the corner of the room where the suitcase had been and crouched there, her face down, her arms around her knees.

'You're breaking the communication!' Rebecca said. 'We have to finish the clearance!'

'She's ill! You're preying on someone vulnerable. And look what you did to Zoe! You're despicable. I'll pay you whatever you need – just get out of my house.'

Rebecca gripped Richard's arm, and there was a wildness in her face that Zoe hadn't seen before.

'Don't you understand? This is dangerous! We've disturbed the spirits! If we don't finish the clearance, this house will be *unlivable*.'

Zoe sat in the middle of the floor, paralysed. Richard and Rebecca were arguing above her. It was over; she could go now. She had a very clear sense of what needed to happen next: she must leave Litchfield Road immediately. She would get up, go downstairs and start packing. This was not her home. She would leave tonight.

She looked at Eleanor, hunched in the corner, and thought she might be crying. Richard was trying to hand Rebecca cash and she was resisting, telling him she would have to start again. Zoe stood up shakily and went to the door. This was nothing to do with her; she should get out as soon as possible. Then, just before she reached for the handle, she turned round and went over to Eleanor. She sat down next to her and put her arms around her.

15

Two weeks later, Eleanor sat on her bed, surrounded by empty boxes. The day after the house clearance, Zoe had told them she was moving out. She didn't say why – there was no need to – and she left that day. On Tuesday, they got home from work and all her belongings were gone.

Eleanor wandered round the basement rooms, absent-mindedly picking up the last traces of her: a rusty Kirby grip, a wrinkled paper bag stained with grease, ketchup and crumbs. Zoe had forgotten to clear out under the bed and there was a bra, a book and a glove underneath it, covered in a film of dust. Eleanor brushed them down and put them in a box, to keep. Zoe hadn't said where she was going, but Eleanor was sure she would be in touch.

Eleanor started packing a few days later. She refused to stay in the house and it was unsustainable now: without Zoe, they couldn't afford the mortgage. They would have to sell it. She started looking for flats to rent while the sale went through. Richard resisted: they couldn't get off the property ladder, they didn't have the money to move. They could find someone else for the room. He suggested that they go away, think about it, clear their heads. Eleanor was resolute. They were putting the house on the market.

She rang her mother and asked to borrow some money,

listening patiently while Carolyn told her that she thought she'd got her life back now and she would never have had a child if she'd known she would still be footing the bill for it thirty-seven years later and what if she wanted to go abroad or back to art school? Eleanor calmly explained that there was a problem with the house that was making her ill. They were going to sell it and buy somewhere smaller in a less expensive part of London. She would repay the loan as soon as the sale had gone through, but in the meantime they needed to cover the cost of the move and somewhere to rent. The money arrived in Eleanor's bank account the next day. She knew that if she'd said she was considering leaving Richard, she would have got more.

But it was enough – enough to rent a flat, to retrain, to get a flight, to start something. She hadn't told Richard about it. The money was entirely hers.

So she could leave now, she could go – there was nothing tying her here any more. They would sell the house, Rosie and Isobel's world would be disrupted anyway and they would be too young to remember a time when their parents had been together. Richard would be generous with maintenance. She scrolled through properties online, imagining herself in the kitchen, making meals for the freezer. Richard would have the children half the time: she would have baths, read books, stand outside pubs after work again, relearning how to be chatty and amusing, even flirtatious. She would get the bus by herself and unlock the door to an empty flat. There would be no endless back and forth about swimming lessons and playdates; the day-to-day decisions about Isobel and Rosie would be her own. She would check the locks and windows at night and keep them safe. She could resign, find work that satisfied her. She felt her body loosen as she clicked through floor plans, photographs, local schools.

Her flat would be part of a large block. It would be big enough for the three of them, but small enough for her to know what was going on in every room. It would have two or three entrances – a security gate, an outer door, her own door – and she would sleep peacefully cocooned in the warren of corridors, lifts, staircases and identical front doors. The walls would be solid and new. She could call maintenance if anything went wrong.

The door slammed downstairs. She heard the children chattering and Richard switching on the TV. She heard him say, 'Daddy's just going upstairs for a minute,' and clatter up the stairs. It irritated her, mildly, the way he felt entitled to make that much noise. He burst into the room and knelt down at the foot of the bed, facing her, extending his hand towards her.

'Eleanor, I need to talk to you.'

She felt a jolt of panic.

'I'm sorry I've been fighting you this week. In fact, I'm sorry I've been fighting you since we've been here. I know you're right about the house – I just didn't want to know it. It's crushing to have to leave, but it was never the right thing. It was just too much, for all of us. I see that now.'

She could hear the theme tune of the children's TV programme. She was bluntly, desperately angry. Her new flat. The money. *Please, please don't take this away from me*.

He was looking up at her, his hand still outstretched. 'We should never have bought it; I should have listened to you from the beginning. We'll move, we'll go, as soon as you want. We'll work out the money somehow. I'd live in a cardboard box with you, if that would make you happy.'

Her new kitchen. The security gate. It was all draining

away. She didn't know whether to try and keep hold of it. Richard was staring at her, looking anxious and afraid.

'It's still what you want, isn't it? To move? To start again?'

She thought about empty rooms, her quiet weekends, her career. She thought about family, predictability and home. She paused, studying his face, and then reached for his hand.

'Yes,' she said.

FOUR

1

They didn't see Zoe again until two years later, when Richard spotted her in a cafe on Broadway Market. He'd been surprised when Eleanor suggested they take the girls to the lido; they didn't often come back to London Fields now.

Richard saw her first: she was with a man, sitting on stools at a counter facing the window. He almost didn't recognize her. She still had too much hair, but it was piled on top of her head now, as though she were an actress in a nineteenth-century drama, and although she was still in jeans, she was wearing them with a shirt buttoned up to the top and she looked smarter than she had when she lived with them at Litchfield Road. There was something off about the outfit – sort of frumpy – that Richard identified as a 'look', just not one he could interpret. She seemed bigger as well: her face was fuller and she was taking up more space. She and the man were totally absorbed in each other, obviously thrilled by one another's company. At one point, it had made Richard jealous, seeing couples like that. It didn't any more.

He pretended he hadn't seen her. He got the cake and coffees, hoping Eleanor wouldn't catch sight of her, but just as they were about to leave, Eleanor said, 'Richard, look, it's Zoe.'

'What? Oh God, so it is.'

'We should go and say hi.'

'Oh, please don't, love. Come on, don't start all that again,' he said, but Eleanor was already on her feet. He stayed with the children and watched the women talk. Zoe looked delighted to see her and there was genuine warmth on Eleanor's face too.

They had finally sold Litchfield Road, to an older couple who had grown-up children and were retiring. Richard was privately astonished that there were people who downsized to a four-bedroom house in London Fields, though he was overcome with relief to have an offer. 'We need a project,' the woman had said, running her hands over the green walls.

As soon as the sale went through, they bought a new build further east. Eleanor refused to live anywhere built more than a few years ago and anyway, they would have had to move too far out of London to afford another Victorian property. She had chosen the area, arranged the viewings, organized the money, and insisted the house was the right choice. Richard hated the idea at first, but not having to think about property any more became increasingly seductive. They agreed they would move again in a year if they didn't like it.

But watching Isobel and Rosie run around the garden, eating their tea in the kitchen, he began to slowly enjoy the house. The space was unremarkable, but it belonged to them, something, he realized in retrospect, he'd never felt at Litchfield Road. He started gathering evidence that their area was gentrifying: he kept an eye on the brands in the corner shops and researched proposed transport developments. He started to get interested in minimalism and Frank Lloyd Wright and would eagerly tell people that he thought Victorian architecture was 'a bit twiddly and twee'.

He had given up his MA after they'd left the house.

He couldn't bear to go back to work full-time, so for now, he spent two days with Isobel, and Rosie when she wasn't at school. At first, the days were long and hard, punctuated by terror and dogged with a feeling of inadequacy. But as he got better at it and more comfortable, he started to see how rewarding it could be. Eleanor worked full-time now and he took a perverse satisfaction in translating Isobel's words to her or being able to say, 'Oh, she's been doing that for weeks,' when Eleanor was surprised by something Isobel could do. They agreed that it wouldn't go on forever, just until he worked out what he wanted to do – at the moment, the thing that would complete him was still elusive.

It was such a relief to see Eleanor happier. Perhaps this was it after all – Eleanor, Rosie and Isobel, their ordinary house, his ordinary job – perhaps he didn't need anything else. It would just flare up at unpredictable times – a conversation with Dominic about managing his team, a visit from his parents. He'd be walking the children home from Rosie's school, thinking about what he might do next, and he'd suddenly be floored by the terror of not making any impact on the world. He didn't know whether to nurture this burst of feeling, treat it as a call to action, or suppress it. And then it would pass. You could almost get used to it.

Eleanor came back to the table, a little shaken.

'Was that OK? How was Zoe?' Richard asked.

Eleanor told him that the man she was with was called Joe and he was an artist. Zoe was living on a houseboat in Clapton and working part-time for an art school as their 'communication officer'. Eleanor and Richard briefly discussed what that might be.

They started to pack up. Eleanor picked up the drawings Rosie had done on the pieces of scrap paper he'd brought, and put them in her handbag; Richard corralled the crumbs on the table and deposited them on the plates, and hooked the sugar lump Rosie had just started to suck out of her mouth. When they were a safe distance from the cafe, they talked about how different Zoe looked. Richard said he thought she'd put on weight.

'I think it's just that she looks happy,' Eleanor said.

*

Later that day, Richard told Eleanor he was going for a run and found himself on the Overground in his running kit, his rucksack at his feet, on his way back to Litchfield Road. It was the third time he'd been back since they moved.

The first time, the couple were taking the house apart, just as he'd wanted to. Zoe's basement was a shell. There was a skip outside, filled with doors, wallpaper, carpet. The second time, he'd seen workmen knocking through the partition between the living room and the kitchen, and tried to remember if that had been in his plan. He watched them carry the double doors of the kitchen out to the skip, a curious mix of feelings brewing.

This time, the house was complete. There was a burgeoning rosebush in the area outside Zoe's room. The front door had been replaced and was painted an elegant navy; Richard thought he could identify the exact shade. He peered through the basement window. There was a long dining table, a kitchen island and huge glass doors leading out to the garden at the back. It was still and peaceful.

Richard felt a small ache – perhaps they could have made the house work after all – but the feeling was dim, and more importantly, it was survivable. The life he was living now was not what he would have planned or imagined but he was inhabiting it at least. He picked up his rucksack and ran towards London Fields.

2

Zoe was sitting at the fold-out kitchen table on the boat, scrolling through her phone, looking at pictures of Adam and Kathryn's wedding on Facebook. She flicked through them quickly, as though they were scalding. They seemed to be getting married in some kind of wood and Kathryn was wearing a daisy chain round her head. She was obviously pregnant and her dark red dress clung to her perfectly hemispherical stomach. She made it look sexy.

Zoe wasn't quite sure what it was making her feel. It was as though she were watching an alternative version of her life, even though she knew that it couldn't have been her, or if it could, it wouldn't have been like that. She didn't feel aching or aspiring; just uncanny. She didn't even know why she had looked them up – maybe it was seeing Eleanor and Richard this morning. The eight months in Litchfield Road now felt like a distinct interlude, but they still burned bright somehow. She put her phone down.

After she'd left Litchfield Road, she'd only had to live at home for two months, before Laura told her she was moving in with Nick and she could take her room in the house. She tried living there for a few months and was relatively comfortable, but it confirmed something she already half knew: she wanted to live alone. There was no way she could afford even a studio flat by herself, and that was when she'd thought about a boat.

Living on the boat was miserable and exhilarating. Cycling along the canal path by herself at night terrified her and, at the same time, the glassy surface of the water made her heart burst. When she got into the marina and shut the gate behind her and saw the crammed rows of bobbing boats, she felt safe. Often, she spent the days she was not at work emptying the chemical toilet or sitting in a launderette on the Upper Clapton Road and wondered what the point was. But then on her way home, a flock of green birds would swoop across the marshes and she'd see her red kettle through the window of the boat. She still felt excited every time she looked out and saw the water inches from her face. She felt closer to the sky.

She was sometimes lonely, sitting in the tiny cabin by herself, but it was her own and it was cheap and although she was dependent on her landlord, it felt good not to be dependent on her job or Joe. 'It's hard work,' the owner said, when he showed her the narrow space with its low panelled ceiling, fold-out bed and doll's-house kitchen. 'Not everyone can live like this. They can't bear to get rid of all their stuff.'

'I don't mind – I don't really have any stuff,' Zoe said.

And it was making her draw, every day. She drew the boats and the river and the birds. She had whole sketchbooks full of them. She drew as resistance; she drew because she thought it might save her life. She was thinking about finding ways to introduce colour and was planning to go back to Evering's to ask Duncan for advice. Joe kept asking to see what she was working on, but she didn't want to show him yet. She thought she would let him at some point, but she wanted it to be entirely hers for just a little longer.

She got up – she was meeting Joe again later on. He made

her so delirious, it was almost violent, as if her life had been dismembered. She'd forgotten about everything that was important to her; every other pleasure she'd ever known had been obliterated, apart from drawing. Laura had asked her what it was she liked about him and she couldn't articulate it – even though she knew he was funny and kind and clever, none of that seemed to matter compared to the way it made her feel when he said her name. It wasn't an answer: this kind of delirium couldn't last and might not lead anywhere good. She shut her sketchbook and picked up her coat. On the other hand, it might.

3

Eleanor took a bin bag and threw in the little pile of Zoe's belongings from Litchfield Road. She'd felt bad about not being in contact with Zoe after they left and hadn't wanted to throw them away, but after today, it was clear she no longer needed them. It had touched Eleanor, seeing her looking so crisp, with her piled-up hair and the high-waisted jeans and blouse buttoned up to the collar – it didn't really flatter her, but it made her look more confident. She was so obviously delighted by Joe. It made Eleanor curious and slightly envious. She hugged Zoe harder than she meant to when they said goodbye and said, 'Good luck.'

For the rest of the day, she felt altered, dragged halfway back to that peculiar time in Litchfield Road. From here, she could only see it through a kind of screen. Her memories were gauzy and fractured. She had been unwell; the children had been so young. There were blank stretches: and she couldn't remember what the carpets were like; she'd forgotten Richard had a study until he mentioned it the other day. She hadn't been herself.

And yet some memories remained distinct: the salmon skin in the tea, the pebbles on the front step. The anguish in Mrs Ashworth's expression; Isobel's scream when the coffee spilt. The bird flying at Rebecca's face.

Her public story about the house had merged naturally with Richard's and they both became practised at telling it, until it almost felt true – there was a structural problem causing damp that made Eleanor ill, it would have cost too much to fix, they had no choice but to sell it. Such a shame, but they were both happy in their new home. Things worked out for the best in the end. Sometimes she wanted to know what Richard thought privately – whether he ever thought about the Ashworths or the upstairs room. She occasionally wondered if he thought he'd seen the bird too, but they never spoke about the house clearance. It was safer not to.

There were still moments, though less frequent now, when she thought they'd carried it with them, whatever it was, like an infection. When Rosie suddenly flew into a rage or Isobel's burn flared up or she felt sick for no reason. She feared that it was part of them now, that it would lie dormant, following them to every house they ever lived in, and she would always be waiting for it to express itself.

But there was no doubt that things had got easier. She rarely felt ill; Rosie had grown out of her tantrums and night terrors, just as everyone said she would. Isobel was three and a half now, and she was a much more content child. She knew they were both growing away from her: they could do most things by themselves and needed Richard as much as they needed her. It made her feel sad sometimes, and impotent. But the freedom was glorious.

She'd finally bought herself a new bike and on the days Richard was at home and she didn't have to drop off the children, she'd cycle to work, spinning through the streets, luxuriating in how light she felt. She didn't tell Richard, but sometimes, when the mood took her, she chose a route that took her down Litchfield Road.

She had felt awful for selling it, for passing the house on

to another family. She had told herself there was nothing else she could do and was relieved the couple who bought it were wealthy because they would not be stuck like she was – they could get out if they needed to. Before they put it on the market, she'd finally wallpapered the upstairs room, but she'd still been terrified that the mood of the house would catch, that the sale would not go through.

The couple worked on the house for nearly eighteen months. She wondered if they had found Emily's writing under the wallpaper and what they had thought. Then the skip was gone and the window frames were newly painted and she could see wooden floorboards where the old carpets used to be. They planted a rosebush in the area outside Zoe's old room. She saw them having breakfast together in the morning, at the end of the elegant dining table in the large, light kitchen looking out onto the garden. They seemed content and companionable; she hoped that she and Richard would be like that one day.

*

After a while, she stopped seeing them. The lights were always off when she went past. The rosebush was getting overgrown. She kept returning, just to see, sometimes taking the detour on the way home too. They were not there in the evenings either; the shutters they had put in were never shut, even when it got dark. The curtains in the upstairs room were always drawn. There was no 'For Sale' sign; she could find no record of it on property websites.

A few months after she and Richard had seen Zoe, she left for work a little earlier than usual. When she got to the house at Litchfield Road, she stopped and propped her bike against the front steps. She noticed a clump of post sticking out of the letterbox; the flowers of the rosebush were brown and curling. They had put an outside staircase in, leading down to the basement, and as she stepped down, she was curiously confident that she would not be caught. She made a frame with her hands and pressed her face against the glass of the basement window. The room was still, as it had been for some time now: the dining table a bare expanse of wood, chairs tucked neatly in. She saw the blank surface of the sink: no washing-up liquid, no sponge or bowl. She was satisfied. They were no longer living there.

She didn't tell Richard. She could hear his voice already: *they just changed their routine, flowers die, they went on a trip.* She didn't believe it. But the beautiful, unexpected thing was that it didn't matter. She would not take that route again. She cycled away, released.

Acknowledgements

Thank you to my early readers, for their generosity, honesty and encouragement: Naomi Booth, Helen Francis, Mary Morris, Ben Platts-Mills, Sarah Savitt and Robert Williams. Thank you to Harry Perrin, Hannah Dearden-Watts and Polly Ho-Yen for their advice; Anouchka Grose for helping me see what I was writing about; and Christina Petrie, for long-standing inspiration and support.

Will Francis and Francesca Main, I couldn't have designed a more perfect agent and editor: thank you. Thank you to Victoria Murray-Browne for her wisdom, unstinting encouragement and support, and superior advice. And to my parents, for giving me the space and security to think writing a novel might be a good idea.

This book would not exist without Chris Stork; thank you for getting it started, getting it finished and everything in between.

picador.com

blog
videos
interviews
extracts